Bag Limit

Books by Steven F. Havill

The Posadas County Mysteries
Heartshot
Bitter Recoil
Twice Buried
Before She Dies
Privileged to Kill
Prolonged Exposure
Out of Season
Dead Weight
Bag Limit
Red, Green, or Murder
Scavengers
A Discount for Death
Convenient Disposal
Statute of Limitations
Final Payment
The Fourth Time Is Murder

Other Novels
The Killer
The Worst Enemy
LeadFire
TimberBlood
Race for the Dying

Bag Limit

A Posadas County Mystery

Steven F. Havill

Poisoned Pen Press

Poisoned
Pen
Press

Copyright © 2002, 2010 by Steven F. Havill

First Trade Paperback Edition 2010923845

10 9 8 7 6 5 4 3 2 1

Library of Congress Catalog Card Number: 2010923845

ISBN: 9781590586617   Trade Paperback

Poisoned Pen Press
6962 E. First Ave., Ste. 103
Scottsdale, AZ 85251
www.poisonedpenpress.com
info@poisonedpenpress.com

Printed in the United States of America

For Kathleen

Acknowledgments

Special thanks to Matt Borowski,
Gerard and Martha Havill,
Vergil Hall, and H. L. McArthur.

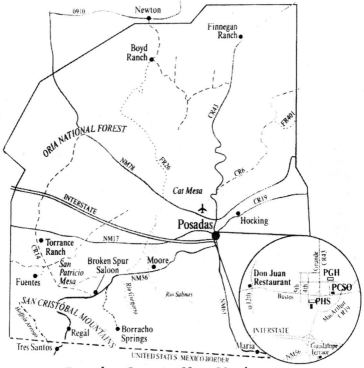

Posadas County, New Mexico

Chapter One

I should have been home, sunken comfortably in my leather recliner with a fresh pot of coffee gradually turning to battery acid in the kitchen and my recently purchased copy of Dayne Mercer's Storm over Chicamauga open on my lap.

Instead, just as the digital clock on the dashboard clicked over to 11:07 p.m. that Friday night, I turned my county car off the pavement of State Highway 56 and maneuvered twenty yards up a narrow fire road on the northwest flank of Santa Lucia Peak, the second highest hump in the San Cristóbal range.

To call the San Cristóbals "mountains" might have been a stretch, except for tourists from one of those midwestern places where the highest promontory in the county is the downtown bank building.

The rumpled, weather-scarred Santa Lucia Peak managed 8,117 feet above sea level—a few feet lower than San Cristóbal to its west. That lofty height would have been impressive had the mountain's base been at sea level, instead of the 5,890 feet that it was.

I had discovered this particular spot on Santa Lucia Peak years before. Skirting a sheer rock outcropping that plunged away from the state highway's serpentine guardrails, the little forest road wandered off to the east to who knows where. I'd never followed it more than the handful of yards.

What I wanted was a vantage point, and by backing just far enough into the little two-track so that headlights of traffic on

56 wouldn't reflect off the bright white of the patrol car, I had myself a quiet, remote nook.

From there, the view of Posadas County to the north and east lay unobstructed. If I had the urge to talk to someone or listen to deputies yammer license plates back to dispatch, the county's radio repeater was a mile behind me on San Cristóbal Peak, as was the mobile phone company's tower. Reception was loud and clear.

Twenty miles northeast nestled the village of Posadas, a tight little collection of lights in an otherwise dark prairie. Running east-west, the interstate formed a winking necklace across the county. With binoculars, I could pick out a few ranches that dotted the void to the north.

Even on a blustery November night, the grandstand view of Posadas County was the best blood pressure medication I'd ever found...the pure recreation of letting the mind wander, to touch first this base and then that, to skip from subject to subject, worry to worry, without interruption.

No one sat in the passenger seat, wondering what the hell I was thinking. No one ran out of patience, drumming his fingers on the vinyl dashboard. No one objected to the cold air coming through the half-open windows along with the potpourri of a thousand scents and wild sounds. No one tried to fill the silence with small talk.

I enjoyed my own company and that was hard to explain to someone who otherwise might think that I was just an old, fat, lonely insomniac. I would cheerfully admit to three of the four.

On that particular Friday night, I was savoring the considerable joys of anticipation. The list was a rich one. If the voters had any sense, come Tuesday Undersheriff Robert Torrez would become the next sheriff of Posadas County, joining a long and sometimes distinguished lineage of lawmen who had all become tired of hearing the question "Sheriff of *where?*"

Unless something had seeped into the drinking water and fermented the voters' good judgment, Bob Torrez was a shoo-in to win the election. Running against him was a daffy woman who had spent twenty years running for every elective office in the county—a woman who could design a hell of an overpass for the State Highway Department, but who didn't have an iota of law enforcement experience.

Torrez's only other opponent had been Mike Rhodes, a retiring state police sergeant. After a lackluster campaign that won him the Republican nomination, Rhodes endured some well-publicized in-law problems. He had given up the idea of elected office, pulled out of the election, and moved his wife and family to Missouri.

As far as I was concerned, Bob Torrez would be undersheriff on November 6, and when the votes were tallied on November 7, I planned to toss him the sheriff's badge and the keys to my desk. He could call himself whatever he wished: sheriff, acting sheriff, sheriff-elect, undersheriff-until-January...whatever. I didn't care what the state constitution might say about the orderly transition of the powers of elective office. For me, November 7 was my last day as sheriff of Posadas County.

In the past, circumstances had prompted me to put off retirement more than once, and I currently held an office to which I neither had been elected nor to which I had aspired. Enough was enough. November 7 was it.

That was the extent of my retirement planning—but not of my anticipation. On Sunday afternoon, Francis and Estelle Guzman were flying into El Paso from Rochester, Minnesota, in company with my two godurchins, Francisco and Carlos. I hadn't seen them in more than five months, and the delight of that reunion was tempered only a little by concern.

In a moment of weakness I'd offered the Guzman family accommodations at my rambling, spacious old adobe on Guadalupe Terrace, since the electricity and water were shut off in the place they still owned on South Twelfth Street. The thought of the two high-powered children racing through the dark sanctum of my fragile old home gave me pause.

My promise to handcuff four-year-old Francisco Guzman to a tree outside if he didn't behave himself produced nothing but a cackle of glee.

Choosing Election Day for a family holiday wasn't as bizarre as it might first seem. Estelle Reyes-Guzman had spent nearly a decade with the Posadas County Sheriff's Department herself, including a week-long stint as undersheriff just before she, her physician husband, and the two kids had moved to the wilds of Minnesota. Two years before that, she'd tried her hand at politics when she ran for sheriff and was soundly trounced. I had planned to retire then, too.

I knew that the Minnesota life was in flux for the Guzmans, but had tried to stay out of their way. I even refrained from sending them care packages of green chile or decent salsa, that cruel trick that New Mexicans do to other New Mexicans who are forced to suffer outside the state for any length of time. I didn't know what the Guzmans planned. If Estelle wanted to confide in me, she would do so in her own good time…I'd learned that over the years. I was just pleased that they had timed their arrival so that they could help the new sheriff-elect celebrate.

The clock on the dashboard clicked to 11:30, and four miles away I could see the wink of headlights as someone pulled out of the parking lot and headed west from the Broken Spur Saloon down on Route 56. In a few minutes, if they didn't turn north at County Road 14, they would start up the long twisting slope toward Regal Pass, taking them past my parking spot. For most of their trip, I'd have a grandstand view as their headlights sliced open the night.

No sooner had the car straightened itself out on the pavement and headed west than another set of headlights popped on, this time a quarter mile east of the saloon. Winking red lights blossomed, and I grinned. I leaned forward and turned up the police radio. The sound of car engines carried in the quiet night air as currents wafted up the back slope of the mountain.

The flashing lights pulled close behind the first car, but it didn't slow. As if tied together, the two cars plunged past the intersection with County Road 14, both heading west. When the car started up the hill without slackening its pace and managed to pull away from the county vehicle, I keyed the mike.

"Three oh eight, three ten is at the top of the hill. You want me to cut him off?"

"Negative, sir. I'm backing off. I know where the kid lives."

Even as Undersheriff Robert Torrez said that, I saw the interval between the two vehicles stretch. In theory, what Torrez was trying to do should have worked. With a dangerous, winding mountain road coming up, there was no point in pressing a senseless chase until someone ended up crashed into a canyon or pulped against a scraggly juniper, grinding up himself and his passengers.

Torrez knew the driver, knew where he lived, knew that if he dropped back, the kid would slow down, stay alive, and pull into the home driveway thinking he'd beaten the deputies again. That's the way it should have worked. But that's not what the kid did. Taking his cue from all the highly paid, sober Hollywood stuntmen he'd watched in the movies, the kid tried for magic.

For a brief minute or two, as it snarled up the sweeping, smooth highway toward Regal Pass, the charging car was out of view, skirting around a couple of dry, brush-covered foothills. I could hear that he was still pushing pretty hard, a little engine flailing away. I saw a flash of lights through the trees and then, with a squawl of tires, the kid stood on the brakes and swerved into the narrow fire road...the same dirt two-track in the middle of which was parked the aging sheriff of Posadas County.

Chapter Two

What the driver couldn't know was that after his car left the pavement, he had no more than fifty feet to haul his vehicle to a stop. That wasn't enough, even for a union-scale stunt driver with two or three rehearsals.

I had time to recognize the oncoming missile as some sort of little compact car, and I grabbed the steering wheel to brace myself. Just before his car T-boned mine, his headlights flicked off. It must have been a hell of a surprise. One instant, he was cleverly reaching for that switch to kill the headlights, and in the next found himself collecting an aging Ford Crown Victoria as a hood ornament.

The little car crashed into the left rear passenger door and quarter panel of 310, sending a shower of busted glass that sprayed the back of my head. The impact jolted the patrol car sideways, uncomfortably close to the yawning open spaces.

For about three seconds after that, things were pretty quiet. I could hear my heart pounding, and then a quiet tinkle as a few fragments of glass tilted out of the remains of the window behind me.

Without taking my eyes off the car, I reached out slowly and picked up the microphone. "Three oh eight, I've got company."

The radio squelch barked twice, but I was more interested in the voices coming from the little car. I didn't know if they had actually seen me sitting in the patrol car or not—it was possible that the driver had hit the lights before my presence registered on their hyperactive little pea brains.

The driver bailed out in a drunken dance that left him on his hands and knees, one hand clutching the open door, the other on the ground.

At the same time, with my flashlight a comfortable weight in my hand, I opened my own door, taking my time. I snapped on the beam and framed the wild-eyed face. The kid was sloshed. He let go of the door frame, reared to his feet, and took a staggering step toward the back of his car. I could smell the alcohol, the concentrated aroma from a six-pack that's had a wild ride around the inside of a car.

"Just hold it right there," I barked. He flattened against the car as if without its support his spine might turn to Jell-O and he'd fall on his face. He wasn't bleeding, and all four of his limbs bent in the right places. He just didn't know what to do with them.

With my free hand I fished the handcuffs from the back of my belt. "Turn around and put your hands on the car," I ordered. The other two occupants hadn't budged, and as long as they stayed put, things would be fine.

I twitched the light just enough to take a quick glance at the kid riding shotgun. He was rocking back and forth holding his face, blood pouring over his fingers. No doubt the dashboard had tap-danced across his mouth, lacing a few teeth through his lip. In the back a third party animal braced both hands against the seat in front of her, staring bug-eyed at me. Fourteen years old and the daughter of an acquaintance of mine, she had reason to be scared.

The kid standing by the car hadn't moved, and I gestured with the flashlight. "Turn around," I repeated. About that time, more lights poured through the trees, and Bob Torrez's patrol unit almost slid past the fire road. He turned in, the stiffly sprung vehicle jouncing on the ruts.

The kid took one look at the flashing red lights on the roof of the Expedition and spun away from me, darting around the back of the little car. He tripped over something and fell hard, then got up and lurched off down the lane toward the darkness.

At one point he was headed straight for a thick grove of scrub oak, but he changed course at the last minute, picking up speed as he went.

Torrez appeared, framed in the headlights. He and I stood and watched as the kid zigged out of the beam of my flashlight.

Torrez showed no inclination to spring into action, and instead said, "Well, that's neat."

I wasn't sure what he meant by that, but I sure as hell wasn't going to run after the kid. At seventy years old and three days from retirement, I wasn't about to run after anything.

Torrez turned the beam of his own light into the car. "Pretty good idea you had, to let Matt drive your car, Toby," he said. He bent down and rested his forearms on the windowsill. The kid was in no mood for sarcasm, and responded with a pathetic whimper. "Let me see your face," Torrez said and reached into the car. With one hand on top of the kid's head, he held him quiet. The youngster still managed to cringe downward, his hands trying to ward off the undersheriff's monstrous paw.

"Move your hands," Torrez commanded, and the kid let them sink halfway to his lap, poised and ready should some part of his injured anatomy decide to fall off. With my light from the other side, Torrez could see the damage, and after a moment he said, "Sit tight. You'll be all right."

He turned the light on the girl in the back. "Nice night, eh?" he said. "You all right?"

She managed a nod.

"No cuts, no hurts?"

She shook her head.

"You sit tight too," he said, and turned back to me. "If you'd request an ambulance, I'll get something for Toby's face."

"I don't need no ambulance," the kid said thickly, the first coherent words I'd heard him utter. He leaned forward toward the dash. He looked as if he was about to throw up.

"I'm sure you don't, tough guy," Torrez said. "Stay in the car." He grinned at me, and then hustled back to the Expedition. I waited until he returned before turning to the radio to hail dispatch.

Now that Torrez had put a name to him, I recognized the injured youngster as Toby Gordan. His mother, Emilita, was going to be really pleased. She worked as a custodian at Posadas County Hospital and lived just a handful of blocks from her work. That was convenient too, since her only car was now a couple of feet shorter than it had been.

With an ambulance on the way, a clean compress holding Toby's remaining teeth and lip in place, and the girl snuffling but otherwise behaving herself in the backseat, I said to Torrez, "What do you want to do about the driver?" I indicated the darkness into which he'd fled.

"Like I said, I know where he lives," Torrez said. He straightened up and rested a beefy arm on the roof of the car. "That's Matt Baca, my uncle Sosimo's oldest kid." He ducked his head and looked in the car. "That's who was driving, right?"

Toby Gordan managed a "mmmph" through his tears and loose teeth, but the girl in back, Jessie Montoya, nodded.

"Where'd you guys get all the beer? Did Victor Sanchez sell it to you?" Torrez asked, but Jessie just looked down at the floor mats. Sanchez owned the Broken Spur Saloon on State 56 where the chase had started, and he knew better. Torrez sighed and glanced at the luminous dial of his watch. "I just caught a glimpse of him, but it looked like our runner was wearing a T-shirt and jeans," Torrez said. "No coat."

"That's it," I said.

Torrez leaned away from the car and looked up into the night. The scrub oak leaves were fitful against a clear and star-studded sky. The moon had slipped behind the bulk of Santa Lucia. The kid would be running by feel and by guess. As drunk as he was, he wouldn't have much luck with either one.

"It's not going to freeze tonight," Torrez said. "He'll be all right as long as he doesn't trip and break his neck."

"Which he's apt to do," I said. "You've been down this road?" I realized that it was a dumb question before the words were out of my mouth.

"Lots of times," Torrez said. His passion was hunting, and wherever anything with fur or feathers went, there went Robert. "It dead-ends about two miles to the east, along this ridge. If he makes it that far, he'll have to run another three miles cross-country to reach the power-line access road over the top. He ain't going to do that. Not at night." He looked at the sky again. "Well," he said, and glanced at me. "I'm going to stroll on after him a little bit, just in case he discovers some sense out there and changes his mind." He shifted his handheld radio on his belt a bit, fiddling with one of the knobs. "I'm on channel three."

The two kids in the car seemed content to sit and snuffle in relative silence, so I made constructive use of the time to fill in most of the blanks on the Uniform Traffic Incident report. I had almost finished when another patrol car, followed by the ambulance, added their light show.

Deputy Thomas Pasquale and two EMTs hustled into the glare of headlights. I looked up at the deputy from where I sat behind the wheel of 310. "And here I was, parked in the middle of everywhere, minding my own business," I said.

"Are you all right, sir?" Pasquale asked, and before I said, "Fine," the two paramedics had found the blood in the other vehicle. Despite their gentle, professional ministrations, we were treated to a pathetic series of yelps, groans, and whines as they got the kid out of the car and strapped to the gurney for the trip back to Posadas General.

I got out of the car and tossed the clipboard and report on the seat. "She's going to need a ride," I said to Thomas. "Let's see what she wants to do."

What Jessie Montoya wanted to do, no doubt, was slink out into the woods somewhere and wait until the world went away. She was the picture of absolute humiliation, cringing away from the young female paramedic who was ready to crawl inside the car if need be for the answers she wanted. Finally satisfied that the girl was unharmed, the EMT backed out of the car.

"She's all right," the paramedic said, and glanced at the front of the vehicle. "Not much of an impact. If the kid up front had

had his seat belt on, he probably wouldn't have smacked his face." She grinned. "You have a good night, Sheriff."

"Thanks," I said, and the EMT stepped out of my way. I bent down with one hand on the roof for balance, keeping the flashlight beam out of Jessie Montoya's face. The harsh headlight beams through the back window haloed the hair around her head, hiding her eyes. The smell of urine had overpowered the beer.

"Jessie, why don't you step out of the car." I tried to sound as if she had a choice. "Let's make sure everything still works, okay?"

She murmured something that I couldn't hear. I held out my hand. "Come on." She turned a bit sideways, swinging one blue jean-clad leg out of the car. "Are your folks home?" She didn't respond, still struggling with the humiliation of being caught with soiled pants. "If they are, we need to give them a call."

"I'll find my way home. Just let me go," she said, and there was a quiver to the petulance.

Tom Pasquale appeared at my elbow. "Here's the number, sir," he said, and handed me his notebook. I shined the light on the page and could have imagined that there was writing there. Jessie Montoya shrank back on the seat, out of Deputy Pasquale's view.

"Tell me what it is," I said to Tom, and dug the small cell phone off my belt. Before I dialed, I said to Jessie, "What time were your folks expecting you home?"

"I don't know."

"Do they know that you're with Matt and Toby?"

That brought a little shake of the head.

"What stops did you make before the Broken Spur?"

"Before the what?"

"The saloon down in the valley. Your last stop before this mess here."

"We were just like...around, you know? I don't remember."

"You don't remember any specific place?"

"No."

"Who had the booze?"

No matter how she answered that, Jessie Montoya could see trouble on the horizon, so she ignored the question and turned her attention instead to the task of getting out of the mangled little car. She stood with her back to Tom Pasquale.

I dialed the number, and in a moment, a pleasant contralto voice answered the phone. "Donna?" I said. "Bill Gastner here. How are you folks doing tonight?" I didn't bother apologizing for the late hour. Young Jessie could do the apologizing later. I tried to keep my tone light, and apparently succeeded. Maybe Donna Montoya thought it was a last-minute, midnight campaign solicitation.

"Sheriff! So nice to hear from you. We don't see much of you anymore."

"Busy, busy, Donna. Look, the reason I called. Jessie's going to need a ride home, and I just wanted to make sure one of you was going to be there when we drop her off. We should be back in Posadas in another half an hour or so."

A dead silence followed. "Jessie? What do you mean?"

"Jessie, your daughter. She's here with me."

"With you? How's that possible? She's in her bedroom, sound asleep, Sheriff."

"Take a minute and go check, ma'am," I said. "I'll hold." She did so, and I glanced at Tom. "The old 'out the window' trick," I said to him, and Jessie ducked her head and slumped her shoulders another notch.

In less than a minute, Donna Montoya was back on the line, this time with considerable urgency in her voice. "Sheriff, where are you? What's going on?"

"Jessie is fine, Donna. She was out with a couple of other kids, and they managed to bang their car up a bit."

"Oh, my God. You're kidding."

"No, ma'am. We're about half a mile from Regal Pass on Fifty-six."

"Oh, for God's sakes."

"Uh-huh."

"And you're sure she's all right?"

"Yes, ma'am. She's fine." Describing Jessie Montoya just then as "fine" was a bit of a stretch.

"Do you want us to come down to get her? I mean, who was she with? Are they all right?"

"She was a backseat passenger in a vehicle operated by Matt Baca, ma'am. Toby Gordan was also in the vehicle, riding up front. And no, it won't be necessary to come get Jessie. I'll just have Deputy Pasquale drop her off on his way back to the office. He's about ready to leave now. You might keep a watch out the window. It should be about twenty minutes."

"Let me talk to her, please," Mrs. Montoya said, and I could hear the coiled cat-o'-nine-tails in her tone.

"Sure." I extended the phone toward the girl. "Mom wants to talk to you," I said. Jessie pushed away from the car, took the phone, and stepped away a couple of paces, her back to us.

"Thomas," I said, "make sure she rides in the backseat, and make sure the first thing you do is radio in time and odometer to dispatch. Do the same thing the instant you park in front of Montoya's."

"Yes, sir." The reminder was probably unnecessary. Circumstances were rare when we provided taxi service, and I wasn't about to summon a matron all the way from Posadas to escort a fourteen-year-old drunk. We didn't need a couple of distraught parents on the highway either, not when the deputy was headed in. But there was no point in taking chances. She could enjoy the ride behind the wire mesh with doors that had no handles or window cranks. Maybe it would make an impression.

I stayed close to Jessie, but she didn't have much to say to her mother. When she finally said, "Okay," and handed the phone back to me, I took her by the elbow to steer her toward Pasquale's car.

"Here's Bob," the deputy said, and I turned to see Torrez strolling toward us, flashlight extinguished and by his side.

"No luck, eh?" I said. He hadn't been gone long enough to make more than a perfunctory effort, and even that was a waste of time.

Torrez shook his head. "He could be anywhere," he said. "But I guess he'll turn up eventually. I'll run on down to Regal and let his father know." He rapped the back fender of 310 with his flashlight.

"You want me to come back out and give it a try?" Pasquale asked, but I waved him off.

"Take Jessie home. You might tell her mother when you get there that we'll be wanting to talk to her again in the morning, after she sobers up."

The deputy escorted the youngster to the patrol car, with Bob Torrez walking behind them. As Pasquale's unit pulled out of the narrow road, the undersheriff reached into his truck and turned off the light display, leaving us in comfortable darkness.

"You'll be all right until the wrecker arrives? I'll probably be back before they get here," he said. "We'll run the tape before they move anything."

"Sure." I swung my flashlight and looked at 310 again. The impact in front of the wheel had caved in the rear door. "It'll probably make it back to town, once the wrecker pulls this other piece of junk out of the way. And if not"—I shrugged—"it's a nice quiet night to watch the stars."

Chapter Three

During the twenty minutes that Bob Torrez was gone, I leaned against the front fender of my car, listening to the mountain. I could hear the occasional car or truck miles away, and more than one dog's yap floated on the night breeze. Other than that, the high country was quiet—just a faint whisper of moving air through the scrub oak and juniper.

If Matt Baca was working his drunken way through the brush down the southwest slope of Santa Lucia Peak toward the tiny village of Regal, he was stepping quietly. I tried to picture how a staggering drunk might navigate at night through oak brush, over jagged and loose rock outcroppings, and around vast cactus beds. If he was depending on dumb luck, the pattern of the evening's events thus far should have made him a bit uneasy—assuming that he had sobered enough to ponder such things.

Just before Torrez arrived, I heard Deputy Thomas Pasquale inform dispatch that he was stopping at the Montoya residence to drop off his passenger. I wondered if, when they drove past the convenience store on the northeast corner of Bustos and Grande, Jessie Montoya had said, "You can just drop me off here. I'll be all right." It was going to be a long night for the young lady.

The Expedition's headlights swung through the trees, and I ambled down the dirt two-track a few steps to meet it. "I was hoping maybe he'd just stroll out of the woods along the roadside," Torrez said as he climbed out of the truck.

"Stagger, you mean."

"That, too," the undersheriff said. "His father isn't home. This hour of the night, he's probably shacked up with somebody."

"Old Sosimo does that, does he?"

Bob grunted in disgust. "That would be why Josie left him two years ago. You haven't heard anything?"

"Not a peep."

"Maybe Matt's found himself a nice spot to sleep it off. And by the way, I talked to Pasquale a minute ago, right after he dropped off the girl. Apparently Matt drove his old man's pickup into town, and then he and Toby linked up at the pizza place. It was Toby's idea to talk Jessie into cruising around with them."

"So Toby's sweet on Jessie," I said. "What'd he take his mother's car for? Dumping the girlfriend in the backseat while the guys ride up front is what passes for a date these days?"

Torrez shrugged. "Sosimo's pickup is so full of junk that three people can't fit in the cab. And it stinks. He chews tobacco, and about half the time he doesn't get it in the cup."

"Well, one or another of them will show up eventually," I said. "The next question to ask Toby, as soon as the doctors cut his lips loose from his teeth, is why he let Matt drive."

"Probably because Toby doesn't have a license yet," Torrez said. "I haven't checked, but I think he just turned fifteen. If I remember right, Matt's going on nineteen. I don't remember for sure."

"For all your relatives, you'd need a directory," I said. "And I don't guess that it's too hard to find someone who's willing to sell a kid a few six-packs without a background check." I scanned the interior of the little car with the flashlight again, catching the glint of three open beer cans but no mother lode. "And it doesn't look like they succeeded in buying anything from Victor Sanchez, either."

We heard a truck approaching, and as it slowed the undersheriff reached into the Expedition and turned on the red lights for a pulse or two so that the tow-truck driver would know where to pull off into the trees.

In less than five minutes, Stubby Lopez had hooked up to the remains of the Nissan, and with that out of the way, I slid into 310 and started it up. It ran just fine, and since the bodywork hadn't crushed into the wheel or tire, I saw no point in towing the car back.

"I'd be happy to make a second trip," Stubby said hopefully.

"Not necessary," I said. "But let me go on ahead of you, just in case." I could have just stayed where I was, content to enjoy a second installment of pretending I was a wart on the side of the mountain, but the mood had been spoiled.

I drove back to Posadas without incident and parked the battered 310 over behind the gas pumps. Both Torrez and Pasquale would be off duty just as soon as they cleaned up their paperwork. Jackie Taber was the only deputy scheduled for the midnight-to-eight slot that particular day. On a quiet November Saturday morning, one deputy would be adequate.

September and October had been so slow that all of us had started to look at a routine speeding ticket as excitement. Bob Torrez had even managed to find the time to erect a handful of campaign signs around the county. That was the extent of his efforts.

More than once I had suggested a couple of radio spots, or maybe a newspaper ad or two—or an appearance at the local Rotary Club luncheon. Each time, he shook his head and grimaced. Maybe he was right. Maybe no one was going to vote for Leona Spears, his only opponent. If all of Torrez's relatives voted for him, the election would be a landslide.

I finally came to the conclusion that it wasn't that Robert Torrez didn't want the sheriff's job. He did—he'd spent the better part of fifteen years with the department, and he had his own ideas about how a tiny, broke county could finance the modern computer age of law enforcement. He just didn't have any patience with the politics that went with it.

After the sudden shot of adrenaline while having my car assaulted, I wasn't the least bit tired when I walked into my office shortly after midnight. My desk was clear of projects. I knew that if I went home, I'd sit up and read most of the night, and

I didn't want to do that, either. If I remained in my office, odds were good that someone would want to talk to me, and I wasn't in the mood to play father-confessor. Those were generally the only conversations to be had in the middle of the night.

I suppose what I really was avoiding was having to answer the irritating question, "So, what are you planning to *do* with yourself now that you're retiring?" I didn't know, and I didn't want to explain to anyone just then that I didn't know, and have to listen to a list of suggestions that didn't interest me. Somehow, people couldn't bring themselves to believe that I didn't *mind* not knowing.

I took the unmarked car that the civil deputies often used during the day, and headed toward the Broken Spur Saloon on State 56. I knew that a chat with the owner, Victor Sanchez, was on Torrez's short list. Sanchez would be closing the saloon in another hour or two, and maybe he'd loosen up a bit. Victor and I had crossed swords on several occasions, and I knew that he wouldn't bubble with enthusiasm when he saw me walk through the door.

I pulled into the saloon's lot and parked between a red Jeep Cherokee with New Mexico plates and a Chevy Suburban with Arizona tags. Two or three other vehicles, all pickup trucks, were widely spaced across the gravel.

The Broken Spur made up in darkness what it lacked in eye appeal. The small foyer was posh in wrinkled black velvet, a dark little hole to wait while the patrons decided which door to choose. To the left were the old-fashioned swinging half doors that led to the saloon. A gaping double doorway to the right opened into the small dining room.

As my eyes adjusted, I could make out a young couple seated in the dining room, hunched toward each other, deep in conversation. A single candle flickering between them. I pegged them for the Arizona plates.

No one was behind the short counter on whose glass top rested the bowl of mints and the stack of menus. Under the glass, the light winked on the gleaming collection of fake silver, fake turquoise, and really dead scorpions encased in genuine plastic. I turned left, toward the music. The saloon was darker than the foyer, and I moved slowly, the Loretta Lynn crooning from the jukebox just about the right tempo for my shuffle.

The long bar hosted a handful of customers, all of them men. I slid onto one of the bar stools out of easy talking range from the nearest, and rested my elbow on the bar. The air was thick with smoke, and it smelled good. I had told my oldest daughter Camille that one of the things I was going to do when I retired was take up smoking again. She hadn't thought the remark was funny.

Two of the tables off to the left were occupied, but at that distance and in the dim light, the figures were little more than muted shapes.

"What can I get you?" The gal's voice was a pleasant contralto, loud enough to be heard over Loretta, but not enough to jar frayed nerves. I didn't recognize her, an experience that always surprised me. After thirty years minding the business of a small county, I had grown used to seeing familiar faces around every corner—or under every rock.

"Do you still have some coffee?"

"Sure. Do you need a menu?"

I smiled with surprise, and looked at my watch. "What time is it, anyway?"

"About one-thirty. Plenty of time."

"Well, then…sure. No, wait. Don't bother. If you can find a green chile burrito back in the kitchen, that'd suit me fine."

"Smothered?"

"Sure. Smothered is wonderful."

She nodded and slipped away, returning in less than a minute with a mug of coffee. She was an attractive kid, and it was pleasant to watch her move.

"Busy night?"

"No, actually, it's been really quiet," she said, and rolled her eyes. "Really quiet. That burrito will be right up."

I nodded and relaxed, letting the warm, stuffy air meld into my bones. I realized I had gotten chilly standing out on that mountainside. If I sat in the Broken Spur very long, my eyelids would come crashing down.

True to her word, the bartender arrived in less than five minutes with a pretty respectable green chile burrito—nothing on a par with what the Don Juan de Oñate Restaurant in Posadas served, but fragrant and savory nevertheless.

"And Victor says to tell you that Matt Baca didn't buy anything when he came in here earlier," she said as she arranged the hot plate in front of me.

I looked askance at her, and then turned toward the kitchen. The swinging door was closed, but I suppose old Victor could see through the little diamond-shaped window.

"Victor says that, does he?" I tried a small mouthful of the burrito. It was pretty good—just a touch on the wet side, one of those constructions where the chef doesn't know enough to let the green chile stand alone, but pollutes it with a soup base to turn it into a sauce. "In what prior lifetime did you and I meet?"

She smiled, resting both hands on the lip of the bar. I was willing to bet there was a whole population of old drunk ranchers who stopped by the Broken Spur regularly, just on the off chance that her one-hundred-watt smile would favor them.

"The first time was about three years ago. I was one of the alternate jurors for that Wilton kid's trial. You testified quite a bit."

"Sure enough," I said, not remembering. I remembered the trial, all right, but not the jurors. I looked at her again, and decided that she was in her late twenties.

"And your picture's been in the paper off and on since then." She leaned forward a bit and lowered her voice. "You can't hide."

"I guess not." I laughed. "What's your name? My memory leaks."

"Christine Prescott," she said. "You know my folks."

"Ah, indeed I do. And I haven't seen either one of them in months. How are they doing?" The Prescott ranch, two miles north of Moore off Route 56, was a tough operation in the best of times. Gus Prescott had never been lucky enough, or positioned just right, to land himself one of the federal grazing leases. Instead he made do with a couple hundred acres of his own. With creativity and hard work, those acres were enough to keep the family right on the line between destitution and poverty.

She hesitated a bit too long and took a deep breath. "Okay, I guess."

One of the patrons farther down the bar caught her attention, and she excused herself before she had the chance to elaborate. I made a mental note to stop by her parents' place sometime. I knew damn well that I'd lose that note in the vast brain-pile of the misplaced, ignored, or forgotten—a pile that grew like a huge landfill, swelling every year.

Christine Prescott showed no inclination to gravitate toward my end of the bar for several minutes, but eventually returned to refill my coffee.

Before she had a chance to turn away again, I asked, "You said Matt Baca came in earlier?"

She nodded, but like the good bartender she was, didn't volunteer any elaboration.

"But he didn't buy anything?"

"Not for want of trying," she said, and stepped away to set the coffeepot back on the hot-plate. She returned and stood with her back to the rest of the bar. Her posture said, "You're going to ask, so get it over with."

"Was anyone else with him?"

She shook her head. "He came in for just a minute, but he sure didn't need anything else to drink."

"Had a little trouble navigating, did he?"

"Just a little," she said, rolling her eyes with the understatement. "He wanted a twenty-four pack, but I told him no, and he fished out his driver's license. I guess he thought I was refusing him because he was underage. It took him a while to get it out."

"So you checked his age and refused him anyway?"

Christine grinned. "No. I never got a chance to see the license. Victor came out of the kitchen, saw Matt, and told him to beat it."

"And Matt didn't argue with him?"

"Well, he started to, but you know how Victor can be."

"Indeed I do."

"Victor told him, 'I don't care whose ID you got. You just go away.' I guess he and Matt's dad have known each other for years."

"And Matt left after that?"

"Yep. And the chase was on." She smiled and pointed at the single window that faced the highway, most of the glass area taken up by the bright neon tubes of the beer logo. "We saw the red lights." The smile faded. "And then later the ambulance went by, and then the tow truck. Was that Matt? I assumed that it was when I saw you walk in."

I nodded. "They're all right. There were three of them in the car. No big deal." I was sure that none of the teenagers would have agreed with my assessment. I turned to see Victor Sanchez emerge through the kitchen's swinging door. Wiping his hands on his apron, he ambled up behind the bar, pausing to say something to each one of the patrons. But I knew exactly where he was headed.

Christine Prescott saw him too, but didn't make a show of being busy, and didn't step away.

"Victor," I said by way of greeting.

He stood for a minute regarding me, hands locked in the folds of his much-used apron.

"What you doing, drinking that stuff this time of night?" he asked, and jerked his chin at the coffee. "You ought to take something to help you sleep." I knew that it was as close to humor as Victor Sanchez was apt to drift.

I laughed and pushed the remains of the burrito to one side. "That was good, by the way."

"Sure it was good," Victor said. He was a squat, homely man with heavy facial features to match his rounded, muscular shoulders and thick waist. He brought the faint, cloying aroma of the greasy kitchen with him.

"You want to know about Matt Baca, you go ask Matt Baca," he said.

"There's not much I need to know about him, Victor," I said. "I know he stopped by here not too long ago, and was refused service. Either he was intoxicated, or underage, or both. It doesn't matter."

"Did he get hurt, or what?"

"No, he's all right," I said. "No big deal."

He rested a beefy hand on the bar. "You guys can put a man out of business," he said.

"Not likely, Victor. You've been here, what, thirty years?"

"Sure. But now we got your man sitting up the road there, all the time. Hell, he might as well sit his ass right in the parking lot, you know? Bad for business." He shook his head slowly. "Bad for business."

I knew that Undersheriff Robert Torrez's pet peeve was drunks. He had lost a younger brother to one years before, and I knew that on occasion, as he had this night, he prowled within easy reach of intoxicated saloon patrons as they staggered out into the parking lot. Counting the four establishments in the village of Posadas that sold liquor, there were nine licensed hot spots in all of Posadas County. In the course of a month, I listened to enough radio traffic to know that Torrez didn't single out the Broken Spur Saloon as his prime target. But there was no point in arguing statistics with Victor Sanchez.

"Cheer up, Victor," I said, and fished a ten-dollar bill out of my wallet. "After the election in another couple of days, Bob will be too busy to sit on his ass anywhere."

"How come you didn't run?" Sanchez asked, and the question caught me by surprise. I didn't figure Victor for the type who would get away from his diced onions and chicken tenders long enough to concern himself with politics. I couldn't imagine that he cared one way or another why I had chosen to retire.

I handed the ten bucks to Christine Prescott and waved away the change. "Because I'm old and tired, Victor. That burrito and coffee will give me just enough energy to get home and into bed."

I zipped up my jacket and thrust my hands into its pockets. "The undersheriff is a good man, Victor. He'll do a good job."

"We'll see about that," Victor said.

Chapter Four

When I left, the Broken Spur was shutting down for the night. I should have shut down too, but my system had other ideas. Sosimo Baca, his wild son, and two daughters lived in Regal, and the dead of 2:00 a.m. that Saturday morning seemed like a perfect time to idle through the tiny village to see who was still burning the candle at both ends. When times are dull, it's easy to start inventing tasks like that, easy to think they might be productive.

There was always the off chance that Matt would be trudging down the state highway, no doubt sobered by his mountain romp. But State 56 was quiet. I crested the pass and started down the long, serpentine curves toward the intersection with what locals called "the Douglas Road," the state highway into Arizona—and beyond that, the village of Regal.

Regal was no more than a dark spot out of range of the arc lights that blasted the days-only border crossing gate a mile south of the Catholic mission, La Iglesia de Nuestra Señora.

The town settled on the humps and bumps where the southern feet of the San Cristóbal range rose out of the prairie. Maybe sixty people lived there, depending on how many illegals were napping in the church at any given moment. Once or twice, we'd made the gentle suggestion to Father Bertrand Anselmo or various church elders that locking the church at night might be a modern thing to do, and make our job a little easier. An eyebrow or two was raised at such a suggestion, and that was that.

I didn't pursue the matter, since a modern lock on an ax-hewn door would have been its own form of sacrilege.

West of the church, a number of arroyos cut through the village, and the dirt streets dipped down into them as they wound from property to property, around shacks and woodpiles and clotheslines and derelict trucks.

If a modern community planner had tried to make sense of Regal, the first thing he probably would have done would be to straighten out lot lines and establish street right-of-ways. And then developers could hang cute street names—picturesque, tourist-pleasing tags like *Palo Verde Lane, Rincon del Sol,* or *Calle Encantada.*

But such was not the case. If any community planner had ever lingered within the boundaries of Regal, he was probably buried behind someone's doghouse with a rude juniper cross marking the spot.

The village had gradually grown into a wonderful hodgepodge as the families grew. The scuff in the dirt that led from house to shed had deepened and widened with the years, and when a son wanted to build his own home, the foot trail between generations had taken on the formality of a two-track. And that had been extended babies later, winding around this barn or that house until Regal's maze of lanes and byways held the village together like a fisherman's net.

I suppose most of the kids who lived there held the place in contempt, champing at the bit, eager to get out into the real world—a place far dirtier, noisier, and uncaring than their quiet Regal homes, despite any shortcomings.

A hundred yards before the driveway to the church, I turned right onto a lane where a small wooden sign proclaimed SANCHEZ with a little black arrow. Victor had lived in Regal once, now preferring the mobile home that was tucked behind the Broken Spur Saloon. His brother Edgar still called Regal home... along with half a dozen other Sanchez relatives.

I knew roughly where Sosimo Baca lived, and I idled the county car along as the dirt lane meandered westward, sometimes passing so close to the front of a house that I could have reached out a hand and streaked the living-room window.

Driving no more than two or three miles an hour, I rounded the corner of a rambling adobe whose front porch corner post had been nicked a time or two by careless bumpers, and damn near ran into a dark figure trudging along the road. He carried a wooden walking stick and had already begun the process of seeking higher ground, but by narrowly missing a mailbox on the left, I was able to swing around him.

I didn't know Sosimo Baca well, but I recognized his face in the glare of the headlights as he turned to ponder this intrusion into his quiet, dark, no doubt well-lubricated world. Stopping the car, I rolled down the window on the passenger side.

"Good morning, sir," I said. He was wearing a dusty, earth-colored coat that blended perfectly with the dark shadows of Regal.

"Now who's that?" he said, stringing out the last word a little bit in an accent that was rich and thick.

"Bill Gastner, Sosimo. We met a time or two, a while back."

"Oh, yes." He stepped closer and I could see that the walking stick was carrying a lot of weight. He transferred his left hand to the roof of the car. "What are you doing?"

"Oh, just out. Can't sleep."

"Yes." The single word carried so little inflection that it could have run the gamut of meaning from "me too" to "oh, sure, I know you're up to something."

"Mr. Baca, we need to talk with your son."

"Mateo?"

"Yes. He's got himself in a little trouble."

Sosimo moved his right arm so he could rest the walking stick against the door of the car, supporting himself. "You know that boy," he said after considerable thought. He turned and looked off to the east. "You know, I was just over at Ibarra's place."

"Is that right?"

"They got a good thing with that cider this year."

"I bet." *And you've sampled more than your share,* I thought. "Are you expecting Matt home tonight?"

He turned back and peered in at me. "Well, I don't know. He took the truck, you know."

"Right. It's in Posadas."

"Well, then, that's where he is," Sosimo said slowly, and patted the roof of the car as if he was sorry that I was so slow-witted.

"Sosimo," I said, "Matt wrecked a friend's car up on the pass. He was driving a vehicle that didn't belong to him, and ran into another car. The kids are all right, but he took off running."

"You don't say so? He's pretty good at that."

"Yes, he is. I thought he might have hoofed it down here since then."

"Well, you know…he might have. But I haven't been home, you know."

"You mind if we check?"

"No. You can do that."

"Get in and let me give you a lift. You can point me in the right direction."

"That sounds good," he said, and it took him a long moment to find the door latch. When he settled into the seat, his stick caught in the door, and I waited patiently while he extricated it.

"There," he said, after the door slammed. His fragrance filled the car. I left his window down and lowered mine as well.

"So that cider's a pretty good brew, eh?" I said as I pulled the car into gear.

"It sure is. It sure is." He rocked forward a couple of times to add emphasis. "That Lucy Ibarra, she makes pretty good cider."

I wondered if Lucy Ibarra's husband had been home during the sampling, but that was none of my business until the whole crowd started shooting at each other.

"Right here," Sosimo said. We had driven no more than a hundred yards and awakened a couple dogs. Sosimo could have walked the distance in the time it took him to get in the car.

The Baca place was one of those adobe houses that had shed its plaster long ago. The faces of the individual adobe blocks were rounded and contoured by age and weather to a soft brown weave that no modern building material could match.

All but one of the *vigas* had busted or rotted off flush with the wall, but other than that, the place was tidy, squat, and square, ready to dust off the worst that southwestern weather could throw at it, whether it be broiling sun or driving west winds that moved Arizona dust into Posadas County.

"The light's not on," Sosimo said. "You can park right here." The "right here" was a vague wide spot on the shoulder of the road that put my door right against the old juniper limb-wood of Baca's fence. I stopped half in the roadway so I could open my door.

"They've all gone to bed," Sosimo said as he levered himself out of the car. "Me too," he added with a grunt. He reached the front gate and stopped. "If he's not here, maybe you can come back tomorrow."

"That's a possibility," I said. "Bob Torrez will probably swing down this way."

"Oh, yes." He stopped with one hand on the first gate picket, remembering something. Maybe it was a moment of parental concern, perhaps felt more strongly when he was sober. But he shrugged off whatever the thought was and headed for the house. He walked like a man of eighty-five, even though I knew he was younger than me.

Across the street, two dogs had waited long enough. Convinced that we were now headed in the opposite direction and were no longer a threat, the mutts set up a rhythmic yapping.

The Bacas' front door wasn't locked, and even in the harsh-shadowed light of the headlights I could see its delightful rhomboid shape. It was the sort of authentic Z-braced territorial door that would fetch a mint in an Albuquerque antiques shop, the nailheads square and rough, drizzling little tongues of rusty stain down the gray wood.

The lintel was low, no more than an inch over my head, and I stood five feet ten only if I straightened my sore back and threw my shoulders out of joint. If Bob Torrez came charging through that door without paying attention, the rough wood would catch him right in the chin.

"There's a light here somewhere," Sosimo muttered, as if the furnishings of the front room hadn't been rooted in the same spots for the past forty years. He found the switch, and as the sixty-watt power flooded the room in pale yellow, I saw that it wasn't just pillows that contoured the old sofa along the south wall.

Matt Baca lay stretched out facedown, his head buried in an old comforter. One hand was curled down beside him in one of those postures only possible when deeply asleep.

"Well, he's here," Sosimo said, and paused, uncertain of what to do next.

Since young Matt was half a century or so younger than I was, and in far better shape even when drunk, I thought it prudent to take advantages as they presented themselves.

"Don't bother to wake him," I said as Sosimo took a hesitant step forward.

"Oh, no," he said, as if the idea had never crossed his mind. "You two go ahead and talk all you want," and he turned toward the door to the left of the sofa, just beyond his son's feet.

I reached around under my jacket and slipped the handcuffs off my belt. The curled right arm I didn't worry about, since the weight of Matt's body would keep it pinned until I was ready for it. I stepped across to the sofa, reached down and took his left wrist and pulled it around behind his back, slapping the cuffs on as I did so. He managed a disoriented "Whuh?" as I snicked the cuffs on his right wrist.

"Now you didn't say..." Sosimo started, but let it trail off.

Matt startled fully awake, twisting so violently that he pitched himself onto the floor, landing hard on his left shoulder. With the resiliency of youth, the maneuver didn't prompt so much as a grunt.

"Just take it easy, Matthew," I said. Earlier, by the time he found his way home and passed out on the sofa, he'd hiked a good deal of the liquor out of his blood...enough that he'd remembered to kick off his Nikes. I toed them toward him. "Put on your shoes."

He muttered an expletive and pushed himself up until he could sit on the sofa, eyes locked on me.

"You've had quite a night," I said. He didn't make a move, so I indicated the shoes. "Put 'em on."

"How the fuck am I supposed to do that?" he said, and the venom was pretty good for the hour and the circumstances.

"Don't care." I shrugged. "If you can't manage, then Robert can carry you out."

Matt's eyebrows darted together and he glanced at the open door. He could see the headlights of my car, and little else. But his expression made it clear that Matthew Baca didn't want to deal with his cousin, Undersheriff Robert Torrez. He scrabbled the nearest shoe upright and stabbed his toes into it, stamping it on with practiced ease.

"Do you have your driver's license on you?" Matt hesitated. "I need to see it."

He leaned sideways and managed to pull his wallet from his back pocket. I reached over and took it. "Where'd you buy the booze last night?" I asked.

"I didn't buy nothing," Matt Baca said.

"Oh, sure," I agreed pleasantly. The wallet included seven dollars and a valid New Mexico driver's license that showed a sullen Matt Baca and a birth date of December 13, 1982. I slipped the license into my shirt pocket and handed the wallet back to Matt.

"Sosimo," I said, "your son is charged with leaving the scene of an accident, providing alcohol to minors, driving under the influence, and half a dozen other things. The best thing for you to do is to come down in the morning and have a chat with Judge Hobart."

"The judge," Sosimo said.

"That's right. The judge. We'll have a preliminary hearing about nine o'clock. Unless you want me to wake Judge Hobart right now. He's apt to be a little sore if you did that."

"No," Sosimo said.

"And you're not in any shape to talk with him now anyway." I stepped toward Matt and took him by the left elbow. "The boy will be safe in the county lockup until morning."

"So you're going to drive up there now," Sosimo said.

"Yes," I said. Sosimo looked like he wanted to say something else, but waved a hand. The whole thing was too much for his cider-laced brain. "You have a good night," I said, and turned Matt toward the door. He shuffled along, letting me steer him into the glare of the lights.

I opened the back door of the Ford and he ducked inside before I had a chance to say, "Watch your head."

It was only as I was turning the car around on the narrow lane that he said, "Where's Bobby? I thought you said he was out here."

"Apparently not," I said, and Matt Baca settled back and ran through his entire four-letter vocabulary in both Spanish and English.

Chapter Five

I lost a bet with myself. I figured that the first thing Matthew Baca would do after he settled down in the backseat was to squirm his cuffed wrists down around his legs so that his hands were in front of him. That wouldn't accomplish much, but at least he'd be able to pick his nose. About half the kids that we put into cuffs managed to accomplish that maneuver, and I suppose that every one of them hoped that we'd be surprised as hell, thereby showing us a thing or two, by God.

Matt didn't bother with that stunt. Instead he lay on his back and let fly at the right side window with both feet.

The safety glass was pretty strong, and for the first few kicks he was off balance and experimenting. I slowed the car and twisted around to look through the heavy steel grille that separated front from back. Matt Baca was a dark, featureless shadow, but he could see my profile clearly enough.

"The last time one of those windows got busted," I said, "the court made the young man who kicked it out pay a hundred and eighty bucks to replace it. And that's in addition to all the other charges. You might want to think about that."

Matt did think about it, for about ten seconds. Reasoning wasn't on his agenda. He set to kicking again, this time with a vengeance. The *thud, thud, thud* rocked the car. Either he was tuckered from his trek on the mountain, or the soles of his nifty sneakers were too well padded. The window refused to break.

His muttered display of colorful language came in short bursts as he sucked in air between assaults on the window.

"Son," I said, "I've never actually seen anybody climb out through a bunch of broken glass while the car was moving," I said. "Especially with handcuffs on. That's going to be quite a stunt to watch."

Maybe young Baca was sober enough by then to imagine himself hanging half in and half out of the window—feetfirst or headfirst didn't matter much. It wasn't a pretty picture.

For a couple of miles, the only sound I could hear was his rhythmic breathing. I turned up the volume on the police radio and keyed the mike.

"Posadas County, three ten."

Enough seconds elapsed that I was raising the mike to repeat myself when Brent Sutherland finally found the transmission bar on the dispatcher's end. "Three ten, Posadas County."

"Posadas, three ten is ten-fifteen, one adult male. Request that three oh one ten-nineteen. And give the undersheriff a call. Advise him that his rabbit is in custody."

There was a moment while Sutherland digested that I was inbound with a prisoner and wanted Deputy Taber's assistance when we arrived and had to transfer the young hothead in the backseat to a jail cell.

"Ten-four, three ten."

Jackie Taber's husky voice added, "Three ten, three oh one copies."

I clicked the mike a couple of times and hung it back on the radio. What my backseat passenger thought of the cryptic conversation was hard to tell, but whatever he thought, it served as a trigger. He realigned and let fly again. Just as we passed the abandoned mercantile at Moore, the passenger-side back window let loose with an expensive *whump* and a shower of glass.

My first impulse was just to let the little shit lie in his own glass until we reached Posadas. I snapped on the dome light and saw that Matt was continuing his craftsmanlike job of removing the entire window in a hail of stomps and kicks.

A pair of headlights popped into view in the rearview mirror, and I slowed and pulled off on the shoulder, swinging into a dirt lane that was blocked a car-length ahead by a locked gate.

Brilliant red lights blossomed, and at first I thought that Deputy Taber had pulled in behind me. As I got out of the car I caught a glimpse of the horizontal green stripe on a field of white. Two figures got out of the Border Patrol unit, and I recognized the short, blocky driver instantly. His gait reminded me of someone walking across a pitching ship's deck.

"We saw the feet," Scott Gutierrez said with a laugh. "Who you got in there?"

"A frisky teenager," I said, and extended a hand. "You timed it just right."

Gutierrez crunched my knuckles in a quick handshake and flicked his flashlight toward his partner. "By the way, this is Taylor Bergmann, Sheriff. He joined the crew a week or so ago. We were taking a little tour, showing him the sights."

"Lots of those," I said, and shook Bergmann's hand. "Especially in the middle of the night. I'm Bill Gastner."

"I've heard plenty about you, sir," Bergmann said, and the tone of his voice left it unclear just what he meant. He turned to watch a truck as it approached from the east, the driver riding the Jake when he saw the red lights flashing on the opposite shoulder. From his confident posture, I guessed Bergmann to be retired military. The truck thundered by in a bow wave of air and a lingering cloud of diesel.

"Have you met Bob Torrez yet?" I asked, and Bergmann shook his head. "With any kind of luck at all, after next Tuesday, he'll be the new sheriff." The three of us chatted for a few minutes as if Matt Baca didn't exist.

And while we talked, not a peep issued from the backseat of my car. Young Matt had the brains to appreciate how the rules of the game had changed.

Gutierrez stepped to the busted window and shined his flashlight in Baca's face. "Hey, my man," he said pleasantly. "Why'd you break the sheriff's window?"

Baca didn't answer. He blinked into the light and lay perfectly still—the first thing he'd done right all night. Gutierrez turned to me, still keeping the light in the boy's face. "What've you got him on?"

"Oh, a number of things," I said. "No big deal. He rammed my car, for one thing."

Gutierrez stepped back and swung the light along the unmarked Ford's flanks. "Not this one," I added. "This is his second wreck for the night."

"A leg tie or two would fix that," Gutierrez observed, and I shrugged agreement. The flashlight swung back into Baca's face. "We were going to hit Tommy's in Posadas for a sandwich anyway. Let's throw him in the back of our unit and we'll drop him off for you. That way he won't sue you for making him sit in a pile of busted glass."

"I'd appreciate that." I stepped to the back door and opened it. "Matthew, time to change wagons. Slide on out of there. And you might want to be careful of the glass."

The kid took his time, and as he swung his legs out, Gutierrez said, "And that unit is brand-new, kid. You so much as breathe on it, we'll take you out into a field somewhere and leave you there."

Gutierrez was about my height and outweighed me by twenty or thirty pounds, no mean stunt in itself. But his was youthful brawn. Bergmann was the better part of six feet three with a wonderfully ugly face that would have looked right at home in a barroom brawl. It was reasonable to assume that the three of us could handle a half-stoned kid who weighed maybe one-forty dripping wet.

None of us knew what was going through Matt Baca's head. Because another vehicle was coming, this time from the west, and because the driver was slow to change lanes to give us a wide berth, both Bergmann and Gutierrez hesitated. Matt Baca hadn't stood up yet, and Scott Gutierrez was in the process of pulling a couple white nylon ties from his back pocket.

Baca lunged out of the backseat of the car, driving hard against my right hip with his shoulder. That didn't move me much, but it spun him around so that he lost his balance, back-pedaling away from me. If he hadn't been cuffed, he could have just extended one hand as he went down, using it as a pivot.

Instead, his flailing body danced backward away from the door and my frantic grasp. The oncoming vehicle wasn't a tractor-trailer, and it wasn't burning up the pavement. Maybe the driver's gaze was attracted by the blinking red lights, and not the shadows beside the vehicles. His front bumper and Matt Baca merged with an awful thump. Because the kid had already started a downward sprawl when the truck hit him, he had no chance.

So quickly did the collision happen that the driver didn't hit his brakes until the front tires, undercarriage, and rear duals had finished the job of pulverizing the young man. Then, amid billowing clouds of blue tire smoke, the truck skewed across the oncoming lane and plunged into the soft sand of the shoulder, finally jarring to a halt with its left front fender thrust through the highway right-of-way fence.

I didn't want to take the handful of steps that would carry me to Matt Baca's side. Bergmann and Gutierrez were quicker. The thought came to me unbidden that Sosimo Baca's last contact with his son had been when they were both drunk. Odds were good that Sosimo would wake up with a pounding head Saturday morning and not even remember that I'd been in his house the night before, that I'd taken his son away. I wondered what Sosimo's last sober memory of his son would be.

Chapter Six

Travis Hayes had been on his way to Posadas, about a third of his nighttime food-service delivery route completed, when Matt Baca staggered backward into the path of Travis' International. The truck's violent slide into the sand had scattered Jorgensen's Blue Label Dairy Products around the inside of the rig's reefer unit like small, frozen missiles.

If there had been heavy traffic, Hayes might have been the second fatality, because he launched himself out of the cab and dashed onto the highway without a glance left or right, only to be grabbed in a bear hug by Bergmann.

"My God," Hayes cried, "I didn't see him. He just…"

"We need you to stay back, sir," Bergmann said.

"He just…" Hayes repeated, and tried to take a step toward the shapeless lump on the pavement. As I approached from the other side, the steel of the handcuffs winked in the headlights of the Border Patrol unit. One of the cuffs was empty and flung wide.

There was no point in feeling for a pulse, but Gutierrez did anyway. Reeling as if someone had punched me, I made my way back to my patrol car and rummaged for the mike.

"Posadas, three ten."

"Three ten, go ahead."

On automatic pilot, the words that would summon the troops spilled out. Deputy Taber estimated her ETA at six minutes, with Undersheriff Torrez right behind her. The ambulance would take twice that long. As far as Matt Baca was concerned, there was no hurry.

I slumped back in the seat and waited. Mercifully, the highway was deserted, as if the world were recoiling in hushed silence. One of the federal officers found a black tarp and highway flares, and the other moved the Border Patrol unit so that it completely blocked the eastbound lane, lights flashing.

I watched the amber numerals on the digital clock on the dashboard, but after a while even they drifted out of focus. My gaze was fixed somewhere out ahead, through the windshield and off across the dark prairie toward the south.

"Are you all right, sir?"

Startled out of whatever world I'd been in by the soft voice and a gentle hand on my left shoulder, I turned and looked up into Bob Torrez's face.

"No...I mean, I'm fine," I said, and shook off the mental cobwebs. The first word out of my mouth had been the accurate answer. I hadn't seen Torrez drive up, but now the area was practically daylight in a brilliant symphony of flashing lights that captured half a dozen moving shadows.

"Deputy Taber is taking a statement from the truck driver," Torrez said. "What he says jibes pretty much with what Gutierrez and his sidekick say happened."

"I'm glad everybody goddamn agrees," I said, and pushed myself out of the car. "How the hell long have you been here?" An ambulance was backing up carefully toward the black plastic-covered lump, the vehicle's tires straddling the center line. A hundred yards to the east, another set of red lights blinked where Taber's patrol unit blocked the highway.

"Just a couple of minutes."

I don't know why that irritated me, but it did. I had the mental picture of them all tiptoeing around me, careful not to disturb the old man sitting off by himself. What the hell did they think I had been doing, writing memoirs with a DO NOT DISTURB sign hanging from the door handle?

I leaned against the rear fender of my car and watched the paramedics try to decide which part of Matt Baca's remains to lift first onto the gurney.

"Baca had his feet out of the car when Officer Gutierrez walked back to his unit," I said. "For a few seconds, I was the only one immediately beside the kid. He bowled into me, and twisted, and I wasn't fast enough to grab him. He took a handful of steps, lost his balance, and went backward out into the high-way, right past the back of the car, here." I patted the back fender of the unmarked Ford, and then lowered my voice. "The driver of the truck hadn't pulled over to the left very much. And he didn't spike the brakes until after he hit the kid." I took a deep breath, and my fingers groped at my shirt pocket where I used to keep the cigarettes. "Just like that. I don't think that the driver ever saw him. He certainly didn't have a chance to swerve or brake."

Torrez nodded and watched the paramedics. "Sosimo is home now?"

"Yes. He's drunk to the world, but he's home. I suppose the two girls are too. I didn't see them when I went in after Matt."

"Somebody's going to have to let them know," Torrez said. "When we get things cleaned up here, I'll go on down there."

"No hurry," I replied. "If you woke up Sosimo now, he wouldn't remember a thing. Let him sleep it off."

"Hell of a deal."

"Yes, it is. And I've been thinking and thinking, and I haven't come up with any answers." I turned and faced Torrez. "Number one, up on the pass, what's the first thing Matt did after his car rammed into mine?"

"He bolted."

"Damn right he bolted. He didn't wait two seconds to see if his friends were hurt, or to see who he hit, or any of that. He just flat ran. And it looks like he ran all the way home, too. When I got to the house, he was crashed out, dead to the world on the couch. Flat busted."

"Did you have any trouble with him?"

"That's what I'm getting at," I said. "I had the cuffs slapped on him while he was still asleep. For a little bit, he was pretty belligerent, but when I mentioned that I might have you carry him out to the car, he just calmed right down."

"We've had our share of run-ins in the past." He hunched his shoulders as if the cold was beginning to seep through his jacket. "You may remember that he was the one who fell down the stairs a couple of years ago, back when the juvenile cell was on the second floor."

"I'd forgotten that. He took a swing at you then, as I recall."

"Sort of."

"Well, whatever the reason, the peace and quiet didn't last. About the time we passed the saloon, maybe a little later, he starts kicking the glass. Now what the hell is he going to do when it breaks? The door's locked, so he can't get out."

"Maybe he hadn't figured that part out," Torrez said.

"Maybe not. But he worked away at that window until he popped it. And then when he had another chance to bolt, he took it." I shook my head in disgust.

"What did he say to you? Anything at all during the drive?"

"Just a colorful vocabulary."

"Anything to the two officers?" He nodded toward Gutierrez and Bergmann, who were in conference with Jackie Taber and the truck driver.

"Nope. He didn't say squat from the time I woke him up until this. Other than cussing me and my ancestors. And you and yours. Half of it was in Spanish. Probably all the good stuff." I stood up straight and tried to stretch the kinks out of my left arm. "Why did he run, Bob? Like you said before, we know where he lives."

"There's no telling what goes through their heads, sir. Especially when they're half-blasted. Something that seems dumb as shit to you or me makes perfect sense to them. At least we know where Matt bought the booze."

"We do? Where?"

"I talked to Tommy Portillo. He remembers that Matt stopped by the convenience store shortly before ten. Beer and a couple of pints."

"Tommy knows better than that," I snapped. "Jesus, he's got kids who go in there all the time, and we've never had a complaint of sales to minors. I always thought he was one we didn't have to worry about."

"He maintains that Matt had a valid ID that showed he was twenty-one, going on twenty-two. He says that he doesn't know Matt all that well, so he glanced at it, saw that it was all right, and let it go. Matt's one of those kids who could pass for anything between fourteen and legal."

"Like hell it was a valid ID." I pulled the driver's license out of my shirt pocket and handed it to Torrez. "I took this out of his wallet. He had this and seven bucks. The license says he turns nineteen in December."

Torrez nodded his head slowly. "He would have been nineteen on the thirteenth of December." He tapped the plastic card against his thumbnail. "Portillo didn't look very closely."

"Shit," I said. "Damn right he didn't look close. Either that or he can't read, the dumb son of a bitch. I can't believe he'd do a thing like that. Hell, he knows what kind of a heller your cousin is…he has to." I grimaced in frustration. "And he couldn't look out his own damn store window and see a carload of kids? Where the hell does he think the booze is going, anyway?"

"He said the car was parked over on the side, where the newspaper vending machines are. Portillo said he glanced that way, and when he couldn't see anything, didn't pursue it. Out of sight, out of mind."

"Terrific. He doesn't see much, does he. Did you check whether there was anything else Matt was carrying? Something I might have missed in the wallet? It's possible he had some other form of ID that he was using…something that a store clerk like Portillo would accept."

"We're looking, sir. Taber's working on that."

"Let's see what she's got." I pushed myself away from the car and glanced down the highway. It was long and dark, stretching away empty in both directions.

The ambulance pulled away, and the driver of the truck waited by his vehicle, his back to the road and one arm thrown up and resting against the massive hood and front fender, face buried in his coat sleeve. Bergmann stood beside him, talking to what didn't look like much response. Gutierrez intercepted us as we walked out on the asphalt.

"This is a real mess," he said. "Tell you what we'd like to do, Sheriff, if you're about through with us here. We'll go on into Posadas and stop by the S.O. and write you up a deposition. You'll be wanting that, am I right?"

"Yes. I'd appreciate that."

"No problem. Starting Sunday, I'll be on leave for a while, so we might as well get this all wrapped up right now."

I nodded. "Thanks. Beyond the deposition, I don't see any reason to tie you guys up with this mess. Enjoy your days off."

"I'll be around, though, if you need anything else. My stepfather's visiting from down south, and him and me and my sister are going to get in a little deer hunting down this way."

I shook my head in frustration. "If you figure out in a sudden burst of inspiration just what the hell happened here, you let me know."

Gutierrez frowned. "We just aren't ever going to know." He reached out a hand and I took it. "You take care, now." I knew he was right. Maybe the red lights on the Border Patrol unit had spooked the kid. Maybe it was the three of us standing around, jawing. Maybe if I'd just driven on into Posadas without stopping, the worst-case scenario would have been a few shards of glass to pick out of Matt's hair. Who the hell knew?

Bergmann strode across the road, and when he reached us, he stepped so close that I could smell his cologne. "You've got a basket case over there, Sheriff. I wouldn't leave him alone, if I were you."

"I don't intend to, thanks."

Deputy Taber had expended the better part of two rolls of film, and Gutierrez raised a hand toward her. "All right to move it?" he called, pointing at the Border Patrol unit. The deputy nodded, holding up the camera to indicate that she had all the photos that she needed.

When the two feds had left, I walked over to Taber. "About wrapped up?"

"Yes, sir," she said. "I wanted to roll a few more measurements, but that will only take a minute."

"Did you find any kind of ID other than this?" I handed her Matt's driver's license. "I took this from him at the house. It was in the wallet, along with a few bucks."

She pulled her clipboard out from under her arm and thumbed the laminated license under the clip. "The wallet itself and the contents of his pockets are bagged, if you want a look. They're over in my car."

I shook my head. "Nothing else? No other ID? No other driver's license? Nothing like that? Something that has a different D.O.B.?"

Taber shined her flashlight on the license I'd given her. "Looks like December thirteen, 1982."

The undersheriff leaned close so that he could scrutinize the license. "And that's the right one. The family Bible never lies, sir," Torrez said.

"So either Portillo was lying, or the kid had another ID with him. One that we haven't found. Maybe back at the house."

"We've never had trouble with Portillo before," Torrez said. "But I guess there's always a first time."

"First and last," I muttered. "What the hell is the point of asking for an ID, and looking at it, if you're not going to enforce the date?" I held out a hand. "Let me take that license. I'll see how well Portillo reads." Deputy Taber hesitated for an instant, then unclipped the license and handed it to me. "Thanks." I slipped it into my pocket, took a deep breath, and stepped over to the truck driver.

He lifted his head out of his arm, but didn't meet my gaze. In the psychedelic light from the various sets of flickering roof racks, it was tough to read his expression.

"I'm Sheriff Gastner," I said. "We haven't had a chance to talk yet."

"God, I wish you could have grabbed him," the man said, and as he turned a bit more, I could see his face was wet.

"You and me both," I said. "These things happen sometimes."

"I couldn't stop. I didn't even see him until just before…"

"I know that," I said. "Right now, my concern is getting this rig out of here, and you safely into town."

"I'll be all right."

"You'll be able to drive?"

"I guess so." He tried a faint chuckle. "We'll see."

"Undersheriff Torrez can drive the rig in for you. That might be better. You can ride in with the deputy."

He shook his head and backed away from the truck. "No, that's all right." He took a couple of steps until he was even with the big chrome bumper, looked down, and then jerked his head up. He turned his back to the truck. It was too dark to see anything, of course, but just the idea of what had happened was replaying in his mind—and would continue to do so for months, sneaking back to jar him awake in the night, or to make him wince in the middle of a meal or the middle of a movie.

"Do you need me for anything else?" he asked.

"The deputy has everything," I said. "If she needs any additional information, she'll give you a call. She'll want you to sign a formal deposition when she finishes, but that'll be later today."

He nodded. "Well, okay," he said and walked around the front of the truck. There was just enough room between the left front fender and the barbed-wire highway right-of-way fence for him to squeeze through.

"You're sure you're going to be all right?" I called after him.

"No, but I don't guess there's anything you can do about that," he said, and swung himself up into the truck. His knees still must have been jelly, because he stalled the rig three times before he managed to back it away from the fence and then judder through the loose sand to the pavement.

Chapter Seven

Tommy Portillo had owned his convenience store on Grande Avenue for seventeen years. Before that it had been a vacant lot that collected weeds, junk, and disparaging comments from the folks who wanted Posadas to be something.

Portillo bought the lot and built his store with a design that featured plastic, shiny metal, and vivid colors, reminiscent of the automobiles of the same period. For a while, the place was an optimistic reminder of what was new and stylish. After a while, it was as much of an eyesore as most old cars are.

I knew Tommy Portillo well enough that we usually stopped to chat for a few minutes when our paths crossed downtown.

Of the nine merchants in the county who owned liquor licenses, I knew of five who had sold to minors at one time or another. Sometimes it was just an ignorant or sloppy employee who made the sale. Regardless of the reason, one slap on the wrist by the state Alcoholic Beverage Control Board was usually enough that even folks with gray hair found themselves carded.

Because the Handiway store was within eyesight and an easy two-block walk of Posadas High School, Tommy Portillo had lots of opportunity. But I had no reason to think that he took advantage of it.

In fact, on one occasion I'd been in his store browsing through a magazine when I overheard a heated conversation between Portillo and one of his suppliers. All the heat was from Portillo's end as he blistered the man up one side and down the other, and then told him to "get those damn things out of my store. What the hell do you think you're doin'? That's just what kids need. You ought to know better." And so on.

After the harangue died down, the salesman left mumbling to himself. I ambled up to the counter.

"Hey," Portillo said. "I didn't see you over there."

"What was he trying to sell you?" I asked.

"You should see this," he said, and reached down. "I threw it in the trash." He straightened up and held out a vinyl sleeve, the bright red and white of a popular brand of soda.

"What's this for?" I said, and then figured it out for myself.

"You just slide that over a can of beer, see, and the whole world thinks you're drinkin' soda pop."

"Clever way to make a buck. I'd think this would be a hot seller."

Portillo snorted. "Of course it would. That's why they make 'em. That's all we need, is those things out and around."

"You mind if I keep this?"

"You just help yourself," Portillo said.

I had kept the slick little plastic sleeve, and still had it somewhere in my desk. This time, though, despite all of Tommy Portillo's show of righteous bluster on that day, one thing was certain now: three teens had had a roaring good time for a while, and by his own admission, he'd supplied the fuel.

The clock ticked 3:15 that Saturday morning when I pulled into the parking lot of the county's Public Safety Building and switched off the car. The Border Patrol unit was parked in the spot marked RESERVED DA. At least they hadn't taken my slot. I was too tired to walk an extra step.

I was exhausted, both physically and mentally. I sat for a moment and stared at the adobe wall ahead of the car, and my own private cinema replayed the film. I had missed grabbing Matt Baca by a hairbreadth after he stumbled into me.

Somehow it reminded me of that ludicrous poster with the old biplane that had crashed into the top of the only tree in the middle of a huge field. One tree, and the pilot had found it. There had been one truck, and Matt Baca had found that, too.

I swore a single heartfelt expletive and hauled my carcass out of the car. I didn't head for the side door, the entrance used by employees. The front door was two dozen steps closer, and didn't require that I fumble for a key.

Three straight-backed leather chairs and a matching bench lined the foyer, with large framed photographs of former Posadas County sheriffs lined up on the wall behind them. I had refused to sit for a portrait, but Linda Real, our department photographer, had snapped a pretty good shot of me sitting at my desk, scowling at the computer screen.

I thought that the scowl was a pretty good comment, and since the photo didn't feature the unphotogenic lower three-quarters of my body, grudgingly allowed the picture to join the rogues' lineup.

I was startled to see Tommy Portillo sitting in the chair under my picture.

"Hello there," I said. "Can't sleep?"

He got to his feet, a hand reaching out to the arm of the chair for support. He reminded me of a doughnut—pasty complexion and round through the middle. If anything was worse for the waistline than long hours in a patrol car fleeing boredom, it had to be working in the very source, the mother lode, of fresh junk food.

"Who can sleep?" he said.

I knew what was on his mind. "Come on in. Let's collapse together," I said. He tried a little chuckle, but it didn't work.

Behind the dispatcher's console were the neat rows of mail slots, and I could see the bouquet of "WHILE YOU WERE OUT" notes taped to the lip of mine. They could wait. Before I had a chance to disappear into my office, Brent Sutherland surfaced from the conference room.

"Are Gutierrez and Bergmann in there?" I asked.

"Yes, sir. And…" He stopped when he saw Tommy Portillo in trail. "Mr. Portillo wanted to see you."

"We'll be in my office. Did Bob Torrez go home?"

"Yes, sir."

I nodded and reached out a hand to usher Portillo through the door of my office. "Get comfortable," I said. I sat down and swung my feet up on the corner of my desk, relaxing my head back against the old leather of the chair. After five slow, deep breaths, I turned my head and looked at Portillo.

He was sitting on the edge of the chair in front of my desk, hands folded between his knees, shoulders hunched, head down as if he were trying to think away an inflamed prostate.

"You've been listening to the scanner, eh?" I asked.

He looked up and met my gaze without flinching. He was wearing an Oakland A's baseball cap, and I realized that I couldn't remember ever seeing him without it. I'd have to go to a service club meeting just to find out what was under it.

"The undersheriff stopped by to see me," he said.

"So I understand. I'd like to hear about it."

"I told him that Baca came in around ten o'clock. That's as close as I can estimate it."

"And you told him that Matt Baca showed you a legal ID of some sort?" I reached into my shirt pocket and pulled out the New Mexico driver's license that I'd retrieved from Matt Baca's wallet. The photo showed a good-looking kid, dark and lean-featured, embarrassed to be sitting in front of a camera without quite knowing how to look tough.

Portillo watched me, and could figure out for himself what I was holding. He waited until I was finished and then reached over for the license when I extended it to him.

Frowning, he turned the plastic card this way and that, and then shook his head.

"This is not the license that Baca showed me."

"I can't remember which side of the bed I'm supposed to get up on most of the time," I said gently. "After a quick glance, there isn't a chance you could be mistaken?"

"No, I mean this isn't the one. And I look, you know? I mean, I really do. Not just a glance."

"All right." I kept my tone noncommittal.

"This is the old style. Here." He handed it back to me. "The license that Matt Baca showed me earlier tonight was the new kind." He dug in his pocket and pulled out his own wallet, then extracted his license. "Like this. I got this on my birthday last month." He held it up so I could see it.

"The new style," I said, as if we didn't deal on a routine basis with the licenses issued by the Motor Vehicle Division.

"The new ones—with all those state seals on them. They kinda shimmer, like."

"Uh-huh." I tapped Matt Baca's license against my thumb. "He showed you a brand-new license. That's what you're saying?"

Portillo nodded. "That's why I came in. First, the undersheriff stopped to talk to me…I guess it was about midnight. And then later I heard about…" He let it trail off with a helpless wave of his hand. "When I talked to Torrez, you didn't have the kid in custody yet, is that right?"

I nodded.

"When I heard about what happened, I knew that you guys would be wanting to talk to me again. But believe me—if I'd thought that Matt Baca was underage, I wouldn't have sold him the liquor." He shrugged helplessly. "I just wouldn't. I wanted to come in and tell you that."

"That's thoughtful of you," I said. "Did you happen to notice his date of birth?"

"I remember that it was before this date in 1980. You know, that's how we do it. Just has to be before…" He let it drift off, realizing that he was lugging coals to Newcastle.

"But you don't remember the year that was on the license?"

"No. Seems to me that it was '79. I don't remember for sure. I mean it was close to that, but as long as it's before 1980 what's the point of paying attention, if you know what I mean."

"Did you happen to notice the date of issue?"

"Date of issue?"

"It's on the license, in small print."

"I didn't notice that, no."

"It had his picture, though?"

"Yes."

"Same one as this?" I held up Baca's license.

Tommy Portillo leaned close and squinted. "No." He settled back in the chair. "It wasn't the same picture."

"You're sure."

"Yes."

"Huh," I said, and leaned my head back against the chair again. "That's something to go on, anyway."

"I just wanted you to know. It was nagging at me, you know? You know how that goes?"

"Oh, yeah. I know how that goes."

"I think maybe I can go home now and get some sleep."

"I appreciate this, Tommy. I really do. We may want to talk to you again."

"Anytime, Bill. Just anytime."

After he left, I put Matt Baca's license back in the small, tagged evidence bag. My intuition told me that Tommy Portillo was telling the truth. He had good reason to make any attempt to cover his ass, especially now, with a fatality involved—however tangentially.

A second license explained the boy's reaching for ID in the Broken Spur. If Tommy Portillo was correct, Matt Baca had been about to show the bartender his freshly minted license. Victor Sanchez stopped the game before it had even begun.

Victor was no threat to Baca—he might not honor the bogus license, but he wouldn't report the kid, either. The kid was free to go elsewhere. It made sense that he'd head for home, where Sosimo was known to keep a bottle or two. But when the red lights blossomed as the trio left the Broken Spur, Matt Baca had reason to run. His cousin, the undersheriff of Posadas County, knew exactly how old he was.

Having the fake license was one thing. Explaining where he got it was another story entirely.

Chapter Eight

I spent a couple of hours drafting my own written explanation of the night's events. It was a simple enough incident, and ordinary circumstances would have required just a few minutes to whack out the necessary paragraphs of the deposition, beginning with the collision of Matt Baca's car and my own.

"Ordinary circumstances" would have been if the incident had happened to someone else. As it was, I lingered over every sentence, letting my mind search and sift, looking for something that might strike a spark. I knew exactly why the kid had been mangled by the delivery truck. He was fast, I was slow. It was that painfully simple. Discovering why he'd decided to run in the first place wasn't so simple.

Later in the morning, one of the deputies would have the chance to talk at length with Jessie Montoya, the young lady in the backseat. And maybe Toby Gordan would be able to mumble a few words past his stitches. The rules of the game had changed since I'd last seen those two kids—there was no need now for them to worry about protecting Matt Baca, or even saving face in front of their friend.

Whether or not Matt had told them where he got the license was another question. I was confident that he had, since humans are notoriously blabby when they've done something stupid of which they're inordinately proud. I was sure that if Toby or Jessie knew, they'd tell us.

Shortly after five that Saturday morning, I finished the affidavit and walked out to dispatch. The deep, predawn hush included the Public Safety Building. Gutierrez and Bergmann, the two Border Patrol agents, had long since left, Deputy Taber was somewhere in the county prowling the shadows, and dispatcher Brent Sutherland was trying his best to remain alert as the adrenaline rush from earlier in the night wore off.

"Dig out your seal, would you?" I asked, and Brent looked grateful for something to do and eager for an excuse to use his freshly minted Notary Public commission. A few minutes later, as I slid the notarized statement into Taber's mailbox, I said, "I'm going home, Brent." At the same time, I leafed through the messages taped above my name…the same messages I'd ignored earlier and that were now stale as day-old toast.

One didn't require a response, and a second recorded that Cliff Larson, the district livestock inspector, had called at 9:30 Friday evening. "What did Cliff want, did he say?"

"No, sir. He said that it could wait until today sometime. I gave him your cell phone number, but I guess he didn't call."

"I guess not. And Frank?" Frank Dayan, the publisher of the *Posadas Register,* had called shortly after 10:00 p.m.—a good hour before all the action started. No doubt Frank would be gnashing his teeth that we'd been inconsiderate enough to make important news a week before his next issue hit the street. A central joy in his life was beating the big-city dailies to the hot stuff. I was sure that most of the time, the metro papers didn't know they'd been scooped…or care.

"He didn't say, sir. Just that it wasn't important."

"Huh," I grunted. "If it's not important, why do these people pick up the phone in the first place. One of the mysteries of life, I suppose." The fourth note, recorded in Brent Sutherland's careful printing, said that Dan Schroeder, the district attorney, had called from his home in Deming at 2:55 a.m. to tell me that a meeting at 9:00 a.m. was just fine with him.

"The DA doesn't waste any time, does he?" I muttered.

"Sir?"

I waved the note. "The DA."

Sutherland looked a bit uncomfortable. "The undersheriff said I should call him because of the fatality," he said. "Because it involved us."

"Not *us*," I said laconically. "*Me.* And both you and the undersheriff did the right thing, and nine a.m. is just fine." I crumpled the note and chucked it in the trash basket. "Like I said, I'm going home for a couple of hours. Is there another vehicle handy? I'll try my best to keep it in one piece."

I ended up taking the keys to 306, the Bronco that Deputy Tom Pasquale drove most of the time.

The breeze outside had freshened, driving the November chill down into the town from the San Cristóbal Mountains. It was the tonic I needed before meeting with the district attorney. If I went home and fell asleep, I'd wake groggy and unkempt for a meeting where Schroeder would expect me to be sharp and cogent.

The better strategy was a good, solid breakfast with enough strong coffee to see me through the morning. Then, after the DA was satisfied, I could go home and crash.

I bounced the stiffly sprung truck out of the parking lot and turned west on Bustos. The Don Juan de Oñate Restaurant opened at six, but I knew that the owners were there early and the side door would be unlocked.

I slowed at the intersection with Grande when I saw the aging pickup truck stop for the northbound light. Cranking the wheel hard, I turned south and then braked to a halt right in the middle of the intersection. Bob Torrez rolled his truck forward until we were window to window.

"I was going to get some breakfast," I said. "Join me. My treat."

"I thought of something that I wanted to ask you," the undersheriff said without preamble. Not many words were wasted in the Torrez household, I had decided long ago. I wondered what constituted small talk when Bob and his wife Gayle were feeling blabby.

"Over a burrito," I said. "Ask me anything over a smothered burrito." A car emerged from one of the side streets to the west, and turned away from us. "And don't tell me you've already had breakfast. Gayle's not about to get up at this hour, and the only time you ever cook is over a campfire."

"Now that's true," Torrez said, and the grin was a welcome break in what was otherwise a pretty gloomy face. "I'll follow you."

I nodded and continued my circle through the intersection. With a belch of smoke, Torrez's pickup fell in behind. As an unmarked vehicle, his truck would certainly fool somebody once. Mostly flat black mixed with a little gray primer here and there, the old Chevy was a monstrosity. There was enough junk in the back, behind the ornamental iron scrollwork that protected the back window, that the rig must have weighed three or four tons.

The front door of the Don Juan was open, but I paused with my hand on the handle, regarding a large, neatly printed sign. When Torrez joined me, I said, "What's with this?"

Rather than hasty black marker, someone had taken the time to letter the sign in beautifully decorated calligraphy.

The Don Juan de Oñate will be closed
all day Nov. 7.
We will reopen Nov. 8 at our usual time.

He shrugged. "No liquor sales that day anyway until the polls close at seven. Fernando must have decided to take a vacation."

"Fine timing." I pulled open the door. "Where are we supposed to celebrate your win?"

Torrez caught the door and followed me inside. "At home, maybe?"

I led the way around various dividers, tables, and the empty salad bar unit and settled in the third booth from the back, where the window faced the parking lot and a fine view to the west. When I slid all the way into the booth, I could see the alcove of the front door.

Arleen Aragon, the owners' daughter-in-law, appeared around the divider. "Hey, you guys," she said. In one sweeping move of her right hand she collected two mugs, and with her left hefted the full coffee carafe.

"Some night, huh," she said as she clunked the two cups down on the table in front of us. Apparently everyone in the world had a scanner tuned to the Posadas County hit parade. Or maybe she'd just overprepped the hash browns, blackening the edges. I didn't pursue what she meant.

"I guess," I said. Arleen filled the cups within a hairbreadth of the rims and started to turn away.

"Neither of you take cream, right?"

I shook my head.

"Breakfast?"

I nodded. She replaced the coffeepot and returned to stand with her hands on her ample hips. "You, I can already guess," she said, looking at me. "Burrito Grande green, extra smothered, sour cream on the side."

"Perfect."

"How about you, Bobby?"

The undersheriff took a deep breath. "I don't know how hungry I am," he said, and started to reach for a menu.

"You gotta eat," Arleen said. "That's the number one rule around here. A burrito would do you good. It looks like that wife of yours is starvin' you." At six-four and 230 pounds, Robert Torrez wasn't my idea of undernourished.

Torrez retreated from the menu. "All right," he said. "The same."

"Except no sour cream, right?"

Torrez grinned. "Right."

"I didn't think that you liked that gringo stuff," she said, and punched me on the left arm. "It'll be a few minutes," she added. "You kinda caught us before the normal breakfast rush."

When she had gone, I took a long sip of the coffee and then said, "You heard about the nine o'clock meeting with Schroeder?"

Torrez nodded. "I told Brent to give him a call. I didn't want the DA hearing it from some other source."

"Have you been out to see the old man?" Sosimo Baca was ten years younger than I was, but his love of alcohol in any form as long as it was in quantity had his family counting Sosimo's birthdays in dog years.

"I went out about four or a little bit before. I woke up Father Anselmo and had him go along." Torrez grimaced. "Father said he'd been expecting something like this for a long time. He calls Matt *el cachorro impetuoso*."

"Meaning?"

"A wild pup. Roughly."

"And when you two went to Baca's, are you sure that Sosimo understood what you were talking about?"

"It appeared so. I made sure that the two girls were awake, too, just to be sure. Sosimo still smelled like a brewery, but the kids understood. I tried to keep it simple." Torrez paused and took a deep breath. "I said that apparently Matt had kicked out a window in the patrol car, and that during the process of transferring him to another unit, he bolted into the path of traffic." He shrugged. "Father Anselmo was still talking to them when I left. Matt's two sisters seemed to take it all right. Maybe with enough coffee in him, Sosimo will be able to understand what happened. By noon or so. I was planning to go back down in a little bit." He glanced at his watch. "Talk to my uncle again. I'd like to look through Matt's private stash and see what I can find."

"Want me to come along?"

"That's not necessary."

I leaned forward and lowered my voice so that the coffee urn wouldn't hear me.

"I've been playing this thing over and over in my mind. I can't get a handle on it."

Torrez shook his head. "From what Gutierrez and Bergmann told me, there wasn't much you could do. Not much anyone could have done."

I waved a hand in dismissal. "I don't mean that. Sure, if I'd been a bit quicker, I could have grabbed him. Hell, so what. If that had happened, maybe he'd have dragged both of us in front of that truck...and then I'd really be pissed. No"—and I shook my head—"that part I can live with, all right. What I don't understand is his determination, Robert."

"How do you mean?"

"On the highway, as soon as you turn on the red lights, he runs. Up on the hill, he crashes into me, and then takes off into the trees. All right, I can understand that. He's scared, as any stupid kid would be. He knows that if you catch him, you're probably going to beat the crap out of him. At least he *thinks* that you are. And maybe the fact that he stumbled on home, right where you knew he'd be, just goes to show how really drunk he was."

"He couldn't have wanted to get away very badly," Torrez said. "Unless he was just too sloshed to know better."

"Right. So we chalk up the first episodes to being young, stupid, and drunk. I come in and slap the cuffs on him. He's had a couple or three hours to sleep, and some of the booze has worn off. He should be able to put two and two together, with a little fresh air to help wake him up."

"And instead, he kicks out the window."

"Right. Now what's that going to gain him?"

Torrez pushed his coffee to one side. "Nothing, but he doesn't know that."

"What, he thinks that I'm going to stop the car, and he's going to have a chance to run off into the night again? In the middle of nowhere, with handcuffs on?"

Torrez shrugged. "We don't know what he was thinking. But that's exactly what he did. Or tried to do."

"Well, it's true. We don't know what he was thinking. But regardless of what his addled little brain was concocting, wouldn't you think he'd put it all on hold when two Border Patrol cops show up? I mean, I'm old and fat, and I know it. And Matthew knew it too. But Gutierrez and Bergmann aren't. So why did he pick that time to bolt?"

With his elbows on the table, Bob Torrez folded his hands together as a support for his chin. He thought for a long time, his gaze taking in the dimly-lit details of the room. About the time my impatience was about to prompt me to ask if he'd forgotten the question, he said, "I don't think it was a rational thing."

"I'll agree to that. But it was a *desperate* thing, Roberto. And there has to be a reason. Why would seeing a couple of Border Patrol agents trigger that reaction?"

"We don't know that's what triggered it, sir."

"No, we don't. I never mentioned them. If he was listening, all he heard was my call to Sutherland, to tell him I was inbound."

Arleen Aragon appeared with two generously heaped plates billowing steam and fragrance.

"That's some breakfast burrito," Bob said, and leaned back while Arleen coasted the platter in for a landing.

"That's our dinner burrito," Arleen corrected. "The sheriff doesn't do those dinky little things on the breakfast menu." The second plate landed in front of me with a heavy thud. "It's hot, so be careful."

"Brain food," I said. "Maybe something will occur to me."

"When he sobers up, Sosimo might have some answers," Torrez said.

"Don't hold your breath."

Chapter Nine

District Attorney Daniel M. Schroeder looked like a lawyer—perfectly fitted and pressed dark suit, spit-polished black wing tips, gold wire-rimmed glasses, a bulging, old-fashioned top-opening leather briefcase, and a gold Cross pen that flicked indecipherable notes on a fresh yellow legal pad.

He was sitting by himself in the Public Safety Building's conference room when I returned. With him looking so damned formal, I was glad I'd taken a few minutes to go home, shower, shave, and spruce up. Not that Dan would have cared how I looked. Over the course of twenty years, I'd come to the conclusion that District Attorney Schroeder was an interesting fellow, one of those rare folks who didn't immediately transfer what he thought about the world to other people as a requirement for what *they* should think.

Still, I had to admit to a certain small uneasiness. No matter how the story was told, no matter how the excuses fell, it was my fault that Matthew Baca was dead. The kid had been in my custody. With that in mind, I had a personal interest in what conclusions the district attorney reached.

Schroeder looked up from his pad when I entered the room, and his round face cracked in a neutral smile. "Morning," he said as he pushed the chair back and stood up. Not "good morning," or "rotten morning," or "how are you." Just the single word into which I was free to read whatever I liked. We shook hands, and his grip was neutral, too—not forced hearty, not perfunctory or limp.

"Do you want the undersheriff here for this?" I asked.

"Ah," he said, and looked down at the legal pad. "Not right away. Let's just you and I talk for a bit." I started to pull out a chair, but he was already gathering up his things. "Let's use your office," he said. "We might have fewer interruptions there."

Interruptions weren't the issue, but I appreciated the gesture and didn't object. If I had to be grilled, it was more comfortable to be well done on home turf. I appreciated an unspoken second gesture, too. Donald Jaramillo, the assistant district attorney who generally worked Posadas County, was not present. I didn't care for the little weasel, and Schroeder knew it.

As I closed my office door behind us, I said, "Go ahead and use the desk."

"This is fine," he said, and settled in one of the two leather-padded captain's chairs.

"Coffee or something?"

"No thanks. I'm fine." He waited until I'd finally settled in behind my desk. With his elbows on the arms of the chair, he held his pen in front of his face, one end in each hand, and slowly spun it as if he were searching for imperfections in the gold finish. After a minute, his gaze switched to me.

"I understand that you witnessed some or all of the under-sheriff's initial pursuit of Matthew Baca?"

"Yes. I was parked up on the mountain, just this side of Regal Pass. A little after eleven o'clock. I could see the lights of the Broken Spur Saloon from where I was parked."

"And you saw the Baca vehicle arrive at the saloon, and then leave shortly thereafter?"

"I didn't see it arrive. Or at least I didn't notice it arrive. That might be more accurate."

"How long had you been parked when you saw the vehicle leave? When you saw it drive out of the saloon's parking lot?"

"Maybe twenty minutes. Maybe twenty-five."

"Do you think that Baca had been at the saloon all that time?"

"I doubt it. The bartender at the saloon said the kid was just in and out. Tried to buy beer, was refused, and left."

"So you just missed his arrival, then. Somehow."

"Somehow."

"Undersheriff Torrez said that he was parked at the old windmill about a quarter mile down the road. To the east. Is that your understanding?"

"Yes. I saw his vehicle when he pulled out on the highway with his emergency lights on. I don't know how long he'd been parked there."

"So he wasn't just driving down the highway."

"No."

"Does he do that often? Park and watch?"

"Sure. We all do." I almost added, "As you well know."

"When the undersheriff began his pursuit of the Baca vehicle, what did you do?"

"I radioed Bob to ask if he wanted me to head the kid off at the pass."

Schroeder grinned at that. "And did you?"

"No. The undersheriff had dropped back then, and said that there was no point in continuing pursuit. He said that he knew where the kid lived. There was no point in pushing the chase and risking an accident."

"We've been there before, haven't we?"

"Yes, we have."

Schroeder nodded and clicked his pen. "And he turned off his red lights?

"Yes, he did."

"Would the kids have seen the lights go out, or was Bob too far behind them?"

"I have no idea. They were intoxicated, excited, scared—all those things. And there are lots of trees, curves, the whole bit. My guess would be that they still thought they were being pursued. Otherwise, I don't know why they would have turned off the highway onto the dirt lane."

"Your lights weren't on?"

"No. My engine wasn't even running."

"That must have been a hell of a surprise, when they turned into that side road. Did they have a scanner in the car, do you know?"

"No, they didn't."

"So they couldn't have known that you were there."

"I don't think so."

"Would a sober driver have had enough time to stop before hitting your vehicle if he had pulled off the highway in the same fashion?"

"No, not at that speed. We're only talking a few yards from the highway shoulder to where I was parked."

"And when the vehicle came to a stop after plowing into yours, Matthew Baca immediately got out of the car?"

I nodded. "Yes. Driver's side."

"He didn't talk to the others?"

"Not that I saw or heard. He got out and stumbled around toward the back of his car. About by the left rear wheel. I got out at the same time and told him to stop, or turn around, or some such. I don't remember exactly what. He looked like he might cooperate. It appeared that when he saw the lights of the undersheriff's vehicle as it pulled off the highway into the lane, he bolted."

"Torrez's red lights were on at that time? He had turned them back on?"

"Yes."

"And the kid just ran off into the boonies."

"Yep."

"And you didn't chase him?"

"Nope. Bob followed him for a ways, but didn't find him."

Schroeder shook his head in wonder, still gazing at me. "And it wasn't exactly the sort of thing you'd bother organizing a search party for, either."

"Hardly. The kid's over eighteen. If he wants to camp out, that's his choice. It wasn't a felony that was involved, after all."

Schroeder smiled briefly. "No, certainly not. So he ran from you, maybe hid somewhere until you guys left, and then made his way home."

"That would be my guess. When I met two or three hours later with his father and then went into their house in Regal, the kid was there, conked out on the living-room sofa."

"Where did you see the father? That's Sosimo, right? The undersheriff's uncle?"

I nodded. "He was walking down one of the dirt lanes in Regal, headed home. He was intoxicated. That would have been about two a.m."

"He was intoxicated to the point he didn't recognize you?"

"No, he knew who I was. Once he got a good look. I told him we wanted to talk with Matthew."

"Did he invite you to his house?"

"No. I offered him a ride home, and he accepted. I asked him if I could check to see if Matthew was there. He agreed."

"Matthew wasn't awake when you entered the house?"

"No. He was sleeping on the couch in the living room. I put handcuffs on him, and that's when he woke up."

"He didn't struggle?"

"No. He was pissed, though, and looked like he might resist if the opportunity presented itself. I made some comment about Bob carrying him out to the car if he didn't cooperate."

Schroeder smiled. "And the threat worked."

"Yes. We got to the car and he called me every name in the book when he found out that Bob wasn't there. Other than that, he behaved himself for a few miles, then started working on the back window with his feet."

"You told him to stop?"

"Yes. And he did, for a while. I called dispatch and told them I was headed in. We were about ten miles from Posadas at the time." I stopped and frowned, remembering. "I also told Sutherland to let Torrez know that I had the kid in custody."

"And Matthew would have heard you say that."

"Sure. And almost immediately after that, he let fly at the window again. It broke and it looked like the kid was going to get his legs out the window, so I pulled over and stopped the car. Another vehicle had come up behind me, and it turned out to be a Border Patrol unit. They saw the kid's feet out the window and stopped as well."

"Red lights on?"

"Theirs were. Mine weren't. I pulled into a little two-track. My unit was perpendicular to the highway."

"So Matthew Baca might have thought that the undersheriff had joined you."

"That's possible, I suppose. In the glare of headlights, he couldn't have seen the markings on the unit."

"Did the Border Patrol agents identify themselves?"

"Yes. Casually. We talked, and Scott Gutierrez introduced me to a new officer. Taylor Bergmann. We talked for a few minutes. The kid would have heard the whole thing."

"The topic of conversation was the chase earlier, and then your subsequent apprehension of Baca?"

"Yes."

"And during that whole time, Bob Torrez never arrived at the scene?"

"No. He'd been off duty for a couple of hours. As far as I know, he was at home."

Schroeder frowned and regarded the notes on his pad. "Who made the decision to transfer the kid to the Border Patrol unit?"

"As I recall, Agent Gutierrez offered. He said that they were headed to Posadas anyway. I accepted, since it made sense not to have the kid lying in a pile of broken glass for another ten miles."

"Do you recall what the officers said to Baca at the time of the transfer? How was that done?"

"Gutierrez had mentioned that a couple of ankle ties would help. And then he said something about how their vehicle was brand-new and if the kid scratched it, they'd take him out into a field somewhere."

Schroeder winced. "They were kidding, of course."

"Of course. It's the kind of thing you say in jest, to make a point."

"What was the kid's reaction?"

"Nothing. He never said a word. He didn't move."

"When you actually started the transfer, were all three of you—Gutierrez, Bergmann, and yourself—in the immediate vicinity of your vehicle?"

I leaned back in the chair, closing my eyes, trying to remember. "I was the closest, right at the left rear fender, by the back door. I think that Gutierrez was walking back toward his vehicle to make sure...I don't know. To make sure that the seat was clear, I suppose. And I remember him fishing in his back pocket for a couple of nylon ties. I don't recall exactly where Bergmann was, but he was behind me, somewhere. Within a step or two, I suppose."

"And then?"

"And then the kid swung his legs out of the car. I reached for him, at least I think that I did. He dove forward and slammed into me."

"Did he knock you down?"

"No. In fact, I'd describe it as him bouncing off of me. He stumbled backward, losing his balance."

"His hands were still cuffed behind him?"

"Yes."

"And so basically he was stumbling backward, toward the highway, in the process of falling."

"Yes. With his hands cuffed, he had no way to catch himself."

Schroeder fell silent, the clasp of the ballpoint pen pressed into his right cheek. "According to the skid marks, the driver didn't apply his brakes until after the impact."

I nodded but said nothing.

"And the skid marks show that he wasn't in the westbound lane. The Border Patrol unit's emergency lights were fully visible. Did the truck driver say why he didn't pull over to give you folks some room?"

"No. I assume he was tired and just not paying attention."

"There wasn't any oncoming traffic?"

"No."

"If his truck had been fully in the opposite lane, would it have been possible for him to avoid hitting Baca?"

"I don't know the answer to that."

Schroeder's eyes narrowed a little. "Give it your best guess, Bill."

"The lane is, what, about twelve feet wide or so? Matthew was in the process of falling backward from a point off the shoulder of the road. A collision wouldn't have been likely, unless the kid continued to scramble out across the pavement after falling."

"So the truck could have missed him?"

"The driver would certainly have had more opportunity to try," I said. "Who knows what would have happened."

Schroeder pursed his lips and frowned. "Are you planning to charge the driver of the delivery truck?"

"No."

"Why not? The Border Patrol's unit was parked at the side of the road, with its emergency lights operational. The trucker should have been able to see figures moving around. A prudent operator, with no oncoming traffic in sight, no double yellows, would have naturally moved into the opposite lane."

"Maybe, maybe, maybe," I said. "But my car was parked on a dirt road that headed off the right-of-way. My car was perpendicular to the highway with its back bumper toward the pavement. It would have partially blocked me from the trucker's view, and certainly the driver wouldn't have seen Matthew until he fell backward, right in front of the truck."

"Which wouldn't have happened had he pulled into the opposite lane," Schroeder added.

"I suppose not."

"And since your unit was parked perpendicular to the highway, it wouldn't appear to matter which back door of your car you chose to use. There was no 'off-road' side, in this case."

I held up both hands by way of answer. We could play the "what if" game all day, and it wouldn't change things.

Schroeder took a deep breath. "We may file against...what's his name?" He lifted up one of the pad's pages. "Mr. Haynes. It's pretty clear to me that he acted in a less than prudent manner, even though he was given ample opportunity to do otherwise."

"If you're asking my opinion, I'd prefer that you let it go," I said.

"The skid marks show that when he finally did slam on his brakes, his right side tires were less than three feet from the white line on the right side of the road. That means that his outboard tires hadn't even kissed the center line. He never pulled over."

"I know that. But we see that all the time. Some folks tend to let their cars drift toward what they're looking at. Anybody who walks along the side of the highway will tell you the same thing. Half the time, oncoming traffic drifts toward the pedestrians as the driver looks their way."

Schroeder's gaze drifted up from the legal pad and he regarded me with interest for several seconds. "You think this is your fault, don't you."

"It *is* my fault, Counselor." I shrugged. "I should have had my hand on Baca long before he exited the vehicle, before he started to stand up. I should have been fully blocking the exit route from the vehicle. I wasn't."

Schroeder's eyes didn't leave mine. "Monday morning quarterbacking is easy, isn't it?"

"Sure is."

Schroeder appeared to be doodling concentric circles on his legal pad. "What did the other two kids have to say for themselves?"

"The deputies are talking to them this morning. Toby Gordan has a mouthful of stitches, so we might not get much out of him for a little while."

"What's your theory?"

"About?"

"Why the kids spooked," Schroeder said. "And why every chance he got, the Baca kid tried to take off."

"For one thing, we're pretty sure that he had a fake driver's license. Tommy Portillo—the owner of the convenience store on Grande—saw it, and sold him some beer earlier in the evening. Later on, when he wanted to buy some more at the Broken Spur, Baca was about to pull it out to show the bartender. But

Victor Sanchez kicked Matt out of the bar before the deal went through. The gal who was bartending never saw the license."

"Why would Sanchez kick him out, no questions asked, unless he knew him, and knew how old he really was?" Schroeder said. "He probably borrowed someone else's license and pasted his own picture over the top of the other. Kids try that all the time, and sometimes it works if the clerk really doesn't give a shit."

"Portillo says it was a real license."

"He has every reason to want to be convinced of that," the district attorney said. "He knows that if the Alcoholic Beverage Control Board comes down on his head, it's going to cost him a bundle in fines and lost business. He's not going to admit to making a mistake. But this is all penny-ante stuff, Sheriff. I'd like to know..."

He stopped in midsentence as the door behind him opened without even a perfunctory knock. I looked up in irritation, but caught my tongue when I saw Gayle Torrez's face.

"Sir, Bobby just called from Regal requesting another officer. From Baca's."

For a moment, my brain refused to register what she meant. "Who'd he send down there?" I said, rising to my feet. "Is he on his way now?"

She shook her head. "No, sir. I mean, it's Bobby. He called from there. Tom Pasquale was in the office, so I sent him. Howard Bishop is up north, but he's on his way down, too."

"What now?" Schroeder said, twisting in his chair so he could see Gayle. I knew exactly what he meant. In the seventeen years that Robert Torrez had worked for the Posadas County Sheriff's Department, he had never asked for assistance. Not once. Not for bar fights, family quarrels, or rabid dogs. Usually, it was his own hulking figure that arrived, to provide backup for another grateful deputy.

I charged out of the office, and it was only as I was slamming the unmarked car into reverse that I noticed that Dan Schroeder had piled into the passenger side, yanking his seat belt tight.

Chapter Ten

I saw the wink of red lights as Sergeant Howard Bishop approached the corner of Bustos and Grande from the north, skirting around Pershing Park. I accelerated hard, plunging our car out of the county building's parking lot onto southbound Grande. In another block, Bishop's unit blew by us as if we were parked.

"Christ," Schroeder muttered and grabbed the padded dash. Bishop drifted the county car into the oncoming lane to pass a couple of panicked tourists whose idea of responding to emergency lights was to jar to a stop in the middle of the street. I passed on the right, and then both of us cleared the little knot of traffic and headed southwest on State 56.

"Find out where three oh six is," I snapped, and Schroeder fumbled the mike out of its bracket.

It had been twenty-one years since he'd left the state police for law school, but he managed to clear the mental cobwebs.

"Three oh six, three ten. Ten-twenty."

We waited for half a dozen heartbeats and then I heard Tom Pasquale's tense voice. "Three oh six is coming up on Moore."

There was no way to wave a magic wand that would vaporize the miles. Regal was twenty-six miles southwest from the intersection of Grande and State 56 at the outskirts of Posadas, and even at a hundred miles an hour that was a long sixteen minutes.

I could picture several scenarios in Regal, none of which would take sixteen minutes to play out. I reached over and took the mike from Schroeder. "Three oh eight, do you copy?"

Silence followed, but all that meant was that Torrez wasn't standing beside his car, or within reach of a radio. We were all more apt to use the cellular phones if we had the time, keeping our business off the public airwaves. I lifted the mike again, but Gayle Torrez's voice beat me to it.

"Three ten, be advised that three oh eight has requested an ambulance at the residence. They're on their way."

I glanced at Schroeder, and then acknowledged the message. "Gayle, contact any Border Patrol or state police that might be in the immediate area."

"We'll just have to wait and see," the district attorney said when I was finished, and pulled his seat belt tighter.

From the pass through the San Cristóbals twelve minutes later, we could look down at the tiny village of Regal, and off to the south I could see the ruler-straight line that was the international border fence. The border crossing was open, and if an agent was available, he'd be only seconds away from Torrez's location.

As we came down off the pass, a thin veil hung over Regal, a haze that was equal parts fragrant wood smoke and dust kicked up by traffic on the narrow, winding dirt lanes. The dust plumes led right to Sosimo Baca's scruffy little adobe on the west side of the village.

When I had arrived at Sosimo Baca's place the night before, there had been room for another vehicle to pass by on the dirt lane if I parked carefully, snugged in close to the fence. Now the west side of Regal was a goddamn parking lot, beginning just after "porch corner," where the road nicked around someone's front porch so close that over the years the corner column had collected a fair sample of automotive paint chips.

"This is going to be a mess," Schroeder muttered.

I saw flashing red lights off to the left, where Tom Pasquale had taken a shortcut through first a backyard and then across a shallow arroyo, sliding his Bronco to a stop by a collection of rotten poles and sticks that might once have been Sosimo Baca's back fence.

Weaving and dodging fenders, we managed another fifty yards before the road was corked by a fancy diesel pickup truck, last in line behind several other vehicles. Two men stood by the pickup's front bumper, in animated discussion. Beyond the truck and a row of seven other vehicles including one with the green and white U.S. Border Patrol logo, I could see Sergeant Bishop's patrol car. He had managed to skirt off to the right through a neighbor's side yard, narrowly missing a chain-link enclosure that housed a pair of frantic yellow mutts. A board fence had stopped him within a dozen yards of Torrez's Expedition, parked with its nose just east of Baca's gate.

"We know it's not a wedding," Schroeder said. He braced his hands against the dash as I bounced the car over a hump of bunchgrass and a low rock border garden to the right. The dogs went nuts as I pulled past their enclosure, and I parked beside Bishop's car.

One of the men who had been holding up the front of the Dodge pickup hustled toward us, as if I'd arrived with just the information he needed. "Hey, Sheriff," he called, and I recognized Steve Parker, a county highway department foreman.

"The first thing you can do," I barked before he had a chance to ask his question, "is to get all those goddamn vehicles out of the road so we can do our job. And no, I don't know what the hell is going on." Apparently that answered whatever question he had, because he stopped short.

Baca's tiny front yard was a mass of people. If it had been the church, I'd have guessed that they were waiting for the bride and groom to come out. Then they would let fly with the rice. I picked what looked like the easiest route toward the front gate and then the passage across the dirt yard to the front door. That door was wide open—with the incomprehensible din of rapid-fire Spanish. The flow of people was outward from the house, though, and that's what was causing the ruckus.

As we went through the front yard gate, Deputy Thomas Pasquale appeared from inside the house with his nightstick held in both hands like a bumper, herding a knot of jabbering sightseers out of the house. Schroeder and I stood to one side as the deputy escorted six people, every one of whom was talking a mile a minute, across the front yard toward us.

I held the little rickety gate as they passed through. Three I recognized by name. The others were only familiar faces I'd seen many times but never formally met. The largest and noisiest of the group was Clorinda Baca, Sosimo's older sister. She was proving that she could talk louder and faster than her niece, Mary Silva, or Mary's sister, Sabrina Torrez.

"We got here as quick as we could," Pasquale said to me, "but it's a mess." I wasn't sure to what he was referring, but unless the gathered herds were corralled and controlled, any evidence there might have been would be stamped to dust, regardless of what had happened to spark the crisis.

No doubt irritated that the deputy wasn't paying any attention to her, Clorinda latched on to my forearm and directed her torrent of words at me, never bothering to switch languages so that I might understand.

I pried myself loose and held up a hand, shaking my head. "Not now, Ms. Baca," I snapped. Off to the left, Scott Gutierrez appeared, his dark green Border Patrol uniform looking as if he'd been lying on his back under a car. He spun a large roll of yellow crime-scene tape across the side yard, looped it around a sagging juniper post at the corner, and headed across the front of the yard toward us.

"Where's Torrez?" Schroeder asked, and Pasquale ducked his head toward the rear of the house.

"Backyard," he said. "He wants the place cleared out to the road, no one inside."

In another five minutes, without knowing anything about events that may have transpired, we had established a semblance of order with most of Regal's population outside the yellow ribbon. Ten people wanted to talk to me at once, but I ignored them and entered the house, stopping just inside the door to let my eyes adjust to the dim light. Nothing had changed in those few hours since I'd found Matt Baca asleep on the old sofa.

Bob Torrez appeared in the doorway that led to the kitchen, and he ducked to avoid cracking his skull on the low, narrow archway.

"Sosimo Baca's out back. He's dead," Torrez said cryptically, and beckoned Schroeder and me to follow. The kitchen would never grace the pages of *House Beautiful* magazine. A dingy little room, it had stopped looking fresh and appealing sometime around 1937.

A white drop-leaf table stood in the center of the kitchen floor with four chairs neatly placed. That was the extent of any order. The old round-topped refrigerator graced a dusty corner under a two-door cabinet that had been first painted yellow, and then, probably years later, layered with not quite enough gloss white to hide the previous color. The door of the fridge, dented, scarred, and stained, stood ajar a couple of inches.

Several meals' worth of dishes waited beside and in the old cast-iron sink, and underneath, jammed between the two-by-four sink supports, sat an incongruously bright and cheerful blue plastic trash can.

"Be careful," Torrez said when he saw Schroeder beginning to drift toward the back door. The door swung inward, and was unlatched. Torrez toed it open with his boot. The upper glass door pane had been broken long ago and then repaired with cardboard and tape, the whole affair painted white to match the frame. The lower pane had been shattered outward, leaving long, ragged shards projecting from the glazing. The screen door, dilapidated to begin with, had been flung open so hard that the frame split and sagged against the side of the house, held in place by remnants of torn screen. The recoil spring hung limply along the doorjamb, a chunk of wood still attached to the eye hook that had pulled free.

"A little ruckus, it looks like," I said, taking a careful step through the broken glass. Two concrete blocks served as a none-too-steady step to the backyard. A dozen paces beyond the house, its bright, shiny black stark against the bare earth, lay a plastic tarp.

"Sosimo?" I asked.

Torrez nodded. "We've got some clear shoe prints, so stay well over to the side."

I took a step or two toward the tarp and then stopped, turning back to look at the house. I could see a knot of people who had drifted along the fence to the east so that they could see past the building, hoping for a glimpse of something. "What about the two girls? Where are they?"

For a moment, the undersheriff looked as if he hadn't heard me, but then he said, "Josie was here earlier this morning. Father Anselmo was still here. Clorinda and a couple of others were too." He saw the blank look on Schroeder's face and added, "Josie is Sosimo's wife. Clorinda says that Josie came and got the two girls. Maybe around seven-thirty or so."

"She wasn't living here? The wife?" Schroeder asked.

"No. She hasn't been for almost two years now."

"They were divorced?"

"No."

"And who's this Clorinda person?"

"My aunt. She's Sosimo's older sister."

"Married?"

"Nope."

"Terrific," Schroeder said. "So the ruckus was with her? The wife? Ex-wife? Whatever she is?" I looked back at the shattered screen door, trying to picture what might have happened.

"We don't know that," Torrez said. "But the way the relatives were piling in here, I thought I'd better get some help…before everything was trampled."

I sighed and regarded the tarp. The lump under it didn't look big enough to be the man who'd been sitting in the passenger seat of my car less than twelve hours before.

Torrez bent down and peeled the plastic tarp away. Sosimo Baca was lying on his face, right knee drawn up and his arms under his body as if he'd been crawling and then collapsed. His eyes were open wide, staring at the dirt.

"Is Perrone on the way?" I asked.

"Yes, sir."

"Any ideas about what killed him?" I asked.

"Doesn't look to be any wound that I can see," the undersheriff said. He knelt down and gently touched what he could see of Sosimo's left hand.

"Christ," Schroeder said. "So he could just as easily have had a heart attack, or stroke, or something."

"That's possible," Torrez said, and rose to his feet. "Dr. Perrone will tell us for sure. But I don't think all that damage to the kitchen door is consistent with him having a heart attack."

"Why not?" Schroeder said. "He panics, tries to go out the door. If he was off balance, he could ram his elbow through the glass as easy as not. Just his weight against that flimsy screen would do some damage."

I looked at Torrez. His expression was skeptical. "What time did you arrive?" I asked.

He glanced at his watch. "A little after nine. Maybe a minute or two. The ladies were here at that time."

I frowned. "The ladies? You mean Clorinda and..." My brain drew a blank. "The sisters? Your cousins?"

"Yes."

"So when you arrived, and the women were already here, Josie and the girls were gone, and Sosimo was lying out here?"

"And who found the body?" Dan Schroeder asked before Torrez had a chance to answer.

"One of the neighbor kids, sir. She and her mother are sitting in the backseat of my car at the moment."

I looked at Torrez incredulously. "How did that happen? And I glanced at your vehicle when we drove in. I didn't see anybody."

"I'm sure they're making themselves very small, sir."

Schroeder thrust his hands in his pockets and frowned with exasperation. "So what the hell do they say happened?"

The undersheriff took a deep breath and held it as he regarded the corpse of his dead uncle. "Josie and the girls left here about seven-thirty. The neighbor girl didn't know that the girls were gone. She didn't know about Matthew yet, or any of the events the night before."

He turned and gestured off to the west. "She lives down this lane a ways, in that little stone house right below the water tank. She wouldn't have heard anything if there was a ruckus. She says that she came over around eight, maybe eight-thirty, to play with the two Baca kids. She walked right in without knocking, which is what she usually does."

"In a village like this," Schroeder said, "she probably lives over here half the time anyway."

Torrez nodded. "She said that no one appeared to be home—at least she didn't hear anything. She came into the kitchen, happened to glance out the window by the sink, and then saw Sosimo's body lying in the dirt outside. She ran home and told her mother. The mother's first reaction was that Sosimo had blind-staggered drunk into something."

"And the mother obviously didn't call the police, since dispatch in Posadas didn't know anything about all this when you responded," Schroeder said.

"No, sir, she didn't call the police. She called my aunt."

"That would be Clorinda? Wonderful," the district attorney said. "The village grapevine." He grinned at me without much humor. "Or more like kudzu, maybe." He stretched with both hands on the small of his back, grimacing. "You think he struggled with somebody?"

Torrez nodded. "Yes, I do. For a couple of reasons."

"The damage to the door and what else?" I asked.

"The refrigerator."

"Oh, please," Schroeder muttered. "You could dent that thing a hundred times, and it'd just blend in with the custom finish."

"That's not what I mean, sir," Torrez said. He stepped closer and lowered his voice. "The refrigerator door doesn't close. It doesn't stay closed. Let me show you."

He turned and strode off toward the house with Schroeder and me following. At the back step, the district attorney glanced at his watch. "I need to get back to town. Do you have someone you can spring free to take me back?"

"Just take the car," I said, and handed him the keys.

He nodded his thanks, and went inside.

"This," Bob Torrez said, and indicated the battered old appliance. Sure enough, the door had drifted open two or three inches. With the corner of my handheld radio, I nudged the door shut. The latch didn't click or catch, and when I released the pressure, the door opened again.

"Neat," I said, and repeated the effort two or three times for Schoreder's benefit.

"They propped one of the kitchen chairs against the door," Torrez said. He took out his pen and indicated a faint horizontal scuff mark below the handle.

"Anything could make that mark," Schroeder said.

"True enough. But when I was here at four this morning, I saw the chair in place. Father Anselmo, Uncle Sosimo, and me all sat around the table. One of the chairs was under the latch on the fridge."

"You've got to be kidding."

"Nope. That's where it was. When I came in here after Clorinda's call, all four chairs were in place. Neatly around the table, the way they are now."

"And the fridge hanging open?" I asked.

"The fridge open."

Schroeder took a few seconds to survey the little kitchen, turning a full circle with his head held high as if sniffing the scents from the four corners of the room.

"Keep me posted, Bill," he said finally. "I've got to run back over to Deming for a while, but I'll be back later this afternoon. We'll see what we've got by then." He reached out and shook hands with Bob Torrez. "And you be very, very careful," he added.

Chapter Eleven

By late Saturday morning, the ogler gallery had reached some conclusions all by themselves, and most had retreated to their homes to leave us in peace. Whether the spectators' theories about what had happened were right or wrong, even the most hard-core gossips had learned a few things.

Yes, Sosimo Baca was dead. The heart attack scenario was the path of least resistance. After all, the old drunk had been through a lot in the past hours, beginning with consumption of about a gallon of hard cider, and then progressing through the death of his son and the arrival of his estranged wife who snatched the two remaining children. In less than a day, fortune had taken Sosimo from bleary-eyed contentment to some seriously twanged heartstrings.

No, we weren't going to let all of Regal gawk at the corpse or let friends and relatives into the house to rummage for souvenirs. No, we weren't going to hold a question and answer session out front.

In addition, a stout southwest wind gradually built, driving the bite of chilly November air. Without a circulating hot coffee vendor, folks who hadn't dressed for the occasion quickly wearied of leaning against cold trucks, waiting for us to attend them. A heart attack wasn't *that* interesting, after all—even an incident as odd as this one appeared to be.

While Linda Real, Tom Mears, and Tom Pasquale worked to photograph and lift every square inch of the interior with special concentration on the Bacas' kitchen, Sergeant Howard Bishop, Scott Gutierrez, and a pair of state troopers scoured the back and side yards of the tiny house. That alone accounted for some of the spectators lingering beyond their welcome, since it's unusual when a heart attack attracts so much law enforcement attention. That added interesting fuel to the gossip fires.

Eventually the coroner, Dr. Alan Perrone, allowed the EMTs to remove Sosimo Baca's corpse. Perrone's examination at the scene was just enough to establish that someone hadn't driven a blade under the victim's ribs, or popped a .22 in Sosimo's ear. "I would guess that it was his heart," Perrone said quietly, and left. We agreed with him. Sure enough, Sosimo Baca's heart had stopped. Exactly when and how was a puzzle.

Undersheriff Robert Torrez and I tackled the seemingly endless job of sorting out who had actually been in the house, and when and why they'd been there.

We didn't know who had been the last person to see Sosimo Baca alive, so we started on the other end—we knew who had been the first to see him dead. Little Mandy Lucero had walked into the middle of things, took one look at the victim, and ran screaming home to her mother. Mandy adamantly maintained that she hadn't touched anything in the house other than the front and back doorknobs. She remembered that both were closed when she arrived. An honest little kid, Mandy didn't remember if she'd closed either when she ran out.

Mrs. Lucero hadn't simply taken her distraught daughter's word and then called the police. She'd hustled over to Baca's herself to make sure, adding her own shoe and fingerprints to the mix. And then she'd telephoned who to her was the logical choice...the formidable Clorinda Baca.

The hamlet politics of Mrs. Lucero's choice were simple enough—and perfectly natural. If she had hot news, she didn't call the newspaper. She called a favorite neighbor...and in this case, the closest relative of the deceased.

The police were the outsiders, those folks who clomp around for a while and then vanish, leaving the village to sort out the forced changes in social hierarchy. Mrs. Lucero hadn't given her actions a second thought. After all the smoke cleared, she would have to live in the same village with Clorinda—not with us.

Ms. Clorinda Baca, a solidly built, square-shouldered woman in her late sixties, sat on one end of the old couch in her late brother's living room. She wore khaki trousers and a blue denim workshirt, with a paisley bandanna forcing order on a full head of wiry, salt-and-pepper hair. It was a uniform that would serve equally well for a day spent pulling ragweed or baking apple pies.

She had deflated a bit from her earlier moments of brassy panic, and now sagged pale and trembly-lipped against a couple of pillows. She hugged one of them under her left arm, fingers fussing with one frayed corner.

I shifted forward in the single overstuffed chair in the opposite corner of the tiny room, just a couple of strides away. For a moment, the two of us were alone. The undersheriff had gone outside with Mandy Lucero and her mother, and I could hear his quiet voice beyond the closed door.

"Clorinda, I'm sorry about your brother," I said.

She nodded absently, picking at the pillow. When she spoke, each word came slowly with careful enunciation, as if she were afraid I might misunderstand. "Sheriff, he was *not*...a *bad*...man."

"I know he wasn't, Clorinda," I replied. "But there are some things we have to know. We need to move quickly, and I think maybe you can be of some help. You've been through a lot, but I want you to focus now...all right?" She either didn't hear me, or didn't care what I had said. Instead she smoothed the tassel on the pillow and repeated herself.

"Sosimo was not a bad man, Sheriff. I want you to know that." Her implication was clear. We were not to think that her brother had suffered a heart attack as some sort of divine retribution for his actions, whatever they might have been. Clorinda and God were evidently in agreement about that.

"Clorinda, my first concern right now is the two girls. Tell me what you told the undersheriff earlier."

"What did I tell him?" Her brow furrowed with either true confusion or a hell of a good act. I didn't answer. "Now what happened," she added, and clutched the pillow a little tighter, glaring at the floor as if the old carpet held the answers. "Their mother came and picked them up."

"What time was that?"

"Maybe it was seven. Seven-thirty, maybe."

"And you were here at the time? Here in this house?" She nodded, closed her eyes, and pressed her lips tightly together. "Clorinda, who called Josie? Who told her about Matt?"

"Lucinda did that," the woman said, and I wasn't able to tell from the tone of her voice just what she thought.

"Lucinda is the oldest daughter, right?"

"Yes. Thirteen, and such a good girl."

"I'm sure they'll both be all right," I said. "We've got someone over in Lordsburg right now, making sure."

"That Josie," Clorinda said, but didn't elaborate.

"And it was the oldest daughter who called you earlier this morning? To break the news? That was Lucinda?"

She looked heavenward. "When the telephone rang this morning, *por Dios,* I knew it was something awful. Lucinda told me that Father Anselmo and Bobby were at the house, and that Matthew had been *killed.*" Clorinda heaved a great sigh. "And she said that her father was drunk, and she didn't know what to do. And that I should come over right away."

"And so you did."

"Yes."

"Do you remember what time that was?"

She shook her head. "It was still dark, you know. Pitch-dark. The middle of the night, sometime."

"And so when you arrived, the undersheriff and Father Anselmo were here, along with your brother and the two girls. That's it?"

"Yes."

"You didn't bring anyone with you?"

"No. Who would I bring?"

I ignored the question, remembering that part of the joy of really good gossip was controlling the exclusivity of it. "Did the undersheriff explain to you what had happened?"

"Of course he did," Clorinda snapped. "Bobby said that Matthew had been taken away because of something he did earlier in the night. Something about a car wreck. And then he said that somehow the boy broke loose or something, and got in the way of a truck." Her eyes misted and her jaw muscles clenched. "That was just a matter of time, you know. Before something terrible happened. *Como padre, como hijo.*"

I nodded as if I understood completely. "Did Sosimo fight with his wife Josie?"

"What do you mean, fight?"

"Just that. Did the two of them get along? I understand that Josie walked out a couple of years ago."

"So, they don't fight," Clorinda snapped. "She's gone."

"Did they fight before that?"

"I suppose so. Well, no, they didn't. Sosimo didn't fight with anybody. He just went his way, and figured that things would work out, you know. Josie was always after him to quit his drinking, to find some work, to do this, to do that." She shrugged. "Sosimo, he just kind of liked to take things real easy, you know."

Clorinda dabbed her left eye. "Josie was real...how do you call it..." Clorinda sat up straight and made a flourish with her hand, like a flamenco dancer. "She was so proud, you know." She settled back against the sofa cushions. "I don't know why she stayed as long as she did, if you want my honest opinion."

"Who knows why folks do what they do," I said. "So Lucinda, the oldest daughter, called Lordsburg to tell her mother about Matt's death. Do you remember about what time that might have been?"

Clorinda's brow furrowed again. "Sometime, I guess."

"Had the undersheriff already left?"

"Oh, yes. He didn't stay too long," and the tone of her voice made it clear that perhaps Robert *should* have.

"Father Anselmo was still here?"

"Yes." She nodded. "We...the father and me...we were pouring the coffee into Sosimo, trying to sober him up some more. The girls were crying. *Por Dios*, such a time. It was Father Anselmo who said that Josie should be notified and Lucinda, right away she was on the phone to her mother."

"And Josie came right over from Lordsburg?"

"She must have come straight over. It wasn't very long, you know." She looked up quickly as the door behind me opened. The undersheriff closed it behind him and walked over to the sofa. Clorinda moved over and patted the cushion beside her.

"You sit here, *sobrino*." Torrez did so, and Clorinda reached out and patted the back of his hand.

"Clorinda, did you call anyone? Did you ask anyone to come over?" I asked.

She glanced at Robert, but nothing in his expression gave her a clue about how she should answer. She drew her hand away from his and latched on to the pillow corner again. "I called Mary, because Raymond would want to know. They don't see each other much, but he'd want to know, just the same."

"That would be Mary Baca?" I asked.

She nodded, and Robert said quietly, "Raymond Baca is Sosimo's younger brother. Mary is his wife."

"Did they both come over?"

"No. Raymond said he had to open the store. But Mary, she came on over."

I glanced at Robert, whose Uncle Raymond was manager of the Posadas Town and Country Hardware, as ambitious and commerce-oriented as his late brother had been soggy.

"Just her?" I asked.

"She brought Sabrina along, too."

"Sabrina Torrez," Robert added. "Mary's sister."

I didn't bother to ask if Sabrina was related to him in any way but by marriage. It wasn't genealogy we were after just then. "Clorinda, this is important," I said, and leaned forward, pointing a gentle finger her way. "The undersheriff left you all 'sometime.' Before dawn, let's say. Lucinda, the oldest daughter, called her mother shortly after that, and Josie Baca arrived from Lordsburg about seven-thirty or so. Fair enough?" She nodded.

"Now," I continued, "Josie left, taking her two daughters back to Lordsburg with her. When did Father Anselmo leave?"

That really made her forehead pucker. "Maybe sometime after that," she said, and I sighed.

"So there was a time when it was just family, right? Just you, your sisters-in-law, and Sosimo? Right?" She hesitated and I added, "The girls are gone, Robert here is gone, Father Anselmo is gone."

"Yes."

"And what time would that be?"

Clorinda did a good job of looking helpless. "I just don't know for sure, you know." I glanced at her wrist, the one partly buried in the comfort of the pillow. Sure enough, there was no watch there, and no pale stripe.

"What happened then?" I asked.

"Sosimo wanted to go to town and get his truck. And I told him he was crazy, just to leave it be for a while. I knew what was going to happen if he did that. I told him he should get himself cleaned up so we could all go in and"—she stopped suddenly, with a little twist of anguish—"the boy's lying in that hospital somewhere, or they got to do an autopsy, I suppose. If Josie's not going to handle it, then it's up to us, you know. Up to Sosimo. That's what I told him. We didn't need him to go off and jump in the bottle again. Somebody's got to take care of the arrangements."

"And Sosimo didn't want to do that?"

"He did." Clorinda nodded. "But he wanted to be able to drive himself. But we knew what would happen. He'd find his way into Posadas, and that would be that. He'd go off and get drunk again." She shook her head vehemently. "Not just when we've got the poor boy's funeral to think about. We just didn't need that."

"Did Sosimo ask you to take him?"

"Yes. And we all said no. That we'd find a way to get that damned old truck back for him. Sosimo, he wasn't in any condition to drive."

"But he went anyway?"

"Yes. He just walked out. He said he'd find a ride."

"And so the only ones here, in this house, were you, your sister-in-law Mary Baca, and *her* sister, Sabrina Torrez." I saw a ghost of a grin slip across the undersheriff's face.

"After Sosimo walked out, we all went home," Clorinda Baca added, and she forced the pillow down into the corner of the sofa, looking as if she was planning to get up.

"It's really important to know what time that was," I said.

"Well, I just don't know," Clorinda said flatly.

"Who called you to tell you that your brother was dead, Clorinda?"

"Elva Lucero," she said promptly, and her tone made it unnecessary for her to add, "as well she should have."

"And you came over here again, saw your brother's body, and called your nephew, at his home." I pointed at Torrez, and Clorinda nodded.

"That's what I did," she said.

"And you're not sure what time that was?"

"No," she snapped. "I'm not."

"Maybe it'll come to you," I said gently. "Clorinda, you saw your brother every day, I'm sure. Off and on, anyway. Was he having trouble with anybody? Arguing with anybody that you know of?"

"My brother didn't have trouble with a living soul," Clorinda Baca said quickly. She pushed herself off the sofa and stood with her arms folded across her chest. "Not a soul. He was a drunk, but he was a good man, Sheriff." She pointed at the small notebook in my left hand. "You write down that I said that. He was a good man."

I slipped the notebook into my shirt pocket. Having made herself abundantly clear, Clorinda Baca left the house. I glanced over at Robert Torrez. "What time did she call you?"

"I was on the phone with her at eight fifty-seven. I pulled in here at twenty after nine."

"Between about seven-thirty and the time the neighbor kid walked in here, we don't know what the hell happened, do we?"

"No, sir. We don't."

"Your aunt doesn't think her brother crossed swords with anyone in the world. If you're right, your uncle sure as hell had trouble with somebody," I said.

"Yep," he said philosophically. "And if I'm right, that means Clorinda is wrong...that just doesn't happen much in this family."

Chapter Twelve

Fifteen minutes. Maybe half an hour. Maybe an hour. The unaccounted for minutes in the Baca household formed their own little black hole. In the predawn hours, the undersheriff had come and gone, as had Father Anselmo. Josie Baca had arrived in Regal and picked up her two children. There hadn't been much of an argument—at least no objection that Sosimo had voiced, no chair-throwing shouting match.

Shortly after his wife's departure with the two little girls, Sosimo Baca had found himself left alone with his sister and her small brigade of moral support—all of whom knew exactly what direction his life should take at that very moment—three women who knew what was good for him.

It didn't surprise me that Sosimo had decided then and there that of all the things in this world that he needed most, his old battered truck headed the list—no doubt along with a nip or three. And so he had left the little adobe in Regal…sometime that morning, most likely before eight o'clock.

Without the children or the father to fuss over, Clorinda Baca and her two sisters-in-law had left the house about the same time…whenever that was. And an indeterminate time later, little Mandy Lucero, innocent of all the upheaval in the Baca household, had arrived for a day of play with the Baca girls. What she found instead was an empty house—and Sosimo's corpse in the backyard.

Another hour spent with Mary Baca and Sabrina Torrez failed to produce anything useful. We talked to them separately, we talked to them together. The black hole of time during which Sosimo Baca had returned home to die in his own backyard remained inviolate.

"The aunties," I muttered as I watched the women leave. "We need to find someone who looked at a goddamn clock this morning, Robert. Nobody knows when they did a damn thing."

The undersheriff stood with his hands on his hips, surveying the small living room. For a moment, the house was silent. The deputies had finished out in the kitchen, but I wasn't optimistic that the prints they'd lifted would shed much light.

"Illegals, you think?" I asked, knowing full well that would be the most lame scenario. Mexican nationals streamed across the border at night in an unchecked flow. It wasn't hard to find a place to hop the fence out of sight of the Border Patrol agents. I knew folks who routinely—and illegally—crossed into the United States on a daily basis to work, their own version of a commute. We knew that illegals frequently took their rest inside La Iglesia de Nuestra Señora, the small Catholic mission on the knoll at the east end of Regal. The place was never locked, and the handful of wooden pews served as a peaceful resting spot.

"No, sir, not illegals," Torrez replied. "It makes no sense that someone is going to hop the wire, and then walk all the way over here, through all the barking dogs, to pick on about the least promising place in Regal. And last night—early this morning—there wasn't even a car parked in the yard. Nothing to steal, if that's what someone had in mind."

"And any help they needed or wanted, Sosimo would have cheerfully provided, I'm sure," I added.

"That's right," Torrez said. He had stepped over to the east wall and examined a small photo that hung in a cheap gold frame beside a gaudily painted crucifix. "Most of them don't come to the United States to get themselves arrested." He reached out and straightened the photograph.

"Happier times," I said, looking past him at the portrait of a younger Sosimo, his wife, and three children. Matthew looked to be eight or nine, a sober, black-haired child frowning at the camera. Lucinda was backed in tight against her father's knees, and Josie cradled the infant Linda in her arms. They were posed in front of a small flower garden, with the freshly painted fence behind them.

"Why did Josie leave him?"

Torrez thrust his hands in his pockets. "Nothing we haven't heard a thousand times before, sir. She grew up here in Regal, and I guess she probably thought Sosimo was her ticket out of here. He was working for the railroad over in Lordsburg when they got married. And then he inherited this place from his father, and that was that. He quit the railroad, settled here, and Josie couldn't pry him loose."

"She's been trying, though," I said.

"Sure. You'll get a different story depending on which relative you talk to. But the bottom line is that she met somebody else who promised her more than my uncle could—or would—and she jumped at the chance."

"That was two years ago?"

"About that. Remember when we arrested Matt and two of his buddies for breaking into the farm supply? That happened just after Momma left."

"For all of that, Josie only got as far as Lordsburg? She decided to try her luck there again, eh."

Torrez nodded. "The big city."

"Well, compared to Regal, I suppose it is. Is she still living with the guy?"

"I don't know, sir." He grinned. "But by the time Deputy Taber gets through with her, we'll know all the gritty details."

I glanced at my watch. "And that should be now. Let me find out what she's got. And Perrone should have a preliminary for us. In the meantime, I want this place turned upside down. Every hair, every print, every everything. And by the way, do you know who lives in that corner house? The one where the porch is parked right in the damn road?"

Torrez stepped to the single, dreary front window. "Right there? The white adobe with the blue trim? That's Emilio Contreras."

"I don't know him."

"No, but you know his wife, Betty."

"In the assessor's office. That Betty? I'll be damned. Are they related to you?"

Torrez smiled. "No, sir."

"One of the few. Where's he work, do you know?"

"I don't think he does, sir. He's on disability of some kind. When he can get out of the house, he usually puts in time over at the church."

"I'll find him," I said. "And by the time the deputies talk to every other living soul in town, we might get lucky." I gestured toward the kitchen. "You don't smash the hell out of a window and tear a screen door off its hinges without making a ruckus of some kind. Somebody had to have heard…it's that simple. You breathe deeply in a place like this, and everybody knows about it."

I went toward the front door, and my cell phone chirped as if the motion had triggered its tiny electronic brain.

"You boys campaignin' pretty hard down there?" the caller said when I snapped the thing open. The reception wasn't the best, but I recognized Cliff Larson's cigarette-strained voice.

"If Bobby loses any more relatives, there won't be anyone left to vote," I replied. "Cliff, what are you doing? Sorry I didn't return your call last night, but things got a bit hectic around here."

"Gayle tells me that old Sosimo Baca passed away," the state livestock inspector said.

"Yep."

"And it was his son who got killed last night?"

"Hell of a deal."

"Well, Christ," Cliff said, and I could visualize him pausing to suck on the cigarette, just the way he did while leaning against a corral, one boot on the lower rail, scrutinizing the brand of each steer as it was herded by. He coughed and I waited for him to get to the point. "Listen," he said finally, "I need to get together with you. I know you're busy, but hell, there comes a time when you got to leave all that shit to the young bucks anyway, you know what I mean. What have you got left, about three days? Tuesday's it for you, right?"

"That's it," I said.

"Well, then, there you go. I need a favor from you, and if you could break away from there for a few minutes, I'd appreciate it."

I knew that "a few minutes" could be the rest of the day when Cliff Larson was involved. His idea of rapid response was second gear in his battered Ford pickup. In his mind, he was running on the same "few minutes" he'd been using when he'd called the office the night before. "What do you have brewing, Cliff? Can't one of the deputies help you out?"

He paused. "Don't think so, Bill. Let me tell you why. I got a little bit of a problem that I think maybe you can help me with."

"What would that be?"

"I ain't positive yet," Cliff said. "But you know just about every living soul in this county, and I thought that maybe I could pick your brain a bit."

I laughed. "I'm finding out there's all sorts of folks in this county that I don't know, Cliff. Who do you want to know about?"

"You know Miles Waddell, of course."

"Sure. He's what's left of Waddell Brothers. They have a spread up north, outside of Newton, don't they? Don't they supply livestock for rodeos?"

"That's it. Well, here's the deal. Sometime Thursday, Miles thinks late evening, well after dark, someone backed a livestock trailer up to one of his pens and helped themselves to eighteen head of ropin' calves."

"That would be easy to do," I said. "There aren't very many watchful eyes up in that part of the world, and an awful lot of empty acres. And lots of trucks and trailers." I looked across at Bob Torrez and then looked heavenward. "Besides, the village of Newton isn't in Posadas County. Better to give Sheriff Hernandez a call."

Larson made a rasping, coughing sound that might have been a laugh. "The village ain't, but the corrals where Waddell keeps his stock are. The actual theft occurred in Posadas County, Sheriff."

"Okay."

"Well," he said, stretching out the word, "it's no big deal, but like I said, I'd appreciate the help. I'd appreciate your expertise."

"What little of it there is left," I said.

Cliff coughed again and cleared his throat. "Well now, I'll take any help I can get. I trust your instincts, anyway."

"It's going to cost you lunch," I said. "You know the Contreras place in Regal? Big adobe that sits right on top of the lane? White-painted front porch?"

"Sure enough," Larson said.

"I'll be over there. Either there or at the mission down the road. I don't have a set of wheels at the moment, so if you want to cruise on down here and pick me up, that would be the easiest way."

"Now be a good time?"

"As bad as any, Cliff." Because I knew that Cliff Larson's "now" could encompass any time between the next moment and the next weekend, I added, "If I'm not there, check with one of the deputies at Baca's. They'll be in touch."

"Done deal."

I closed the phone and glanced again at Bob Torrez. I shook my head in resignation. "I'll be at Contreras' if anyone needs me," I said. "If Cliff Larson shows up, point the way. This is just what we need right at the moment. Somebody stealing a bunch of goddamn calves."

"I heard you say up in Newton?"

"Yes. But unfortunately, the calves were corralled in our county, Robert."

"Take three oh six. Tom can ride with me," Torrez offered, but I waved a hand.

"I will if I need it, but right now, a walk sounds good. It'll give me time to think," I said. A hundred steps would take me to Emilio Contreras' front door, and if necessary, another five hundred yards would take me to La Iglesia de Nuestra Señora. At the rate I walked, that would fit in with Cliff Larson's schedule just fine.

Chapter Thirteen

Deputy Tom Pasquale looked up from his clipboard as I walked by. He was working on a schematic drawing of the yard, adding measurements as Tony Abeyta and Howard Bishop called them out. Pasquale was far from being the department's best artist—Jacqueline Taber held that honor—but with his careful sketches and Linda Real's still camera shots and videotape, we had the place covered. Not one of the deputies asked why we were being so thorough with what appeared to be a heart attack case—a simple unattended death. Evidently they had learned either to trust Bob Torrez's intuition, or to keep their mouths shut.

"Do you need the unit, sir?" Pasquale asked, nodding toward his Bronco. Perhaps he mistook my head-down, hands-in-pockets shuffle for discomfort. The west wind was fitful and cold when I turned to face it, but the sun felt good.

"No, thanks," I said. "I'm going to take a stroll downtown. Work out the kinks."

He grinned. "We're about finished here, I think."

"Take your time." I slipped under the yellow ribbon and made sure the gate was pulled closed behind me. The minute my boots hit the dust of the lane, the two dogs across the way settled in for another long fit of barking.

I stopped in the middle of the road and regarded them, and as soon as they saw that they had my undivided attention, the two of them set out to deliver the entire lecture. The larger female, gray starting to tinge her golden muzzle, cocked her head and looked sideways when she barked, a steady two-followed-by-three pattern. Between each salvo she looked at me. The other dog, smaller and younger, was probably her son. He stood on his hind legs, front paws on the chain link.

Their enclosure was connected in the back to a shed, a building that looked as if it would tumble with the wind the instant the dog run was removed. Behind the shed was a mobile home. Most of its windows were boarded with weathered plywood. I walked across the road to within a dozen feet of the dogs and they stopped barking, the younger male's tail lashing from side to side as if I held his food dish.

"You saw all this, didn't you," I said. Both tails wagged frantically. The dogs had suffered their fill of being ignored all morning. "So who the hell takes care of you two?" The nearest occupied dwelling on the same side of the lane was across the lot to the west. The tramped trail from house to dogrun was clear in the red dust, winding its way through the ragweed, bunchgrass, beer cans, and discarded plumbing fixtures.

I turned and looked back toward Baca's place. Tom Pasquale had moved close to the gate, brow furrowed in concentration as he worked with paper and pencil.

"Tom," I called and he looked up. "Who lives there?" I pointed toward the square adobe with the metal-clad mansard roof.

"That's the Sisneros place," he said. "Archie Sisneros?"

"The principal at the elementary school in Posadas," I said, bringing to mind a jowly, jolly little pudge of a man.

"Yes, sir. He and his wife Ernestine."

"Cousin of whom?" I muttered.

"Sir?"

"Nothing. Thanks. Be sure you talk to them."

"I believe that Tony was over there earlier, sir. They weren't home."

I looked at the dogs. "These guys belong to them?"

"Yes, sir."

The animals watched as I walked past their enclosure. With the wind at my back, I trudged along the lane, the dust powdery under my boots. Sixty-seven paces later, the lane started a graceful curve first to the south, and then around the corner of Emilio Contreras' front porch. A large white cat appeared from underneath the step and rubbed against the wooden latticework that enclosed the porch foundation. He clearly expected me to bend over and deliver a little ecstasy. I ignored him and climbed the three steps to the porch.

Betty Contreras answered the door and greeted me with a warm smile. She was as much of a county fixture as I was, keeping the assessor's office organized and running during the week regardless of whom the voters decided should be the name on the door. As such, Betty had the inside track on where one could find the lowest valuation in the county. Regal headed the list.

"How about some coffee?" she said, and held the door open for me.

"No, thanks." I went inside. Their home was a riot of colors in traditional Mexican style. A dozen images of Christ and the Virgin Mary protected the home—some nothing more than a picture clipped from a magazine and hung with a cheap dime-store frame, others delicate *retablos* or pounded and pierced tin reliefs.

"You look like you've been up all night," Betty said. "How about some breakfast?" She looked at her watch, a motion not lost on me. Clorinda and her gang might not know morning from noon from night, but Betty would. "Or lunch, by now."

"Nothing, thanks. I'm sure one of the deputies has already been over to talk to you folks."

"Tony came by," she said. "Tony Abeyta and Scott were making the rounds."

"Scott?"

"Gutierrez."

"Ah," I said. "Both you and Emilio were home earlier this morning, then?"

"Oh, we both were," Betty said, and turned to one of the rockers. I remained standing, knowing that if I sat down now, I'd be there for the duration.

"This is such an awful thing," she said. "One of my neighbors called practically at daybreak with the news about Matthew. Such an awful thing." She looked down at the green carpet. "Of course, we've expected something like that for a long time, but still. He could be such a good kid when he put his mind to it. There was so much potential there."

"I'm sure there was," I said.

"It just broke his father's heart, is what I think. Elva Lucero called me to break the news about Sosimo. I couldn't believe it." She sighed philosophically. "Although the way that old fool carried on sometimes, I don't know why any of us would be surprised by anything that happens." Her eyes turned soft. "The girls went with their mother. Is that right?"

"They're fine, Betty. What we're particularly interested in right now is the time around seven-thirty. Maybe seven-thirty to eight this morning. You and Emilio were both home?"

She nodded. "I was here. Emilio had already left for the church."

From where I stood, I could look out the window and see Betty's little blue sedan parked in the narrow driveway. "He drives?"

"Oh, no. Every morning, he walks. Every blessed day, no matter what weather the Lord sends his way, he walks. And now, with his bad hip, he uses a walker." She shook her head in admiration. " 'I'll just leave a little earlier,' he says."

"What time did he leave the house?"

"It would have been at seven." She said it as if for Emilio, no other time would do.

"And you were up then, too?"

"Oh, sure. If we waited for the sun to make it over the mountains, half the day would be gone. And besides, there was enough noise next door to wake anybody."

I moved to the west window and bent slightly so I could peer out through the lace curtain. Sosimo Baca's house was partially obscured by a large elm tree, but even at night, Emilio or Betty could have seen the front gate clearly—if there had been either a porch light or headlights.

"I'm a heavy sleeper," Betty said. "It takes a nuclear explosion to wake me up before the alarm goes off. But Emilio, he's up and down all night. Like I told Tony Abeyta, if you want to know what happened last night, you just talk to Emilio."

"Actually, it's not last night that concerns us. It's between seven-thirty and eight this morning."

Betty shook her head. "I confess. I wasn't glued to the window, Bill. I was in the kitchen. Meat loaf. It's my answer to all the world's problems." She giggled. "But really. We all have to eat, you know."

"So you didn't notice folks coming and going next door?"

"No, I'm sorry. Once, I heard what I thought was someone walking by. Sosimo, I think. He kind of mumbles to himself when he walks. I remember being a little surprised that it was him, but I was in the middle of something, and before I could get to the front door, he'd walked on by. I wasn't about to shout after him and disturb the whole neighborhood."

"At that time, did you happen to glance out the window? Look next door?"

She nodded. "Clorinda's big old Mercury was there."

"You didn't hear her leave?"

"No, but she would have driven out the other way. Her house is just down around the corner, there. Just a stone's throw from the Sisneroses' place."

"About a two-minute walk," I said.

Betty Contreras laughed. "Clorinda Baca does not walk, Bill."

"And from then until the parade started, nothing special that you remember?"

"No. One of the federal units went by about the time I finally got around to feeding the cat, but they cruise through here all the time, night and day."

"Border Patrol, you mean? What time was that?"

She nodded. "I think so. Probably about eight. I just glanced up and saw the white and green. I didn't see who it was. Scott Gutierrez said that it was probably him."

I took a deep breath, my stomach acutely aware of the time of day and the aromas from Betty Contreras' kitchen. "If you should happen to think of anything else, you'll give me a buzz?"

"Certainly." She frowned as she rose from the chair, and looked sideways at me. "You think that there's something going on? More than a heart attack or something? When Elva called me, that's what she said it looked like."

"We're not sure, Betty. But, as I'm sure you're aware, anytime there's an unattended death, we tread kind of carefully until we know the answers. Emilio is down at the church, though?"

"Oh, he'll be there most of the day. He'll want to make sure that everything is just so. Weddings and funerals—they're important shindigs in a place like this. The whole town gets out."

"They sure do."

She reached out and touched my arm. "And are you ready for the big day?"

I laughed. "As ready as I'll ever be, I guess. For a while there, I thought things were going to stay nice and quiet. And then all hell breaks loose down here." The moment I said it, I was acutely aware of the various painted eyes around the room, watching me with disapproval.

Chapter Fourteen

Betty Contreras wasn't the only resident of Regal with food for funerals on her mind. As I walked down the narrow lane that skirted first one home and then another, various aromas wafted out to greet me. It was going to be a hell of a feed.

In another two hundred yards, the lane curved around an old adobe whose back wall bulged out to leave a gaping cavern under the eaves. A hole in the roofing had allowed the infrequent rainwater to reach the earthen bricks. The windows were gone, with just a few cross sticks remaining, broken askew by swiftly pitched rocks and bleached gray by the weather. Gravity had started the war, but the old house was tough.

I had wandered through Regal for the first time nearly thirty years before, and the house was vacant then, too. Sometime in the next decade, the back wall would crumble, leaving the guts of the place yawning open and vulnerable. Gradually, with the remaining walls dissolving and tumbling bit by bit, the structure would settle into a collection of rusted roofing metal, corroded nails, and the last of the adobe nothing more than a pile of clay and gravel.

Sosimo Baca had been no genius of home maintenance. But any living presence, no matter how neglectful, helped a house survive the seasons. With Sosimo and his son gone and the two remaining children wafted off to Lordsburg, the process of collapse had started. I wondered how long it would be before the first rock whistled through one of the windows at what eventually would be known as "the old Baca place."

I couldn't picture Josie Baca and her new boyfriend returning to Regal. The property would be tied up in probate court for so long that by the time Josie was free to sell it, no one would want the place. Maybe in fifteen or twenty years, one of the Baca girls would convince her husband to bring in a bulldozer to level the lot. Then the process could start all over again.

I ambled along with my hands thrust deep in my pockets, ruminating about stuff like that…an old man walking through an old village in the heart of November with a hard breeze at his back. It was positively poetic. Enough to make me want to seek out a gnarled old walking stick and take up pipe smoking.

A few steps on the hard, impersonal asphalt highway that led toward the church's driveway and, farther on, the international border crossing were enough to break the mood. The wind was chilly, and I quickened my step. I'd managed about fifty yards along the left shoulder when I heard a vehicle coming up behind me. It slowed even as I turned around.

Cliff Larson stopped his Ford and regarded me with a raised eyebrow. "Headin' for Mexico?" He glanced in the rearview mirror and without bothering to pull off the highway popped the gear lever into neutral. At the same time, he dug out a cigarette from his shirt pocket. I walked across the oncoming lane and rested a hand on the top of the truck.

"My morning constitutional," I said.

"Oh, sure." He grinned and looked off into the distance, his face a weather-beaten mass of lines and wrinkles. Larson was one of those men who had never known the burden of a single ounce of extra fat. He was as rail thin now, at fifty-seven, as he'd been at sixteen. How his system managed, I didn't know. It wasn't from hard work. Lifting the cigarette was about the extent of any exercise I'd ever seen Cliff Larson do.

I had always thought that Cliff took a quiet, private delight in sounding like an uneducated hayseed, despite the bachelor's degree in animal husbandry and a master's in range management from the state university in Las Cruces. He'd made more than one impressive arrest by simply sounding stupid at the right time and place, digesting information that others assumed was just passing in one big ear and out the other.

He inhaled deeply and coughed out a blue stream of smoke. "So...has Bobby about figured out which one of his relatives did what to who?" he asked.

I shrugged. "It looks like Sosimo had a heart attack."

Larson looked askance at me. "Quite the party of cops for just a heart attack."

"Well, there are a few things that don't quite add up. We want to be sure."

"Such as?" He shifted his gaze to the wing mirror and we watched a large white and blue RV approach. "Suppose I ought to get out of the road," he said.

"You're all right," I said, and watched the vehicle roll past in the passing lane, two sets of eyes staring at us. "For one thing, there are signs of a struggle in the kitchen."

"That happens sometimes. He mighta kinda thrashed around some. They do that now and again."

"Uh-huh, they do. But not quite like that. And I'd think that maybe he'd thrash his way toward the telephone, or maybe a neighbor's. The glass in the back door was broken outward, then that door was opened, and the screen door broken. Somebody or something hit it so hard it was torn off a hinge."

"Huh."

"Of course, the door was in such rotten shape it wouldn't have taken much."

"No blood?"

"No. But Torrez is being careful. We might get lucky and turn a good set of prints, or some tissue, or something like that."

"Is this tied in some way with last night? With the kid that got himself killed.?"

I took a deep breath. "I don't know. We've got some gray areas there, too. Some things that don't add up."

"Well, let's us do some addin', Sheriff, if you've got the time. Come around and climb in."

"Before I get sidetracked, I need to talk with Emilio Contreras for just a minute. He's up at the church." I nodded toward the driveway.

"Drivin's faster than walkin'."

La Iglesia de Nuestra Señora had been built on a knoll just east of the highway, positioned so that its buttressed, window-less back wall faced Mexico. A perfectly painted sign beside the entrance steps, dark blue letters against a white background, read simply:

La Iglesia de Nuestra Señora
1826

The graveled parking lot was empty. Larson let the pickup roll right up to the wide front steps. "It don't look like anybody's here."

"His wife says that Emilio walks down from the house," I said. "Every day."

Without comment on what he must have regarded as Emilio Contreras' daily monumental waste of energy, Larson switched off the truck. "Wetback hotel," he said, and coughed a laugh. "I'll wait for you."

"You're welcome to come in," I said. "I'm not going in for confession or anything."

The livestock inspector laughed again. "I don't think so." He reached down and turned up the volume on the police radio. "I'll keep track of your boys for you."

"I'll be just a minute," I said, and got out of the truck. The carved wooden door of the church faced north and swung on enormous iron strap hinges, with a simple thumb latch for security. I pushed it open and went inside.

Little had changed since the first finishing coat of whitewash had been slathered on the walls in 1826. Light poured in through five tall, narrow windows on each side. The ripples in the colored glass and the dark patina on the leading would make an antiques dealer's pulse pound.

Emilio Contreras was working near the third window on the west side, and he didn't look up as I approached.

"Hello," he said as I came up to him. A small scraper and a patch of sandpaper rested on the wide sill. He held a pint can of paint in one hand, and what looked like an artist's brush in the other. With his mouth held just so, he was running a bead of white paint down the lower mullion, the loaded brush bristles following the seam between glass and wood with precision.

I watched in silence until he finished the stroke and lifted the brush.

"If I tried that, you'd have a white window," I said. "How are you doing, Emilio?" Resting against the nearest pew was his cane—one of those modern aluminum things with four feet spread wide, a sort of one-handed mini-walker.

"I'm doing okay," he said, sounding surprised. "How about you?"

"I've been better," I said, and he shot me a quick glance as he straightened away from the window. I'd once heard that Emilio was twenty years older than his wife. I knew Betty was pushing sixty, but in the shadows of the church, I wouldn't have guessed that Emilio was much older than that. Barely five feet tall and slight, he moved with a dancer's grace unless the maneuver required use of his left leg.

"I need to ask you about this morning, Emilio. I'm particularly interested in the hour between seven and eight—what you might have seen or heard."

"You mean over at Sosimo's?" He pointed with the handle of the small brush. "What a shame, eh."

"Yes."

He regarded the window for a long time, can of paint in one hand, brush in the other. "I walked over here at seven," he said judiciously, and turned to look at me. "And there were a lot of people over there, even then. That's unusual." He grinned. "Sosimo doesn't get up so early." He set the open can of paint carefully on the windowsill, and rested the brush across the top.

"But you didn't go over?"

"No, I didn't go over. Clorinda was there." He flashed a quick smile. "Her big old barge was parked out front. The last thing I needed was to be corralled by that woman." He shuffled to the pew and lowered himself to the seat, stretching his leg out with a grunt. "She always wants me to fix something or other." He frowned suddenly. "We heard about the boy. That was too bad, wasn't it?"

"Yes, it was. When you walked over here this morning, was there any traffic?"

"No, not then. Maybe later, when Sosimo was walking up the hill." He gestured toward Regal Pass to the north.

"You saw him walking then? What time was that?"

"Maybe seven-thirty, maybe quarter to eight." He indicated the plastic two-and-a-half-gallon water container on the floor, and the coffee can. "I went outside to clean this brush. It gets loaded, you know, and the paint starts to dry. That makes it hard. So I went outside to clean it and take a breather." He grinned again. "I like to see the village waking up. And Sosimo, he's walking up the road."

"You're positive that it was him?"

"Oh, sure." He didn't explain why, at two hundred yards or better, in oblique morning light shaded by the mountain's bulk, he could recognize Sosimo Baca from the back.

"And he just walked up the hill?"

"As far as I know. I came back in here. I got work to do."

"You mentioned traffic. Was it just the usual border traffic on the road, or someone specific that you recognized?"

He nodded. "The usual," he said. I turned and surveyed the small church, and found myself idly wondering who from the next generation was going to lavish the attention on its wood, plaster, and glass. "Emilio, I'm thinking that this morning somebody was over at Baca's place, alone with Sosimo sometime between seven-thirty and eight. It looks like he died right around then. Mandy Lucero says it was about eight or maybe a little after when she found him."

"It's a shame that Mandy had to walk in on something like that," the old man said. He narrowed his eyes and frowned. "And maybe it's a blessing that she didn't walk into that house a few minutes earlier, if what you say is true."

"For sure. If you happen to remember anything, give me a call, will you?"

He nodded, and picked up the brush, politely waiting for me to stop interfering with his drying latex.

The women needed to cook and bake in preparation for the funerals. Emilio needed to paint and spruce up La Iglesia de Nuestra Señora. I walked out of the church with the feeling that everyone in Regal was ready to close the book on Sosimo Baca and his son. The daughters were out of sight and out of mind, and a good meal and some organized wailing would take care of the last vestiges of that branch of the Baca family.

Cliff Larson saw the expression on my face when I walked out, and he grinned through a fresh plume of smoke. "Didn't see a thing, did he?"

I sighed and settled into the truck. The door, slightly buckled just behind the hinges, closed with a groan. "No. He didn't see anything."

"I coulda told you that before you went in there."

I laughed. "You gotta cover all the bases, Cliff. Actually, there was something. Emilio did say that he saw Sosimo Baca walking up the hill, toward the pass. That's what the three women said—that he set off toward town. Emilio saw him too. That's something, at least."

"So he started to feel bad, and turned around and walked back home. No mystery there."

"Nope. No mystery there."

Cliff frowned. "What's the problem, then?"

I didn't want to launch into a dissertation about a refrigerator, or Bob Torrez's reservations, or just my own sense that we were missing something, so I shrugged and let it go by saying, "I don't know what the problem is, Cliff. Intuition, I guess."

"Well," he said, starting the truck and pulling it into gear, "that'll screw you up every time." He glanced at his watch. "Let's give you something else to think about. Bobby can handle this end of the county. Hell, he's related to half of 'em."

"And I don't know if that's part of the problem or not," I said.

Chapter Fifteen

The livestock inspector kept his truck in third gear for two cigarettes' worth, all the way up through Regal Pass. Other than a grunt or two about the weather and what kind of winter it was going to be, Cliff didn't say much. It was as if his concentration helped the truck manage the grade. He was mentally fussing with something, I could see that. He tongued the cigarette from one corner of his mouth to the other, but I didn't prompt him. He'd get around to whatever was nagging him.

We crested the pass and the northern two-thirds of Posadas County stretched out before us. The wind during the past several days had kept the prairie stirred up just enough that the murky air on the eastern horizon reduced the Posadas skyline to a black smudge twenty miles away.

"The whole problem is," Cliff Larson said suddenly as we started down through the east slope esses toward the Broken Spur Saloon, "there ain't a whole lot to go on. You know how these things are. A few tracks, things like that." He grinned at me, his slate-gray eyes just about disappearing behind the wrinkles. "You want a snack of something before we head on over to Newton?"

"Coffee, maybe," I said. "Where exactly is the holding pen that Waddell was using? Are you talking about that complex of corrals south of Newton, on Johnny Boyd's property?"

"That's the one."

"We don't need to drive all the way out there, do we?" I glanced at my watch. "I don't know as I have the time. This is a bad day."

"I'd really appreciate it," Larson replied doggedly, and the way he said it told me that he had something on his mind that he didn't feel like turning loose just then. "Let's get a cup of coffee first, though." He shrugged his shoulders as if a chill was whistling through the truck. "Damn, I get cold awful easy nowadays. Old age ain't what it's cracked up to be, is it."

I shifted on the uncomfortable seat. "How and when did Waddell find out that his cattle were missing?"

"Well, see, Miles told me that he was up in Albuquerque for the day. He come home Thursday late, and he drives out to feed the stock, and everything is just dandy. Everybody is accounted for. He goes out again Friday mornin' just to check things out, and damn if a handful of 'em ain't missin'. See," and he smiled, "he says he was sure they was all there the night before." Cliff hesitated while he braked for a sweeping corner that could safely have been negotiated five times faster than our current rate. "So sometime between eight-thirty Thursday, and about seven in the mornin' on Friday. That's the window we got to look at." He snapped ashes in the general direction of the ashtray.

"So what have you gathered so far?" I asked. "Cast of the tire tracks? Photos, I suppose. Anything else?"

"I took some pictures. I'm not sure just how great they're going to be, but I took 'em. A cast would help, for sure. I was hopin' that maybe you could help with some of that."

"Of course we can. I can have Linda Real out there sometime this afternoon for photos. That's easy. Tom Mears does the best job of plaster-casting tire prints. We can spring him free for a few minutes."

Cliff Larson's face crumpled up as he grimaced. I didn't know what he was thinking about, but I supposed he had his reasons for being so reticent. Evidently my suggestions weren't the kind of help he was seeking. The truck slowed as we approached the Broken Spur Saloon. I waited patiently while he swung in, thumping down off the rough shoulder and crossing the gravel. He squared the truck away in the saloon parking lot and the engine sighed to a stop. I sighed too.

"Let's get us some coffee," Larson said, as if all the answers to the world's problems would be solved that way.

As we walked toward the front door of the Broken Spur Saloon, I saw Victor Sanchez's pickup truck parked around the side, and another vehicle I didn't recognize. I didn't see Christine Prescott's car. Larson held the door open for me and we went inside.

"How about right over here," Larson said, and led the way toward a dark booth on the opposite side of the room from the bar. We slid in, and before my hat settled beside me on the vinyl seat, Victor Sanchez appeared at the table.

"Hello, Victor. Just coffee, please," I said, and without response or even indication that he had heard, Sanchez shifted his gaze to Cliff Larson.

"The same."

Sanchez spun on his heel and left, hospitality overflowing. He had his reasons not to like us much.

"So, what's the 'something else'?" I asked. Larson turned sideways and stretched his lanky frame, letting a boot hang off the end of the bench.

"I got to go to Illinois here pretty quick."

"What's in Illinois?"

Cliff took a deep breath. He patted his pocket, and pulled out the remains of the cigarette pack. It was flat. He crumpled it and tossed it in the ashtray, and pulled a fresh one out of the side pocket of his jeans—already pre-crumpled. "Well, my ma's not doin' too good. Had a stroke last week, and Dad, he can't manage. He tried." Larson peeled the foil off and rapped the first butt out of the pack. "Nah, he can't do it. So I need to run me on back there for a while."

"I'm sorry to hear about your folks, Cliff. I didn't know you were from Illinois."

"Yep. Hell of a good place to be from." He grinned lamely. "And it looks like I'm headed back that way, too. Ain't none too happy about that."

"That's why you called earlier? Whenever it was?"

He nodded and sat back while Sanchez placed the two cups of coffee on the table between us. "Nothing else, Victor," I said pleasantly. "Thanks for asking." I grinned at him, and that just made matters worse. If I'd been a young sprout, he'd probably have tossed me out on my ear. As it was, his upper lip just twitched a bit.

After he'd left, Cliff Larson leaned forward. "Here's what I'm thinkin'. Come election, you're gonna hang it up, right?"

"Sure enough. November eighth. That's twelve-oh-one a.m. this coming Wednesday."

"Going traveling?"

I frowned. "No, I hadn't planned on it."

"Not going to spend two weeks at each one of the kids'? What, you got four of 'em. That eats up eight weeks, right?"

"I don't think so. If they want to come here to visit, I've got plenty of room." I knew damn well what he was getting at, so I said with a grin, "Get to the point, Cliff."

"I want you to fill in for me."

I laughed. "Not in this lifetime."

"Now you think on it for a minute."

"It won't take even that long, Cliff. Why would I want to do that, anyway? The New Mexico Livestock Board can hire its own inspectors. Get some young buck fresh out of school at Las Cruces. They don't need me. And on the other side of the same coin, I can't imagine that they'd *want* me, either."

Cliff Larson took a sip of his coffee and made a face. "You think on that for a minute," he repeated.

"I already did."

"Here's the problem," he said, ignoring my response. "I'm flyin' out the later part of next week. There ain't no time to bring somebody new in and train 'em from the ground up. But I could get together with you and show you the ropes."

"I wouldn't know what the hell to do, either."

"Sure you would. And it's the kind of work you'd like, Bill. Most of the time, it's outdoors. Drive around, talk with people. Check brand scabs, lip tattoos, paperwork. It's no big deal. Write a few permits, collect fees, turn 'em in. It's who you know, most of the time—and hell, you know this county and the folks in it every bit as good as me."

"About the last thing I'd want to do is jump from one job right into another," I said.

"Why the hell not?" Larson laughed. "What the hell else you going to do? Sit around and read until your arteries crust over?"

"That sounds sort of pleasant."

"Shit. You know that ain't true. You want to be out smellin' the sage and breathin' that good air." He dragged deeply on the cigarette.

I didn't respond to his pastoral image, and Cliff shook his head with impatience. "You ain't ready to park it," he said. "Anyways, it might not be for too long. Soon as I can square things away back home, I'll be back. Hell, it might only be for a week or two. You never know."

"Right. That's how these things start," I said. "I know how it works." Draining the last of the not very inspired coffee, I set the cup down and added, "Do we still need to drive to Newton?"

"Yep, we do," Larson said. "There's a few things you need to see."

Chapter Sixteen

From the Broken Spur Saloon, there was no easy way to reach Newton, a simple thirty-five miles due north as the crow flies. County Road 14 snaked up that way from its intersection with State 56, a stone's throw from Victor Sanchez's saloon, but if we drove north on CR14 fast enough so that we wouldn't spend all afternoon eating dust, we'd be pissing blood instead. The road was bad in spots, awful in others. Sometimes it was little more than a rock-strewn slash gouged through the rimrock by the county's battered road grader.

Instead, we drove the twenty-three miles back to Posadas, then headed out of town again, this time northwest on State 78. As we passed the airport, Larson actually goosed the pickup up to the speed limit for a while, and less than an hour after our last sip of coffee at the Broken Spur Saloon, we turned right on 0910, out of Posadas County and eastbound to the hamlet of Newton.

In the center of Newton, across from the small convenience store, Our Lady of Sorrows Church, and the cinder-block community center, we turned south on a wide, paved street that had probably suckered in more than one tourist. Wide and paved for a hundred yards or so, it narrowed to gravel, still smooth and well crowned. Newton had grown by a couple of mobile homes since summer, and a run of new chain-link fencing enclosed the yards along the shoulder of the road.

Two miles farther, we passed the small metal sign that announced the Posadas County line, and gravel gave way to two ruts worn in the prairie. Another sign cheerfully announced that COUNTY MAINTENANCE ENDS.

"Now this here leads us over to the stock pens," Larson said, ever the thoughtful tour guide. We turned onto an even worse two-track and ahead I could see the corrals, stark against the cholla, greasewood, and scant bunchgrass. Maybe planning someday to corral angry Cape buffalo, Miles Waddell had used railroad ties liberally.

Larson let the truck roll to a stop fifty yards from the corral where the two-track split, one branch leading to the loading chute, the other toward a windmill. "Let's hoof it from here," he said.

With no mesas to block it, the wind was hard and cold, blowing in from Arizona. I pulled my jacket collar up around my neck and scrunched my hat down hard on my head. Before we'd walked twenty paces, I heard a vehicle.

"That would be Waddell," Larson said. We watched the big pickup jounce toward us, wind scudding the dust in swirls through the cholla. He parked next to the state truck. Larson raised a hand in greeting. Two men rode with Waddell, and they all piled out, ducking their heads against the wind so they wouldn't end up chasing their hats through the cholla.

"Hello, Miles," Larson said as the trio approached. "I expect you know Sheriff Gastner."

"'Spect I do," Waddell said, and extended his hand. "How's everything goin' with you? Haven't seen you in a while."

"Things are going okay," I replied. His grip was firm, the skin of his hand rough as an old fence rail. It wasn't the wiry, redheaded Waddell who interested me just then. I eyed the two men with him. The taller one, going to fat and bundled against the growing November nip in an expensive parka, eyed first Waddell, then me, then Cliff Larson, as if waiting to be told what to do. I had either met him, or seen him a time or two, but couldn't bring his name to mind.

The other man was shorter than Waddell, a compact bull of a man with a broad face and heavy features. He wore a black baseball cap without logo or insignia pulled down on his head so that the bill was a couple of fingers above the bridge of his nose, military style.

Waddell reached out a hand toward his companions, pointing at the taller of the two first. "Sheriff, this here is Mark Denton. He's one of my partners." I shook hands with Denton, and he pumped my hand eagerly. He didn't look much like a rancher. "Mark lives over in Animas," Waddell added. "And this is Ed Johns."

"Mr. Johns," I said. His grip was perfunctory along with the slightest of nods, but as if an electrical switch had been thrown, the moment our hands touched I remembered who he was. "You still with Catron County?" I knew that he wasn't, but didn't recall the circumstances of his parting company with that Sheriff's Department.

"Nope," he replied, and let it go at that.

"So what did you find out?" Waddell asked. He thrust his hands in his pockets, hunched his shoulders, and looked expectantly first at the livestock inspector and then at me. When Larson's answer was too long in coming, he added, "You know, I talked to Kirk Payne, over in Broadus. We was over there, just a bit ago."

"And what did he have to say?" Larson asked.

"Well, I think it'd be worth your while to talk to him." Waddell nodded. "He says that Dale Torrance stopped there Friday morning early, and filled up with diesel. He was pullin' a livestock trailer, and Payne says that it looked like the kid was pullin' a load."

I frowned. "Dale Torrance? And pulling a load of what?"

"Well, cattle, I suppose," Waddell said, as if the matter were settled.

Cliff Larson glanced at me. "I stopped by the store in Broadus yesterday, askin' around. Payne told me the same thing. He says it was a load of calves that Dale had." With a shrug, he added, "Can't picture young Dale havin' anything to do with stealin' stock, but stranger things have happened, I guess."

"Now wait just a goddamn minute," I said, and I could feel my blood pressure rising by leaps and bounds. I didn't like people pussy-footing around me, feeding me only what they thought I should know. I took hold of Cliff Larson's sleeve. "Show me these tracks." The others started to follow, and I held up my hand. "Stay put, gents. Give us a few minutes before we track all over every goddamn thing in the neighborhood."

It wasn't the truck and trailer tracks that concerned me. Blown sand *might* yield a track cast that *might* be good enough for a bluff, but not for court. I held my tongue until we were sheltered by the mass of the corral and loading chute.

"See, he backed right in here," Larson said. "Pretty clear. Last set of tracks right there." He bent down. "Nothin' on top. That's the last set."

"Yeah," I said. "Sure enough. Now listen. What the hell is going on here? You've got a whole bushel of things you aren't telling me, Cliff. What's this about Dale? What other little surprises do you have going here?"

Larson sighed and glanced back at the three men, now lounging against the front of their pickup. "Kirk Payne says that he saw Dale with a stock trailer, loaded, early Friday morning, right around six o'clock. He was fillin' up with diesel. Sixty bucks' worth in cash."

"And so?"

"I happened to talk to Herb Torrance on Friday, just kind of casual like. Saw him downtown, as a matter of fact. At the bank. He was goin' in as I was comin' out. I asked him if they were plannin' to move any stock, told him that I was goin' out of town for a few days, and if they needed anything, maybe it'd be good to catch me before I left."

"And Herb said they weren't," I added.

"That's right."

"Was this before you knew about the theft?"

"Sure enough was."

"So you hadn't talked to Kirk Payne, either." Larson shook his head slowly. "Did you talk to Dale since then?"

"Not yet."

"Shit," I muttered. "Dale would have needed a permit from you, wouldn't he? If he had cattle trailered as far away as Broadus…and he was obviously heading somewhere else, since he was fueling up."

"Yeah, he would."

"But neither he nor his father received a travel permit from you in the past few days?"

"Nope."

"Have you talked to Herb since?" I asked, and Larson just shook his head again. Try as hard as I might, I couldn't see an easy way around it. Maybe there was a logical explanation, but I found myself stalled. "Trouble is, Cliff, we both know Herb Torrance too well."

"Now that's a fact."

The epitome of the hardworking, law-biding rancher, Herb Torrance made a living as best he could in tough, hardscrabble country—and kept his good humor at the same time. I counted him a good friend. We'd had a few hard times with his eldest son, Patrick, a couple years before—woman trouble that had blindsided the boy into making ill-considered mistakes. That had worked itself out.

Dale Torrance was nineteen, I knew, and had decided to work at home, despite his father's encouragement to take a couple years and see if university life held any attraction. I knew that the boy loved the rodeo circuit, and chasing the silver buckles would keep him flat broke most of the time.

With my hands in my pockets I faced into the breeze, taking a deep breath as if I could smell answers on the wind. "What else?" I asked.

Cliff Larson looked down at the ground and scuffed dust with the toe of his right boot. "The calves are in Lawton, Oklahoma. I know that much."

"Jesus Christ, Cliff," I snapped.

"Okay, now here's the deal," Larson said, holding up both hands as if to ward off blows. "It don't take no rocket scientist to figure this one out." One hand froze in the air and he stopped, taking time to think. "If it was Dale, and I got no reason to think that Kirk Payne wouldn't know, then he was eastbound with those calves. Broadus is ten miles from here more or less. Gettin' fuel was just somethin' Dale didn't think about. So he goes east."

"And there's millions of choices where he could go," I said. "Why Lawton?"

Cliff grinned. "I learned over time that if there's a way a relative could be involved, it's worth it to check that out first. Families just kind of work that way."

"And there's Torrance relatives in Lawton?"

"Nope, but there is in Hulen, just a bit south. I called an inspector friend of mine over that way, and asked him to do some checking around. He says word has it that there's a dealer or two around Lawton who might be persuaded to bend the rules a little."

"Take stolen cattle, you mean?"

Larson nodded. "He checks to see if there's any critters that he might call into question, and sure enough. He checks one of the stockyards and finds himself about eighteen head of yearlings with the Waddell brand. That simple."

"Who is the relative that lives in Hulen?"

"That's Herb Torrance's younger sister. She's married to some farm equipment dealer over that way."

I heard voices and looked back to see Miles Waddell and his two buddies walking toward us. Apparently their patience was running thin.

"The cattle are being held in Lawton, then?" I said.

"Yep."

"What's the timetable for Miles getting them back?"

"Well," Cliff said, and hesitated. "The livestock is impounded, all right. But feed bills run high. Authorities want us to move pretty quick. They don't want to baby-sit a herd of cattle if they can help it."

"I'm sure of that. I wonder what the hell Dale thought he was doing."

"Beats the hell out of me," Larson said. "I ain't got that far yet."

I smiled at him and shook my head in exasperation. "And you're taking off to Illinois?"

"Got to," he said. "No way around it."

"Around what?" Miles Waddell said as the three men reached us.

"Miles," I said. "we've got a lead that we're following up. Give us until Monday, all right?"

"Shit, by that time, my stock will be a thousand miles down in Mexico, brands changed to read 'Lazy Runnin' Mex' or some damn thing."

"I don't think so, Miles."

"Well, I tell you what. "We was going down to talk with the Torrance boy. That sure as hell seems like the place to start."

"Forget it, Miles."

He looked sharply at me, catching the tone in my voice. "Listen, Sheriff," he said, "eighteen head of stock don't come cheap. I ain't going to stand around with my head up my ass, hopin' that those calves will kick the boards out of whatever pen they're bein' held in and wander their way on home."

"You've got a business to run, Miles. Why don't you just do that, and let Cliff and me do what we're paid to do."

"Look, I'm just sayin'…"

"I know exactly what you're saying, Miles. This isn't a hundred years ago. Stealing cattle is a felony. So is transporting livestock across a state line without proper permits." I thrust my hands in my coat pockets and regarded Waddell for a moment. "And so is playing vigilante."

His eyebrows shot up at that. "Look, Miles," I said. "We've got us a royal mess here, a royal screwup. You just give us time to straighten things out. It's not going to accomplish anything to have you three gentlemen bust in on Herb Torrance and his boy with this situation. Let us talk with them. You'll get your cattle back. Guaranteed. All right?"

"Goddamn yes, I guess it is," Miles Waddell said. "You don't have to get so jumpy. I never said anything about playing vigilante. I just want what's mine. That's all."

"Then give us a couple of days. It's a bad weekend, Miles," I said. "We're all just a little bit on edge."

"If you're talkin' about that boy gettin' killed down in Regal, I heard something about that."

"So you know," I said. "Give us a break. We aren't going to drag our feet on this. Just the fact that I took time out to drive up here with Cliff ought to prove that we're not about to let things slide." Miles Waddell ducked his head in agreement.

"We'll be talkin' to ya," Cliff Larson said as the three of them turned to walk back toward their truck. He let out a long breath and groped for a cigarette. "Jesus, Bill," he said. "Give you the diplomat of the year award." He snapped his lighter. "You want to go talk with Dale?"

"Now would be a good time," I said. "What else do I have to do?"

Chapter Seventeen

Larson and I parted company at the Public Safety Building in Posadas for a few minutes. For one thing, if events conspired and we needed to take Dale Torrance into custody, I didn't want to have to lash him into the back of Larson's pickup truck.

I also wanted to talk to the undersheriff and bring him up to speed, since he was bound to inherit the whole mess in about seventy-two hours, whether he wanted it or not.

We were still operating on Cliff Larson's version of "now" anyway, so I rationalized that a few more minutes couldn't hurt. The truth was that I hadn't figured out just what to say to Dale's parents, Herb and Ann Torrance.

I agreed to pick up Cliff Larson at his home later that Saturday afternoon, after I'd had a chance to procrastinate. I knew there wasn't much point in prolonging the inevitable. The whole affair cost me my appetite, but what the hell. The boy was old enough—hell, he wasn't a boy anymore, either—to know that what he'd done was not only illegal but stupid to boot. One thing was for sure: he'd be a lot smarter after the Oklahoma and New Mexico courts were through with him.

I surprised myself when I discovered I was musing over the livestock inspector's job offer. With a fresh cup of coffee in hand, I visited the Sheriff's Department library—a single small bookcase in the corner of the conference room. I found a 1978 edition of New Mexico statutes Chapter 77 that covered the animal industry...everything from defining what a cow is to what fee to charge for watching a rancher dip his sheep. If the slim collection of statutes rested on the corner of my desk for a while, it might do some good.

Intending to brush up on the statutes that involved the Torrance kid's transgression, I leafed through a few pages, opening at random to the section on "commuting" sheep. I grinned at the mental image of neatly coifed sheep carrying briefcases, waiting patiently in traffic.

"Sir?"

I looked up with a start. Gayle Torrez stood in my office doorway. "Sorry, sir. But the undersheriff asked if you would come over to the county maintenance barn."

"I can do that," I replied, and tossed the book of statutes on my desk. "What's going on?"

"I don't know, sir. He just called and asked for you. And by the way, Catron County returned my call. Edward Johns quit that department in March, '99. Ortiz said that if he could have found an easy way to fire him, he would have. But Johns just quit. Sheriff Ortiz said that he had an attitude problem."

"It's hard to picture Eddie Johns working for Lorenzo Ortiz anyway," I said. "What's he doing now, did Ortiz say?"

"The last he heard, Johns was working for University Real Estate in Las Cruces. I called and confirmed that."

"Real estate?" I frowned, trying to picture Johns showing a two-bedroom bungalow with white picket fence to a newly married couple. Warm fuzzies all over the place. "That's a start. Thanks, Gayle. And now I need some wheels."

The only vehicle remaining in our parking lot was an aging Bronco whose transfer case sounded as if it were full of gravel and whose windshield sported a fascinating pattern of cracks. I took it, figuring that if three was a charmed number, the old Bronco was a good choice for something to wreck.

The county barn one block south of Bustos on Fifth Avenue was a bulky Quonset building that overlooked the vast boneyard of equipment, both functional and long-dead, that kept the county in business.

Puzzled, I parked the Bronco so it joined the lineup of other department vehicles. The confab apparently had moved from Regal to here. The massive roll-up door was closed, so I entered the shop through the white steel door with the single word OFFICE stenciled at eye level.

The office included three desks and a variety of bookshelves, with every available flat surface covered in a vast avalanche of junk, from empty coffee cups to reams of computer verbiage to a case of oil filters with an invoice that, before the next week was over, would probably be filed by the gravity system. All of it was untended, but I heard voices out in the shop.

I stepped through the side door that sported the eye-level warning AUTHORIZED PERSONNEL ONLY. Perhaps there were a surprising number of people who wanted to tour the place, hoping to catch a tantalizing glimpse of a county road-grader having its blade changed.

The unmarked county car in which I had been transporting Matt Baca during those almost surrealistic early morning hours was parked in the far west rear corner of the building. It was snuggled between the sorry remains of the marked unit that had been T-boned earlier through young Baca's efforts, and an elderly dump truck with its uncovered differential in a thousand pieces.

Skirting the yawning lube pit that had been built long before the county could afford a decent hydraulic lift, I made my way across the dark, oily concrete floor. A burst of light exploded inside the unmarked car, followed by another. Undersheriff Robert Torrez saw me and broke away from the party. I saw Tom Pasquale leaning inside the car, and could make out the top of Linda Real's head where she manipulated the camera.

"What's up?" I asked.

"Sir," Torrez said. "A couple of interesting things. First of all, did Alan get a hold of you?"

"Alan Perrone? No, why?"

Torrez glanced back toward the two cars. When he turned back, he lowered his voice. "He's got some interesting preliminaries for us. In a nutshell, he thinks that Sosimo was struck, maybe more than once." He put his hand on his own belly, just under the ribs. "And he thinks that at least one of those blows may have contributed to the rupture of an existing aortic aneurysm."

I frowned. "He's sure?" It was a pointless question, since I knew damn well that the sober, methodical Dr. Alan Perrone didn't make wild guesses or jump to unfounded conclusions.

"Yes, sir."

I took a step backward and leaned against the rear tire of one of the county's tractors parked beside a set of welding tanks. I regarded the polished brass valves of the welder, but my mind wasn't there. "So very likely there was a struggle in the kitchen, like you said. They bang around, smash the window in the back door, and somehow Sosimo breaks away and plunges outside, taking part of the screen with him. And by that time, if the aneurysm burst, he's already dead on his feet." I held out my hands. "And that's it."

"Could be." Bob Torrez's face was its usual, noncommittal mask, and he waited while I fumbled with the pieces of the puzzle.

"You have thoughts otherwise, Roberto?"

He shook his head. "That's the way I see it. We just don't know who was there."

I thrust my hands in my pockets. "Let me ask you something. I know they're family and all, but Clorinda and the other ladies… they're quite a crew. Could one of them be involved somehow?"

A faint smile cracked Torrez's face. "Sir, my aunt Clorinda can make up some of the wildest stories. But it's against her nature to hide things, or try and cover-up. I think that if she had to hold a secret for any length of time, she'd explode." He shook his head. "No, if Clorinda knew anything, she'd tell me. And she'd tell everyone else, too. I really think that what she says happened is just about what *did* happen, as far as she or the other ladies know. Sosimo left the house to find his truck, or just to get away from them…and when he did that, they left the house, too. There was nothing else for them to do there, with everyone else gone. And that's all they know. They didn't see Sosimo return. The next time they plug into events is when Elva Lucero telephoned them with the bad news."

"We've got a goddamn fifteen-minute gap, maybe half hour," I said. "A gap when nobody knows what the hell went on." I pushed myself away from the tractor and nodded across the building where Linda Real continued burning up film. "And you didn't call me over here to tell me about Perrone's findings. What gives with my car?"

Torrez beckoned and I followed him through the litter of hoses, tools, and cartons full of who knows what.

"Deputy Pasquale had an idea," Torrez said as we reached the front of the car, and he looked sideways at me.

"Oh-oh," I said.

Pasquale heard us and turned around. He'd been using the roof of the car as a desk, filling out the plastic evidence bag label with a black marker. Surgical gloves clad his hands. He grinned at me and stepped away from the car. The backseat cushion had been removed and leaned up against the wall.

Torrez didn't add to his explanation, and I looked quizzically at Pasquale. "So tell me," I said.

"Sir, we were searching the residence down in Regal, and I was going through the couch in the living room, looking under the cushions and what not. It was at that time that I realized that none of us had turned the car."

"Turned the car," I murmured, amused at the young deputy's tendency to turn to Hollywood for his phraseology. The brief flash of amusement was replaced by the familiar sick, hollow feeling of seeing the broken window and having my mind replay the events of the night before. "So what did you find?" I leaned inside. Lying amid five years' worth of dust and litter was a shiny, plastic laminated driver's license. Catching the light, Matt Baca's photo looked up at me.

"I'll be damned," I said and glanced up at Linda. She stood by the left rear car door, camera at the ready. "You were able to get all this?"

"Yes, sir."

"Good. Thomas, you knew this was here before you moved the seat?" I straighted up with an audible popping of joints.

"No, sir. But I got to thinking. It made sense to look every place that Matt Baca had spent some time. We knew that he had some sort of fake ID, and that he had to stash it somewhere. It wasn't in the house, unless he plastered it inside one of the walls. And he didn't have time to do that."

"No fresh plaster," I said.

"No, sir," Pasquale said, taking me dead seriously. "And then I remembered that you said that you arrested him when he was lying on the couch. If he had a fake ID, he wouldn't want to be caught with it. You said that it wasn't in his wallet, which is the logical place to keep it."

"That's where his regular license was—the legitimate one," I said.

"Yes, sir." Without the least apology, he added, "When I was a kid and carried a fake ID, I always just slid it into my back pocket. Takes too long to fumble in a wallet."

"Is that right?" I looked at him with amusement.

"That's what got me to thinking about Matt. If he had a fake ID, he might just have slipped it into his other back pocket where he could get it easily. If he didn't do something about it, we would have found it when he was processed for the detention center. And down at his house, he might not have had the chance to slip the fake license out of his pocket just then. You were watching him every minute." Pasquale looked at me expectantly.

"But he did have the time once he was inside the car," I said. "Lying on the backseat, with me busy driving. It's dark, and he's got lots of opportunity to work out his problem. He sticks it down behind the seat. And what are the odds that anyone would look there?" I regarded Tom Pasquale with interest. "Your prior education is coming in real handy, Thomas."

Tom's eyes flickered over to Bob Torrez, who remained studiously silent. "Just outstanding, Thomas," I said. "Don't you have to unbolt the seat to move it? It doesn't just flip up like the seats in the SUVs, does it?"

"No bolts, sir. It just lifts up and out. Takes just a second. No problem."

I frowned and turned slowly to the undersheriff. "Was Matt smart enough to figure all this out?"

"What do you mean, sir?"

"Slip the license down behind the seat. And we can take it one step further. Is he smart enough to kick out the window, knowing that the car will end up in the shop? When it does, he can come grab the license."

Torrez looked skeptical. "I don't think so, sir. It's possible, but I don't think so."

"Does he know anyone who works here?"

"I imagine he does."

"Well, then…maybe that's it. But why run, then? That doesn't make sense." I turned to Tom Pasquale. "And you didn't feel down in there first? Before you moved the seat?"

"No, sir. It's too snug. And if there was something there, I didn't want to touch it. I knew that we'd want photos. And I knew that it'd be easy for something to slip down where I couldn't feel it anyways." He shrugged. "So that's what I did."

I turned and grinned at Torrez, then reached out and took Tom Pasquale by the shoulder to rock him back and forth. "Wonderful, Tom," I said. "Just outstanding." I bent over and peered at the license again. "Damn, you're good."

"If Linda's through, let's get it out of there," Torrez said, and Tom Pasquale jumped to it as if he'd been stuck with a cattle prod.

Chapter Eighteen

The discovery of the license did a lot for my mood. I was impressed as hell that somebody had thought to look behind the seat of the car in the first place. I certainly hadn't. And I was doubly impressed that Deputy Tom Pasquale hadn't just rummaged behind the seat and grabbed the thing without thinking—as he would have done just a couple of years before. He'd been methodical and careful, and it had paid off.

The license provided a new piece for the puzzle. Everything on it was right, too right—except Matt Baca's birthdate. That had been sealed in plastic as December 13, 1979. With that in hand, Matt had grown up fast.

Discovery of the fake license restored my faith in Tommy Portillo, too. Under normal circumstances, I had occasion to visit his convenience store a dozen times a month. It would be nice to be able to wish him a pleasant day and mean it.

A high-quality forgery of a state license was no small crime, and it wasn't something Matt Baca could do in his bedroom with a rubber stamp and lettering kit. Someone who could make such a fine copy would see no reason to stop at just one.

With any luck at all, the smooth plastic would reveal some high-quality fingerprints—Baca's, Portillo's—and if we held our breath just right, maybe some surprises.

But even if luck smiled on us, a whole landslide of unanswered questions remained. On top of all that, Dale Torrance was still enjoying the profits from his recent foray into cattle rustling, and that needed resolution.

On the way out of the county barn, I explained what I knew of the case to Torrez, and he shook his head in wonder. "Give me a couple hours to finish up a few odds and ends, and we'll take a run out there," he said. "Something else you might want to check, by the way—you know who Dale is trying to impress, don't you?"

"Impress? Stealing cattle is a hell of a dangerous way to impress somebody. Who?"

"He hangs out around Christine Prescott a lot." He grinned. "At least his tongue hangs out a lot. What better reason to want a wad of cash, don't you think?"

"And how do you have this gem of information?" Remembering Torrez's habit of bar-baiting, I could picture him watching the Broken Spur from his parking spot east by the windmill, binoculars in hand. The undersheriff grinned, and I waved a hand in protest. "Better yet, don't tell me. Holler at me when you're ready to go on out. We'll pick up Cliff on the way."

I slid into the Bronco, fumbling for a moment before I found the keys. The old engine settled into a fitful rumble. It sounded as tired as I felt. I dug out the cell phone and auto-dialed dispatch.

"Gayle, I'm going to be home for a little bit. If Cliff Larson calls there, have him come over to the house. Otherwise, I don't want to talk to anybody."

My plans called for a fresh cup of coffee, a shower, and a Saturday afternoon nap. I'd been running for the better part of thirty hours without conking out, and was acutely aware that the gears in my inner clock were starting to slip and miss.

I wasn't one of those fortunate souls who could catch a little shut-eye at the office or in the car. The previous sheriff had been fond of referring to me as "badgerlike." Whether that referred to my disposition or to my preference for diving back into my own private hole when I needed rest and relaxation I wasn't sure, but I preferred the latter.

The thick, carved door of my rambling, dark adobe home on Guadalupe Terrace locked out the world's noises and the eighteen-inch mud walls muffled them into silence. It was a good place to think.

South of the interstate exchange, I turned the grumbling Bronco off Grande onto Escondido, then took the hard right onto Guadalupe. Parked directly in front of my garage door was a blue Corvette, one of those models with the enormous humpy fenders and pointed shark nose. I idled the Bronco in behind it, close enough that I could read the Texas license.

Puzzled, I climbed out and walked the length of the car, pausing to rest my hand on the hood. It was still warm. A sticker on the front bumper allowed parking at Chase Field Naval Air Station in Beeville, and I grinned. "Well, I'll be damned," I said aloud, and turned toward the house.

The front door was locked. I finally sorted out the right key and let myself in. The interior air lay undisturbed. I walked quickly back to the kitchen, confirming that no one was inside. It was when I paused for a moment that I heard the faint voices, out behind the house.

The adobe, a vast, sprawling structure built room by room until everyone had run out of ideas, sat on the front edge of five acres. Those five acres separated me from the interstate and from neighbors. The acreage's location made it perfect for a truck stop or motel, and I knew with grim satisfaction exactly what the land was worth.

I stepped to the back door, shot the bolt, and pulled it open. The five acres were a mini-wilderness, choked with whatever would grow without attention. Immediately behind the adobe, a series of enormous cottonwoods presided, their canopies stretching autumn-bare branches over the house. The thick carpet of leaves crackled underfoot.

"Hey!" A shout from off to my right drew my attention, and I turned and watched two men walking toward me from the rear of the property. I'd been told a number of times that my youngest son looked more like me than I did. He scuffed through the leaves with his hands in his pockets, turning his shoulders just enough to dodge a bramble or low-hanging limb. Wide through the shoulders and thick-waisted, William C. Gastner, Junior, was going to have to work hard to avoid tipping the scales a little more each year until the copy of his father was complete.

I couldn't recall just then if his son Tadd was a junior in high school or if Tadd was a senior and some other grandchild was the junior. Whatever the case, this grandson towered over his father by a good three inches, taking his height from his mother's side of the family. He smiled broadly as they approached, a pleasant, open face with the clear, olive skin inherited from his grandmother's Peruvian blood.

Without a word, Buddy took his hands out of his pockets and bulldozed into me with a powerful hug. About the time I knew I was turning blue, my grandson said, "Okay, it's getting late. Time to go." My son and I stepped apart, and the kid added, "My turn." He opened his arms wide and clamped me in his own version of a vise hug. His mother's side of the family hadn't contributed much padding to his frame.

"I'll be damned," I said finally, looking at the two of them. "Isn't this something. What's the occasion?"

Buddy shrugged. "Tadd here talked me into stretching the beast's legs on Interstate Ten."

"That's a hell of a stretch, but what a great idea." I thumped Tadd on the arm. "That's quite the car you have there. What time did you leave?"

"We pulled out of the driveway at oh three hundred hours, right on the dot," Tadd said. He scrutinized his watch, one of those enormous things with all the knobs, buttons, and dials. "Eleven hours and twenty-five minutes."

"That's not bad for seven hundred and fifty miles, counting stops."

"Seven hundred eighty-one miles in six hundred eighty-five minutes," Tadd said instantly. "That's sixty-eight point four miles an hour, on the average."

"On the average." I laughed. "I wish I'd known you were coming. I could have had a brass band out front, or something.

Or a checkered flag. Come on inside." I turned toward the door. "Did you call dispatch, or what?"

"No," my son said, "but we swung by the office when we saw you weren't home. Gayle Sedillos told us where you were, and that you'd be heading home in a few minutes. So I thought, what the hell. We'll just come back and tour the grounds."

"It's nice that she let me know," I grumbled.

"Nah. I told her not to," my son said. "Leave it as a surprise. One of those spur-of-the-moment things. I tried to call you last night, but I guess you weren't near a phone."

"Not if I can help it. And she's Gayle Torrez now, by the way. She and Bob finally did it."

"Well, good. It took 'em long enough." We stopped by the back door and my son stood with his hands on his hips, regarding the house. "The place looks great, Dad."

"A jungle."

He turned and nodded toward the back forty. "I was trying to find the spot where that old man buried his wife. Way out back. Remember that? Tadd thought I was making up that story."

"Right across the street from the old Apodaca place. Directly across," I said. "There's a tangle of box elder saplings there now. I think their roots found the village water line."

"We weren't even close to the spot, then."

"There's not much to see now, except a little scuffed dirt." I ushered them inside.

"So how does it feel having just a couple of days to go as *el alguacil mayor del condado?*" Buddy asked. "Are you going to wake up on Wednesday and regret not being stud duck?"

"I'm going to wake up feeling wonderful," I said without elaborating. "How about some coffee? Or there's some beer in the fridge, I think. Or better yet, how about some real food? You guys must be starving." I looked at the clock. "I've got an hour and a half before I need to be at the office."

"The Don Juan," Buddy said.

"That'll work." To Tadd, I said, "You hungry?"

"The bottomless pit is always hungry," my son said before Tadd had a chance to answer.

We took the Bronco, with Tadd sitting in the backseat behind the wire mesh like a good prisoner.

"This thing is the pride of the fleet?" Buddy asked. He reached forward and traced a finger along the major windshield crack. "It reminds me of a couple of the old Orions they retired down at the base."

"We've had an expensive couple of days," I said. "This is the only thing with wheels at the moment." I backed the Bronco out of the driveway, the gravel in the transfer case growling loudly.

"So what's at five o'clock?" Buddy asked as we rattled our way up Grande.

"I told the livestock inspector that I'd help him take a kid into custody. Remember the Torrance family? They own the H-Bar-T out west of town, on County Road 14?"

"Vaguely."

I shrugged. "Well, no reason you should. One of their boys pulled a stupid. He rustled a bunch of roping calves and trucked them on over to Oklahoma to sell. Only he knows why."

"You're kidding."

"Nope. That's what he did. Bob Torrez says that the kid has a girlfriend. Or maybe more accurately, would *like* to have a girlfriend. Who the hell knows. From what I know of the girl, I'd put my money on it being a one-way romance."

"So what's at five? Are the courts getting so bad now that you have to make an appointment to arrest somebody?"

"Not yet. We're making progress in that direction, though." I shot a smile at my son. "We just wanted a few minutes to get all our cards in order. It also gives Cliff Larson, the livestock inspector, a bit of time to communicate with the Oklahoma folks and find out what they want to do at their end."

"Amazing," Buddy said. He watched first Grande and then Bustos slide by. "Posadas hasn't changed much, Dad."

"Nope."

"You think you'll stay here?"

"Sure." I surprised even myself by answering so quickly. "It suits."

Buddy grinned and turned to glance at his son, as if my reply had confirmed an earlier conversation between the two of them.

"I hope you can stay a little while," I asked. "This isn't just a one-nighter, is it?"

"We thought we'd stay through Wednesday," my son replied, and braced himself as I thumped the Bronco up into the Don Juan's parking lot. "If you've got room and can stand the company. Aren't Francis and Estelle coming down sometime soon?"

"Tomorrow."

He nodded. "We can stay down in the Posadas Inn, if that makes it easier."

"Like hell, not when we have four bedrooms to fill. Estelle and Francis can take Camille's room, and their two terrors can bunk in your old digs. You and Tadd can take the third. I'm just sorry Edie couldn't come with you."

"Couldn't fit Mom on the luggage rack," Tadd said.

"She wanted to come, but she has got classes she can't afford to miss," Buddy said. "Lawyer stuff, you know. She has just the one semester left before she takes the bar exam." He grinned. "Getting a little bit nervous about it all."

"She'll do fine," I said. We parked and entered the restaurant. My usual booth was empty, and we slid in. For the next thirty minutes, we ate and talked, and I was amused at the number of times Janalynn Torrez, our waitress, found an excuse to return to the table, either with water or coffee. My grandson had her eye, that was for sure.

I had just cleaned up the last bit of lettuce, cheese, and green chile when she appeared again, this time carrying the telephone. I groaned. My own phone was out in the Bronco, hidden under the refuse where it belonged. Janalynn handed me the damn thing, managing to do so without taking her eyes off my grandson.

"Thanks," I said, and turned sideways, elbow on the table. "Gastner," I said.

"You about ready to go, sir?" Robert Torrez asked.

"Yep. Give me five minutes to finish up here and then run my son and grandson home."

"We'll pick you up on the way."

I switched off and sighed. "So much for peace and quiet," I said.

Chapter Nineteen

Cliff Larson rode with the passenger window open, letting the brisk air suck out the smoke from his incessant cigarette. I had traded the aging, clanking Bronco for the unmarked sedan that Howard Bishop had just parked, its interior still pleasantly warm.

A thousand yards behind us were Undersheriff Robert Torrez and Deputy Thomas Pasquale.

During the past two hours, Larson had done more than encourage his emphysema. He'd spent time on the phone, and added to our log of information. None of it improved my mood.

The dealer in Oklahoma, Mickey Emerson, caught with stolen cattle and ready to make any kind of deal that might save his own hide, had cheerfully told Comanche County sheriff's deputies everything they wanted to know. And it all pointed at Dale Torrance, the nineteen-year-old kid from Posadas, New Mexico.

Emerson had a copy of a transportation permit for the eighteen calves signed by Cliff Larson, and the sheriff's investigator in Oklahoma faxed us a copy. Mickey Emerson had used that document as all the background he needed to cut a bill of sale. He didn't look at it too closely. He paid Dale Torrance in cash, $285 for each late yearling steer—a nice bundle, even though considerably below the market price at the time.

"Pretty slick," Cliff mused. He had his briefcase open on the seat beside him, with the year's file of permits. "But dumber'n a post. Dale used permit two eight one oh eight." Larson held up the clipped file. "I wrote that to his dad earlier in the summer when he was movin' stock from the home ranch over to a Forest Service lease on Johnny Boyd's spread."

"He didn't even change the number of the permit?"

"Hell no. Course, that's harder to do." He held up the permit, assuming I could glance over and see the number at the bottom of the page. "He did fudge some other changes, though."

"And the name? How did he pass that off? The cattle belong to Miles Waddell, not Torrance."

"Well, see, that's the beauty of usin' correction fluid, and then makin' a fresh copy on somebody's copier somewheres."

"The permits aren't color-coded?"

"Hell yes, they are. But who's going to keep track of that? White, blue, goldenrod, yellow, green. You think if he got stopped by a trooper on a spot check that the cop would give a damn? Or even know in the first place?" He grinned. "State police would say that's not their job. And a cowpuncher with a load of calves in a goose-neck trailer ain't all that suspicious in ranchin' country. And Oklahoma authorities don't have the same system we do. And it don't appear that Mickey Emerson looked all that close. Or wanted to."

"I wouldn't have thought that the livestock market was so hot that it'd pay. What did he get? Two eighty-five? That's a good price, but what's Emerson stand to gain at sale? A few bucks a head. As much as a hundred per calf at the most? Why did he bother?"

"Because he could," Larson said. "Ever wonder why somebody goes to all the trouble to take a crowbar to a parkin' meter for a few lousy nickels and dimes?" He shrugged. "I mean, first the son of a bitch has to steal a crowbar, right? For a few minutes of his time, Emerson picks up maybe a hundred bucks apiece, and that's almost two grand that he didn't have before." He crushed out his cigarette. "I imagine you've seen a lot worse done for two thousand bucks."

"Of course," I said. "Over and over and over. And it still never ceases to amaze the hell out of me. This Emerson fellow is positive it was Dale?"

"One hundred percent. I faxed the Comanche deputies a copy of Dale Torrance's yearbook picture. No question about it. Emerson said he'd swear to it in court. And he's got Dale's signature on his copy of the bill of sale."

"They're going to want to extradite him, I'm sure."

"Don't count on it. They're willing to impound the cattle for us, but they want them *gone*. It's a pain in the ass for them and Oklahoma sure as hell doesn't want to pay feed bills on eighteen head of hungry steers that are New Mexico's problem. But we'll let Dan Schroeder figure all that out. Hell, even if they wanted to prosecute over in Oklahoma, they'd have to stand in line. By the time New Mexico gets through with old Dale, he ain't goin' to be a teenager no more." I wasn't sure that I shared Larson's grim satisfaction.

About twenty-five miles west of Posadas we turned south on the washboard gravel of County Road 14. Torrez kept his distance. There was no point in eating our dust. More important, by staying far enough back, we wouldn't look like an ominous convoy bearing down on the prey. The last thing I wanted was to spook the kid.

I didn't know what would be going through Dale's mind. I didn't know if he felt confident that he'd pulled off the perfect crime, or if he was a little jumpy, looking over his shoulder like a scared jackrabbit. He wasn't stupid by nature. He had to know that what he'd done would land him in a world of trouble if he were caught.

If the heat were turned on, Dale had an example to follow, and that made me uneasy all over again. When Dale's older brother Patrick had gotten himself in a pickle a couple of years before, he'd headed for Gillette, Wyoming. His had been woman troubles, too—but in Patrick's case, the gal who'd twanged his heartstrings was a real wild hare who didn't think about the legalities of what she did for more than a couple of seconds. Patrick had decided that running *from* her was the smartest thing he could do at the time.

I didn't think that younger brother Dale was going to run away from Christine Prescott. Less than twenty-four hours before, I'd gotten the impression that Christine was a good deal more than just a beautiful face and stunning figure. To be a successful bartender for Victor Sanchez's Broken Spur Saloon, she needed to be hardworking, levelheaded, honest, and tolerant. Sanchez was barely on the up side of nasty. Her boss may have had the personality of a sun-struck rattlesnake, but as long as he stayed in the kitchen, none of his customers much cared, and Christine Prescott could cope with his moods.

We all assumed that Dale Torrance had stolen eighteen head of cattle for ready cash. Whether he needed that $5,130 to impress Christine somehow, or for some other reason only he knew, it couldn't be news to Dale that a century before, that stunt would have earned him a new rope.

Five miles farther south, we passed under the entryway for the H-Bar-T. The archway was one of those fancy scenes plasma-cut into black iron, this one featuring a cowpuncher on horseback chasing a herd of cattle through the yucca, lariat in full loop over his head.

The Torrance home was as out of place in that bleak, stark country as a Rhode Island license plate. The two-story affair was one of those things offered in catalogs back in the fifties, the white paint trying its best to gleam after a season of pounding sun.

Just before the driveway, the ranch road forked, with a trail leading around a paddock, shed, and copse of leafless elms to an older model, red-and-white mobile home.

"I think we're late for the party," Cliff Larson said, and my heart skipped a beat. Herb Torrance's pickup, habitually crusted with mud and range dust, was pulled up in front of the front steps of the house. Another older model pickup with dual back tires was nosed in beside the mobile home. No amount of road dirt could hide its battle scars, the fenders and flanks dented and torn from a long, hard life.

Parked immediately behind it, half blocking the driveway, was the truck we'd seen just a couple of hours before carrying Miles Waddell and friends.

Chapter Twenty

Step into a crowd of people, and sometimes it takes a few seconds to sort out who's who—and who's doing what to whom. This time, it was easy.

Even from across the open spaces of what passed for a front yard, I could see Miles Waddell's red hair. He, Mark Denton, and Ed Johns were standing by the front of Miles' new truck. I pulled in immediately behind them, missing the back bumper by a hair breadth, and Johns turned slightly to see who had arrived. The others were riveted on the action and could have cared less.

In this case, the action was Herb Torrance and his son Dale... and one of their blue healer pups. Two dozen steps away from the three men, Dale was backed up against the side of the mobile home, pegged there by a father whose face was livid. The dog was frantic, darting this way and that, yapping his fool head off, unsure whether to leap into Herb's arms, jump on Dale, or bite them both.

I got out of the car just in time to see Herb come up with his right hand, hard. The blow took Dale on the face, a crack that I could hear across the yard. The kid's head snapped around and for a moment he lost his balance. His right hand swung out against the side of the trailer for support as his feet flailed, one of his boots catching the dog in the face. At the same time Herb's hand flashed again, and this time Dale sprawled against the trailer's skirting.

Waddell leaned against the grille of his truck, his arms folded in satisfaction over his chest. He glanced at me as I rounded the side of their truck, and then nodded at Cliff Larson.

"I thought I told you to stay away from here," I snapped, and Waddell shrugged.

"You took your own fair time getting here," he said. "And hell, we're just watchin'."

As I advanced on Herb and his son, I couldn't hear what the older man was saying, even if the dog hadn't been hysterical. It was no yelling match. Herb bent down and grabbed Dale by the shoulder, their faces no more than an inch apart, Herb's voice a hoarse croak.

"Just hold on there," I bellowed as I approached. Two strides separated me from Herb's back when Dale's foot lashed out and caught his father on the ankle. At the same time, the boy twisted, taking advantage of his father's loss of balance. Using both hands and feet, Dale scrambled wildly out of his father's grip. He flailed wildly for traction even as Herb slammed his hand against the trailer to stop his fall.

"Dale!" I shouted, but the boy was a human jackrabbit. He'd gotten his feet under him and sprinted along the side of the trailer, Father in pursuit, blue healer dancing around them. Lame as Herb was from years of winter knees and livestock kicks, he managed a credibly fast sideways lope, his left leg dragging stiffly.

"Eeee haw," Waddell cried with delight.

I heard Bob Torrez's vehicle pull in behind mine. If there was chasing to be done, better someone sure of step, fleet of foot, and strong of heart. Waddell and his buddies weren't about to help, and Cliff Larson would cough himself to death before he ran twenty feet.

For whatever reason, Dale Torrance headed toward the paddock area and the complex of loading chutes. What good that was going to do him wasn't clear, other than to put some railroad ties between him and his father. Just when he had his father beat in their foot race, something caught the toe of his left boot and he went flying, crashing into the bottom two-by-six face first.

The rough wood caught him across the mouth. It must have hurt like hell if he'd been in the mood to notice. But his father was bearing down on him.

Herb slowed enough to scoop up a length of splintered fencing, a chunk of wood about four feet long and maybe two inches square—about twice the size of a broom handle. The dog made a grab for the other end and missed.

Within range of the boy, Herb let fly and I could hear the wood sing. Dale had scrambled to all fours, blood streaming from his mouth. The swat caught him solidly on the rump, a hard *whack* that raised dust from the seat of his pants.

"Sir?"

I turned and saw Tom Pasquale at my elbow. A few yards away, the undersheriff was moseying toward us, in no hurry. Years before, I had heard him tell another deputy that the best way to survive a career of being called to break up nasty bar fights was to "arrive late and arrest the loser." As sound advice as that might have been, it wasn't Pasquale's style.

I held up a hand. "If he starts hitting him in the head," I said. "Otherwise, they're having a little family discussion on family property."

Herb made pretty fair use of that chunk of board, driving his son across the small corral that fed the loading chute. He connected two or three times, and by the second time, the healer decided that if Herb was hitting the kid, it was okay to bite him, too. On the other side of the corral, the dog got a mouthful of jeans just above the boot, and that put Dale off balance. The kid took the opportunity to roll under the fence, dog still tussling.

The seven of us had gravitated toward the corral, and if the fight went on much longer, we'd look like seven spectators at a rodeo. All we needed was to hike boots up on the bottom rail, nestle our elbows on the top, and chew idly on a wisp of straw, observing the action, making sage commentary, and placing side bets on the winner.

Herb was running out of breath, and when Dale went under the fence, the older man hesitated, bent at the waist, heaving and puffing. His face was blotchy, and if he kept it up, somebody was going to be practicing CPR.

Dale, under the fence and with the dog deciding they were playing after all, hesitated long enough to suck in three lungfuls of dust and air. He staggered to his feet and once more set off running, this time around the back of the trailer.

Herb remained rooted, his hands on his knees. He looked over at me and shook his head in disgust.

"You better go after him," I said to Pasquale, and the young deputy took off like a shot. Dale Torrance had the head start he needed, and he was on familiar territory. He cut around the mobile home and emerged at the other end, in the clear. Two more strides brought him to the door of his truck, and he snatched it open and dove inside.

The diesel lit on the first crank. He pulled it into gear just as Pasquale dashed around the end of the trailer. The old Dodge surged backward in a cloud of dust and exhaust. The back bumper was one of those stout black creations that ranchers weld up out of scrap iron—sharp corners and edges. The bumper slammed into the left front fender of Miles Waddell's fancy truck, driving the shiny bodywork in until chrome, steel, and plastic molded themselves around the tire and suspension.

The sound of the crash hadn't died away when the back tires spun another dust storm as Dale surged his truck forward. I saw and heard Tom Pasquale's hand smack down on the hood, but the deputy could see what none of the rest of us could. He had a straight-on view of the kid's face. He made the right decision and jumped sideways, the front tire of the Dodge narrowly missing his foot.

"Goddamn," Waddell said, groping for something intelligent to say. "He backed into my truck."

"Well, now," the livestock inspector added. The dual rear tires spewed fountains of dust and gravel as Dale Torrance floored the accelerator, feeding that turbo-diesel for all it was worth. The Dodge spun half a donut and careened through a small knot of juniper sprouts, jouncing airborne as it crashed over the old parent stump.

Undersheriff Torrez had kicked himself into motion, and he sprinted to the idling unit parked behind mine. The Torrance boy drove a beeline for the gate, and Torrez spun the Expedition in its own length, avoiding my car as he did so. He paused just long enough for Deputy Pasquale to grab the door and yank it open.

"Where do you suppose he's headed?" Mark Denton mused.

"Damn," Waddell said, watching the chase in wonder.

By this time, Cliff Larson had walked back to the unmarked car, waiting for me. "That wasn't exactly what I had in mind when we come out here," he said laconically as I yanked open the door. "You want Herb along?"

"No," I said. As we shot back out the long driveway, I glanced in the rearview mirror. Herb Torrance was leaning against the fence. The other three were gathered around the front of Waddell's truck, yanking on the bodywork in an attempt to free the front wheel.

Up ahead, young Torrance's truck reached County Road 14 and tried to turn south. He was going so fast when he hit the gravel that the truck plowed across the road and into the bar-ditch, bouncing hard enough that a piece of back fender flew off. Torrez had better luck, throwing the Expedition sideways before he hit the county road. He slid the vehicle onto the gravel facing in the right direction.

The two vehicles, a dust storm engulfing the Expedition, hurtled down County 14 nose to tail.

As I straightened the sedan out on the county road, I grabbed the mike off the dash.

"Back off, Robert," I said, but the undersheriff had already lifted his foot. As the county road changed from gravel to red clay, Torrance's pickup kicked a plume of dust thirty feet high, like a great vapor trail behind a jet. After a quarter of a mile he'd pulled far enough ahead that Torrez and Pasquale could breathe.

"Well, this ain't good," Cliff Larson drawled.

"No, it isn't," I said. Some fourteen miles of county road lay ahead of Dale Torrance before he jumped out on State 56. The first handful of miles were straight, relatively level, and fast. Then the road wound up the backside of San Patricio mesa, a narrow, rock-strewn cut not much more than one truck wide. The road snaked up through juniper and brush until it broke out on top, where the mesa was scarred by water-cut arroyos and massive, crumbling fissures in the rimrock. That was the good part of 14. If Dale managed that without crumpling his truck into a ball of tin foil, he still had the final six miles, where the road meandered down the face of San Patricio mesa, switchback after switchback, toward the state highway.

The radio crackled into life, and Torrez sounded as if he were asking for some more fried chicken at a summer Sunday picnic. He'd waited until he'd crested the backside of the mesa, within range of the repeater on the San Cristóbals across the valley.

"Three oh four, three oh eight. Ten-twenty."

"Three oh four is Abeyta," I said, and Cliff Larson nodded. He'd pulled his seat belt tight, and for once left the cigarettes in his pocket.

"Three oh eight, three oh four is in Regal. Ten-eight," Abeyta responded after a moment.

"Three oh four, we need you at the intersection of State Fifty-six and County Road Fourteen. Right at the cattle guard. A red and white Dodge dually is headed your way. Don't let any traffic northbound on Fourteen, and if he makes it that far, don't let him out on the highway."

"Ten-four," Abeyta said.

"How's he going to do that?" Larson asked.

"Don't know," I said. "He can block the cattle guard easily enough."

"You think you'll have any cars left when this is all over?" Larson managed a nervous laugh.

"It's not the cars I'm worried about," I said.

Chapter Twenty-one

On Friday night, everything had gone wrong for Matthew Baca. Less than eighteen hours later, Dale Torrance was determined to try his luck. I could guess at his mental state—but at least he wasn't drunk.

Working in Hollywood, the celluloid high-speed getaway artist might have thundered south on County Road 14, the vapor trail of dust from his speeding car snaking down the face of the mesa. Cheek muscles twitching with the easy determination of someone who'd read the script, he'd actually be looking forward to the roadblock down at the state highway.

Maybe the deputy would park in the approved Hollywood roadblock fashion, diagonally across part of the right-of-way so that his unit could be thrown to one side in a theatrical crash that did little more than crumple the speeding thug's fender. As the car sped by, demolishing the police units in great flaming explosions of inexplicably ruptured fuel tanks, the cops would fire wonderfully ineffectual shots with their shotguns.

I prayed that Dale Torrance hadn't been paying attention to the movies. Both he and Undersheriff Robert Torrez *had* paid attention to details over the years on various hunting trips, and they both knew that three miles from the intersection with the main road, a little-used scratch in the sand and rocks forked off to the east.

In my nocturnal wanderings, even I had had occasion to amble along the path—it was little more than that. Once upon a time the trail had provided access to a cattle tank, but the gears and rods in the windmill motor had long since fused together into a hundred pounds of useless iron. Most of the blades had fallen from the fan, and the reservoir below was choked with blow sand.

Hunters used the path regularly. Since hunters used it, over the years they had extended it eastbound in search of wily javelina, antelope, and desert mule deer. After meandering past the windmill for two miles or so, the trail's route was blocked by a deep river wash. The arroyo's vertical sides plunged nearly thirty feet.

At one time, before cattle and juniper moved in to the range, there had been water in the Rio Guigarro. Now it roared and carved its path only after a torrential storm. Otherwise the gravel arroyo bed lay dry, a nasty drop below the rolling contours of the prairie.

The arroyo stopped the trail and turned it south. If a hunter squinted and looked in just the right place through the brush and around the various limestone outcroppings that jutted up along the skirts of San Patricio mesa, he could look directly south and perhaps a mile and a half in the distance, straight into the back door of Victor Sanchez's Broken Spur Saloon.

Dale Torrance may have crested the edge of San Patricio mesa and seen the glint of a vehicle in the distance, parked at the cattle guard just a few yards off State 56.

With that route closed, he'd plunged another mile down the mesa face and taken the trail east. It's possible that was what he had been planning all along. The maneuver might have worked if Bob Torrez hadn't hunted these same hills and mesas himself.

Enough dust lingered in the air above the scuffed ground where Dale had hauled the big old truck off the road that the undersheriff, following a half a mile behind, could tell in a heartbeat that's where the kid had gone.

"Three oh four," Torrez's voice said over the radio, "he's turned east on the base trail. The only place he can come out is the saloon, unless he goes cross-country. Move on over there. Be careful. Don't press him into something stupid."

Abeyta acknowledged. By the time Cliff Larson and I made it to the rim of San Patricio, with a commanding view of the valley, I could see the dot that had to be Tony Abeyta's vehicle pulling into the parking lot of the saloon.

The Ford Crown Victoria for which I had traded the worn-out Bronco was a handful on the loose, downhill gravel. Several times, Larson stretched out a hand to the dashboard for support and once when the front wheels broke loose on a particularly nasty, washboarded switchback, I heard an almost plaintive "whoa" from his side of the car. A touch of the gas busted the back wheels loose and pointed us pretty much in the direction we wanted to go.

"Three oh four, he's turnin' south toward you," Torrez radioed.

"Ten-four. I see him." All Tony Abeyta had to do was sit quietly in Victor Sanchez's parking lot and wait for the old pickup to burst up out of the brush.

At one point, we had a clear enough view of the state highway out ahead of us to see the white and green Expedition of the U.S. Border Patrol when it flashed by, eager to join the fun.

In his rush to dive off the main county road, Dale Torrance had done a fair job of blocking himself in. Looking ahead toward the saloon, the bulk of the building would block his view of Tony Abeyta's county unit, and the general roll and rise of the prairie would block the paved highway from view. Others could follow his dust plume with ease, but he would have no way of knowing what lay in wait.

Unless he stopped in just the right spot to watch the twisting trail behind him, he would never have seen Bob Torrez as the undersheriff slammed the back door on Dale's escape route.

Trying to crawl into the mind of a petrified teenager to understand his actions was futile, but I found myself doing just that. If Dale assumed that all the cops who had been chasing him had been faked out by his clever ruse, then he had to assume that we were at that moment still on County Road 14, closing in on the state highway—with that intersection just a quarter of a mile west of the saloon.

When we reached the pavement, Dale knew we'd have a choice…if he was thinking at all, that is. Would we assume that Dale had headed southwest for Mexico or Arizona, and turn right to follow? Posadas to the left didn't offer much refuge, and if we didn't know that the kid had turned on the rough trail, then heading east on the state highway didn't make much sense.

I grimaced as we jounced over a particularly badly installed cattle guard. "He's going after the girl," I said.

"Don't doubt it," Larson replied.

"He thinks he's going to sneak in from the back. He thinks he can hide the truck from the road that way."

"Got to be," Larson agreed. "That boy ain't the sharpest tool in the box."

"Panic time," I said, and slowed for the second cattle guard that marked the boundary of the state highway's right-of-way. "He's not thinking at all. Even if Christine wants to go with him, where does he think he can go?"

"Maybe he thinks we just don't care all that much."

"Oh, sure."

"Well, when Bobby dropped back there at the beginning, that thought might have crossed his mind."

"Three oh eight, three oh four." The voice in the distance prompted me to reach out and turn up the radio a bit.

"Three oh eight."

"Three oh eight, he's stopping behind the bar."

"Does he know you're there?"

"Negative. He can't see the unit."

"We'll be there in a minute or so. Let him go on inside, and block his vehicle."

"Ten-four."

Once on the pavement I accelerated hard, approaching the saloon from the west just in time to see Abeyta's unit disappear around the backside of the building.

"Three oh eight, the truck's parked and the driver's door is open," Abeyta said. "He's gone inside."

"Ten-four. Just block the vehicle. Don't go in."

I slowed to turn into the parking lot and saw a fair-sized convention. Victor's truck was parked near the kitchen door on the west side, as usual. Since it was late Saturday afternoon, the bar traffic was picking up, with an assortment of vehicles nosed up to the railroad tie barrier in front of the saloon. Last in line was the Border Patrol unit, and I saw Scott Gutierrez leaning casually against the front fender.

My back tires hadn't left the pavement when the kitchen door burst open. Dale Torrance was doing a fair imitation of flying backward, pursued by Victor Sanchez. The bar owner's shoulders were hunched for combat. Torrance bounced off the side of Victor's truck, but he was game. He lashed out a quick blow that caught Victor on the cheek. Whether Victor was stunned or just goddamned surprised that someone would have the guts to hit him back wasn't clear, but it gave the Torrance boy an opening. He shot back through the door, into the kitchen.

Victor Sanchez found his footing and lunged after him.

"Well, shit," Larson muttered.

I pulled to a stop beside Sanchez's truck and even before I was out of the car I could hear the bar owner's voice bellowing inside, followed by a metallic crash.

Tony Abeyta appeared from behind the building, and I heard the approach of Torrez's unit, chewing its way up from the arroyo.

"Tony, go around and make sure he doesn't skip out the front," I said, and the deputy nodded. "Scott's out there, too."

Abeyta broke into a jog toward the front of the building.

"Let's see what kind of party we've got," I said to Larson, and he nodded dubiously. I agreed with him. It might have been better retirement insurance to wait patiently outside, ready to grab and bag whatever pieces of Dale Torrance sailed out.

Chapter Twenty-two

The kitchen of the Broken Spur smelled of grilled chicken, chile, and onions, spiced by the tang of broiled hamburger and good strong coffee. Under other circumstances, it would have been a marvelous place to spend some time. No one was in the kitchen, though. Three burger patties spat and dripped on the grill, and off to the side, a mound of hash browns sizzled—all untended.

From the other side of a narrow doorway, I heard a shout, then another shout followed by a loud metallic bang, as if someone had walloped the bar top with a frying pan. Immediately on its heels came something akin to a rebel yell.

I made my way through the kitchen to the swinging door into the barroom. My hand was about to push it open when it slammed inward toward me, the painted plywood surface smacking the palm of my hand and sending shock waves rippling up through my elbow and shoulder.

Jerking backward, I stepped first on Larson's foot, heard him grunt, and then regained my balance by using him as a wall.

Victor Sanchez halted in the doorway. He was breathing heavily, mouth firmly clamped shut in a thin line livid with anger. His nostrils flared with each inhalation. His black eyes regarded me for about the count of three, and then he turned slightly to indicate over his shoulder.

"That worthless little sack of shit is in there," he said. "Get him out of here." I saw his eyes shift and narrow. Undersheriff

Robert Torrez strode through the kitchen door from outside, followed by Deputy Tom Pasquale.

Sanchez pushed past me, studiously ignored Torrez and Pasquale, and picked up the grill spatula. He dabbed gently at the patties while the grease hissed.

I pushed the doorway again and entered the saloon.

"Ho!" somebody said, and from off in the corner somewhere I heard somebody else reply to that observation with a snicker. At about the same time, Tony Abeyta appeared in the main entrance, with Scott Gutierrez's blocky form behind him. I hesitated for a moment to let my eyes adjust to the smoky darkness of the place.

One man was standing at the bar, both arms under him as he stood on his tiptoes, leaning his weight on the lip of the counter so that he folded at the belt buckle. It gave him a good view of the floor behind the bar, an area of apparent interest for him and several others.

"Nobody needs to call the cops," the guy leaning over the bar said as he glanced our way. The snicker repeated itself, maybe with good reason. Damn near half of the Posadas County Sheriff's Department, with backup from the U.S. Border Patrol, had secured Victor Sanchez's saloon.

Mindful of my elbows and all the neatly stacked glassware, I made my way behind the bar. About halfway up, right behind the draught beer dispenser handles, order gave way to mess, the floor covered with busted glasses and two bottles that lay on their sides, gurgling themselves empty on the rubber mat.

Christine Prescott got to her feet when she saw me approaching. Two men were with her, and about that time I could see the soles of a pair of boots, toes pointing up.

Christine wiped her face with the back of her hand and said something to one of the men. He glanced over his shoulder, saw us, and scrunched to one side. Christine pushed past him.

"Are you all right?" I said when she was close enough that I didn't have to yell. I reached out a hand and rested it on her left shoulder, looking her hard in the eye.

She nodded and turned, not out from under my hand, but so that she could look behind her at the figure on the floor. She turned back and took a deep breath.

"Victor clocked him when he grabbed me," she said.

"Okay. Stay put." I squeezed her shoulder once and then slid on past. Dale Torrance lay on his back in a welter of glass, chips, dip, and peanuts. Kenny Salazar moved out of my way, but the other young man whom I didn't recognize remained near Dale's head. He was holding a folded bar rag against the kid's scalp.

I used the shelf under the bar as support and dropped to my knees. With two fingers I felt the left side of Dale's neck. The pulse was strong and rapid.

"I think he's okay," the man holding the rag said. "He just fetched a good clip upside the head with that billy."

I looked where he was pointing and saw the wooden fish billy on the shelf. I grinned. Victor Sanchez was one of a kind. He had made efficient work of the situation and then went right back to his job. Whoever had ordered the burgers and hash browns wouldn't be inconvenienced for a moment.

Dale Torrance's face bore the blank expression of someone who'd finally drifted into deep sleep and was planning to stay there for a long time. His breathing was steady. "Is he bleeding badly?"

The man shook his head and drew the cloth away. The club had caught Dale right above the left ear. The scalp laceration oozed blood, the tissue already beginning to swell. The man put the cloth back. "Don't move him," I said. "We'll get an ambulance here."

"He ain't going anywheres," the man said, and I pushed myself to my feet. Bob Torrez was talking on the cell phone, and I beckoned to Tony Abeyta and Tom Pasquale.

"Make sure he doesn't move," I said. "If he regains consciousness, don't let him sit up. Don't let him roll over. Don't let him do a damn thing." They nodded and slid past me.

I took Christine by the elbow. "Give me a few minutes," I said, and she nodded. "Where's a good place to talk?"

Before she had time to answer, the kitchen door swung open and Victor appeared, three plates expertly balanced on his left arm. He moved around the small room as if the troops weren't there, but on his way back to the kitchen he paused at the door. He glared at me and jerked his chin toward Christine.

"I got to have my help," he said. "Don't be wasting her time." With that, he disappeared back into the kitchen.

"What a sweetheart," Cliff Larson said.

Christine Prescott led us out into the dark foyer and then into the small nonsmoking dining room. No one was there at the moment, which wasn't surprising. Victor did as little as possible to encourage the room's use. Why he bothered with it, I didn't know, unless the health department had ordered him to have it available.

The girl sat at the table nearest the east-facing window, and she kept glancing toward the door—no doubt awaiting another appearance by her boss.

"Christine," I said, "what was Dale after?"

"Me, I guess," she said. Her voice was husky.

"What did he say to you?"

Christine took a deep breath and closed her eyes. "Really weird," she said at length. "He ran in from the back, from the kitchen. He said something like, 'Come on. We gotta go.' I don't know what he meant." She shrugged.

"And then what happened?"

"Well, Victor was right behind him, maybe ten steps. I said something like, 'What are you talking about?' And then Dale grabbed my right arm. He said something like...let's see. He said, 'Come on. I'll explain later.' And that's all he had time for. Victor came up behind him and took him from behind, one hand on each biceps, like this?" She stretched out her arms, hands clawed into clamps. I could picture Victor doing just that.

"When he did that, Dale jerked around and took a swing at him. I think he hit Victor on the right shoulder, kind of a glancing blow. And then Victor kind of drop-kicked him out of the bar and into the kitchen." Christine half smiled and looked heavenward. "He opened the door with him, headfirst."

"And then he came back in? Dale came back?"

She nodded. "He just ran in. He said, 'Come on. I got the money now.' He grabbed me by the arm, real hard. I said something like, 'Let go of me,' and that's all the time he had. Victor caught up with him again, grabbed the billy from underneath the bar, and hit him with it. One pop."

"And went right back to the burgers," I murmured.

"Sir?"

"Nothing. Christine, do you know what Dale Torrance wanted?"

"Other than that I was supposed to go with him just then, no. I don't."

"Had you been seeing him?"

"Oh, yeah." She smiled ruefully. "He kinda got so that he was hanging around here regularly, whenever he could. Most of the summer, as a matter of fact. Maybe too much. Victor said to make sure not to serve him any alcohol. And I never did."

"Did he have a crush on you?"

"Yes," she said without hesitation or embarrassment. She grinned. "A *mega*-crush."

"Did you ever go out with him?"

"Sure. A couple of times."

I regarded her thoughtfully and she took that as a prompt. "Well, not really *out*," she said. "I mean, once I went with him to pick up a horse that he'd bought from some guy over in Eunice. It was my day off, and I didn't have anything to do. He called and asked if I'd go along, that he could use a hand." She shrugged. "So I said yes. I didn't see anything wrong with it. Dale's kind of sweet. He's fun to be with."

"And other times?"

"Last week, he stayed until I was done work, at closing. My car was broke down again. He tried to fix it, but couldn't. He just took me home."

"That was it?"

"Well…" she hesitated, then added, "well, sorta that was it."
She actually blushed. "Stupid car," she said. "That's one thing I
plan to do working here. Get enough money together to make a
down payment on something that runs more than half the time."

"Did you tell Dale that?"

"Oh, sure, I suppose. We talked about stuff like that."

"And that's all that happened? You don't know what spooked
him today?"

"No, sir." She looked across at Cliff Larson. He hadn't said a
thing, but he sure wanted a cigarette. He had held one unlighted,
fiddled with it this way and that, for most of our conversation.
Christine Prescott knew exactly who he was, too. She turned
back to me. "You were after Dale for something?"

I nodded.

"Can I ask for what?"

"It appears that he took eighteen head of roping stock belong-
ing to someone else."

"No," Christine said. She smiled in disbelief. "Why would
he be so dumb?"

"I was hoping you could help with that," I said. "He drove
them out of state and sold them."

"You're kidding," she said.

"No. I wish that for his sake we were."

"What's going to happen to him now?" Christine asked.

"First, he goes over to Posadas General to make sure his skull's
not cracked," I said. "We'll see from there."

"Is Victor in trouble?"

I laughed loudly. "I don't think so." Off in the distance I
heard the wail of a siren. To Larson I said, "Would you go out
front and make sure he gets loaded all right?" Larson nodded
and got to his feet, free hand already grubbing in the pocket of
his jeans for his lighter.

When he'd left, I turned back to Christine. "There's another
question I need to ask you. It has nothing to do with Dale
Torrance or this mess today."

She folded her hands and waited. "Remember back to Friday night," I said. That made it sound longer ago than the twenty or so hours that it actually was. "Last night. When Matt Baca came into the saloon. Remember?"

"Of course."

"What exactly did he do?"

"I don't understand."

"Just that. What did he do. When he walked through the door, what happened?"

Christine frowned. "He walked in, kinda spaced. I could see that right off. He lost his balance a little and leaned first against the doorjamb, and then against the bar when he made it over that far."

"What did he ask you?"

Christine bit her lip, brow furrowed. "He said, 'I need two twelve-packs of Coors.' I was busy making a margarita for another customer, and I said something like, 'Not in this lifetime.'"

"And tell me why you said that. Right off the bat, no hesitation."

"Because I knew that Matt Baca wasn't twenty-one."

"You knew that for a fact?"

Christine frowned again. "Well, no...I guess I don't know it for a fact. But he sure didn't *look* twenty-one. I've seen him around, you know. I know that he hangs out with kids who are a long, long way from twenty-one."

"So you just refused him."

"I didn't have to. Victor happened to come out of the kitchen and saw him. Right away, he told him to beat it."

"He didn't ask to look at any ID?"

"No. He knows who Matt is." She grimaced. "Who he was."

"Okay. Now think back. When Matt asked for the beer, and you said, 'Not in this lifetime,' what did he do? Exactly?"

"What do you mean, *do?* He was just standing there."

"You said earlier that he put one hand in his pocket, as if he were going to pull out an ID and show you."

Christine looked up at the ceiling. "Yes. He was reaching into his back pocket when Victor came out of the kitchen."

"Like for money? Or an ID?"

"Maybe. It could have been."

"Which pocket?"

"Oh, wow." She closed her eyes in thought, brought both hands up, and rested her fingertips on her temples. "Right. Right pocket. Right back pocket. I remember that because he was grubbing a fistful of peanuts out of the bowl on the bar in front of him. That was the hand closest to me. And I was on his left."

"You're sure?"

"No. But I think so. What difference does it make?"

I sighed. The wallet had been in Matt Baca's left back pocket. If the fake ID had been tucked in his right pocket, I wouldn't have seen it when I took the kid into custody at the house and searched his wallet. It looked like Tom Pasquale's scenario was right on target.

"It probably doesn't make any difference," I said, and got to my feet. "Christine, thanks for your help. We appreciate it. Sorry to cause such a ruckus in your life."

"What happens to Dale now?"

"I don't know," I said. "There'll be an arraignment with Judge Hobart. The young man's bought himself a whole string of problems. We'll see what develops."

We left the dining room just in time to see the gurney loaded with Dale Torrance's quiet form wheeled through the foyer, maneuvered by the two white-uniformed paramedics. Holding the front door for them was a pale-faced Herb Torrance.

I took a step toward him, but before I had a chance to open my mouth to speak, Victor Sanchez's gravelly, irritated voice stopped me.

"Why don't you bring a few more Gestapo with you next time," he said. "Maybe you could bring the National Guard in on it, too."

"Victor…" I started to say, my patience running thin.

"Here," he interrupted, and handed me a fat brown envelope. He swatted my arm with it, to make sure he'd made contact.

"What's this?"

"Kid dropped it in the kitchen," Victor said with a slight inflection that might have passed for humor. "He had it in his back pocket."

The brown envelope was rumpled and folded. I opened it just enough to see the considerable amount of money inside.

"I figured it didn't belong to him. Otherwise, you guys wouldn't have been chasing him. Right?"

"Thanks, Victor," I said, but I was already talking to his back.

Chapter Twenty-three

"Thanks for not chasing the boy off into some tree stump somewheres," Herb Torrance said. He had good reason to look and sound miserable. He watched the ambulance pull out of the parking lot and shook his head wearily. He turned back to Larson and me. "Thank God his momma wasn't home. Jesus." He heaved a great sigh. "I don't guess you all know for sure what happens next."

"No," I said. "First things first, Herb. Let the doctors check him out. He took a hell of a rap, so they'll probably hold him overnight. There'll be a deputy at the hospital to make sure he doesn't do something foolish if he wakes up in the middle of the night."

I tried a sympathetic smile, but I was weary myself. As soon as the Torrance kid had spun that pickup truck out of the yard, my nerves had replayed hell with my system. On the drive south on County Road 14, my imagination had conjured all kinds of awful scenarios, each one ending with Dale Torrance splattered over the New Mexico landscape.

"You don't need to worry about him getting out of that room. He ain't goin' nowheres," Herb said emphatically. "The wife wasn't home when all this happened, thank God. But I'm going to pick her up now, and we'll be at the hospital in just a few minutes. And we'll be there, as long as it takes."

"That's good, Herb. I'll talk to Judge Hobart as soon as we get back to Posadas this evening, and see if he can arrange a preliminary hearing for the morning…assuming Dale's released by then. You understand that he's in our custody right now?"

"Yep," Herb Torrance said. "I understand that, all right. The boy's gotten himself in a hell of a mess." He thrust out his hand. "Thanks again." He grinned and ducked his head in embarrassment. "I don't guess I handled this all too good."

"It happens."

"Shouldn't have, by God. And by the way, what's the deal with Waddell's steers, now? They're impounded over in Lawton?"

I nodded. Cliff Larson cleared his throat. "And the Oklahoma authorities sure as hell don't want a feed bill, so they're eager to have someone truck 'em out of there."

"I'll take care of that," Herb said. "Give me tonight, to make sure the boy's going to be all right. Then I'll go over first thing in the morning, or whenever Judge Hobart is done with us."

"That'll work," Larson said. "They're at Emerson Livestock, right on the south side of town. I'll fix you up with paperwork so you can get 'em back."

Herb nodded and again shook first my hand, and then Larson's. Cliff and I watched him trudge back to his pickup. "Ain't that a sorry mess," Cliff muttered. He looked at me and grinned, the stub of the cigarette jerking as his lips moved. "See why I need you to fill in for me?"

I glowered at Larson and mouthed an obscenity at him. That split his grin even wider.

By 6:30, the last patrol car pulled out of the parking lot of Victor Sanchez's Broken Spur Saloon, leaving him in relative peace and quiet. I had no doubt that by closing time, the story passed from drunk to drunk would include at least eighteen officers converging on the saloon from all sides, with Victor alone able to subdue Dale Torrance, saving the fair damsel behind the bar from who knows what fate. What the hell. It was all good for his business, even though he would be the last one to admit it.

I dropped Cliff off at the Public Safety Building where he'd stashed his truck. With things quieting down, we had an extra vehicle or two, so I took the unmarked car home with me.

I didn't know what direction Bob Torrez's investigation of Sosimo Baca's death was taking, but at the moment I was too tired to ask. It was his ball game, anyway. If he needed something from me, he'd say so.

When I walked into my house on Guadalupe Terrace, I could hear familiar theme music. In the sunken living room off the kitchen, my grandson was hunkered down in front of the television watching Gary Cooper stand uncomfortably in front of the church congregation. "Now you all know what I think of this man," the on-screen mayor was saying self-righteously.

My son was settled deep in the leather folds of my favorite chair, a book open on his lap. "We couldn't find where you store the rest of your tapes," Buddy said with a wide grin. He knew perfectly well the answer to that mystery. He'd given me a VCR and the tape of *High Noon* for Christmas several years before, I suppose figuring that would kick off my collection.

It didn't kick off anything. I'd watched the movie countless times, and could probably recite most of the dialogue by heart. During a burglary of my home two years before by local teen-agers, the original VCR had been stolen, but not the tape. So much for taste. I'd replaced the VCR, but never added to the tape collection.

"This is cool beans," my grandson said, nodding approvingly as Cooper walked out of the church, a disgusted man.

"How did your afternoon go?" Buddy said, and pushed himself out of the chair. "Sit. I'll make some coffee."

I waved a hand and glanced at my watch. "Even better. Let's go get something to eat."

"You ready for that?" my son said to Tadd, and the kid launched up off the floor and snapped off the VCR and television. "He's always ready to eat," Buddy added.

"We going to the Don Juan?" Tadd asked. "That's a cool place."

My estimation of my grandson clicked up another notch. And this time, we managed a meal that was uninterrupted and leisurely. By the time we finished eating, we were all ready to go to sleep right there in the restaurant. I knew that with close to thirty hours to wakefulness behind me and my belly full of fresh green chile I could go home and conk out for at least twelve hours. By that time it would be Sunday, the day that Estelle and her family would arrive from Minnesota.

Back at the house, we settled comfortably while Tadd watched Will Kane make preparations to face the vengeful brothers.

"So what happens after Tuesday?" Buddy asked. He rested his arm on the back of the sofa and looked at me. I tipped my mug slightly and regarded the steaming surface of the decaffeinated coffee he'd made for dessert.

"I thought maybe I'd figure that out on Wednesday morning," I said. "Cliff Larson offered me a job today." I shrugged. "He's the livestock inspector. Maybe that would be interesting for a little while."

"What sort of work would that entail?"

"Not much." I grinned. "Basically, anytime a rancher moves livestock in New Mexico, he has to have a travel permit. The brands have to be inspected. Or lip tattoos on horses if they're headed for a race track. You make an accurate count. Check for obvious signs of disease. That sort of thing."

"Do you have situations very often like you had this afternoon?"

"Hopefully not," I said. "But there's a surprising amount of livestock theft that goes on. Our department has helped Larson clear several larceny cases over the years. And there's more and more trouble with the border traffic. Especially with racehorses moving back and forth." I sipped the coffee. "I don't know. I haven't decided yet." I set the cup down on the end table. "When's your tour over?"

"In January," Buddy said. "January twenty-sixth is my last day. Twenty-five years."

"God, that got here in a hurry."

"Yes it did."

"And you're only forty-seven years old!" I said in wonder.

"So the more immediate question is, what the hell are you going to do with yourself? Edie is not going to let you stay at home all day long and have all the fun while she's swapping lies with other lawyers."

My grandson glanced over at us. On screen, Katy Jurado was explaining the facts of life to Grace Kelly. "Did you tell Grandpa about our place in San Antonio?"

"You haven't told me anything," I said. "Great state secrets abound in this place. What's with San Antonio?"

"We'll be moving up there right after Christmas," Buddy said. "I've got some accumulated leave, and Edie and the kids will be done with the semester. We've bought a place there."

"This is all pretty sudden, isn't it? But hell, San Antonio's a pretty city. Why not."

Buddy nodded enthusiastically. "You can't imagine how happy we are to get out of Beeville. I signed on with the Texas Department of Public Safety, and San Antonio's where I'll be based. It worked out great, since Edie got an offer from a law firm there as well. It's the firm she wanted."

I held out my hands. "Whoa. You signed on with DPS?"

"Aviation division. I get to watch chases like you had this afternoon, from the air."

"I always assumed that you'd end up with one of the airlines," I said.

"Nah," Buddy said with a grimace. "Bus driving is not for me. Shuttling those heavies from one city to another, full of a bunch of cranky passengers—that's not my cup of tea. Anyway, for the last ten years or so, I've been in choppers."

I smiled. "Well, good. If that's what you want, that's good." I felt as if I needed sticks to prop my eyes open. I thumped the arm of the chair, and watched the TV for a few seconds. A very young Lloyd Bridges was trying to talk Cooper into saddling a horse and lighting out of Hadleyville.

"This is the same guy who was in *Hot Shots,*" my grandson said with considerable wonder.

"Forty-five years younger," I said. "And since I know how this movie ends, I'm going to go to bed. You guys are welcome to watch movies all night, if you want. There's even a video store downtown, if you get desperate." I pushed myself to my feet with an audible symphony of joints.

It was nearly nine. The phone had left me in peace for three hours. In my bedroom at the opposite end of the house, I couldn't hear a sound—not my grandson chatting with his father, or the gunshots as Gary Cooper settled accounts, and certainly not the gentle little *chunk* as he pitched his badge in the dust at the end of the movie.

The cool silence enveloped me and for once chased away the devils of insomnia and the kind of circular, unproductive problem-solving that inflicts the prone and the wakeful. Maybe it was just the pleasure at having good company under my roof once more, with the anticipation of more to come the next day. Maybe it was profound relief that Dale Torrance had suffered nothing more serious than a rap on the head—something he probably needed anyway.

Whatever the reason, I slept like a dead man, deep and hard. It would have been nice to awaken refreshed and rested, with the sun of Sunday morning just peeking through the cotton-woods. Instead, I jerked awake soaked in sweat, the house silent and black. My mind had been working, even if the rest of me hadn't.

"Son of a bitch," I said, and sat up straight. The clock on the dresser said forty minutes after two. I fumbled for the telephone and managed to find the right buttons for the Posadas County Sheriff's Department.

Chapter Twenty-four

I sat on the bed and listened to the circuits click, the light from the number pad soft in my peripheral vision. After five rings Brent Sutherland answered. I could hear voices in the background, and, as he brought the phone to his ear, Sutherland said, "No, I don't think so," to someone.

"Posadas County Sheriff's Department, Sutherland."

"Brent, this is Gastner. Is everything all right down there?"

"Yes, sir. Jackie just brought in a DWI. We were finishing up the Breathalyzer."

"Who was it?"

"Out of town." I heard papers shuffle. "A Mr. Bruce Whitaker, from Socorro."

"Passing through, or staying in town?"

"Apparently he was passing through. Jackie stopped him on Seventy-eight, just beyond the airport. He told her that he'd had trouble staying awake, and had one too many cold beers."

"That's brilliant thinking," I said. "Everything else quiet?"

"Yes, sir. Dead."

I glanced at the clock on the dresser. At 2:43, deputies had been home from the swing shift for a couple hours, long enough to have settled comfortably in bed. "I need Tony Abeyta's home number, Brent. I don't have the roster in front of me at the moment."

"Just a second, sir." I could picture him leaning across the desk, consulting the neatly printed chart taped to the green filing cabinet. "That's nine seven seven, three zero zero six," he said after a minute.

"Thirty ought six. That's easy enough to remember," I said. "Thanks."

"He's not there, though. At least I don't think he is. He and Tom Mears were planning to do something with Tom's car. I don't remember what. But he was going over there. Do you want Tom's number too?" I said I did and he read that off as well. I hung up, rolling the number around in my head enough times that I'd remember it.

I started to push the buttons and then hesitated. Both Tony Abeyta and Tom Mears were married, Tony for less than a year. I hated to haul a spouse out of bed in the middle of the night with the harsh ringing of a phone if it wasn't an emergency.

I hung up and sat in the dark for a few minutes, mulling over what my memory had told me, trying to decide if I was just imagining connections that weren't really there. In five minutes, I knew I'd never fall back to sleep. I got up, showered, shaved, and slipped into my favorite red-checkered lumberjack shirt and corduroy trousers.

In the kitchen, I glanced out the window at the thermometer. The temperatures were taking November seriously, touching twenty-seven degrees. There would be frost on the car, but by midmorning it might be fifty degrees. A light breeze rocked and rattled the few cottonwood leaves that clung to the tree just off the back deck.

While I waited for the coffeemaker to do its thing, I rummaged in the front hall closet and found my down vest. I slipped it on and was in the process of running my belt through the hi-rise pancake holster when I damn near collided with my bathrobe-clad son.

"Well, good morning," I said.

"Just barely morning," Buddy replied. He watched as I slid the pair of handcuffs off the kitchen counter and hooked them through my belt at the small of my back. "You don't have enough seniority yet to avoid working the graveyard shift?"

I sighed. "The mind," I said, tracing circles around my right ear. "The mind won't shut up."

"I know how that goes," Buddy said.

I set two cups on the counter, poured, and slid one across to my son. "I hope you haven't inherited my sleeping habits," I said. "Or lack thereof."

He grinned. "I think I'm working on it."

The coffee did the trick. I could feel the rest of my senses spooling up to speed. "You want to go along?"

He raised an eyebrow. "To where?"

"I need to talk to one of my deputies," I said. I set the cup down on the counter and drew irregular patterns on the wood. "It's like a big puzzle." I looked up at Buddy and lifted a finger. "I woke up thinking that maybe I'd been shown another little piece and just didn't recognize it."

"Ooookay," Buddy said slowly. "If you can give me a minute to get dressed. And I'll leave a note for Tadd."

"Oh, we'll be home long before he gets up," I said, but Buddy shook his head.

"You'd be amazed."

While Buddy got dressed, I refilled my cup and snapped the coffeemaker off, then went outside. The air was crisp and clear, the great star-wash of the Milky Way so bright that it rivaled even the pervasive glow from the interstate exchange over to the northwest.

I had no outside lights around my home, figuring that all they did was make life easy for burglars. On more than one occasion, when I'd nearly tripped over a skunk at night, I'd briefly considered a simple entryway light over the door. I'd never done anything about it, preferring the darkness.

My son stepped out and closed the door. "Nippy," he said. "Want to take my car?"

I almost refused, then shrugged. "Why not, if I can get in it."

With the tiny door of the Corvette open, I regarded the challenge dubiously. "It's easiest to slide your left leg in first," Buddy instructed. "All the way. And then just kind of slide down into the seat."

"This may not be such a good idea," I said as I did as instructed. With plenty of grunting, I settled in place, the seat hugging me in a dozen spots and the center console under my left elbow. I slammed the door and regarded the interior with interest. "Not much room for radios," I said. "And you're going to have to carve out half the dash and punch a hole in the roof for the shotgun rack."

Buddy laughed and fished the ignition keys out of his jacket pocket. "A real pisser for high-speed chases, though." The massive engine cranked half a cylinder before erupting into a gruff idle that shook the entire car. He blipped the throttle gently as the beast warmed up, and I could feel the whole thing twist with the torque.

"What engine?"

Buddy grinned. "That's worth more than the rest of the car. It's a four twenty-seven that a friend of mine on the base had. It's actually from a '68 'Vette that mated with a telephone pole. He salvaged the engine, and I bought it from him. She's been tweaked, too. We figure somewhere around four-thirty horses, give or take."

"I'm impressed."

"It's a hell of a lot of fun," Buddy said. He pulled up the hypodermic-shaped lifter on the gear lever and found reverse. He idled the sports car around the back of the unmarked county car and then we headed out the winding driveway through the trees to Guadalupe and Escondido. Buddy drove the thing as if it were made of handblown glass, letting the idle carry us along in first gear.

At the stop sign on Grande, he glanced over at me. "Where to?"

"Just up the street to the second right. MacArthur."

I lowered the window, enjoying the icy air on my face. The curb passed by just below head level, the pavement only inches under my rump. "This isn't so bad," I said. "There's even room in here for a wallet and maybe some spare change."

We turned onto MacArthur and I pointed up ahead. "The street just this side of the middle school."

"Crosby."

"Right. When was the last time you were in Posadas, anyway?"

Buddy sighed. "I guess about ten years ago. Not much has changed, that's for sure."

"Nothing," I said. "Turn left here." We swung north on Crosby, a narrow macadam street that skirted the dilapidated middle school building. I looked across at the building's hulk.

"Did you go there? I can't remember."

"Eighth grade," Buddy said without pausing to calculate. "We moved here in the fall of '66." He slowed the car to a crawl. "Lots of places out behind that building to do stuff," he added.

"Stuff," I mused. "They still do stuff. Just more of it." I shook my head. "I don't want to think about how long ago that was." I craned my neck to see over the long, sloping hood. "There's a little side street about a block up here on the right. It'll go right behind the athletic field. We'll want to try the fourth house on the left. There'll be a race car on a trailer parked in the driveway."

We turned onto Ithaca Place. The little concrete-block houses looked as if they'd been poured from the same mold, rectangular two-bedroom units that had been built in the late fifties in response to the mining boom. Each had been dinked with and added to over the years, but there was no hiding their pedigree.

A blaze of lights marked Deputy Tom Mears' home. Sure enough, number *18* squatted on its white trailer. Huge fat tires were enclosed by bodywork whose every square inch was rumpled, dinged, or torn. Mandy Mears' red Honda was parked at the curb, with her husband's old Suburban in front and Tony Abeyta's yellow Camaro behind.

The garage door was up, and inside I could see the two young men leaning over the front suspension of yet another race car, this one an open-wheeled thing with a monstrous wing on the back and a stack of polished chrome carburetors thrusting up through the hood.

"This is it," I said, and Buddy let the Corvette idle to the opposite curb. The engine died with a final *whump* and shake.

Mears and Abeyta had straightened up and were watching us with rapt attention.

"I could use an ejection seat," I mumbled, and Buddy laughed. There was no easy way, but by swinging a leg out and then pretending I was going to fall on my face in the gutter only to save myself at the last moment, I managed to exit the beast.

Mears ambled down the driveway, wiping his hands on a rag. He was a small, slender blond-haired man whose twin brother was a loan officer at Posadas National Bank...and at first glance looked more at home there than Tom did in the deputy's uniform. But looks were deceiving. Mears had been with the department for nearly fifteen years, a good, steady, levelheaded cop.

He extended a hand. "Commander," he said to Buddy. "Nice to see you again."

Buddy flashed a smile. "Thanks," he said. "That's quite a memory you've got."

Before I had a chance to walk around the car, Mears had introduced my son to Tony Abeyta. "And as I remember," Mears said, "the commander flies things considerably faster than this." He patted the Corvette's left rear haunch. I frowned, embarrassed to think there had been a time when I had talked enough about my family that Tom Mears would remember all the details.

"I need to chat with you guys for a minute," I said.

"If it's to decide who gets to use this new undercover car first, it's my turn," Mears said instantly.

"No, no." I waved a hand in dismissal. "Tom Pasquale's already called it."

"Oh, shit no." Mears burst into laughter.

"Let's go in there," I said, nodding at the garage. "Out of the wind. And where the neighbors won't ogle."

For the next few minutes, we chatted about the Mears racing stable, and then I lifted a small toolbox off the seat of a ratty metal folding chair and sat down. "Tony," I said, "yesterday morning, you and Scott Gutierrez talked to Betty Contreras down in Regal, right?"

"Yes, sir."

"I did too, a little bit later in the morning. There's something that she said that kind of bothers me, and I should have followed up on it." I shifted my feet and leaned back in the chair until I felt it start to flex under my weight. "Betty told me that when she was talking to you guys, she mentioned to you that she saw a vehicle drive by on Saturday morning."

Both deputies looked puzzled. "This would have been about eight o'clock. She said that she was outside, hanging up clothes or some damn thing. No...she was feeding the cats. That's what she said. While she was doing that, she recalls seeing a vehicle drive by. She said it was white with a touch of green. She told me that she assumed it was the Border Patrol. They drive through there all the time. When she said that to you guys, Scott Gutierrez told her that it was probably him."

Abeyta frowned. He looked down, regarding the front right tire of the sportster.

"You remember that conversation?"

"No, sir, I don't."

"You don't recall Mrs. Contreras mentioning the white and green vehicle?"

"She didn't mention it," Abeyta said. "Not to me." He lifted the Dallas Cowboys cap off his head and scratched his scalp, trying to agitate the memory cells. That didn't help. He shook his head. "I don't recall her saying anything like that. And as far as I remember, Scott never said a word, all the time we were there."

"Huh," I said. "Maybe she was dreaming."

"I would have remembered, sir. That's the time period we're interested in, and if I knew that Scott Gutierrez, or anybody else, had driven through the neighborhood just then, I sure as hell would have asked them about it. And Scott would have said something, for sure."

"Was there ever a time when she was alone with Scott, and might have mentioned it then?"

Tony Abeyta shook his head emphatically. "No, sir. We went in together, talked to her for a little while, and left."

I crossed my arms over my chest. "Why did Gutierrez go with you in the first place?"

Nonplussed, Tony Abeyta turned to Mears. "I don't know. I guess we just sort of fell into teams, you know."

"Rick Knox went with me," Tom Mears said, naming one of my least favorite state troopers. "Tommy and Bob were busy in the house and stuff. You and Schroeder were together until the DA left. That's just the way it worked out."

"It was kinda good talking to Scott," Abeyta added. "He's real savvy. He knows a lot of people. He gave me a lot of good ideas to follow up."

I shook my head and stood up. "I'm not debating that, Tony. And I'd be the last person to object. It's just that I've known Betty Contreras for the better part of thirty years. I'm trying to puzzle out why she'd lie to me."

Chapter Twenty-five

My son waited patiently for me to saddle up, and when I'd slammed the door, said, "Now what?"

"I wish to hell that I knew," I said, nodding at the clock on the dash. "Tell you what…it's still early. Want to take a little ride?"

"Sure. I'd even be sort of curious to see where all this happened."

"Then south to the border it is. Back under the interstate, and then take Fifty-six to Regal."

We rolled out onto Grande and a few minutes later, as we drove southwest on the state highway, I filled in the details of the past couple of days for Buddy. He let the car amble along at fifty-five, lugging in fourth gear. Even so, the healthy exhaust note combined with open windows made whispered conversation impossible.

The highway was deserted, and when we passed the Broken Spur, the saloon was just a dark lump on the prairie, its one sodium vapor light casting shadows through the cholla and greasewood that outlined the parking lot.

We started up through the esses toward Regal Pass, and Buddy downshifted into third as we swept through the first bend. I had been in the middle of recounting my conversation with Emilio Contreras at the church, and I hesitated as the sports car leaped forward.

"Nice road," my son said.

"Lots of deer, too," I shouted back, picturing the car's shark nose slicing under a mule deer's belly, pitching the critter through the windshield and into our laps.

With the car holding just enough speed to make the twists, turns, and switchbacks a continuous graceful ballet, I relaxed back into the support of the seat.

"The point is, no one saw anyone," I shouted at Buddy. "Not the neighbors, not anyone. We've got a big, ugly gap."

"In a town where everyone knows and sees everything," Buddy replied. "That's interesting. You think they're holding back because of Torrez? His being related and all?"

"I don't think so. But it's hard to say. I've known Bob a long time. The one thing I am certain of is that he wouldn't try to cover up anything. But I don't know about the others."

As we approached the divide, I pointed off to the left. "That's where I was parked when the kid crashed into my car."

We shot through the pass and started to nose downhill toward Regal. Where the highway curved in a sweeping turn to the left, the right shoulder had been bladed into a turn-out. Parked in that turn-out, lights off, was one of the Sheriff's Department Broncos.

"Whoops." Buddy lifted his foot, but if the deputy had his radar on, we were already nailed. "Are you in good with these guys?" My son watched in the rearview mirror for a couple of seconds until the lights disappeared around the curve. "Maybe he's asleep," he said.

"That would be Deputy Jackie Taber, and she wasn't asleep. Guaranteed." Even as I uttered the last word, headlights popped into view behind us. My son had slowed the car to under the speed limit by then, but since we'd been cruising at well over eighty when we passed, it took the deputy a couple of miles before she was riding on our back bumper.

"It takes her a few seconds to get a response from dispatch when she calls in the plate," I said. "Assuming everyone's computer is up and running, and assuming that none of us is asleep."

The road wound the six miles down toward Regal, and just as we approached the last switchback, the deputy behind us flipped her headlights quickly to high beam and back, braked abruptly into a wide parking area at the apex of the turn, and swung around in the road to head back north.

"You still have clout"—my son laughed—"at least for another two days."

"Damn right." I wasn't so interested in that as in the view ahead. From the flank of the hill above Regal, I could estimate where the old church would be off to the left, nestled in its comfortable darkness. A mile farther south the harsh lights at the locked border crossing illuminated the gate and barbed wire. A sprinkling of porch lights dotted the village.

Any vehicle driving through the village was exposed to view from a dozen directions. "It's hard to imagine anything happening in secret here," I said. "Take the first right, where the sign says SANCHEZ."

We turned onto the dirt lane with a clink of stones against undercarriage, and Buddy slowed the Corvette to a walk. "I don't have much clearance. Does this get worse?" he said as we scraped over a hummock of dried grass in the middle of the lane.

"No. Just go slow."

With the engine thumping at idle, we eased around the Contreras' front porch. From inside, it must have sounded as if we were about to turn into their bedroom.

"This is the Baca place," I said as we drew in front of the adobe. For once the two dogs across the street weren't in their chain-link run. When Buddy nosed the Corvette close to Sosimo Baca's front gate and switched off the ignition, the only sound we could hear was the ticking of the cooling engine.

"You know what strikes me as odd?" Buddy asked. He sat with his head propped on his left fist, regarding the dark house. "I always associated crime with the evening hours—the saloon hours, know what I mean?"

"Sure. The swing shift is our busiest, usually."

"And all this happened right around daybreak. That just strikes me as unusual. Most folks are wound up at nightfall, not dawn. That's the ebb tide, so to speak."

He turned and looked at me for explanation. "That's because we started the party," I said. "The Baca kid visited the saloon at about eleven. That's the usual time for hijinks, as you say."

"And then he spent the rest of the night sobering up on the mountain somewhere."

"Right. And made his way back to his house..." I stopped, trying to estimate Matt's arrival home. "Hell, I don't know. Sometime." Clorinda Baca's vague answers came to mind, and I chuckled. "I was out and around, and like you say—at dawn, the vast majority of people are asleep, or at least so groggy they don't function too well. That's the best time to bust in on somebody. I swung by here long before that, though, just in time to catch Sosimo walking home from *his* night of guzzling the hard cider. I took the kid into custody a few minutes after that. If things had gone right, he would have been in jail when dawn broke."

"There's nothing you could have done about that," my son said gently.

"That's what I tell myself. That it was just the luck of the cards. When Bob Torrez drove back down to break the news to Sosimo it was an hour or so before dawn."

"After that, the old man went for a walk, headed toward Posadas," Buddy said. He turned back and looked at the house. "Huh. Somebody was up and around early to meet up with him."

"That's what I think. But..." I turned first to the left and then to the right, indicating the village that surrounded us. "Lots of these folks get up at the crack of dawn. The coroner says that Sosimo died sometime around eight. Hell, by then the day's half over. And even though it's three thirty-five right now," I said, leaning forward and tapping the clock, "I'm willing to bet that there's at least one or two sets of eyes watching us at this moment."

"Or one or two dozen." Buddy laughed. "We can't exactly tiptoe with this car."

"That's for sure," I said, and then was interrupted by the chirp of my cell phone.

"Now I'm impressed, Dad. Such high-tech stuff," Buddy said as he watched me fumble the little thing out.

"You betcha. We're feetfirst in the twenty-first century." I found the correct side, the one with all the buttons. "Gastner."

"Sir," a soft feminine voice said, "this is Deputy Taber."

"Jackie, what's up?"

"Sir, I'm parked up on Regal Pass. That was me that came up behind you and your son a little bit ago there, up above the village."

I twisted in my seat and looked up the hill. It was a waste of energy, since there was nothing but the black featureless hulk of the mountains through the tiny window. "I thought it might be. I'm giving my son the grand tour."

"Yes, sir. I was wondering if I could ask you to do me a favor."

"Name it."

"There's a vehicle parked over behind the church. When I was driving down the hill toward the village the first time, I saw him start up and head out of the lane you're on right now. He had been parked at the Baca place."

"And now he's over behind the church?"

"Yes, sir."

"Were you able to identify the vehicle?"

"No, sir. But it's a white or off-white SUV of some sort. Maybe Border Patrol. I couldn't be sure."

"Well, that doesn't surprise me," I said. "What do you want me to do?"

"Just go over and talk to whoever it is, sir."

"All right. That's easy enough," I said. "What are you fishing for?"

"I'm not sure, sir."

I laughed. "I'll be in touch." I closed the phone and looked at my son. "There's a vehicle parked over behind the mission. Deputy Taber wants us to find out who it is."

Surprised, Buddy tried to look past the scrubby elm that blocked his view to the east, toward the church. "If Taber knows there's somebody over there, why doesn't he just go talk to whoever it is himself?"

"Herself," I corrected. "Deputy Jackie Taber is a her. And I don't know why. I just do what I'm told these days." I gestured toward the ignition. "And let's try not to wake the entire village on our way over there."

Buddy was reaching for the keys when we heard a vehicle approach from behind us. The silky smooth engine was little more than a whisper of the various fans and belts, accompanied by the crunch of tires on gravel.

Contrasted to the low, wide profile of the Corvette, the boxy-shaped vehicle loomed like a tractor-trailer as it idled up behind our rear bumper and stopped.

"Who's this?" Buddy asked, and the answer was not long in coming. A bright spotlight beam lanced out and blasted through our back window.

Chapter Twenty-six

"Just hold on a minute," I said quietly. "Give him a chance to run the plate." And sure enough, in another minute, the spotlight flicked off, and I heard the door open.

"Everybody's kind of nervous around these parts," my son observed. He rested his right hand on top of the steering wheel, with his left arm on the windowsill.

"Evening, gentlemen," a voice said, and at first I didn't recognize it.

"Good morning," I replied. The Corvette's roof line was so low that all I could see was a green uniform from the belt down, outlined in the harsh glare of the headlights.

The Border Patrol agent bent down and I saw that it was Taylor Bergmann. "Sheriff Gastner, we met earlier yesterday. I'm Agent Bergmann." He spoke with the rigid formality of the rookie trying to make sure he did everything just right.

"Right. I remember. Thanks for your help, by the way. This is my son, Commander Bill Gastner." I figured a little formality in return couldn't hurt.

"Commander," Bergmann acknowledged. He bent down a little farther so that he could look directly across at me. "This is the latest thing in unmarked cars, sir?"

"Absolutely. It's the new Stealth unit. Doesn't show on radar." I shifted in my seat a little so that I could talk without busting my neck. "So what are you hunting, Agent Bergmann?"

"I'm trying not to get lost," Bergmann said with a grin. "So far, I'm doing pretty good. I came in from the west, on the Douglas highway, and I thought I would swing up around here, through town. Agent Gutierrez drove me through Regal the other day, but you know how that goes."

"A blur," I said. "Who's riding with you?" A solo Border Patrol agent was unusual, especially a rookie. Their patrons tended to arrive in groups, and a single agent was at a distinct disadvantage, especially at night, and especially in the back border country. Why a single deputy sheriff in the same territory was perfectly acceptable with county commissioners I had never been able to figure out.

"Agent Tomlinson is riding along tonight," Bergmann said. I looked into the tiny rearview mirror on my side, and apart from the ominous message that OBJECTS MAY BE CLOSER THAN THEY APPEAR etched into the mirror's glass, I could see nothing but the dark shadow mountain of the Expedition. I would recognize Agent Gordon Tomlinson on the street if I saw him in uniform, but that was it.

"Scott's off?" I asked.

"Yes, sir. He took a couple days annual leave."

"Well deserved. He gave us a hand this afternoon…make that yesterday afternoon now. We had us another little problem to resolve."

"That's right. I heard about that. And I thought that since there had been an unresolved situation here on top of that"—he stopped in midsentence as my cellular phone chirped, and then added as I opened the gadget—"that it wouldn't hurt to cruise through the area."

"Sure enough," my son agreed, and Bergmann straightened up away from the window.

"Gastner," I said into the phone.

"Sir," Jackie Taber said, "the vehicle now parked behind you came in from the west. The other vehicle is still behind the church, as far as I can tell."

"Okay. Thanks. We'll wander over that way when we're finished here."

"Yes, sir."

"Stay put."

"Yes, sir."

I closed the phone and scrunched down so I could see Bergmann. He was standing with his hands on his hips, surveying the Baca house.

"Is there anything in particular that you needed, Taylor?" I said, and he turned around quickly.

"No, sir. I saw your vehicle parked here and thought I'd check. That's all."

"I appreciate it. We can always use an extra set of well-trained eyes, believe me."

"Commander," Bergmann said, and patted the roof of the Corvette, "nice to meet you. Have a great visit."

"Thanks," my son said. "It's been interesting so far."

Bergmann almost laughed. "I bet," he said. "We'll talk to you gentlemen later."

We heard his boots crunch on the dirt and then the door of the Expedition open and close. The engine had been running, but produced just a gentle whisper as Bergmann reversed to clear our back bumper. He drove around us and continued down the dirt lane to the Sisneroses' driveway, where he turned around.

"He's not going to chance any more of Regal's back streets," Buddy observed.

"This one doesn't go much farther anyway," I said. "Down around the corner to Clorinda Baca's, and then it just kind of peters out beyond her woodpile."

"Whoever she is," Buddy said, chuckling.

"She's..." I started to say, but he held up a hand.

"I don't need to know, Dad," he said. The Border Patrol unit eased past us heading eastbound, and I raised a hand in salute, catching a glimpse of Agent Tomlinson's round, pleasant face in the passenger window. "Do you want to go over to the church now?"

"Our last stop on the grand tour," I said. I gestured after the two agents. "And I wouldn't be surprised if they do the same thing. The mission is one of the traditional stopping places for illegals who jump the fence in this area. It's never locked, which makes it easy."

"Is a full-time border crossing in the cards for this place anytime soon?" Buddy asked. He ignited the Corvette and let it idle for a few seconds.

"Probably within the next year," I said.

We used the Sisneros driveway too, and I could picture Archie Sisneros lying in bed blurry-eyed, wondering if he should turn his dogs loose. I could hear the two of them barking inside the house.

We drove back out the dirt lane. Ahead of us, the Border Patrol unit halted at the pavement, a nice full stop just like the sign ordered. The left directional signal flashed a couple of times, and Bergmann pulled out on the highway and accelerated on up the hill. "I'm surprised he didn't check out the mission," I said.

"Maybe he figures that's your turf." We reached the pavement, and Buddy leaned forward, pulling himself up against the steering wheel. By easing up and over the edge of the asphalt obliquely, my son was able to avoid leaving serious parts of his car behind. "What time do Estelle and Francis fly in today?" he asked as we straightened out on the pavement.

"Their plane arrives in El Paso a little after two this afternoon," I said.

"I look forward to seeing them again. The last time I was here, Estelle was just breaking into detective work. As I remember, she was about to take her sergeant's test. And she was still single, too. Gorgeous and single."

"Pull into the church," I said. "And none of that applies anymore, except maybe the gorgeous part. She's happily married, two kids, no longer in police work. As far as I know. She doesn't talk much about herself."

We turned off the asphalt and I leaned forward. "The deputy says that someone's parked behind the church, so let's go around the back side."

"It's gravel all the way?" As if to punctuate his question, a stone pinged against the exhaust pipe directly under my rump.

"No ruts. It'll be all right."

We drove around the west side of La Iglesia de Nuestra Señora, and at the back corner there was just room to skirt the large chamisa plants that kept the inattentive from nicking the adobe corner of the building. The rear wall of the church, its smooth brown adobe expanse broken only by a single window that filtered light the length of the nave, rose more than fifteen feet from the ground to the rounded tops of walls.

My window was down, and even before we started to nose around the east corner toward the side of the church opposite the highway, I heard an engine start. "I don't think whoever it is plans to stick around and chat," I said.

But I was wrong. We rounded the corner and pulled in behind a late-model white Dodge Durango with Texas plates. Our headlights picked up the silhouette of a single occupant before we pulled so close that the back of the vehicle blocked the light.

My son turned on one of the little aircraft-style interior lights so I could see the cell phone, and I dialed dispatch. "Hopefully young Sutherland is awake," I said. Young Sutherland was, and answered on the second ring.

"Run a plate for me, Brent," I said. "Texas dealer plate November Hotel niner Baker Thomas six." He repeated the number and I waited, the even rumbling of the Corvette's idle marking time.

"Sir," Brent Sutherland said finally, "that tag is registered to Walsh Chrysler-Plymouth, two twenty-one Parkway Avenue, Del Rio, Texas. No wants or warrants. Just a second, sir."

I heard a voice in the background, and then the rattle of the phone being handed off to someone else.

Robert Torrez's voice came on the line. "Sir, we think that truck belongs to Scott Gutierrez's stepfather, a Mr. Jerry Walsh. He owns a dealership in Del Rio. Where are you right now? Behind the church?"

"That's exactly where we are," I said. "Jackie asked me to check out this vehicle for her. Why, I don't know." If the under-sheriff knew where I was, he no doubt also knew that I was there by Deputy Taber's request.

"Does the driver know you're there?"

"Unless he's asleep or dead, he knows there's a noisy Corvette parked behind him. He would have no way of knowing who it is unless he's psychic."

"Okay." Torrez didn't elaborate.

"Assuming he doesn't drive off in the next ten seconds, do you want me to talk to him?" I prompted.

"Sure. Go ahead, sir."

"Robert," I said, exasperated by his taciturnity, "what are you not telling me?"

"Jackie has reason to believe that the occupant of that vehicle was inside Sosimo Baca's house just a few minutes ago."

I sat silently digesting that. "She's sure?"

"No, sir, she's not. But Archie Sisneros called here a while ago to ask if one of our people was still working the Baca place. Archie says he saw the white vehicle parked in front, and someone inside the house with a flashlight."

"He thought that was kind of odd, did he?" I said.

"Yep. Jackie took the call. On her way down the hill from the pass, she saw a vehicle exit the lane and then park behind the church. She decided it would be better to hang back a little and see what developed."

"Well," I said, "we developed. I'll go have a chat with Mr. Walsh—or whoever has his truck."

"It might be useful if he didn't know that the deputy was sitting up the hill."

"You got it." I snapped off the phone. "Cat and mouse time." I shook my head and looked across at my son. I handed him the cell phone. "That button right there"—and I pointed to one of the white buttons on the left side—"is the auto-dial to the Sheriff's Office."

"Why am I going to need that?"

"Hopefully, you won't. But I have to try and pry myself out of your stealth bomber again. If I get stuck partway, we may need to call for assistance."

Chapter Twenty-seven

I was halfway out of the car, contorted like Houdini, when I started to count down all the stupid things I was doing. If I had caught one of the rookie deputies pulling the same dumb stunt, I'd have chewed his ass up one side and down the other. Had the person waiting in the dark vehicle ahead of us been an armed psychotic in a stolen truck, he needed to look no further for an easy target.

The interior courtesy light of the Corvette wasn't much, but it did a thorough job of illuminating my gyrations as soon as I opened the door. Finally struggling to my feet and taking a deep breath of relief, I pushed the door closed and walked around the front of the car.

The dome light of the Durango snapped on just as I rounded the left rear fender. The driver's side window was down, and I could see an elbow resting on the sill. The headlights of my son's car behind me worked to my advantage.

"Good morning," I said as I came up behind the open window.

Scott Gutierrez leaned forward a bit so that he could twist around to peer at me. He grinned and then turned away from the glare of the headlights. "Good morning, Sheriff. I was wondering who that might be." He gestured toward the northwest.

"I saw you turn into the lane down there, but I lost you through that grove of trees. And then I saw the Border Patrol unit do the same thing. I figured the two of you were having a chat."

"The night shift," I said. "That was Bergmann and Tomlinson chasing coyotes." I moved forward so that I could lean on the Durango's door. "My son and I are roaming around, sharing insomnia on a nice peaceful Sunday morning."

He laughed. "Yep." He stretched, straight-arming the steering wheel with his left while thumping his right hand against the vehicle's roof.

"I thought you were on leave," I said. "That's what Bergmann told me. And you told me earlier that you were going hunting this weekend."

Gutierrez yawned and nodded. "I am. Or rather, we are. My sister and me. And my stepdad. He's visiting from Del Rio." He turned and looked up at me. "The annual pilgrimage."

"He's staying in Posadas?"

"Yes. With Connie French. My sister."

"Aren't you still living in Deming?" Gutierrez caught the puzzled note in my voice and grinned.

"I thought it would be easier if I bunked on sis' floor for the weekend, rather than driving back and forth. We're going out and set up camp this afternoon, over on the north side of the mountains." He nodded at the San Cristóbals. "Then, come first light Monday"—and he held up and sighted an imaginary rifle—"the champion twelve-point buck who's waiting out there is mine."

He put down the rifle. "But see, the problem is that my stepdad sees it as his goal in life to rearrange *my* life to his satisfaction. We always end up arguing about something. There's about a six-hour grace period after he and I show up in the same house. And then, it's anybody's guess."

"I know how that can be."

The young man's expression turned to one of chagrin. "This time I didn't even get the six hours. We had a good row earlier this evening. I went back to sis' place after that ruckus at the Broken Spur, and I made the mistake of mentioning it to my stepdad...you know, about that stupid kid running from the cops." He shook his head ruefully. "That lit the fuse, I guess.

What he really wants is for me to be partners with him in the dealership in Del Rio."

"That doesn't appeal to you?"

"Jesus, no. I can't even imagine that."

"He's trying to bribe you into it by letting you drive this fancy truck?"

"Right." He surveyed the inside of the Durango. "It's not bad, either."

"I hope you left your stepdad a note." I chuckled. "He's apt to wake up, find his baby gone, and go ballistic."

"Not likely. He sleeps like a rock. In fact, he usually misses all the good dawn hunting when we go out."

"So," I said, and paused. "Any brilliant ideas about this mess we've got on our hands?"

"The Baca thing, you mean?" He shrugged. "There's two possibilities that are the most logical. One is that the old man had an argument with a relative over something. Domestics are number one, right?" He laughed. "I should talk."

I nodded.

"With what happened to his son and all, I wouldn't be surprised if that's what happened. And then you gotta figure"—and he swept his hand in a general arc that included all of Regal—"if he's out on the highway, he's fair game for just about the whole world. Somebody saw him, figured to take whatever money he had, maybe brought him back to the house by force." He looked up at me again. "That's what I think, for what it's worth…which ain't much."

I glanced at the digital clock on the Durango's dashboard. "So how long have you been sitting here?"

"Hell, I don't know. A while." He yawned. "I pulled in here on impulse. A good place to do a lot of thinking. You never know what you're going to see."

"Anything interesting?"

"Well, the old lady who lives in that adobe with the yellow window frames"—and he pointed to a single porch light across the way that wasn't blocked by the bulk of the church—"she let her dogs out for about ten minutes, and then called 'em both back in again at three-oh-five. That's big news. The Contreras' kitchen light came on at three-thirty for a few minutes and then went off again, so husband or wife or both were up and got a snack. That's big news." Gutierrez laughed.

"Hot times," I said.

"And then a little bit ago, at about oh four hundred hours, this big, bad-ass 'Vette sneaks down the hill into town. I thought I had something fun going on with that one, until the Border Patrol nailed him."

"I hadn't thought of it as sneaking," I said.

"Well." Gutierrez looked at me sideways with a "gotcha" grin. "You were comin' off the hill like some airplane. I could hear all the way down here. And then you slowed, and didn't come out from behind that big foothill there for a long time. And when you did, you were just kinda of drifting along."

"Lots of deer out," I said.

"Ah," Gutierrez agreed. "Leave some for me, all right?"

I straightened up and stretched, and glanced back at my son sitting patiently in the car. "I have to climb back in that thing," I said. "It's a major undertaking."

"Life's tough." Scott chuckled.

"Did you happen to drive through the village tonight?" Before he had a chance to respond, I added, "See any foot traffic? Hear any dogs going nuts?"

"Nothing." He shook his head. "I didn't have to drive through. I can hear every sniffle and giggle right from here. The whole valley is as quiet as this church." He sighed and settled even farther down in the seat. "One of the things that's on my mind is seeing that youngster get hit. That's one reason I'm out and around. I lie down to sleep, and that's what I see." With a grimace, he smacked one hand against the other. "Bam. Just like that. I don't guess I'll ever forget that sound."

"I sympathize," I said, thumping the windowsill of the Durango with both hands. "It takes a while for things like that to heal—if ever."

"You still don't know why he tried to run?"

I shook my head. "The only thing I can figure is that he was afraid of his cousin. They've had more than one set-to over the years, and Bobby's a little tough on the boy. I've been running it through my mind, and that's all I can come up with. Just before he popped the window, I radioed the office and said I was bringing the kid in. At that point, Matthew was behaving himself. I made the comment that the dispatcher might want to contact Undersheriff Torrez and let him know. That's when the kid went berserk."

"Huh," Gutierrez said. "That might make sense, Sheriff. You stopped your unit and we pulled in on the shoulder behind you. With all the lights on, the kid couldn't tell one unit from another. Bergmann's a big fella. If the kid caught sight of him backlit by all the flashing lights, maybe he thought it was Torrez, comin' to thump on him. So he bolted."

"Maybe so. At any rate, we got one thing cleared up. One of the deputies found a fake license that Baca had been using as an ID."

"No shit?" Gutierrez raised an eyebrow. "You mean a fake driver's license?"

"Sure enough. The little rat had stuffed it down behind the seat of the patrol car. And that makes sense, when you think about it. That's the last thing he wanted any of us to find on him."

"I thought you looked in his wallet. I know Taber did. I saw her do it."

"We don't think it was *in* his wallet, Scott. He had it stashed somewhere else."

"I'll be damned."

"Yep." I pushed away from the truck. "Well, we best be heading back to town." I stopped. "Oh, by the way, Tony Abeyta probably asked you about this already. When you drove through Regal yesterday…no, when the hell was it. Saturday morning? Before the ruckus? You didn't see any vehicles that looked out of place?"

Gutierrez's eyebrows knitted together. "I didn't drive through Regal on Saturday morning. I was at the crossing talking with one of the Customs guys, and caught the call on the scanner. That's the first I heard about it. I heard the call, and drove over. Hell, it's what, a little more than a mile? Half the town was there by then, already."

"Ah," I said, nodding in comprehension. "Somebody's got their timing screwed up. I was told that you had driven around the village earlier."

Gutierrez shook his head. "Not me. I know that Taylor Bergmann is fascinated by this place. It might well have been him. Or maybe one of the other guys. It's kind of on our route." He flashed a sudden smile. "Bergmann's from St. Louis. There are more cars at a single traffic light at any given moment on an average day than in all of Regal." He scoffed. "He thinks Regal would be the ideal place to live."

"It might be," I agreed.

"Who told Abeyta that I drove through?"

"That's a good question. Maybe I heard him wrong." I grinned. "We've heard a different story from every resident of the village. Makes a fascinating set of reports." I reached in and tapped him on the shoulder with my index finger. "Don't be dozing off now. Some illegal would really be tempted by this buggy. I'd hate to have to break the news to your stepfather that you'd been hijacked to Mexico."

"See, that's what he expects," Gutierrez said with a laugh. "That would—how does Bergmann put it—'validate all his arguments.' You guys have a good night. Keep it slow and easy."

Practice was paying off. When I settled into the Corvette this time, it almost qualified as a modern dance routine.

"All set?" my son asked.

"Yep." I slammed the light fiberglass door and struggled with the seat belt. "It's one of the Border Patrol officers, undercover in his stepfather's truck."

"Well"—Buddy laughed—"you're undercover in your son's car, so that makes it even, right?"

He backed up a couple of paces and cranked the front wheels to clear the Durango's chrome back bumper. Despite his best egg-under-foot efforts, the wide back tires of the Corvette kicked a little gravel as we swung wide.

"Where to, sahib?"

I had the phone in hand and pointed up the hill with it. "I want to talk with the deputy. Make sure she hasn't been inhaling the funny smoke or something. Somebody sure as hell is making up stories."

Chapter Twenty-eight

From her vantage point just south of the pass, Deputy Jackie Taber could see the entire village of Regal, and beyond the vast, yawning blackness that was Mexico. A single group of lights twinkled on the southern horizon, the tiny Mexican village of Tres Santos.

"If you swing around and point downhill, we can park door to door, and I can talk to the deputy without getting out of this thing."

"That's not going to work too well," my son said, "but we'll take a shot at it." Cops become expert, over the years, at those door-to-door conferences. You can pass coffee and donuts back and forth, or hand over paperwork, or chew the fat—all those good things that we did while we waited for something exciting to happen.

That didn't work this time. When I turned my head and looked out the window, I'd be looking right at the bottom of the sheriff's star on the driver's door of Taber's unit. Fortunately, the young deputy had anticipated that very problem, and as we rolled in, she got out of the truck to meet us.

She knelt down beside my door. "Good morning, sir."

"Yes, it is," I said. "Have you met my son? Commander Bill Gastner Junior, this is Deputy Jackie Taber."

"Pleasure," Buddy said.

"Nice car, sir." Jackie grinned. She stroked the top of the door with light fingers. "What did you find out down below?"

"First of all, that's Scott Gutierrez hanging out down there,"

I said.

"Really?"

"Really. He's driving a vehicle from his father's dealership. The old man's up visiting for a few days, and Scott decided to find some fresh air."

"Ah," Jackie said. "Okay, that makes sense."

"I'm glad it does to you. This is a long way to drive just to get out of the house. Of course, like the rest of us, Scott's got Matt Baca on his mind."

"Other people have been known to roam the county with no particular destination in mind, sir," Jackie said, and grinned across at my son. She shifted her weight to favor the other knee. I motioned her away from the door.

"Let me get out of this thing so we can talk without torture," I said. Buddy switched the car off. The mountain was silent, just the faintest of winds itching the vegetation along the highway. My son got out with practiced ease.

"Scott is staying with his sister for the weekend," I said. "They're going hunting." I leaned against the Bronco's front fender, the hood just the right height for my elbow. "I don't think I know her."

The deputy nodded. "His sister Connie lives in Posadas, over on South Twelfth Street. About a block south of the Guzmans' place."

"Scott said he took a drive to get away from the old man for a while. But Connie...do I know her?"

The deputy smiled, an expression that didn't wrinkle her smooth, serious face too often. "I would imagine that you do, sir. Connie French? She got divorced last year from Mike French, the guy who runs the Chevron station on the east end of Bustos. She's living with somebody else right now." Her brow wrinkled. "He's a custodian at the high school. I can't recall his name. She works for the Motor Vehicle Division with the undersheriff's sister. I'm sure you've met her."

"You're getting to be a regular gazetteer of Posadas." I laughed. "And I'm sure I have. But the memory is a leaky bucket these days." By stepping around the front of the Bronco I could look out into the darkness. "You say that you can see Sosimo Baca's house from here? And enough detail to guess at the color of a vehicle?" The village was a sprinkle of lights, no more than half a dozen.

"Try these," she said, and handed me a pair of heavy binoculars.

That was the operative word...*try*. The eyepieces weren't designed to use with bifocals, and without glasses all I saw was black. A light flashed briefly and I managed to pin it down so that it created a neat star pattern in the lenses without showing me a damn thing.

"So you decided to park here and check out the village," I said.

"I always do that, if I have time. I like the idea of an overview."

"Outstanding. And you saw the headlights, I assume, over by Baca's. Then you saw the vehicle drive out the lane. As it passed by Contrerases' you'd catch a glimpse of the color, if their porch light was on." I tried to find the Contreras house, but gave up. Without car headlights to serve as a marker, the whole place was just a black hole to me.

"Yes, sir. And then it drove out to the pavement, turned south, and then swung around behind the church. That's where he parked. After about ten minutes, I decided to drive on down the hill and check him out. I was about to get back into the unit when you drove by." She beamed again. "And then after I found out who Thunder Pipes was, I thought it might be useful, if you were touring Regal, for me to stay up here. I wanted to know what the occupant of the vehicle behind the church would tell you. I talked to the undersheriff, and he agreed."

I handed the binoculars to my son. "Can you see anything, Commander Thunder Pipes?"

Buddy cranked the objectives a little farther apart and spun the focus knob like someone who uses those sorts of gadgets on a regular basis. "As a matter of fact, I can. Our white Durango is coming out from behind the church with his headlights off. Ah...now they're on." Even without the binoculars, I could see the beams stab out across the parking lot. "And now he's on the highway, turning up the hill." Buddy handed the binoculars back to Jackie.

"By the way, Scott told me that he hadn't driven through the village, Jackie," I said. "Either tonight, or on Saturday morning, despite what Betty Contreras says." She nodded, and I added, "That confuses me, see. Tony Abeyta said that Betty never mentioned a vehicle driving through the village while he and Scott were talking to her...she certainly didn't mention a Border Patrol vehicle driving through. That's what Tony says. Now Betty says that she did mention the vehicle while she was talking to Scott."

I turned and listened. "You can hear him now, coming up the hill." Looking back at the deputy, I said, "So either Betty is lying, or Tony Abeyta is lying. And Scott Gutierrez *is* lying, about tonight, anyway."

"Betty told the undersheriff the same thing, sir. Just what she told you."

"She did?"

"Yes, sir."

"She told him that she saw the Border Patrol unit drive by her house? Around eight?"

"Yes, sir. She said that she only caught a quick glance, but that it was two agents."

"Jesus H. Christ," I said wearily. "Betty, Betty, Betty." At the sound of an approaching vehicle, I turned and saw headlights pop into view, and a moment later, the white Durango passed us, its aggressive all-season tires howling on the pavement. Scott Gutierrez tapped the horn twice.

As the taillights disappeared around the bend, I said, "Archie Sisneros called dispatch and said that he saw a light inside Sosimo's house while the vehicle was parked there. Is that right?"

"Yes, sir."

"Scott says he didn't even drive into the village."

"You've got an interesting potpourri of what passes for the truth on this side of the mountain," my son said.

"That's what has the undersheriff on edge," Jackie said quietly.

"The obvious thing to do at this point," I said, "other than thinking about finding breakfast somewhere, is to talk with Mrs. Contreras again. Her husband doesn't recall seeing any traffic, of any kind…but part of the time he was inside the church sniffing paint. So…" I shrugged. "Tell you what. Let me talk with Betty again. We'll see what she's up to. In the meantime, I'd like you to find out all you can about Scott Gutierrez."

"The undersheriff is working that way, too," Jackie said.

"Then I need to talk to Robert. He's at the office, or at least he was a few minutes ago."

Buddy held up a hand in surrender. "Dad, we need to head on back to the house. Tadd will be up and around, and maybe we can catch up with you later in the morning." He pushed a button on his watch. "It's about four-forty now, and beginning to look like you're going to have a busy morning. I've got a couple of errands I need to run, myself. Let's try to meet at noon. How about that?"

"Noon for lunch," I said. "If it won't hurt your feelings, I'll ride back in with Jackie."

The only luggage I'd had with me in the sports car was my cell phone, about the size of a pack of cigarettes. It didn't take much to transfer that. The Corvette's bellow was already fading as Jackie and I pulled out onto the highway in the Bronco.

"Your son flies jets in the navy, sir? That's what some of the others were saying."

"That he does." I chuckled. "Choppers too. You can tell?"

"He has that military look," she said. "The big watch, and all." The military "look" was nothing new to Jackie Taber, fresh out of six years with the army when Posadas County hired her. "How long will he be visiting?"

"Through the middle of the week. More if I can twist his arm. Where's your sketch pad, by the way?" The large drawing pad had become a Taber trademark, and her work was stunning. Others might sit in the patrol unit and smoke a cigarette during an off moment. Jackie Taber hauled out her charcoal pencil and drawing pad.

"Under my briefcase," she said, indicating the clutter between us.

"You keep after that," I said. "It's a real talent." I laughed. "You need to talk Sheriff Torrez into moving you to days. The light is a whole lot better."

She made an amused little sound, noncommittal at best. "Maybe swing shift, sir. Then there's the best of both worlds. Lots of gray tones."

As we headed north, both of us fell silent. I didn't have to ask what prompted the occasional impatient drumming of Deputy Jackie Taber's fingers on the steering wheel. The puzzle had enough pieces to keep us all busy.

Something had been on Scott Gutierrez's mind. There was no question about that. Only old, fat insomniacs parked themselves in the dark corners of the county in the middle of the night, listening to the dim pulse of the world. No doubt, Scott had his share of troubles—a recent divorce, a nagging stepfather, the dull routine of chasing people trying to come into the country without a ticket.

A young, aggressive cop with his whole career ahead of him had better things to do than sulk behind buildings just to fritter away time.

There was something on the undersheriff's mind, too, enough to keep him sleepless, despite the best efforts of his beautiful wife. I knew it wasn't the election just two days away. I hadn't met a single person who took his opponent seriously—and Robert Torrez wasn't the sort to lose sleep over politics.

Chapter Twenty-nine

The undersheriff's door was open, two doors downstream from my office and immediately across from the dispatcher's island. One might have assumed that someone of Robert Torrez's size would have sought out an office to match, a place where he could stretch out. Instead, he wore the room like a polished, tight military boot.

Small to begin with, the oddly shaped office featured one corner lopped off at an angle to accommodate ductwork for our recently updated heating and cooling system. Torrez had skewed his large metal desk so that the light coming in from the single tall, narrow window wouldn't blanket the screens of his two computers with reflections. That desk, along with two filing cabinets and two chairs, didn't leave room for amenities.

I stood in the doorway and regarded Torrez. He was leaning back in his swivel chair, one black boot on the corner of his desk, the other flat on the floor. One hand was poised over the keyboard of the nearest IBM, the other balled into a fist under his chin.

His dark brown eyes shifted to look at me. Other than that he didn't move a muscle. His brow was locked in a frown, and after a long moment—during which I wasn't able to tell if he was angry, tired, or just plain frustrated—he puffed out his cheeks and then slowly exhaled.

"That bad, eh?" I said. I hadn't expected to hear a dissertation from Robert Torrez, but a simple "good morning" would have been nice.

Torrez nodded and his eyes flicked back to the computer. He jabbed at the keyboard with his index finger, swung his leg off the desk, and let the chair slam forward. If he hadn't had an elbow on the desk, he would have fallen on his face.

I reached out a hand for the door. "You want this closed?"

He shook his head, then stood up, still leaning on the desk with one hand. "Coffee or something?"

"I'll wait for breakfast," I replied. "My treat."

Torrez grimaced. "I don't feel much like eating right now, thanks."

"That's bad, Roberto," I said, although it was an accomplishment of sorts to have goaded him into a complete sentence.

"Uh-huh." He sat back down, and I unloaded a stack of newspapers from one of the leather-bottomed chairs. He waved a hand at the top of one of the filing cabinets, and I thumped the newspapers there.

"So…explain why I'm paying you so much overtime," I said.

"Don't I wish," Torrez replied.

I tried to squirm myself comfortable in the straight chair, and gave up. I held up both hands, waiting for an answer.

He nodded, leaned back again, and clasped his hands over his belly. "That license that Matt had? The one we found under the seat of the unit?" He stopped there.

"Pasquale's triumph. Any ideas yet about where Matt dug that up?" I asked, and no sooner were the words out of my mouth than a synapse or two fired inside my brain, faces snapped into place, and I knew exactly what was troubling the undersheriff.

"Your sister Melinda works in the Motor Vehicles Division office. She and Connie French. Melinda is the office manager, if my memory serves." Torrez nodded ever so slightly, watching me, no doubt waiting to see what conclusions I had reached. After a moment he opened his desk drawer and pulled out the plastic evidence bag that contained the driver's license.

"It's the real thing, sir."

For a moment I misunderstood. "I thought you said that Matt…"

"No." He cut me off. "The dates are fake. Other than that, the license is real. It's not made-up."

"You mean it's not something that was just pasted together out of bits and pieces, and then maybe run through a plastic laminator at school or something," I said.

Torrez nodded. "I think that was issued by some MVD office. By one of their machines. It's got the seals, the holograms or whatever you call 'em, the whole bit. As far as I can tell, it hasn't been tampered with. It's not something that somebody would just hack together with a home computer."

"But we don't know which office issued this, do we. They don't put the office location code on them anymore." I twisted the license this way and that, looking for its secrets. Both of us were silent for a bit, and then I looked up at Torrez. I saw the dark shadows under his eyes and knew why he wasn't home snug in his bed.

"What does Melinda say?"

"I haven't talked to her about it."

"Are you going to? And you know—she's not the only one in that office, Roberto. Like I said, Connie what's-her-name works there too. Scott Gutierrez's sister."

A flicker of irritation surfaced and was as quickly hidden. "Yes, sir. Connie French. I don't think so."

"I know that we automatically think the worst, but in point of fact, there would be nothing to prevent Matthew from driving to Deming or Lordsburg or even Albuquerque for a license," I said. "Anywhere in the state where there's a field office. But…"

"But what?"

"I'm sure you remember the incident a couple of years ago where some MVD clerks got in trouble for making fake IDs. The state cracked down on that, and with the computerized systems, it's not as easy as it was. I think it would be tough to find a clerk now who'd just take a kid's word for his age, and run him through the licensing process just on his say-so."

"There's too much risk," Torrez said. "And with a kid like Matt, there would be no big money involved."

"Exactly."

He fell silent again, brooding at the computer screen.

"It'd be easier if he knew somebody in the office," I said. "Obviously, it'd be a lot easier." Torrez didn't respond. We both knew that one step better than knowing someone in the office was having a blood relative there. Matthew Baca was first cousin to the Torrez clan, with the undersheriff and his younger sister right on top of the list.

"What have you got there?" I prompted, nodding at the computer.

"I was trying to pull up something about the MVD," he said. "I don't even know what I want." He poked at the keyboard. "Or where to start."

"You need your own personal hacker." I laughed. "And don't look at me. Your wife always bails me out with the complicated stuff. Like how to turn the damn thing on." The corners of the Torrez's mouth didn't even twitch. He was in no mood for humor.

He looked up at the small wall clock above the filing cabinets. "She'll be in at seven-thirty,"

"Did you mention any of this to Gayle yet?"

He nodded slowly, rocking his head for about ten oscillations as if he didn't have the energy to stop the motion once started.

"And she said…" I added, feeling like a dentist trying to extract an impacted wisdom tooth.

"She doesn't think either Miranda or Connie are involved."

I had known Gayle when she'd been Gayle Sedillos in high school. I'd hired her the summer of her senior year as a clerk trainee and on the first day knew I had a rare one in my charge. If Deputy Bob Torrez had noticed the almost exotically attractive teenager that first day, he hadn't let anyone know it. It had taken eight years for their relationship to grow deep enough for him to pop the question. Gayle had been a study in patience.

As much as she loved her husband, I couldn't picture Gayle Torrez avoiding the truth about a Torrez relative just to save her husband some pain.

Torrez twisted away from the computer, dropped his hands in his lap, and regarded me. "I just don't know."

"I'll tell you what bothers me," I said. Torrez raised an eyebrow. "Your cousin was scared of you. Do you know that?"

He nodded. "We've had our encounters. He knew that if I caught him, I'd take care of him first. And then it's the rest of the family's turn."

"So there you go," I said. "Can you imagine Matt Baca doing something so foolish as tricking a fake license out of the local office, and running the risk of having you find out?"

Torrez rested his chin on his fist again. "Sure," he said. "It's called 'rubbing my nose in it.' "

"Meaning?"

"His nickname for me is Big Bad Bob."

I laughed. "Not to your face, I don't imagine."

"Oh, yes. He thinks...thought...that he could run faster than me."

"So you think that he'd pull something like this, just to tweak you?"

"What better time to do that than when Triple B is running for office. Hell, why not. Pull this shit right under my nose. He was a clever kid."

"Almost clever enough," I said. "Almost. Look." I leaned forward and held out a hand as if to stop Robert from doing something rash. He hadn't moved. "Look. How about if I talk with Melinda? Hell, I've known her just as long as I've known you. She's covered for me on more than one occasion when I've forgotten to renew my license. Let me talk to her."

Bob looked skeptical and I pushed ahead. "Really. I've got an idea that I think might work out. And the news isn't all good, Roberto. If your sister's involved..." I paused and watched the flicker of emotion on Torrez's dark face. "If she's hiding something, I think that I'll be able to tell. We're going to have to move and move quickly. But it'd be easier if I did it."

He shook his head. "I think it's something I need to do, sir."

"Bullshit, my friend. For one thing, when it's family like this, it's ten times as hard, election year or not. And no matter how hard you try to be impartial, you'll have a set of family blinders on." Torrez's frown deepened.

"And I've been thinking about something else. The inscrutable one will be here later today." Torrez knew exactly who I meant, and his expression turned guarded. "You know that while she's here, Estelle doesn't intend to sit on my back patio and knit—even if she could find the patio for all the weeds. The gals know each other really well. I think that if I go and talk with Melinda, and Estelle is along, we'll know the truth by the time we're done."

"Melinda's not even in town right now."

"She's not?" My stomach sank.

"No. She'll be back on Monday afternoon sometime. Becky and Melinda and one of their cousins went to Albuquerque this afternoon. A weekend of doing malls or some damn thing." He grinned. "I told 'em that if they weren't back in time to vote, and if I lost…" He let the rest of the implied threat against his two sisters and their cousin dangle. And then his face lost all its brief humor. "And the double funeral for Matt and Uncle Sosimo is Monday afternoon at five. They have to be back for that."

"The MVD office is open Tuesday, Wednesday, and Friday, right?" He nodded. "Then first thing Tuesday morning, before the herds arrive to take a number, Estelle and I will have a chat with Melinda."

"And say what?"

"For one thing, I want to ask her how a clerk would go about making a fake license like that one," and I jabbed the plastic bag with my forefinger. "We need to know that, regardless of what office is involved."

Torrez's eyes narrowed as he continued to assess what I was offering.

"If Melinda had nothing to do with this, I think it'll be obvious. And I'll have Estelle's judgment to back me up."

"Okay," Torrez said. "Actually, that will work, because Melinda will be by herself on Tuesday. Connie French won't be there. She's taking a couple of days off to do some hunting."

"With her stepdad and brother," I said. "That's what Scott told me earlier."

"And that's the other thing," Torrez said. He took a deep breath, as if he needed to wind himself up like a friction motor to launch into the next explanation. "Now I keep asking myself these questions. First of all, Scott and Bergmann arrived on the scene when Matthew kicked out the car window. Fair enough. I checked with the Border Patrol district office, and Bergmann did just join this region, and a tour wouldn't be unusual—although why at night I don't know, except that's the shift that Bergmann had been assigned to."

He tapped his second finger. "Scott is in the area first thing Saturday morning. In fact, he was the first officer who responded to my call from the Baca house. He was quality assistance, too. He stayed around until we'd cleared the scene. And"—he tapped his third finger—"despite the fact that it wasn't his case, and that he had no connection to it other than as courtesy backup, he stayed in the area most of Saturday. He was in the area and responded to the fracas at the Broken Spur when you took Dale Torrance into custody."

"So he's around a lot. That's his job, Robert."

"And he went on leave sometime Saturday."

"That's what he says."

"He can't sleep, so he's prowling around Regal half the night, and according to Archie Sisneros, was actually inside the Baca house. I have to ask myself…looking for what?" He reached over and tapped the license. "This, maybe?"

"I mentioned to Scott that we'd recovered it, by the way. That might not have been too smart."

"What did he say to that?"

"He was surprised."

"I bet he was." He hooked his little finger. "What about this. Suppose that his sister issued that license to Matthew Baca. Not my sister at all. Maybe Melinda didn't even know anything about it. Connie French issues it, either as a favor, or for some bucks, or because she's got a crush on Matthew. I don't know if she did or didn't, but anything is possible with that kid. If Scott Gutierrez found out about what was going on, he might try to protect his sister."

"Maybe."

Torrez frowned. "During the course of the investigation, he would have certainly heard someone in the department talking about a faked ID, about the interviews with Tommy Portillo at the convenience store, maybe even about Matthew's attempt to buy booze at the Broken Spur. There's lots of talk, and Scott would have heard."

"It's possible. And that might explain why he was inside the house tonight. He was looking for that license. And after I told him that we had it in evidence, he left Regal." I spread my hands wide. "Not in a rush, but he gave up his vigil at the church."

"I don't know," Torrez mused. "What doesn't sit too easy with me is that there are other explanations, too."

I knew what he was thinking and remained silent, letting him sort out in his own mind how he wanted to approach the next step.

"I don't think that my sister would have issued the license," he said after a moment. "But there's that possibility, isn't there?"

"I suppose there is. But I agree with you—it's unlikely." The undersheriff didn't ask me *why* I thought it might be unlikely, and I would have been hard-pressed for an answer other than my high opinion of the Torrez family in general, and my regard for the pleasant young lady whom I saw regularly.

"Suppose Melinda was the one who issued the license. I couldn't guess why she'd do a thing like that, but just suppose," Torrez said, retracing his steps. "And in the first place, with the new computerized systems, I don't even know how she'd do it, but like anything else, I imagine there's a way. If she did that, what's Scott's interest in it?"

"From a cop's point of view, he'd want to protect his sister, and nail Melinda. He'd want to make sure that Connie didn't take a fall for something she didn't do. It's possible Connie got wind of the deal, and mentioned it to Scott."

"Sure. That sort of thing is hardly the Border Patrol's turf, but like you say, it's family." Torrez rested both forearms on the desk and fixed me with an unblinking stare. He didn't say a word for a long time, and finally I broke the stalemate.

"What?" I asked.

"You talked with Tony Abeyta earlier tonight," Torrez said. "Apparently Betty Contreras is saying that she saw a Border Patrol vehicle drive by around eight? Just before the Lucero kid wandered over and found Sosimo dead?"

"That's what Betty says. She told me that she mentioned the incident to Scott, and that Scott then told her that the vehicle was probably him. But that's not what he tells me. Tony agrees—he said the conversation never took place, at least in his presence. And he never left the room while Scott was there."

"So Betty's lying. On top of that, she told me the same thing." Torrez turned and looked out the window. "Why would she do that?"

"I have no idea, Robert. Scott said that he never drove through the village."

"Did you happen to ask him if he picked up Sosimo that morning? While my uncle was walking along the road?"

"No. But if he'd picked him up and took him home, then he would have driven through the village, wouldn't he?" I shrugged. "And he would have said so."

Torrez didn't look as if he was listening. Instead, he said, "If Scott Gutierrez was the one who picked up Sosimo yesterday morning, I'd have to ask myself why he'd bother. He wasn't scheduled to work yesterday during the day. Why is he there at all? If he saw an old man walking along the highway, why would he bother to pick him up?"

"Why not?" I might, if I knew him."

"Sure, *you* would. But Scott Gutierrez wouldn't, unless he had a good reason. If he takes Sosimo back home, what's he want?"

"The license? If he knows about it, even if he doesn't know where it is. He knew that it wasn't in the kid's wallet because he watched Jackie Taber search through it at the accident scene."

"Maybe so. He thinks that Sosimo might have it, or he wants to search the house. Maybe Sosimo isn't so fast to agree to that. A few threats, a scuffle, things don't go quite the way Scott would have liked, and he's out of there. My uncle is dead in the backyard with his arteries blown up."

"But all of that means that Gutierrez knew about the license before that morning, then. Even before we did."

"That's right. And if that's true, it puts a whole new spin on things."

For a moment I studiously regarded the cuticles of my right hand. "Betty Contreras works just down the hall from the MVD office, doesn't she?"

"Sure."

"And she'd have occasion to talk with both your sister and Connie French on a daily basis."

Torrez shrugged. "Sure. At least on the three days that the MVD is open. Tuesday, Wednesday, and Friday."

"Have you talked with Betty since yesterday?"

"No, sir."

"Let me take another swing at her, then." I put both hands on the chair and leaned forward, gathering the ambition to get up. "Give me some time to talk with Betty and with your sister. You hang low for a little bit." He looked uneasy. "I'm serious," I continued. "You're so tired you can't see straight. Go home and get some sleep."

Torrez reached across and picked up the plastic evidence bag. "I want to know how it's possible to make this."

"So do I. Let me find out." I grunted to my feet. "Estelle and Francis should roll in sometime this afternoon," I said. "Like I said, it wouldn't hurt to run all this by her, to see what she thinks."

Torrez laughed. "Just swear her in," he said. "And by the way, speaking of swearing in, the preliminary hearing for the Torrance kid is nine o'clock Monday morning, if I can ask you to go. Dr. Perrone wanted to keep him in the hospital today, for observation. Apparently old Victor really belted him. There's a little bleeding that Perrone's worried about."

"I'll be happy to go, he lied," I said. "I don't suppose there's any chance that Miles Waddell might drop the charges, but it wouldn't hurt to pull him into a dark corner and ask him. It'll be really interesting to see what Judge Hobart says, He's known Herb Torrance longer than I have."

"I heard by the grapevine that Cliff Larson wants you to work the inspector's job for a while," Torrez said.

"That's what he wants," I said, and moved toward the door. "I'd have to give that a really long think. There are other concerns hanging right now that are higher on my list." I saw the undersheriff lean back and swing his boot back up on the desk. That didn't look like movement out of the office to me.

"Go home, Robert. Let it ride." I smiled. "And don't worry. I know what I said, but I'm not going to just drop all this in your lap on Tuesday night and walk away. Not until we find out where that license came from. And not until we find out who killed your uncle."

Chapter Thirty

I pushed open the heavy door and was about to step outside. The first slap of early morning air hit my face, but I stopped in midstride, hand on the brass door handle. For several long seconds I stood rooted in place, letting the November chill waft into the Public Safety Building.

"Huh," I grunted to myself, and retreated back inside. In the few moments I'd been gone, it didn't appear that Torrez had changed position.

"We're missing something," I said, and he glanced up.

"I have the feeling," he said slowly, "that we're missing a whole lot of things, sir."

"No, really. Suppose this. Suppose that Matthew kicked out the window just because that's the thing that you try to do if you're a half-wild teenager out to test the world. He'll show us, by God. Maybe next time we won't be so quick to arrest him."

"Oh, sure," Torrez said, and actually managed a full-fledged smile.

"Think about this, though. Suppose that busting the window isn't really important…no more than just a show of spite aimed as much against you and your department as anything else."

"What's important, then?"

"I pull off the road, the good Samaritan that I am, thinking that the kid is going to cut himself on busted glass or hang himself in the broken window. What happens next?"

Torrez had risen from his chair and walked around the desk. He leaned against the front of it, arms folded across his chest. In the marines, I'd been five feet eleven inches when I was racked at attention, but in the fifty-two years since I'd enlisted, I'd settled some—and expanded horizontally. The undersheriff was a solid six feet four, and even with him leaning against the desk, I had to look up to talk to him. He waited for me to continue.

"Scott Gutierrez and Taylor Bergmann arrived. We chatted for a little bit, and Scott introduced me to Bergmann. And then Scott walked up to my car, leaned down, and shined his flashlight inside. Now, all this time, Matthew had been quiet as a church mouse in the backseat."

"He recognized my nephew?"

"Hard to say. There's no reason that Scott would know Matthew, is there? I mean, they may have crossed trails at one time or another, with Matt living in Regal, and Scott working the area. But there's never been a gathering of the two families, has there?"

Torrez shook his head. "What did he actually say?"

"I don't remember. Nothing threatening at that point as I recall. Scott asked Matthew why he'd broken the window. I do remember that."

"What did Matthew say?"

"Nothing. He didn't say a word. It was at that point that Scott suggested that they take Matthew into Posadas in their vehicle. They were headed toward town anyway." I turned at the sound of footsteps. Brent Sutherland approached, obviously not eager to intrude. When he saw that he had my attention, he quickened his step.

"Sir, Judge Hobart wants you to call him."

"The judge? You're kidding."

"No, sir. He said just whenever you can get to it, as long as it's in the next thirty seconds."

I laughed, picturing the old, grizzle-headed, pock-faced alcoholic sitting up in bed, a glass in one hand, the phone in his lap, waiting for it to ring. The wall clock said it was five minutes before six on that Sunday morning. For the judge to begin his day any earlier than nine o'clock took an act of Congress, so his mood would be delightful.

I nodded at Brent, and he retreated. "I wonder what that's all about," I said, and then retraced my thoughts. "Anyway, that's what we set out to do—transfer the kid to the Border Patrol vehicle. Scott was going to use some leg ties, and I remember that he half jokingly threatened Matt. Something about if he messed up the new Expedition, that he'd take him out into a field and do whatever."

Torrez was staring out into space, and when I paused to take a breath, he turned back and gazed at me, head nodding in comprehension.

"The obvious question," he said, taking care with each syllable, "is, what if my nephew bolted not because he was afraid of me or the thumping I might give him when he got to town, but he *was,* in fact, afraid of being put in the Border Patrol vehicle and taken somewhere."

"Exactly," I said. "What if Matt was running not from you, but was running from Scott Gutierrez?"

"Or..." Torrez said, and stopped.

"Or what?"

"Taylor Bergmann."

"He didn't even know Bergmann," I said. "Not until that moment."

"We're not sure of that."

"No," I admitted. "We're not."

Torrez let his head hang, and he regarded the ugly green floor tiles for a moment. "Why would Matthew be afraid of Scott Gutierrez?" he asked, and then looked up at me. "I can think of one scenario."

"That Matt got his fake license from Connie French, and Scott knew that he had it...and that if we found it, an investigation might backtrack to the source, and Connie would be in worse trouble than the kid. We're back to brother protecting sister again."

He nodded and went back to his examination of the floor tiles.

"Right now, let me see what's on Hobart's mind," I said. "Meanwhile, is there any chance that you can contact your sister up in Albuquerque? Do we need to wait for Monday?"

"No...I can find her. She's staying with an aunt up in Corrales."

"Do that, then," I said. "Get her to cut the shopping trip short. I'd like to talk with her today, before this has a chance to fester."

Chapter Thirty-one

I began to think that Judge Lester Hobart had fallen back on the bed, sound asleep. The phone rang eight times, and I was about to hang up when I heard the click, followed by a fumble and clatter and a muffled, "Goddammit."

"Yes," the judge snapped. "What is it?"

"Good morning, Judge," I said. "This is Gastner."

"I know who the hell it is, and what's so good about the morning?"

I laughed and swiveled in my chair so I could see out the window. The sky was deep indigo to the west, mellowing toward the sunrise. "It looks like a nice Sunday, for one thing," I said.

"I suppose. So what do you need?"

"I don't need anything. You called the office and wanted to talk to me, Judge."

"Dammit, where the hell is my mind," he muttered.

"Haven't seen it," I said. "Same place mine is, no doubt."

"Let me look at my notes a second. Hang on." More rummaging and scuffling followed, and I had the mental picture of the judge sitting on his rumpled bed, papers scattered all over the bedroom, his ancient and disheveled toy poodle cowering on the far corner of the bedspread. "My office is a goddamn mess," he said. "But you ought to see the goddamn clutter here at the house."

"No worse than mine, I'm sure."

"I hear your son's visiting," the judge said.

"Yes, he is."

"The one in the navy?"

"Yes. He and my grandson drove up for a few days."

"Grandson, eh."

"Yep. One of several. He's a nice kid."

"I'm sure," the judge said. "He into drugs yet? Tattoos and earrings? That kind of shit?"

I laughed. "No. Not that I can see, anyway."

"Not even a tongue stud?"

"Nope. He's a pretty straight-arrow sort of kid. The last time I saw him, he was sitting in my living room, watching *High Noon*."

"Damn," the judge said. "Well, clone him, while you have the chance. Let me see, now. Here's the deal, speaking of kids. This Dale Torrance. Shit, I'm surprised Herb hasn't had a stroke. Or killed the kid. Or maybe both. I have on file that the boy is nineteen. Is that right?"

"To the best of my recollection."

"And he's never been in trouble. At least he's never been in my courtroom."

"Up to now, a clean slate. And this one is pretty simple. Dale fell for a girl, and did all the stupid things."

"This is the Prescott girl, right? Christine Prescott?"

"Yes."

"Well, hell, this deposition from Larson says that she's almost twenty-eight."

"Right. I'm not sure that Dale's infatuation is a two-way street, Judge."

"Yeah, well…hell." He stopped as if he were reading something, and I waited. "Okay, here's what I want to happen. Larson already talked to Schroeder, and I guess the DA's got enough on his plate right now that a few head of livestock going for a joyride isn't something that he wants to pursue hot and heavy… assuming that the cattle are returned in fair health and condition to their rightful owner. At the preliminary hearing on Monday, he's going to bring up charges against the kid for grand larceny and exportation of cattle without inspection papers, as well as leaving the scene of an accident. Schroeder tells me that the kid deliberately backed his pickup truck into one owned by Miles Waddell."

"That's correct. He did. And for not wanting to pursue the case hot and heavy, two felonies sounds like quite a start."

"Well, hell," Hobart said, "that's the tip of the iceberg, if Schroeder wanted to play every card in the deck."

"It'll make Waddell happy," I said.

"What's that supposed to mean?" I heard a little bit of an edge creep into the judge's voice. He wasn't up for reelection, but the district attorney was.

"It means exactly what I said," I replied. "I'm sure Waddell wants to pursue this for all it's worth."

"I don't give a good goddamn what Miles Waddell wants to do or doesn't want to do," Hobart snapped. "Miles Waddell isn't the State of New Mexico, much as he'd like to be. Anyway, Herb called me last night, and we talked for a bit, and then I tried to get a hold of you, but I guess you had your hands full."

"Yes, we did."

"Well, here's the deal, regardless. Doc Perrone was going to turn Dale loose this morning, if all goes well. And the minute he does, Larson is going to bring him on over for arraignment. I'm going to turn him loose to the custody of his pappy—if his pappy has five thousand bucks for bond."

"He won't go anywhere," I said, feeling a little less sure of that promise than I would have liked.

"Well, he damn well *is* going somewhere," Hobart said. "The minute we're done here, Dale and his father are going to truck right back over to Lawton to pick up those steers. I'm going to tell Herb that I want the boy to use his own pickup, and to pay for the fuel out of his own pocket. I want to see the receipts with the boy's signature on 'em."

"Fair enough."

"And then when they get back, Miles Waddell is going to hold the cattle in quarantine for thirty days, to make sure that none of them are hurt or sick, or any goddamn thing like that. Dale

Torrance is going to pay for all that, too. All the feed, the inspections, whatever it takes. When Cliff gives the okay, Waddell can have 'em back, to rope or make hamburgers or whatever the hell it is that he does with the damn things. The dealer in Oklahoma gets his money back, Waddell gets his truck fixed, and the world is ready to start over again." He coughed into the telephone.

"By the time we have the preliminary hearing on Monday morning, the cattle will be back in the county," I said.

"They damn well better be. And then we'll decide where to go from there. That sound good to you?"

"It's what should happen," I said, and Lester Hobart read the rest of my thoughts.

"And then on Monday all things being equal, Schroeder will agree to a year's probation and a thousand bucks fine after all the expenses and damages are paid. That ought to get the kid's attention. And after that, we'll see about whether we wipe the slate clean or not as far as the boy's record is concerned."

"That will work."

"All right, then. I wanted to run all that by you, just in case one of the deputies saw the Torrances on the road with a livestock trailer in tow. Didn't want you cops to get excited."

"They'll be aware of the situation," I said.

"I wish to hell the rest of the mess you're in would clean up so nicely." Hobart chuckled. "I can understand why Dan Schroeder is staying over in Deming. He sure as hell doesn't want any of that shit to rub off on him."

I started to say something inconsequential, but the judge interrupted. "And say, I have a question for you."

"What?"

"Who's Bobby Torrez going to pick for undersheriff? Has he said yet?"

"Bobby has to win the election first," I replied.

The judge scoffed. "That's a given, Bill. If Leona Spears wins the sheriff's race in Posadas County, it'll be because she's the only one who voted."

"I hope that's true. For his sake, I'd like to see a landslide."

He laughed. "He'll get it. Now who's on the short list?"

"He hasn't shown it to me," I said. "I wish I could tell you, but I can't." And it was almost the whole truth.

"I've heard some interesting rumors," the judge said.

I took a deep breath. "Well, I tell you, Judge. Consider the source for each one. Unless you hear it from Robert himself, it ain't worth much."

"Well…" he said, turning coy. "We'll see. We'll see."

Judge Lester Hobart was a staunch Republican, and the only candidate in his party had pulled out of the race in late summer. That left Torrez as an Independent running against the loony Leona, the embarrassment of the Democrats. I could understand the judge's desire to bring at least part of the department under the party wing. I didn't envy the taciturn Torrez the politics he might have to play to work smoothly and productively with the Republican-controlled county commission.

"Is what Cliff Larson tells me true?" Hobart quickly added.

"About?"

"You and the livestock inspector's job."

"Yes. I guess it is."

"You've decided to take it?"

"Until Cliff comes back. a couple of weeks. Sure. Why not?"

"Did he tell you the rest of it?"

I frowned. "The rest of what? About his parents, you mean?"

"No. None of that. About why he wants to step down from the job."

"He didn't say specifically that he did. He told me that he wants a break to take care of family matters."

Hobart chuckled that "I know more than you know" laugh. "Sure enough." He cleared his throat, changing leads. "Well, see you Tuesday, if not before."

"I'll be at the Torrance hearing tomorrow morning," I said. "What's on Tuesday?"

Hobart hesitated, then muttered something I didn't catch, and said, "Well, I figured I'd catch up with you one way or another around the ballot boxes. It's going to be a long day."

When I hung up, I sat for a few minutes, doodling mindless circles with a pencil on my clean desk pad. Politics was one of my personal irritations, partial explanation of why, in thirty-plus years, I'd never run for the sheriff's post. I had the distinct feeling that Judge Lester Hobart was playing a political game with me. I didn't like the feeling.

"What the hell," I said to no one in particular. I wrote FRANK DAYAN in heavy block letters, and scribbled a circle around the newspaper publisher's name. If anyone knew which way the political winds were blowing, it would be him.

Chapter Thirty-two

I drove home just as the sun was cracking the horizon. We'd be first in line to sample Sunday breakfast at the Don Juan if I could pry my son and grandson out of the sack. I opened the front door and stopped short as an assault of aromas flooded out of the old house.

The place was accustomed to the fragrance of fresh coffee at any hour of the day or night—that was the staple fuel that kept my system going. But I didn't cook, despite the pleas from my housekeeper. Every once in a while she'd leave something, usually a casserole of some sort, neatly packaged on my kitchen counter in the vain hope that I'd hack out a piece and nuke it for a snack.

What she didn't realize, in her own sweet, innocent way, was that sitting alone at my kitchen counter to eat a meal was the most dismal way I could imagine to spend my time. I saw enough of myself during the day without wallowing in me at mealtimes. I liked to eat on someone else's dishes, with the food served bubbling hot by someone else—and that someone else preferably wearing a nice smile with no personal complications that I was expected to solve.

And so the aroma of breakfast in my own home jolted me to a halt. Coffee, bacon, a host of other things. I advanced cautiously, because I could see Buddy sitting in my large leather recliner in the living room, reading a section of the Albuquerque Sunday paper. That meant someone else was tending the burners, and the only other someone else in the house was my grandson.

Buddy looked up, saw me, and grinned. "Hey there."

"Good morning," I said. "I was going to take you out to breakfast, but it smells like someone beat me to it." Tadd stuck his head around the corner.

"Neat," he said. "You're back."

"I'm back."

"Do you have time to eat?"

"I certainly do." I walked into the kitchen, thrust my hands in my pockets, and surveyed the battleground. "And by the way, I don't think that works." I nodded at the old electric waffle iron sitting on the counter. The single idiot light that indicated preheat was dark, and I stepped over to it. From several steps away, I could feel the hot cast iron.

"I think it's ready," Tadd said, and opened the top. "One of the wires came off the contact in back," he said. "I stuck it back on. It works fine."

"It looks like my timing is impeccable," I said, leaning over so that I could see the wires where they vanished into the chrome housing at the back of the waffle iron. "Where did you come by this interest?" I straightened up and moved to one side, watching as Tadd ladled the waffle batter onto the iron's steaming surface.

"Oh, I don't know," he said with typical teenage vagueness.

"Tell him about Mrs. Hooper," Buddy said from the living room.

"Well, yeah, her," Tadd said, and closed the cover of the waffle iron. "She teaches home ec and foods and stuff. I took Foods I and II, and this year, I'm working in the Hospitality Suite."

"And what's that?"

He shrugged. "The school restaurant. We serve lunch three days a week. It's kind of a big deal. Cloth napkins, fancy silverware, waiters and waitresses and stuff. The whole bit. It's a fund-raiser, too. Most of the faculty eat there. A lot of people from town, too."

I watched the kid move around my kitchen as if he'd lived there all his life. I calculated backward and decided this was the third time Tadd had set foot in my house. The first time, he'd been on all fours as his principle mode of locomotion, and during his second visit, he couldn't have been more than eight or nine.

"You can eat eggs, can't you?" he asked, pausing in midstride from counter to refrigerator.

"I don't have any," I said, but he opened the door and took out a carton anyway.

"We did a little shopping," Buddy said.

"I guess you did. And yes, I can and do eat eggs. And waffles. And anything else you know how to make."

The breakfast progressed from there, served with perfect timing and a flair for presentation—green chile, cheese, and onion omelets, waffles and all the trimmings, along with what looked like a full pound of perfectly done bacon. He even knew how to con the drip machine into making hot, rich black coffee.

I did more than sample, too. I practically ate myself into a stupor, which amused and pleased my grandson no end. Finally, I put my fork down and leaned back, savoring a comforting sip of coffee.

"Amazing," I said to Tadd. "And thank you."

Buddy grinned. "We thought we'd keep him," he said.

"Are you planning on doing this for a living?" I asked.

"*Errrrr,*" the kid imitated a game-show penalty buzzer. "Not."

"I'm surprised," I said. "I would have guessed this is where your interests lie."

Tadd managed an expression that said interests were pretty much classified as a bother, but then reconsidered. "It's a good way to impress the chicks, though," he said.

"I suppose it is," I said.

"I saw this movie once," he said. "This guy, I forget who it was, made this really elaborate gourmet dinner for this girl he wanted to impress and stuff? I remember thinking at the time, 'Hey, it'd be neat to know how to do all that.' " He shrugged. "And Mrs. Hooper makes it fun, so…" He pushed his chair back, arose, and returned with the coffeepot.

"Impress the chicks," I mused as he filled my cup. "Gourmet cooking sure beats stealing cattle."

"Are you about wound down on that one?" Buddy asked.

"Just about."

"And the Regal fracas?"

"Far from wound down. We haven't heard a thing beyond the preliminary autopsy, and haven't found anything in Baca's house to give us a lead. What we're left with is an inconsistency in some statements by the witnesses. That and a puzzle about where the driver's license came from." I blew across the coffee. "First things first. I've got a woman down in Regal who's saying a couple of different things, and I thought I'd start with her. Backtrack a little and see what I can find. You want to come along?"

Buddy held up his hands. "We're going to let you do that on your own, Dad. Tadd and I have a few errands that we need to run after a little bit." He grinned. "Give folks a chance to get out of bed first." He twisted and looked at the wall clock. "What time does the Guzman mob roll in?"

"Their plane arrives in El Paso at eleven-fifty. I suppose that puts them here around two or so, all things being equal."

"That's perfect," Buddy said. "We're going to do some grocery shopping as soon as the supermarket opens."

"That's not necessary."

"Oh, I know it's not. But it's fun. We were going to see if we could get the grill working. Hell, the two Guzman brats would rather tear around your backyard and eat hot dogs than have to behave themselves out in public."

"Just finding the grill will be a trick," I said. "It hasn't seen the light of day in fifteen years." I groped in my pocket and pulled out my key ring. "Take my Blazer. It sits in the garage so much it's starting to mold. You'll have to move it anyway to get at the grill. Don't get caught in an avalanche."

Tadd had started methodically arranging the dishes by the sink, and Buddy caught the bemused expression on my face. "Mrs. Hooper taught them how to clean up *first*," he said. "That's what impresses the hell out of me. She deserves a Nobel prize."

"I'd like to meet this woman," I said.

"Well," Buddy said, and pushed himself away from the table, "if you should ever decide to leave Posadas County, that could be arranged."

"I do leave the county," I said defensively, and took a final swig of coffee before handing the empty cup to Tadd. "Hell, just last week I was in Deming. And this morning, or yesterday, or whenever the hell it was, I drove through downtown Newton."

"Positively cosmopolitan," Buddy said. "Plan on lunch?"

"I'll try my best," I said, and turned to Tadd. "You cooking?"

"Yeah," he said with obvious self-satisfaction, and then, with the odd raised, crooked elbow and three-fingered point of the Hollywood gang-banger amplified by a ridiculous caricature of a Mexican accent, he added, "The man be cookin'."

"Then I wouldn't miss it."

I took a few moments to freshen up. When I left the house, my mood was upbeat. As I turned the car onto south Grande, I found myself still chuckling at my grandson's comment. "The man be cookin'," I said aloud, and then realized with a start that it had been a long time since I'd been preoccupied with something other than work.

Chapter Thirty-three

Betty Contreras was stepping out the back door of her home just as I pulled into her driveway shortly before eight that Sunday morning. She carried a wrapped parcel, the right size and shape for a pie.

"Well, good morning to you," she said brightly and paused on the step.

"Betty, good morning. I need a minute or two of your time. You headed to church?" She nodded. "Is Emilio down there already?"

"Oh, yes," she said. "For sure. He's been there since about six."

"Gets the fire going, eh?"

"This time of year it sure feels good," she agreed. "That big old high ceiling, you know. It's like a barn." She turned first to the left and then to the right, as if she were looking for a place to set the pie. "Why don't we go inside, then," she said.

The kitchen was warm and perfumed by baked apples. The clock over the refrigerator said Betty had four minutes if Father Anselmo was prompt with the 8:00 a.m. mass.

"How about some coffee?" she said, but I shook my head.

"No. You're busy, and this is a bad time. You're about to head out the door. I'll make it quick."

"Oh, don't be silly," she said, and slid the heavy pie onto the counter beside the stove. She turned and waved a hand at one of the chairs at the table. "Sit. Sit."

I did, folding my hands together on the table in front of me. "Betty," I said, watching her smooth, pretty face for some flash of emotion that might clue me into what she was thinking, "I'm confused. Let me spell it out." I tapped the table with an index finger. "You told me yesterday that you saw a Border Patrol vehicle drive by on the road out front. You said just about eight o'clock in the morning. Saturday morning."

She frowned and nodded. "I was out back," she said. "I think I was feeding the cats."

"That's what you said yesterday." I regarded her for a moment, and her face kept the slight frown of puzzlement. But her eyes returned my gaze without flinching. "You told me that you mentioned the vehicle to Scott Gutierrez, and that he said that it was probably him."

This time, I saw a fine line of crimson creeping up her neck. I continued, "Tony Abeyta said that no such conversation took place while he was here, and that there wasn't a time when he left Scott Gutierrez alone with you," I paused, then added, "when such a conversation might have taken place."

She leaned back against the counter, one hand on each side as if she were preparing to launch herself across the room. "Oh, brother," she said, muttering the comment in the same tone that she might use with a county resident complaining about receiving the wrong tax notice.

I waited. Finally she released her hold on the counter and turned to the coffeemaker. "Let's have a fresh cup," she said, her back turned to me.

"That would be fine," I said. "No cream, no sugar." As she rummaged for the filter and the coffee and the spoon, I glanced at the clock. "You don't mind missing mass?"

She laughed, a small, self-deprecating little puff of amusement. "There's always ten," she said. "That old barn will be warm by then." Her voice took on a bit of an edge. "And I guess it doesn't matter if I mind or not, Bill."

When she'd finished prepping the coffee, she returned to the table and sat down at the end, in the chair nearest me. "This is embarrassing," she said. She was an articulate woman, used to dealing with the public who entered the assessor's office in all sorts of moods. I knew that she'd find the right gear if I left her alone.

"When I was out feeding the cats," she said, "a vehicle *did* drive by. And that's the truth. It was white, and I saw just a flash of green. I suppose that's what put the Border Patrol in mind. I don't know what the vehicle was, whether it was a Bronco or Suburban or Expedition, or what. It was one of those big boxy things, though. It could even have been a van. Big and boxy. Of that I'm sure." She turned and glanced at the coffee-maker as it released a loud gurgle and a puff of steam.

"So you're not sure that it was a government vehicle?"

"No, I'm not."

"You didn't see the driver, or the white government plate?"

"No, I didn't."

"Number of occupants?"

"Bill, I think...I think...that there were two. But if I had to swear in a court of law, I'd have to say that I wasn't sure. It seems to me that there were two. That's as close as I can come."

"But you didn't recognize them?"

"No."

"Did something lead you to believe that it might be a Border Patrol vehicle?"

She hesitated. "A natural assumption, I guess. They drive through here all the time. This street is the major one through this part of the village. If you wanted to drive through most of Regal, you'd end up on Sanchez Road, one way or another." She nodded toward the front of the house, where Sanchez Road nicked perilously close to their front porch. "And the patch of green against white is what put the Border Patrol in mind, I'm sure. It wasn't a neighbor's car."

She got up and took two coffee cups down from the upper cabinet, two fragile little things with flowers and vines and the sort of tiny handles that are difficult for big fingers.

"You're sure, absolutely positive, that a vehicle drove by. You'd be able to testify to that in court without a problem?"

She nodded and poured the coffee.

"You could testify that it was white, that it was an SUV, that there was green on it."

"Yes."

"If I asked you if you were one hundred percent sure that it was a government vehicle, or a Border Patrol vehicle, you'd have to say no. Is that correct?"

"That's correct, Sheriff." She was smiling when she brought the coffee to the table. "Nothing in it, you're sure?"

"It's fine, thanks. And I know all this sounds as if I'm holding you over a hot burner, but I have to be sure."

"I understand all that."

I watched as she sipped the hot coffee. "How did it happen, Betty? Who's right?"

"I saw the white vehicle," she said, enunciating each word carefully, "and it wasn't the sort of thing that I put any effort into remembering. You know how that goes? But then, after the deputies left—well, Tony and Scott, I mean—I remembered, and I knew that I *should* have mentioned it to them. I didn't. It was an oversight. I got to thinking about it later, and knew that it might be important. I mean, we're talking timing here, right?"

"Yes, we're talking timing."

"I should have remembered, and I should have mentioned it, and I felt really stupid for not doing so. And then *you* stopped by, and it was a good opportunity. I told you about it. And I made a mistake. Nobody likes to sound stupid. So it was just a manner of speaking, you know? I told you that I had mentioned the car passing by to the boys, and that Scott had said it was probably him. Well, I *didn't* mention it to them, Bill. I didn't mention it to them. I should have, obviously. And I *knew* I should have. So I told you, and stupid me—I made it sound as if I'd already remembered to tell the deputies when they were here."

"Betty, did you tell anyone else, besides me?"

"No, I didn't."

I leaned back and looked out the window. I'd only had a sip or two of the coffee, good as it was. She pointed at the cup and I shook my head.

"That car might be important," Betty said. "That's the point of all this, isn't it?"

"Sure." I turned my gaze back to her. "Especially if you heard it stop at Baca's. Or if you heard anything after that."

"I wish I had," she said. "The radio here in the kitchen was on, and I was thinking of a jillion other things. Who's going to notice a car driving by, unless someone tells you in advance that you *should* be noticing? That's the hard part of being a witness. Tell me beforehand that I should pay attention, and it's easy."

"Isn't that the truth," I said. "One more thing. You told me that it was probably Scott Gutierrez who drove by. Now lots of agents work for the U.S. Border Patrol, and they rotate through here all the time. I could list you half a dozen that the Sheriff's Department sees on a regular basis. Why did you think it might have been him?"

"I suppose because Scott is the one I see most often, and I know him pretty well, what with his sister working just down the hall from me. He stops in once in a while. I got to thinking about it, and he was the last one I happened to see. His name came to mind first. A good assumption."

"If there is such a thing," I said. "When was the last time you saw Scott Gutierrez drive by—and I mean the last time you were *sure* that it was Scott? When maybe you actually waved to him?"

She took a deep breath. "Friday evening," she said.

"You're sure of that?"

"Yes, I'm sure. I'm positive, I'm so sure. Emilio was with me. We were both on the front porch. He drove by then. He had someone else in the vehicle, but it was dark, I couldn't see who it was." This time her smile was strained. "My *assumption* was that it was another agent. Scott leaned forward when he saw us, though. And he waved."

"Do you recall what time that was?"

"I'd be guessing," she said. "Sometime between eight and nine, maybe. No later than nine, certainly. We were only outside for a little bit."

"Stargazing, or what?"

She laughed. "The coyotes were giving a concert. It sounded so comical, like maybe a whole den of little ones were trying to learn how to howl the proper way. We stepped outside to listen." Her face brightened. "And yes...I remember the time. We'd watched the first part of *StarTown*, and it was during a commercial break about halfway through. So that makes it sometime between eight-forty and eight-fifty."

"And you're sure it was Scott Gutierrez who was driving," I said.

"Oh, yes. I'm sure. That's probably why his name popped into my mind the next morning. It made sense to me. So much for trying to be helpful."

I stood up with a sigh. "I'm sorry to have caught you at a bad time, Betty. But I appreciate it."

"I'm sorry that I made problems for you," she said. "It was just one of those things. We sometimes say things without stopping to think." She smiled tightly. "A little embellishment sometimes sounds so good. At the time."

I left the Contrerases' feeling as if all I'd done was slip into deeper, murkier water. Betty had fabricated when she'd first talked to me, trying to make herself sound like a better witness. Hell, that happened all the time...it went with the turf. It was amazing how many witnesses told us what they saw, when in fact they never saw a damn thing. It felt good to tell a colorful story, I guess, to tell an officer what he wanted to hear.

Betty Contreras was unusual. She admitted what she'd done, instead of stubbornly trying to stonewall her mistake. Her years spent keeping track of all those tax numbers helped develop that skill, I was sure.

Scott Gutierrez had told me that he hadn't driven through Regal Saturday morning, and now Betty's recollection neither supported nor contradicted him. He hadn't gone out of his way to tell me that he'd driven through the village on Friday night, either. Perhaps he didn't consider it important. And maybe it wasn't. After all, when the lame jokes of the sitcom *Star Town* were airing and the coyote pups were practicing their howling, both Matt Baca and his father were still very much alive.

Chapter Thirty-four

I hesitated to bother Frank Dayan on a Sunday morning. The frenetic newspaper publisher burned up the sidewalks six days a week trying to keep the *Posadas Register* alive and well, and any questions I had for him about Posadas County politics could wait for Monday. Instead, I went home, planning to spend some time putting the house in order for the imminent Guzman invasion.

What I could do about that order was a mystery, since Maria Ibarra, my housekeeper, thought far ahead of any meager efforts I might make. She hadn't done any grocery shopping, though, and neither had I. My son was taking care of that. He'd even taken the money I'd forced on him and stuffed it into his son's shirt pocket. Tadd would attend to the culinary end of things, I was confident. Evidently, Buddy didn't share my assumption that when hungry, the Guzman kids could just truck on down to the Don Juan de Oñate Restaurant for a Burrito Grande.

The guest rooms were ready, including a whole zoo of stuffed animals that Maria had dragged from a closet. She used them to populate the single beds where little Francisco and Carlos Guzman would snuggle and giggle. I didn't even remember that I'd kept the damn animals, originally part of my youngest daughter's collection. The critters had been jammed away in the dark years ago and then forgotten.

I stood for a while in the doorway of that bedroom, looking at the beasts while their ancient, wise button eyes stared back at me. One small black dog, fur worn by the years of roughhouse handling, had advanced halfway down the bedspread. He stood facing the doorway, small ears at attention.

They should have brought a smile to my face, I suppose. Instead, a great, crashing wave of melancholy swept over me, and I turned away. Part of the melancholy was that I didn't know what Estelle and her husband planned. Despite our telephone and E-mail conversations since they'd moved to Minnesota the previous spring, I knew only that their stay in the northland had had its setbacks. A talented vascular surgeon, Francis Guzman had managed to severely injure his left hand in a biking accident while riding to work. Estelle had told me that much. Whether the young physician was now discovering that tying the tiny, intricate stitches in some patient's ballooning aorta were beyond the limits of his crippled hand, I didn't know.

And only when I'd pressed her about the missing FOR SALE sign had she told me that they'd taken their house on Twelfth Street in Posadas off the real estate market because they weren't sure of their plans. My hopes soared, naturally, knowing that Posadas continued to be a possible option for them.

In one recent communication, Estelle had reported that Francis' aunt, Sophia Tournal, was visiting from her home in Mexico. I'd met Ms. Tournal a time or two, and at the first meeting knew instantly why she was such a successful attorney in her home state of Veracruz.

All of that gave me reason to suspect that the Guzmans' trip to Posadas that November was more than just the opportunity to watch election returns. After all, a card of congratulations or commiseration to Bob Torrez and a "Happy Retirement!" card for me would cover those bases.

Part of Estelle's charm—and sometimes, when she'd been working for the Posadas County Sheriff's Department, what frustrated the hell out of the rest of us—was that the world, beyond mother, husband, and children, operated on a need-to-know basis.

I was godfather to the Guzman children. I knew that Estelle trusted me as unequivocally as I trusted her. I'd saved her life on more than one occasion, and she'd done the same for me. All of that, though, wasn't an admission ticket to her inner circle. That's just the way she was. Join the club with the rest of the six billion.

Shortly before eleven Sunday morning, Robert Torrez stopped by briefly to tell me that he was headed for Regal, and that his sister would be home by two that afternoon.

"I didn't tell her too much when I talked to her on the phone," Torrez said. "But she's upset. I could tell."

"You told her about the license?" We stood at the front door, the undersheriff refusing to come inside. I noticed that he was driving his "tank," an ancient Chevy pickup truck burdened with several decades of junk that filled the back. Wrought-iron curlicues protected the back window from a shifting load. Unshaven and dressed in a bright red and yellow flannel shirt, down vest, and jeans, he looked like a hunter just finishing a week out in the bush.

He shook his head. "No." He regarded Buddy's Corvette impassively. "But she knows that I wouldn't bother to call her like this if it wasn't something important. You know how she gets."

I didn't, but nodded agreement anyway, figuring I'd find out soon enough.

"I asked her to meet us at the MVD office at three this afternoon."

"That'll work," I said. "Do you mind if I bring Estelle along? If she's here by then, that is?"

He grinned, started to say one thing, and then changed his mind. "No, I don't mind."

"That's if she wants to," I said. "She may be pooped from the trip. But I have a resident kid-sitter with my grandson being here, so Estelle could break away for a little while."

"Sure, if she wants to."

"I talked to Betty Contreras, by the way. She was being a good witness, telling us what we wanted to hear."

Torrez frowned. "Sir?" he said, looking sideways at me.

"She admits that she isn't sure that it was Scott Gutierrez who drove by at eight on Saturday morning. She isn't sure who it was.

In fact, she has no idea at all. She mentioned Scott's name to me because she'd seen him drive by *the night before*. His name just came to mind. She didn't mention him to Tony, like she told me she had." I shrugged. "She's embarrassed, needless to say."

"Well, duh," Torrez said with a straight face, sounding more like my grandson than the undersheriff. "What time did she see Scott Friday night, did she say?"

"About eight forty-five or so."

"Well, that doesn't mean squat," he said. He turned to his truck, rested a hand on the hood, and kicked the left front tire pensively. "See you at three?"

"You got it," I said. "And by the way, Judge Hobart asked me this. Are you planning on announcing who you're going to name as undersheriff before Tuesday? Not that it's any of my business—or his. But voters might like to know."

Hand still on the truck, he twisted and looked at me, one eyebrow cocked. "You want the job?"

"Oh, sure." I laughed.

He returned his scrutiny to the front tire, looking down at the gnarly tread, idly digging at one of the huge cleats with the toe of his boot. "It's not something that I want to rush into," he said. I couldn't remember an occasion when Robert Torrez had rushed into anything. "Did you hear who Leona Spears asked?"

"No. But then again, I'm not on her 'tell first' list, either."

"Eddie Mitchell called me from Bernalillo County. She gave him a buzz."

"She has more brains than I thought," I said. Mitchell had left Posadas the previous spring, and I knew he'd already passed his lieutenant's exam in Bernalillo. "He'd do a fine job."

"Yes, he would. I was thinking the same thing." He sighed and straightened up, pushing away from the truck. "It's a long four months until January, too. We'll see what happens."

"Let me know what I can do," I said.

"I will. Right now, I'm just going to Uncle Sosimo's place. Sit and think. There's got to be something. There's a couple other things I want to check out, too, while I'm down that way."

I patted the faded fender of the Chevy. "We're short of vehicles?"

He grinned. "Nah. It's that time of year."

I knew exactly what he meant. The scoped .308 rested in its back window rack, ready to train its sights on a trophy desert mule deer. "You be careful," I said, and stepped back from the truck. I knew the cloud of fumes that would issue from it the moment he hit the starter. "Happy hunting."

"We'll see," he said, and I knew from his expression that he wasn't talking about mule deer.

Chapter Thirty-five

I had never been a hunter. Or a golfer. Or messed with model railroads or patiently fitted stained glass. I didn't have the patience of a fisherman. At odd moments, I sat down with a book that had something to do with military history, but even then, the collection that overflowed my living-room shelves held many more volumes than I had actually completed…or ever would.

The nearest I came to a consuming hobby was consuming at the Don Juan—and my thoughtful grandson had made sure that wouldn't be necessary for several hours.

Two o'clock on that Sunday afternoon seemed weeks away instead of hours, and that was only if the damn airlines were on time. Mercifully, Buddy and Tadd returned shortly before noon. "Do you think they'll already have eaten?" Tadd asked even before he set the three heavy plastic bags on the kitchen counter. I grinned. The kid was a true Gastner in everything but appearance—and that part was just as well.

"It doesn't matter," I said. "No matter what they do, the two youngsters will be starving. And I've never known Francis to turn down a meal, either." I paused and glanced at the slow-moving clock. "And then there's me." That brought a wide grin from my grandson. "I've got a meeting at three, by the way."

"You're kidding," Buddy said in wonder. "No, I guess you're not." He thumped a heavy wrapped cut of meat onto the counter. "We'll get you fed in time for that." He turned with his hands on his hips. "Come Tuesday night, is it like somebody suddenly throws a big light switch? Do you suddenly get your life back? The phone stops ringing, all that sort of thing?"

"I fervently hope so," I said. "In theory, the sheriff-elect takes office in January. But I told Robert that when he wins the day after tomorrow, he gets the keys to the executive washroom right then and there. Tuesday night. That's it. It's his."

Buddy laughed. "And what if what's-her-face wins?"

"Leona Spears? She's not going to."

"Famous last words."

"They would be, too. If she won, I'd be intensely unhappy, because I'd have to rethink the whole thing. I'm not sure I'd toss the keys to her. I might have to wait until the last second on January twentieth, and in the meantime, hope for an earthquake or something of the sort."

"We're going to eat at exactly two-thirty," Tadd said, not one to be easily derailed from his mission with talk of politics. "If the Guzmans' plane is late, that's tough."

"He has spoken," Buddy said. I watched his son poke at the fresh leg of lamb as if seeking out a weak spot.

"You're not going to have time to cook that whole thing between now and two-thirty," I said, but I should have known better.

Tadd picked up a package of eight stainless-steel skewers. "Lamb ka bobs," he said, beaming.

"Christ, you bought those, too?"

"No. You had 'em inside the grill," Tadd said. "The package had never been opened. Neat-o."

"Neat-o," I said. "I didn't know I had 'em. Anything else you need?"

"Just a really good knife," Tadd said. "So I can hack this thing up." He patted the leg of lamb affectionately.

I turned and pulled open a drawer, viewing the helter-skelter of implements lying at rest. "Define 'really good,' " I said.

"Something that won't snap halfway through a cut and shear off his thumb," my son said, and I detected a note of parental concern. Apparently it was one thing to have a teacher tell you that your son was a culinary arts genius, and another thing entirely to turn over to the kid all the edged weapons without a single apprehensive pang.

Tadd chose a big old heavy thing that had been his great-grandmother's, then settled in with the knife and the sharpening steel to bring the edge up to his specifications.

Buddy and I retired to the living room, with nothing to do but talk and watch the clock…and perhaps keep one ear cocked toward the kitchen in case a sudden gasp from the chef alerted us to a missing digit.

At 12:30 the phone rang, and for the next twenty minutes I talked with my eldest daughter, Camille. More accurately, I listened to the high-powered recitation of life in Flint, Michigan.

Somewhere in midparagraph, I realized that she had asked me a question.

"Pardon?" I asked.

"I said, have you heard from Kerri and Joel?"

"Ah, no. But then it's early. Probably tomorrow. Or maybe even Tuesday," I said. My youngest daughter Kerri would find a working phone only with difficulty in the Peruvian village where she lived—less than ten miles from where her mother had been born and raised.

My oldest son Joel and I didn't see eye to eye on a lot of things, and it wasn't just because as president and CEO of BetaComp International, he was on the other end of the income spectrum from Kerri. It'd been nearly two years since I'd last heard the sound of his voice…and even on that occasion, his secretary had put me on hold for ten minutes. Hopefully, Joel Gastner was finding happiness peddling whatever computer component it was that BetaComp manufactured.

"Big doings planned for Tuesday night?" Camille asked.

"Not if I can help it."

"What"—she laughed—"no victory burrito at the Don Juan?"

"Nope. They're closed all day Tuesday, the bastards. But we've got the last laugh. Tadd's here, and he's cooking up a storm. You want to talk to him while he's still got all his fingers?"

"Sure, but put Buddy on first," Camille said. "I need to talk to him before I forget what I wanted."

"Buddy," I said, and held the phone out to him. "It's Camille. She wants to talk to you."

"Of course she does," my son said, and took the phone into a quiet corner of the living room.

"Anything I can do?" I asked Tadd, bending over his shoulder as he labored.

He shook his head. "Just havin' fun," he said.

"Well, I'm glad you are. Tell your dad when he gets off the phone that I'm out back. I'm going to get some air."

The kitchen door opened without a pry bar, and I brushed aside a couple vines that had spent all summer trying to come inside the house. As I stepped outside into the cool air, I saw that the back door of the garage was ajar. The grill had been hauled outside to sit in the sunshine, lid open to allow the spiders a chance to escape before Tadd touched off the gas.

The dry cottonwood leaves crackled overhead and underfoot. There had been no ripping wind whistling around the house to do my raking for me, and the leaves made a nice, deep blanket over the patio bricks. With hands thrust in my pockets, I ambled out away from the house.

The first cottonwood stood less than thirty feet from the back door. Fully four feet in diameter, its trunk bulged in a series of nodules and carbuncles as if the very weight of the tree was compressing the lower wood. The tree shed limbs regularly, some of them crashing onto the roof of the house. I craned my neck and looked up. The limb that hung thirty feet over the kitchen was gunmetal-gray and without a stitch of bark. At its base, it was more than a foot in diameter.

"Whatcha lookin' at?" Buddy asked. He let the screen door close gently in deference to the rusted hinges.

"That limb." I pointed. "It's drawing a bead on the kitchen."

"That'll be exciting," he said, glancing up. "Camille's telling Tadd how to make an instant marinade for the lamb," he added. "Anything is possible, apparently."

"Your son is amazing, Buddy." I touched his shoulder. "Take a walk with me?"

"Sure." The two of us strolled out into the wilderness of my backyard. A trail of sorts took us through the grove of cottonwoods. Far enough away from the house that roots couldn't reach the waterlines, the vegetation became a hodgepodge of whatever could survive—grasses mixed with New Mexico locust, elm, cholla, creosote bush, three or four species of acacia, and stunted juniper.

"This makes a nice buffer for your place," Buddy said. "Gives you some privacy."

"I guess it does," I said, and stopped at a small grove of twisted oaks, none more than twenty feet tall.

"I remember when those were just sprouting," Buddy said. "Me and Billy Spaulding used to shoot the tips off with our BB guns."

"The two Wild Bills," I said. "Whatever became of him, anyway?"

"Don't know," Buddy said. "We graduated and that was that."

I nodded and took a deep breath. It was too easy to slip into a quagmire of reminiscence. The last thing I wanted to do was spend three maudlin days letting the past take over my life.

"Do you have any objections if I sell this land?" I said suddenly.

Buddy looked surprised and followed me through a thick grove of elm saplings. "Why would I mind?"

"I just thought I'd ask, is all. No sentimental attachments?"

Buddy laughed. "Attachments? No. Other than that this is where you live. If you move somewhere else, that's fine." He chuckled again. "You can run, but you can't hide, Dad."

I didn't tell him that was the second time in forty-eight hours I'd been told that—the first time by a pretty bartender at the Broken Spur. I stopped within view of Escondido Lane, the village street that circled the back of my five acres. Just beyond was the embankment that rose up to the interstate. The earth along Escondido was still freshly torn up after the village had put in a new water line to service the neighborhood to the east of me.

"This property is probably pretty well situated for some business," I said. "I sure as hell don't need it all."

"If you don't mind someone moving in close by," Buddy said. "But hell, you don't need the money. Just keep it. As long as you're living here. Why worry about it?"

"I'm not worried. Just thinking, is all." I flashed a smile at him. "Scheming."

"Well, scheme away, Dad. Put in a helipad while you're at it, and I can scoot over for a visit now and then, when things get slow."

He meant it as a joke, but mention of helicopters crystallized an image in my mind so powerfully that Buddy frowned at the expression on my face. A comic-book panel would have had a huge yellow lightbulb hovering over my head.

"What?" he asked.

"The hospital doesn't have room for a helipad," I said. "They have to drive out to the airport, and that's a long way."

"You're thinking here instead?"

"Why not? With five acres, there's enough room for a clinic, parking, helipad…whatever the hell we want. We're three minutes from the hospital."

This time, the look of enlightenment spread over my son's face. "Ah," he said. "That's ambitious. I didn't know that Francis was serious about relocating back here."

I took a deep breath, surprised that I had been so transparent. "I don't know if he is or not, Buddy. If he is, then maybe some readily available land is just the ticket."

"You think he has the financing to set up his own clinic?"

"He can get it," I said.

My son regarded me with amusement. "No ulterior motives here, though."

"Of course not."

Chapter Thirty-six

The telephone rang at 2:20. My immediate reaction when the phone's bell tingled my pulse was that Estelle Reyes-Guzman was calling to report that their flight had been snowed in somewhere in downtown Minnesota, or that they hadn't been able to find a rental car in El Paso.

Tadd managed to manipulate the phone on the kitchen counter without breaking stride with whatever it was that he was doing…a process that appeared to involve a lot of loose flour.

"Gastner residence. This is Tadd Gastner speaking," he said, and tucked the phone under his chin as he concentrated with both hands on kneading a long roll of dough. "Sure," he said, and listened again. "No, he's right here. Hang on."

A lift of the chin and he dropped the phone and caught it deftly with a small explosion of flour. He extended it toward me. "Mr. Dayan would like to talk with you, Grandpa," he said.

I took the receiver gently and dusted it off. "Frank," I said into the phone, "I was about to call you."

"I thought we had a moratorium against weekend crimes," Dayan said.

"Don't I wish," I replied. Dayan's *Posadas Register* hit the newsstands and the Post Office on Thursday afternoon. A major event happening close to the weekend made him easy prey for the big-city dailies whose circulation reached Posadas—should we have an event that piqued their curiosity.

"I tried to reach you yesterday afternoon, but you were busy, I guess. Pam was going to track you down too, but I didn't hear if she managed or not."

"No, she didn't." Pam Gardiner did most of the editing and reporting for the *Register*, but she was no ball of fire. I was certainly no judge of journalism, but it appeared that her favorite kind of news was the carefully prepared public relations release that she could paste into the newspaper without a second thought.

"Someone was telling me that it's Undersheriff Torrez's nephew who was killed Friday night in that truck-pedestrian accident, and his uncle who died Saturday morning. Is that right?"

"Almost. Matthew Baca was killed Friday night. He was one of Torrez's cousins, not a nephew."

"The other was his uncle, though?"

"That's correct."

"And you're investigating the uncle's death as a possible homicide? Did I hear that right?"

"That's also correct. Your grapevine is pretty good."

"Well, it's Dan Schroeder, and he should know," Dayan said with a short laugh. "How did the old man die, do you know?"

"We're not sure."

"Not shot or stabbed, though? Anything like that?"

"No. It doesn't appear that way. It looks like there might have been some kind of tussle that precipitated Sosimo's death."

"Got a name yet?"

"For whom?"

"For whomever Mr. Baca was fighting with."

"I didn't say they were fighting, Frank. I said some kind of tussle. We don't actually know what the hell *they* were doing, if there was a *they*. Dancing, maybe. And no, we don't have a name."

"Huh," Dayan said, hesitating.

"That's the way I feel," I said. "A great big 'Huh.' "

"Is the undersheriff heading things up?"

"Heading things up? What's that mean?"

"Is it his investigation?"

I sighed. My intuitive feelers sensed the not-so-fine touch of Leona Spears behind that question. There was still lots of time for the daffy candidate to blow things all out of proportion before the polls opened at 7:00 a.m. Tuesday.

"What does Leona say?" I countered, and Frank Dayan laughed.

"I'm surprised she's not camped on your doorstep," he said. "She wants to know if I'm putting out an election eve special edition."

"And are you?"

"Uh, no. But she kindly provided me with two letters to the editor, just in case I change my mind. In the first, she accuses Torrez of trying to cover up the facts about his nephew's death."

"Cousin. And what are the facts that we're trying to cover up?"

"That the incident followed a high-speed chase that resulted in damage to two county vehicles and serious injury to two other teenagers, one of whom is reportedly hovering near death as we speak."

"That's goddamn creative," I muttered, and Tadd glanced over at me and grinned.

"And that following a night spent out on the mountain, the boy was finally arrested at his home." I heard the rustle of paper. "And then the questions start." Dayan cleared his throat. "Why was the Border Patrol involved? Why did they stop the deputy who had Matthew Baca in custody?"

"The deputy?" I said. Despite my best efforts, I could hear my pulse clicking up a level or two.

"Well, whoever. And the last one. Why was the boy allowed out of the car along a busy highway?"

"That's it?"

"That's the gist of it."

"Leona is a head case, Frank. You know that. I'm not going to dignify any of that trash with a comment. Except to clarify the deputy thing. I had the kid in custody, not one of my deputies."

"I know that, Bill. Schroeder set me straight, and said he was going to call Leona and set her straight. I just kept the letter as a souvenir. Something for my scrapbook in the chapter titled 'Life with the Loonies.' If you think that letter's good, you ought to read the second one…just in case I decide to have an election eve special, mind you."

"I'm not sure I want to hear."

Ignoring me, Dayan started his recitation. " 'Despite the United States Border Patrol's best efforts to investigate the death of a prominent Regal resident, the Posadas County Sheriff's Department steadfastly refuses to divulge important information to federal authorities.' "

"Steadfastly. I like that word."

"Me too. There's more. 'None of this is surprising, considering that the victim is a close family relative of Undersheriff Robert Torrez, who heads the investigation for the county.' "

"A *family* relative," I said. "I wasn't aware of any other kind."

"I thought you might appreciate that."

"Your original question is probably valid, Frank. Is Robert heading the investigation? No, he's not. I am, at least until Tuesday when election returns are counted. And when Robert wins the election, *he'll* be in charge. And I, thank God, will be a civilian again, with nothing better to do than sit around and write crazy letters to the newspaper."

Dayan laughed good-naturedly. "I look forward to those, Bill."

"I bet you do. But look…I appreciate hearing about Loony Leona. It's nice to be forewarned, just in case. And I have a question for you, too."

"Shoot."

"In your travels around town, have you heard anything about Cliff Larson resigning as livestock inspector for this area?"

A short pause followed, then Dayan said, "I hadn't heard that, no. It doesn't surprise me, though. I know he has family somewhere back east with an illness, and I know for a fact that he's ill. So it wouldn't surprise me if he called it quits. Why?"

I didn't ask Dayan who his sources were, but it didn't matter. He and Judge Lester Hobart belonged to the same service clubs, where talk was rampant. Cliff Larson looked like death warmed over—maybe because he was. And if that was the case, he wasn't asking me to take over the livestock inspector's job for just a week or two…just as Judge Lester Hobart had implied.

"That's what I thought," I said. "He looks and sounds like hell. But he asked if I'd help him with the job after the election for a week or two."

"A week or two? Maybe that was just to make it sound like a smaller favor than it is, Sheriff."

"You're not the only one saying that, Frank. What's going on?"

He hesitated again, and for an instant I wondered if I was going to regret talking to the newspaper publisher. I had trusted him before with sensitive stories, and beyond that, even though he'd lived in Posadas now for nine years, I knew that he was still considered an outsider—except during community fundraisers, of course. "Maybe you and I should have lunch sometime," he said.

"Why not just tell me right now?" I said with more impatience than I would have liked.

"Some things I'd rather say in person, Bill," Dayan said. "This is kinda interesting. You and I need to talk."

"I can't today, except maybe later this evening. How about tomorrow?"

"That will work, I think." He laughed. "Do I need to ask where?"

"No, you don't. And how about around two in the afternoon? That'll give the lunch crowd time to get out of the way."

"I'll be there. Call me if something comes up so you can't make it."

"Sure enough." I hung up and took a deep breath. Tadd was cutting strips of thin dough and lacing them across the top of a sea of apple and pineapple in one of my old glass baking pans. "Is that cobbler?"

He nodded. "Cool beans, eh?"

"Cool beans," I said. "You're hired."

He grinned. "What's a livestock inspector do, anyway?"

"All kinds of things," I said. "I didn't realize you were tuned in." He shot a quick glance at me to see if I was really as irritated as I sounded. I wasn't, and added, "New Mexico has a pretty comprehensive set of laws that govern how livestock is handled, Tadd. Anytime a rancher wants to move cattle off his own property, for instance, he's got to have a travel permit. That involves an inspection of the cattle, a count, all that kind of thing." I waved a hand in dismissal. "It goes on and on from there."

"You're going to do that after you retire?"

"I've been thinking about it."

He stood back and regarded the finished creation. "You sure find interesting things to do, Grandpa."

"Thank you." I bent down so I could direct my bifocals at the intricate crust. "And when do we get to eat this?"

"Thirty minutes from now," Tadd said, and glanced at the clock. "Timing is everything."

Chapter Thirty-seven

The tornado hit at 2:32 p.m. The only warning was Buddy's calm remark, "I think we have company." At the moment, I was en route to the bathroom. Thankfully, I knew what was coming, and didn't put off my trip to the head.

I emerged from the bathroom and felt the draft from the front door, stepped into the hallway, and heard a loud *"Padrino!"* screeched at the top of Francisco Guzman's four-year-old lungs. He'd been standing outside with everyone else, shuffling leaves with his little shoes and wondering who the hell Buddy was. Then he caught sight of me. The youngster cleared the front steps in a bound and hurtled down the hall.

I dropped to one knee and braced myself, taking the attack on the protective bulk of my girth. Francisco hooked his bony little arms around my neck and locked on. His raven-black hair had that musty smell that marks most little kids too long on the road, and his forehead bashed my glasses painfully against the bridge of my nose.

"Whoa, *keeed,*" I bellowed, and bear-hugged the little squirt. With considerable effort I stood up, taking Francisco with me. A smaller version of him appeared in the doorway, eyes wide. Carlos wasn't quite sure who I was, his dim memories probably blended even further by seeing my son first—a thirty-year younger someone whom he couldn't quite remember anyway.

"Carlos," I shouted at him, and his eyes widened some more as he backed out of the door, both hands coming up toward his mouth.

"Hijo, muy bien," a soft voice behind him said. *"Es su padrino."* Estelle Reyes-Guzman appeared in the doorway, bent down, and scooped up Carlos as if he were weightless. With a deft hoist, she draped him over her left shoulder like a little bag of grain, holding on to his ankles as he let out a screech of delight.

"Hey, there," I said. "You want this one too?" Francisco giggled and locked his hands tighter.

"You can have him, Padrino," Estelle said. She frowned at her oldest son, and all that accomplished was to drive his face harder into my neck, threatening to cut off my already over worked carotid.

I grinned, silly with delight. Estelle and I managed a hug with the two squirming dervishes more or less entwined. "God, it's good to see you guys. It seems like about ten years," I said.

"That would make this *hijo* old enough to drive, and that's a scary thought." Estelle laughed. "Six months is long enough."

"You bet it is."

She heaved a great sigh and stepped back a pace, giving her room to bend over and deposit Carlos on the floor. He latched on to her left leg and regarded me, black eyes just like his mother.

"Did you bring Francis with you, or leave him behind?" I asked.

"Afuera," Francisco announced too close to my ear, and pointed. "Who is that?" he added, and transferred the point over my left shoulder. I twisted at the waist and saw my grandson approaching.

"This is my grandson," I said. "Tadd, I don't know if you've ever met the Guzman clan," I said.

"No, but heard lots," Tadd said. He stepped up, clamped his hands on either side of Francisco's rib cage, and curled his lips in mock threat. *"En especial acerca de usted, chiquito."* For once, at least for a few seconds, Francisco was speechless. Tadd released his hold, grinned at the kid, and tousled his hair, then switched his attention to Estelle. "You must be Estelle," he said, and held out a hand.

She reached past the squirming arms of the two kids and took his hand. Her heavy black eyebrows twitched in amusement as she watched Francisco's expression run the gamut, finally settling on wide-eyed astonishment.

"El Nieto," she said to the child. *"Nieto del Padrino."* She gave Tadd's hand a final pump and smiled at him. "It's nice to meet you after all this time." She turned and looked back out the door. "My husband has been captivated by your son's Corvette. We may never get him inside."

"Is that your car, *Padrino?*" Francisco asked, suddenly regaining his composure.

"Nope. It's my son's."

"Let me show you," the youngster said, but the command was directed at Tadd.

"Okay, show me," my grandson said, and Francisco slithered down to the floor and shot out the door, little brother trying his best to keep up. As he headed outside, Tadd nodded at Estelle and me. "About ten minutes or so," he said.

"He means until dinner is ready, and he's dead serious," I said.

Estelle watched him go. "He looks a lot like his grandmother," she said.

"Yes he does, fortunately for him. His older brother is the tank of that generation. Kendal's in school, though, and couldn't break away."

She squeezed my arm and we headed outside. Dr. Francis Guzman was standing with his arms folded across his chest a pace or two behind the Corvette, regarding it critically while Buddy explained its various merits. He turned at our approach, a broad smile splitting his handsome face. He had clipped his full beard short, and it seemed more liberally sprinkled with gray than half a year before.

"There he is," the physician said. "Bill, you're looking better than ever."

"That wouldn't be hard to do." I laughed. "You guys look like Minnesota is treating you well." He clasped my hand, putting his left over both in a two-handed grip. I couldn't help noticing the heavy, ridged scar that ran across the back of his left hand, from between his index and second finger, diagonally back to his wrist, behind the base of his thumb.

"Most of the time," he said lightly. *"Hijo,"* he snapped. Francisco was in the process of reaching toward the recessed door handle of the sports car, and his hand stopped as if it had encountered an invisible wall.

"He can't hurt it," Buddy said.

"You'd be amazed," Francis replied. Tadd scooped the kid up and with the other hand deftly opened the car door. He sat in the driver's seat, Francisco on his lap. Carlos advanced, uncertain, stopping at his father's leg. From inside the car, I heard the nonstop jabbering of the excited older youngster, all of it in Spanish. My grandson's response was just as rapid-fire, just as incomprehensible.

"I didn't know until thirty seconds ago that Tadd spoke Spanish," I said to Buddy.

"He'd better," my son said. "I think he's been studying it in school since about second grade. And the crowd he hangs out with is mostly bilingual, so…" He shrugged.

"Friends for life," Estelle said, watching Francisco read each number on the tachometer to Tadd.

"Unless we're late for lunch. And then it's all over."

"We ate a little on the plane, and then Francis stopped in Cruces so the kids could tank up," she said. "Don't go to any special trouble."

"No trouble for me," I said. "It turns out the grandkid is a surprise. He loves to cook. That's all he's been doing, all day. You're all starving, believe me."

Between the five adults and two rambunctious kids, we managed to unload the Guzmans' rental van in one trip. I couldn't tell if my big, quiet old adobe was cringing at the ruckus, or was content with the sudden injection of uproar.

When Francisco and Carlos saw their room, they stood in flat-footed amazement. And in silence too, for about ten seconds. After a couple of minutes, Tadd excused himself to return to the kitchen, and Francisco immediately detached himself, following along behind my grandson, one of the larger teddy bears in tow.

As soon as everyone knew where their digs were, I left Estelle and her husband alone, and joined my son and grandson in the kitchen.

"What do you need?" I asked Tadd.

"Are you going to take me for a ride, *Padrino?*" Francisco asked before Tadd had a chance to answer.

"Not now, kid," I said. "Maybe later you can talk *Nieto* here into it."

"Not," Buddy said quickly.

"They can sit on my lap while Dad drives, maybe," Tadd said. He looked down at Francisco. "Right now I need you to uncover the grill outside," he said. "You think you can do that?"

"I'll show 'em," Buddy said, not quite as eager as Tadd to trust the process to the whirlwind.

When the door closed behind them, I repeated my question. Tadd paused, regarding the cobbler on the cooling rack as if all the answers lay there.

"Do you think it's warm enough for the kids to be outside?" he asked.

"Sure."

"Then I think I'll eat outside with them. That way maybe you guys can have a little peace and quiet. Okay?"

I reached up and squeezed the back of my grandson's neck. "You're a good kid," I said. Estelle stepped into the kitchen, and the instant that her shoes hit the saltillo tile, the phone rang.

I picked up the receiver. "Gastner."

"Sir," Bob Torrez said, "my sister's back. She said that three would be fine. I asked her to meet us at her office."

I groaned inwardly and looked up at the clock. "Roberto, the Guzmans just now walked in the door. My grandson's got a dinner prepared for 'em and we're just about to sit down. If I walk out now, he'll shoot me."

"No problem, sir." He sounded more formal than need be. I wasn't sure if he meant that shooting me was no problem.

"Here's the plan," I said. "Why don't you and Gayle come over. When we're done here, then we'll go chat with your sister. Call her and tell her that we'll be a little late. Maybe four, four-thirty. Something like that." I glanced at Estelle and raised an eyebrow. She nodded.

"You're sure?" Torrez asked.

"Of course I'm sure. My grandson has cooked enough for about eighteen people. We'd all like to see you guys."

"Right now?"

"This very moment." Torrez lived four minutes away, up on MacArthur. "See you in a bit." I hung up before he had second thoughts. "He and Gayle are on their way," I said. "I hope you don't mind. He needs to relax for a little while, if he can. Have you heard from Gayle much?"

"We keep in touch," Estelle said. "More from Bobby, though. I just got an E-mail from him this morning, before we left for the airport. He must have been up half the night."

"Is that right?" What I really wanted to ask was what the E-mail had been about, but I knew it was none of my business.

As usual, my thought process was as transparent as glass to Estelle. "He's worried that his sister might be involved in something?"

"There's that possibility," I said.

"Apparently you were going to talk to her this afternoon. Bob asked if I'd consider going along—assuming that we made it here on time."

"We can't ask you to do that," I said, not meaning a word of it and trying to keep the surprise off my face. I found myself more amused than irritated that my undersheriff had extended the invitation to Estelle long before I'd suggested it—and then not told me that he'd done so. "You're supposed to be on vacation."

"Doing a little business makes it all tax deductible," Estelle said. "It sounds kind of interesting. And I know Bobby's worried. He tries not to sound like it, but I know he is."

I let out a deep breath. "I've been trying to figure out how to ask you," I said. "But he beat me to it. It seems like kind of a dirty trick to hornswoggle you into working the minute you set foot in the county."

"It's not really work," she said, and favored me with one of her rare smiles. "And we're going to eat first, anyway."

Chapter Thirty-eight

I knew that Robert Torrez wanted to talk to his sister about the bogus license, but when I'd first broached the idea earlier, I thought that I'd made myself clear—that just I, or maybe Estelle and I if she was so inclined, would go chat with Melinda. We'd keep it informal, unthreatening—but we would keep big brother out of it.

Torrez may have agreed with that idea originally, but when he and Gayle arrived at the house, he seemed determined to accompany us to the MVD office later that afternoon.

Eventually, he grudgingly agreed that if he went along, no matter how silent he remained, no matter how he tried to blend with the wallpaper, it would be a case of big brother hovering protectively over his little sister.

"And that's just a bad idea, Robert," I said.

"You need to let the sheriff and Estelle go," Gayle Torrez said at one point after we all had bandied the idea back and forth. Torrez said nothing, but turned and looked at Estelle. Estelle's head moved, the faintest hint of a nod. Evidently that was enough.

Torrez put his fork down. He hadn't touched most of the food. "Okay," he said. "You two go."

After another half hour, a nap would have been in order, but instead I fueled up on three or four cups of strong coffee and the assurance from Buddy and Francis that the house would be in safe hands during our absence. I saw that I didn't need to worry about the kids. Tadd had both Francisco and Carlos in tow, the two dervishes ready to do anything he asked.

Robert and Gayle Torrez left, and I knew by the look on his face that he'd head for his office and sit there in the silence of a Sunday afternoon, fuming and fussing until he heard from me.

I settled into the unmarked car and watched Estelle slide into the passenger seat. She finally found the other end of the seat belt amid the welter of junk. "Feels about right, doesn't it?" I said as I backed out of the driveway, maneuvering through the clutter of vehicles.

Estelle didn't immediately agree, which was something of a disappointment, but she didn't disagree, either. Instead she said, "Your grandson is a remarkable young man."

"Yes, he is."

"I've never seen Francisco eat bell peppers before. Tadd ate 'em, so he did too."

"It was interesting to watch," I said. "Carlos wasn't so easy to convince, though." I laughed at the memory of the smallest Guzman pushing the unidentifiable green lizards around on his plate, dark brows furrowed in critical concentration. He hadn't been taken in by any smooth talk. Those bell peppers weren't green chile, and the kid knew it. "Can you believe that the last time I saw my grandson, he wasn't all that much older than Francisco? Christ, time just slips away, doesn't it?"

"Way, way too fast."

Robert had called his sister and told her that we'd meet at the MVD office at 4:30, and we were a few minutes early. I idled the car along and Estelle appeared to be examining every building en route.

"I don't guess the place has changed much," I said, and gestured at the supermarket, a new sign molded in gaudy plastic above the door. "The Carter family sold the store earlier this fall. Some outfit from El Paso."

"Old Sam," Estelle murmured, "he was a real creep."

That comment took me by surprise, since the Estelle I knew kept opinions so closely guarded that they could qualify as state secrets. Not that I didn't agree with her assessment. Sam Carter had indeed been a crooked, philandering creep. He'd also been chairman of the County Commission, and on more than one occasion had made our lives downright interesting.

Less than two blocks farther on, the Posadas County complex on Bustos Avenue included a small annex that housed the state's Motor Vehicle Division field office, and I pulled into the parking lot and nosed the car into a slot beside Melinda Torrez's blue Datsun pickup.

"I appreciate your doing this," I said to Estelle. "And so does Bob."

"He's a basket case," Estelle said. "But then, he has good reason to be. I can't even imagine what's going through his mind right now. First his cousin, then his uncle."

"And he liked Sosimo, too, for all his faults," I added. "The old guy was a family favorite."

"That's right. And now this." We got out of the car and stepped up onto the sidewalk. The office door was locked, and I peered inside. A blind on the window and a partition just beyond shielded the office from view. I rapped on the glass with a knuckle, and almost instantly, Melinda Torrez appeared from the left and came in front of the counter. Her key ring still hung in the lock, and she opened the dead bolt.

Three years younger than her brother at thirty-four, Melinda was the oldest daughter of the late Rafael Torrez and his wife, Elsa. There had been nine children livening up that household, with Robert the oldest of four boys.

One brother had been killed fifteen years before. A drunken driver had clipped the boy, pulverizing his motorcycle and throwing him nearly fifty feet into a guardrail on the opposite side of the road. The drunk had been trying to negotiate his way out of the parking lot of a bar. He'd seen the truck that young Torrez was following, but he claimed he never saw the motorcycle.

Robert Torrez had been a Posadas County sheriff's deputy for four months at the time. Mercifully, he hadn't been on duty.

Except for that tragedy, the Torrez children prospered as a diverse, huge, and as far as I could tell, happy family whose holiday gatherings were legendary for grid-locking MacArthur Street.

Melinda hadn't yet found a man she wanted to marry, and she and her mother, Elsa, presided over the family, deferring to the oldest son and future sheriff of Posadas County just enough that he felt in control.

"How are you doing, Melinda?" I said. "I'm sorry to wreck your Sunday in the big city."

"You haven't wrecked a thing," Melinda said. She was a handsome woman, tall and big-boned like her brother, with sharp features and a high, broad forehead. She held open the door and stood to one side, her smile for Estelle wide and genuine. "And look who's here," she said. The two women embraced. "Two minutes in town, and you let the boys drag you out already?" She released just enough of the hug to free one hand. Drilling her strong index finger into my biceps, she said, "See how you are?"

"Yep," I said. "A hopeless case. I admit it."

"And where's the hunk?" Melinda stepped back a pace, holding Estelle with a hand on each shoulder like an elementary school teacher grabbing the attention of a seven-year-old.

"He's back at the house, trying to make sure that *los niños* don't wreck their host's home."

"All right. I can understand that." She shot a look of sympathy my way. "You're a brave man, Bill." She gestured back behind the counter and when we'd cleared the door, turned the dead bolt. "Come on back." She rounded the corner and then stopped. "God, how have you guys been? It's been *forever!*"

"We're fine," Estelle said.

"How long are you here for?"

"Just until Thursday," I said. "Not long enough, I keep telling them."

"Ain't that the truth." She lifted both hands palms up to encompass the entire office. "So here we are. Bobby was… what…a little vague about what was going on? I put two and two together and decided it had to have something to do with Mateo and Uncle Sosimo. Is that right?"

"Yes," I said. I turned the license so that Melinda could read it clearly and laid it on the counter.

"What's this?" she said automatically. She leaned on the counter with an elbow on each side of the license, hands clasped together. For a long minute, she examined it without touching it. Then she turned the license over, scrutinizing the magnetic strip and the empty line for endorsements.

"Oh, boy," she said.

"What do you think?" I asked.

She sucked air between clenched teeth, making funny little noises with her tongue. As if another examination might change things, she picked up the plastic card again. This time she looked so closely her eyes crossed. "Oh, boy," she said again. "Matthew had this with him?"

"It would appear so."

"Oh, boy," she muttered. Her eyes narrowed just a tad when she looked at me. "And you want to know where he got it."

"Yes." My interest was tweaked. Melinda asked her question in that rhetorical tone of voice that hinted she might have heard the same question before.

She turned the license over several times, quick motions with two fingers and a thumb. She would have made a good blackjack dealer at one of the tribal casinos. "God, I hate to see this," she said, and leaned on the counter. "You know, there's just no way to fake one of these things."

"That's what I thought," I said.

Holding up a hand, she added, "Well…I should say that *as far as we know*, there's no way to fake one. Any security device—like these little holograms here of the state seal? They're supposed to help make these things tamperproof. And then there's this," and she ran her fingers along the magnetic strip on the back. "So my first thought is that this was issued somewhere through our system. Sure enough, it was. That's what I'd say."

"That's what I wanted to talk to you about, Melinda."

"You're thinking it was done here?"

"I don't know where it was done."

She cupped her chin in one hand, fingers rubbing her right eye, and regarded me with her left. "If it was done here, then it could have been done anywhere in the state. Anywhere that's connected to the same data system that we are. We don't even use location codes anymore. We used to, but not now. If it was done here in Posadas, then it was done by either me or Connie. We're the only ones who work in the office."

"Or someone who slipped in after hours."

"That's not likely. One of us would have to let them in. And besides"—she turned and looked at the two computers—"this would be tough if you didn't have the training. All the time is logged, things like that. And the preformatted forms that we feed into the printer can be a real pain if you're not experienced."

"So how could it happen?"

She shook her head. "I just don't know."

"Can you pull up information on Matthew for us?"

"I *can*," Melinda said, sounding as if she wanted to add, "but I won't."

"I'd be interested to see what comes up," I said. "Especially about his birth date."

The computer was running, and Melinda circled around the desk and settled into her chair that faced the computer screen.

"Do you leave these running all weekend?" I asked.

"No," she answered. "I booted up just a few minutes ago because I knew you'd want to see something." She grinned at the two of us. "What's to see at a MVD office other than the computers?" Carefully, she placed the license next to the keyboard, and then said, "Let's see what the number brings up."

In a moment, she frowned. "It brings up nothing. Well, it's voided. That's not nothing."

"Meaning..."

Melinda leaned back in her chair and crossed her arms over her chest. "You can void whatever you're working on, anytime in the process."

"Okay. Could someone make a license out of parts?"

"Out of parts?"

"Sure. Take the picture, fabricate the right numbers, put it through the laminator?"

"No. See—"and she leaned forward and pointed at the gadget that took the license photos—"that used to be separate, years ago. Now everything is linked together. The camera takes a photo when the computer tells it to, and the image goes right into the processor. Everything comes together as a package. It's all digital." She meshed her fingers together. "I don't know of any way to make the different parts of the process work independently."

"You couldn't just take my picture now, and not do anything else, you mean?"

"No. I couldn't do that." She frowned and then said with considerable feeling, "Shit." She handed me the license but didn't elaborate on her comment.

"How can I make this?" I asked.

"Well, it's no problem to type in bogus information," Melinda said. "That's not hard to do. We're supposed to ask to see various things, and there's some tick-offs, but..." She shrugged. "Like so many things, who's to know most of the time? I mean, we used to hand-score the drivers' tests, remember that? Santa Fe changed that so the tests are all automatically machine-scored, and the information goes right into the computer."

"But there's nothing to prevent you from giving the correct answers, is there," I asked. "Whisper over someone's shoulder."

"No, of course not. Just the memory of that incident a few years ago when two MVD clerks got themselves led out of the office in handcuffs."

I leaned back and nodded at the small sign taped to the front panel of the counter. "And it says here that they have to present proof of insurance to obtain or renew a registration. You could just let that slide, too, right?"

"Sure. And like most things, no one would be the wiser until something happened."

"So back to the original question. How do I make one of these?"

She leaned back again and surveyed her machinery. Her cheeks moved as if she were puffing a silent tune while she thought, and then she closed her eyes, head moving this way and that. I glanced over at Estelle. Her black eyebrows lifted a fraction in acknowledgment, even though she didn't take her eyes off Melinda.

"The easiest way is just to process it, just like normal," Melinda said. "This birth date is fake, that's for sure. But there's no big bell or whistle that goes off if you type in the wrong date. The customer is supposed to have proof of age the first time he applies for a license, and after that, the D.O.B. is in the system. It's automatic. Here, let me bring this up." She rapped keys and the screen blinked, and eventually Matthew Baca's operator's license information appeared.

"Here's his D.O.B., right there." She highlighted the numbers. "Twelve thirteen, 1982." She twisted in her chair to look at me. "And if my math is correct, that would make him nineteen next month."

"And that's what he was?"

"Yes. Last night, Mama and I were talking about him. Mama remembers birthdays just as good as this thing." She nodded at the computer. "They agree. It's written in the family Bible that she keeps too, so I know this is right."

"How do I fake it? The date, that is."

"Just like I said. Run a license through the whole process, make a few changes, and there you go. But this says that license, the one you have there, never existed. Or was voided."

"Can you void a document anytime in the process?"

"Sure."

"Does the computer keep a record of what the document was that was voided?"

Melinda frowned and shook her head. "Not as far as I know. It's just gone."

I leaned on the counter. "Could you void it after the photo was taken, after the actual license was produced by the computer? After it actually spit it out?"

"I suppose you could. I've never tried it, but I don't know any reason why you couldn't do it."

"Then you'd be left with a bogus license, like this one, and no record of it in the MVD."

"As far as I know, you could do that. But that's only as far as I know. I mean, I don't sit in here all day and play with these darn things." She flashed a smile. "There's plenty to do without that, trust me." Her brow furrowed. "But it wouldn't be worth it, Bill. If you ever got caught, you'd lose your job, maybe go to jail…"

"Obviously it'd be worth it to somebody."

"When do you work?" Estelle asked, and the sound of her voice startled me.

"Well, this is a small office, as you well know," Melinda answered. "We're open Tuesday, Wednesday, and Friday. Three days a week is all the state will give us. It used to be just me, but two years ago, Santa Fe said there should be two of us here. I work Tuesdays and Fridays and Connie works Wednesdays and Fridays."

"She's here all by herself on Wednesdays?" I asked.

"Yes, but I'm here alone on Tuesdays."

"When was the last time you saw Matthew Baca in this office?"

Melinda looked blankly at Estelle for a minute. "God," she said, "I wouldn't know." She indicated the screen. "This says that his license—his real one—was issued in November of '98. That's the last time I *recall* that he was in here. And you know, that's more of just an assumption on my part. I don't remember for sure. I saw Matt all the time at family get-togethers, so it's hard for me to remember the last time he was *here*. Right here, in this office."

"He doesn't hang out here sometimes?" Estelle asked. Her voice was husky and quiet.

"No. Not when I'm here."

"Had he been seeing Connie?" I asked.

Melinda's lips pursed briefly. "They were seeing each other for a while, yes. Well, let me take that back. *Seeing* each other probably isn't the way to put it. I remember that a time or two, she asked me about him. About Matt. It was like she was interested…maybe. I couldn't tell." She looked heavenward. "I remember thinking that there was a bit of an age thing there, you know? I mean, Connie is thirty something and Matt's a crazy teenager. I don't think that would have been going to work too good." She sighed. "That was just after she broke up with Paul French. They got divorced. And then she started going with Neil Sommers, that guy that works over at Custom Auto Parts. He seems pretty solid."

"From your perspective," I asked, "what was Matt's relationship with your brother?"

"With Bobby? Ohhh…"

"Matt stayed out of his way?"

"He tried to. I think that he liked giving Bobby a hard time—when he could get away with it. My brother could be hard on those kids, and they don't always take it in the manner in which it's intended. Bobby's not Matt's father, after all." She flashed an apologetic smile. "I'm sure that Matt thought his cousin was a real hard-nosed son of a bitch. And Uncle Sosimo didn't make it any easier for Bobby. Matt was kind of wild, and his father didn't do much to try and control him."

"Comes a time when that's tough," I said. "Let me just ask you flat out. How much do you trust Connie French?"

Melinda looked directly at me. Her eyes were sad but unwavering. "Connie's a nice person," she said. "She's a hard worker, she's dependable, she's accurate."

I smiled. "That's not what I asked, Melinda. Is she capable of doing something like this?"

"I would hope not." She saw the expression flicker on my face and quickly added, "I know, I know. That's not an answer either."

"But…"

"But that's the best I can do. Sure, she's capable of doing it. So am I. I didn't, though, and I would sincerely hope…*sincerely* hope…that she didn't either. She's another one who hasn't had a life that was just a bed of roses. I know her brother's worried about her, too."

"Scott? When was the last time you saw him?"

"I talked with him just the other day, as a matter of fact."

"Do you remember the day?"

"It would have been Friday."

"During regular office hours, that was?"

"Yes. He came in when—" She stopped suddenly and just stared at me. "He came in when Connie was out on her lunch break. We're supposed to close down from noon to one, but we don't. So many people need that time to run errands. So we split lunch. But that's when he came in."

"What did he want, do you recall?"

"He just asked when Connie worked."

"And you told him?"

"Yes, I did. I told him that Connie went out to lunch, and she'd be back at one, if he needed to see her. I guess it wasn't important."

"Did he ask what days she worked?"

"Yes. Although I can't imagine that he didn't already know. I mean, he's in and around now and then. Why wouldn't he know something as simple as that?"

"He may just never have paid attention to those details before," I said.

"He's a cop," Melinda said quickly. She reached out and tapped the back of my hand, just enough to make the connection. "I'd be willing to guarantee that he pays attention to all kinds of things."

Chapter Thirty-nine

By the time we left the Motor Vehicles Division field office, the sun had dipped below the boot of the San Cristóbal Mountains. The air was still. The last vestige of clouds formed a thin lenticular wisp about thirty thousand feet over Regal Pass. In another hour, we'd be able to stand in my backyard, away from all the streetlights, and see every star in the heavens. And they wouldn't give me any answers, either.

I drew in a deep breath of the nippy fall air and stood on the sidewalk with my hands jammed in my pockets as I watched Melinda Torrez lock the MVD's front door.

"Thanks, Melinda," I said.

"I don't know what for," she replied. "If there's anything else, let me know. This whole thing makes my skin crawl, I can tell you that. Will you let me know what happens?"

"Without a doubt." She nodded and slipped into her little truck. Estelle had opened the door of the county car and was about to get in when she saw that I had settled against the front fender. I slouched there, arms folded over my belly, one boot crossed over the other. I don't know what I was looking at—the scenery was limited to a spread of old adobe buildings renovated to look younger than they were, county gas pumps, and three Sheriff's Department vehicles parked in a neat row between the two elm trees that marked the front entrance of the Public Safety Building.

My back was to her, but I heard Estelle step around the car. She appeared at my right elbow.

"So what do you think?" I asked.

"Too many possibilities," she said quietly.

I grinned. "I was afraid you were going to say that." I turned to look at her. As always, I was struck by how slight she was, even with the extra bulk of the nifty quilted vest that she was wearing. "How well do you know Melinda?"

"I know her pretty well." Estelle didn't elaborate, but it would be tough to work for a decade in a tiny department in a tiny village without forming some lasting friendships—and without learning where most of the dark corners were.

"Well?"

"What are the possibilities?"

"It would be easier to imagine what *isn't* possible."

"All right. Start there."

"For one thing, Melinda is telling us the truth. I can't conceive of her issuing some wild kid a fake license so that he can go buy booze whenever he wants to."

"Especially a relative."

"Especially that. Especially when one of Melinda's own brothers was killed by a drunk driver. In fact, Melinda was one of the prime movers and shakers when the state was trying to drum up support to outlaw drive-up windows at liquor stores."

I stared off into the distance again, chewing on my lower lip. Estelle stepped down off the curb. That put us at eye level with each other.

"Now," Estelle continued, "would Melinda *allow* someone else to do the dirty work? Did she know about it? No. I don't think so."

"Me either," I said. "Do you know Connie French?"

"I think I've met her a few times. I'd be able to pick her out of a crowd, but that's it."

"So if she issued the license, she did it on the sly, when Melinda wouldn't know about it."

"That makes sense. What doesn't make sense is that she'd bother. What's there to gain?"

"Just a favor for a friend," I said. "People have done worse for less. Maybe she had a crush on the kid. Who the hell knows."

"You haven't talked to her yet, then?"

"No. All this reminds me of what downhill skiing must be like. Not much time for side trips."

Estelle smiled. "Well, speaking of side trips. If Connie French didn't issue the license, then that opens a whole new series of possibilities."

"The damn license could have come from anywhere," I said.

"Exactly. But there is something that tells me the license came from here." She nodded at the dark building. "From what you told me, Scott Gutierrez has been around most of the weekend, in one way or another."

"He works in this part of the country. And he has relatives here."

"He works in the area, true. But *he* lives in Deming. Now, you said that he arrived at the scene when Matthew Baca was killed. He apparently spent a good deal of the night in the area, with or without his partner. He was first at the scene when Robert called for assistance the next morning...not at his home in Deming, or not at the field office. And if he'd been on duty with what's-his-name that night..."

"Bergmann."

"With Bergmann, then he wouldn't have been assigned to work the border crossing the next morning. But there he was. And he was around, still using a government vehicle, when you guys chased Dale Torrance into the Broken Spur."

"Sure. I thought about all that. And it makes sense to me."

"It does?"

"Sure. He's an eager young cop. He works long hours. So what?"

"Sir...*you* work hours like that because you can't sleep, and because this entire county is as much home to you as your adobe house on Guadalupe Terrace. But follow it through. Who is sitting in the dark behind the church in Regal in the middle of the night? Isn't that when you said you and Buddy talked to him?"

"Yes. After Jackie Taber saw him drive through the village."

"And he's going on a hunting trip with his sister and stepfather the next day? He's going to be in great shape for that. He'll spend the day sleeping under a tree somewhere."

"What are you telling me, Estelle?"

"Scott Gutierrez is looking for something."

"That's been my assumption. And it only makes sense that it has to do with the license. Why else would he be interested in anything Matt Baca is up to? Why would he go inside their house? A neighbor claims to have seen his vehicle there, when he had no reason to be on the property at all. And when I told him that we'd found a fake driver's license, he left Regal. What's that sound like to you?"

"That he knew what was going on," Estelle said. "That he was looking for the license."

"And now tell me why."

"Too many possibilities," Estelle said, and I scowled with frustration. "The one that comes to mind first is that he's protecting his sister. If Connie issued that license, and if Scott can find it first, then she's off the hook. It's just the say-so of witnesses that Matt Baca used a fake ID."

"That thought had crossed my mind," I said, but I shook my head. "All this for one stupid fake license? I don't believe it. She'd lose her job and God knows what all else. Scott Gutierrez would lose his...and God knows what all else, too. All for some smooth-talking little punk who convinces Connie that if she issues him a fake ID, the whole world will spin faster and truer? Jesus."

Estelle smiled, and even in the poor light, it appeared to me that maybe there was a trace of sympathy there.

"People do stupid things, we both know that. Why were you chasing Dale Torrance?"

That prompted a loud laugh, the sort that reduced my blood pressure a couple of points. "Because he stole eighteen head of cattle so that he could buy his girlfriend a diamond ring or make a payment for her on a new pickup truck, or whatever the hell the money was for," I said. "And he's too stupid to realize that the love of his life wasn't just all that impressed. And he's too thick-skulled to figure out that if he stops for gas at a neighborhood station, someone might remember him?"

Estelle held up her hands in surrender. "You see what I mean."

"Clearly."

"There's one other possibility that we need to explore, though."

I stood up and brushed the fender dust from the back of my pants. I didn't bother to correct her use of the "we." "What's that?"

"Suppose that the license that was issued to Matt Baca wasn't the only one."

I looked hard at Estelle for a minute. "That thought has crossed my mind."

"Exactly."

I slumped back against the car. "Tell me what you're thinking," I said.

Chapter Forty

The undersheriff was in the process of pouring a carafe of water into the coffeemaker when we walked in. Maybe it was just my glasses that needed cleaning, but the water appeared amber, as if it had been used more than once.

With practiced ease, Torrez slid the empty pot under the drip and motioned for us to join him in his office. "I want to show you something," he said. That was an improvement over sitting in a blue funk. Inactivity didn't suit the man.

As he rounded the corner of his desk, he pushed the computer screen so that it turned to face us.

"I finally figured out what I wanted to look for," he said. "This is for the past twelve months."

Estelle scanned the screen-load of data far more quickly than I, but she didn't have bifocals to deal with. "I don't follow," I said. "What am I supposed to be seeing?"

"How many arrests were there statewide for fraudulent or altered driver's licenses, sir?" Torrez asked. He sat down behind the desk.

"Six, it looks like."

"That's six in an entire year, for the entire state."

"Right. That's what it says. Not something that happens all that often."

"What the numbers tell us," Estelle added, "is that there were only six instances when the perpetrator was apprehended. Not necessarily the number of times the violation occurred."

"Well, sure," I said. "We don't know how many attempts there were. Or for that matter, how many successful operations."

Torrez smiled grimly. "Even more interesting…how many incidents were there of an illegal license being issued by a MVD office?"

"Not one."

He leaned forward and turned the screen partially back so that he could view it. "Not one."

"Your sister showed us how it might be done," I said. "All a clerk would have to do is void the thing from the permanent record. Then you've got the license in hand, but with no record of it on file."

"And…" Torrez said, rising from his chair. He held a pencil in both hands, and I could see the wood bending as he pursued the thought. "Suppose an officer stops John Doe for a traffic violation, and asks to see a license. Let's say that Mr. Doe has a fake license, just like the one that my cousin had."

"Unless the cop knows him, or has some reason to suspect the license, he's going to accept the license as long as the photo matches. As long as it's an official license from a MVD office, there would be no reason to question it," I said.

"Exactly," Torrez said. "In point of fact, there is no way for the officer to question it, at the time of the stop. We can't access Motor Vehicle Division records through normal channels. We can't just punch in the number on the license to make sure it's what it seems to be."

"You could call a MVD office on the phone and ask," I said. "But who's going to bother to do that. Unless something tipped off the officer that it might be necessary."

"Right. And those records there"—and he nodded at the state compilation of violation statistics—"indicate that's not happening."

"So where does that leave us?"

"What I got to thinking," Torrez said, "was pretty simple. What if my cousin's little prank wasn't just an isolated thing? What if he got the license not because it was an original idea with him, but because he knew that he could? Maybe he knew somebody else who had one, or heard about it. Family or not, I'll be the first to tell you—my cousin wasn't exactly a rocket scientist."

I sat down and looked at Estelle. "That's what you were thinking, isn't it? That Matt might not have been alone in this?"

"Yes, sir."

"A risky business," I said.

"Well, not really," Torrez replied, and pointed at the screen. "That shows how risky it is, right there. They're not being apprehended, that's for sure."

"If it's happening at all. The lack of numbers may mean just that, Roberto—that we're dreaming up a problem that doesn't exist. Give me a better reason."

"Money," Torrez said promptly. "What if you could sell a license for, say, five hundred or a thousand bucks a pop. That's a nice little bit of tax-free budget helper."

I frowned. "That's not what I meant, but I just answered my own question. I know that anyone will sell anything, given the right price, legal or not. Who'd want one, though? And that's pretty simple, too. What one document makes the whole of the United States fair game? A driver's license. That's what cops ask to see. We don't ask to see a Social Security card. We don't ask for a credit card. We ask for a driver's license."

Estelle nodded. "If I'm a trucker living in Mexico and I want to tap the big money north of the border, I need a license," she said. "A commercial driver's license would be my ticket. No green card complications, no tests to take, none of that nuisance. Nothing. And the money on this side of the border is a whole lot better."

I pinched my thumb and index finger together, holding up the imaginary license. "With a valid driver's license, this country is mine. I can travel where I want, work wherever. A fake Social Security number does the rest, if the employer is playing by the rules and paying over the counter. Otherwise, even that doesn't matter. I'd be willing to bet that a third of the workers in Posadas County don't have W-4 forms filed on 'em." I gestured at Estelle.

"Hell, here's a young lady who could just as easily be a current resident of Michoacan, Mexico, as Michigan or Minnesota. Estelle, you walked through a couple of international airports on your trip down here, and how many times were you asked for identification?"

"Never, sir."

"Exactly my point," I said. "Once you get yourself past customs, get in the county, cops don't check papers. And if you were stopped, they'd want to see a driver's license. Even those of us with half a brain know that cops have profiles. Avoid the profile and avoid the confrontation. Just because someone has black hair, black eyes, and talks with an accent doesn't mean they need a green card."

"There's a catch, though," Torrez mused.

"Sure there's a catch," I said. "If the driver's stupid and gets himself a ticket, even a routine ticket for driving his rig thirty-seven in a thirty zone, then the fake number on his license goes into the computer. Somewhere down the line, some bells and whistles are going to go off."

"But not at the time of the actual traffic stop," Torrez added. "If the driver's careful, he could use the fake license for a long time."

"Hell, a lifetime. And if he does get in hot water, he goes back to Mexico for a while. If the ticket was in New Mexico, hell— drive into Texas or Arizona for a while. No big deal." I grinned. "Our interstate cooperation is legendary, as we all know."

"You want some fresh coffee?" Torrez asked, sounding more as if he were searching for a way to wind me down from my soapbox than anything else.

"Hell, yes. It's been almost two hours since I ate last. I've got some empty corners down there. You want anything, sweetheart?"

"No thanks. I'm fine," Estelle said. Minnesota hadn't changed any of her habits. I waited until Robert returned with coffee for himself and me. "So…do you want to know what your sister said?"

"She wouldn't do it," he said with conviction.

"No, she wouldn't. Estelle and I agree with you on that. And if she knew it was happening in her office, she'd blow the whistle."

"That means if Matt got his license from this office, he got it from Connie French."

"If," I said.

"Nowhere else makes sense," Torrez said with a shake of the head. "Not for Matt. He didn't have two cents to his name most of the time. He's not going to go to some city somewhere and shell out a bunch of money just so he can try to buy a beer now and then."

"But he knew Connie," I said.

"And that tells me why Scott Gutierrez would be so interested," the undersheriff said. "If he was tipped off that his sister was up to something like this, he'd have some hard choices to make."

"And covering up for his sister might be one of them."

"Or not." Estelle shrugged. "There's this other obvious possibility. I don't know Scott that well. I never had occasion to work with him. All of this might be a case of sister doing a favor for brother." The small room fell silent, and Estelle didn't bother to elaborate.

"You mean Scott Gutierrez is lining up the customers?" I said after a minute. "I'd hate to think that."

"Why not?" Estelle said. "He's in the perfect position. He knows the country, he knows the people on both sides of the border, he's got contacts. He'd know when there's pressure on, too. When to back away."

I turned to Robert. "And on the other hand, everything that Scott Gutierrez has done the past few days is consistent with an officer digging around, looking and listening, trying to find some answers for himself. There's every possibility that Connie is involved. If Scott found out about that, he may be trying to pin down who's working with her."

"It's every bit as logical that he might be protecting himself," Estelle said. The room fell silent again. Robert Torrez sat on the edge of the desk, regarding the computer screen.

"What direction do you want to go with this?" I asked.

He reached over and pressed enough keys that the computer sighed into darkness. "I guess I'd like to talk with Neil Sommers first thing in the morning."

"Connie's boyfriend of the moment," I said for Estelle's benefit. "What's he going to tell you?"

"I have no idea," Torrez said, and he actually grinned. "Well, I do have an idea or two nagging at me, and he's given me some pretty good deals on stuff for my truck over the years. Maybe I'll get lucky."

I glanced at Estelle, and saw that she was watching Robert's face. Her expression almost made me a believer in telepathy. I wasn't so blessed. "Ideas like what, for instance?"

"For one thing," he said, "Scott's stepfather is visiting for a few days."

"So Scott said."

"They're all going hunting. In fact, they went this afternoon. This is the last week for the area that includes the San Cristóbals."

"And how does this involve Neil Sommers?"

"He didn't go along, sir. They left this morning, and he didn't go with them. I happened to see him coming out of the grocery store this afternoon. I didn't stop to talk."

"People walk out of grocery stores all the time, Roberto. Maybe they forgot the hot dogs or beer."

"Maybe. He was home later in the day, too. He lives just a few doors down from me. I'm just curious, is all. I wouldn't think a young couple would miss an opportunity for some time around a campfire. I'd just like to know, is all."

"Have at it," I said, shaking my head.

"You always talk about little pieces of the puzzle, sir," Torrez added.

"I know I do. That doesn't mean I know what I'm talking about." I stood up and put on my hat. "Let me know what you find out. I need to take our hostage back to her family." I smiled at Estelle. "Robert, if you need me, I'll be at the house, repairing all the holes in my walls and sweeping up the shattered glass."

Chapter Forty-one

There were no holes in the walls or busted glass in my home. In fact, the scene at Guadalupe was downright peaceful—until I'd hung up my coat and hat and started toward the living room. A cacophony of falling objects, screams, giggles, and other odd noises rolled out of the kids' bedroom. I stopped in my tracks.

"They're playing Idiot Blocks," Buddy said. He and Francis were sitting calmly in the living room, each with a glass near at hand.

"This I've got to see," I said. The bedroom door stood half open, and the three kids—two small and one large—were camped on the floor with the braided rug thrown back. They were surrounded by a welter of wooden blocks of all sizes and shapes, some as large as a shoe box. Off in the corner, I recognized the old battered cardboard box that served as a storage bin on the upper shelf in my garage.

Three large blocks had already been assembled as foundation of the new structure, and I could see that instability was the name of the game. Francisco was holding Tadd's hand so that my grandson couldn't put another block in place.

"C. G. goes next, dodo," Francisco was saying. "You started."

"I know I started, *loco-moto*," Tadd said. He saw me in the door and grinned. "Then C. G., then you. So whose turn is it now?" He wrestled the block free from Francisco's clawlike grip. "It's mine, and this is where it goes."

The exchange was enough to crumble both Francisco and his little brother into a heap of giggles.

"Did everything go all right?" Tadd asked, and the two Guzman kids spun around, prompting the inevitable.

"*Padrino!*" Francisco announced. He scrambled to his feet and flung himself at me. Carlos beamed, but remained near the blocks. He reached out and touched the large, angular blue block. "This one's mine," he said soberly.

"That's good," I said. "And yes. Everything went just fine. Who's winning?"

"Tadd cheats," Francisco said in my ear.

"Well, you'll have to watch him, then," I said, and returned to the living room.

I found a soft spot on the old sofa and collapsed, resting my head on one of the corduroy pillows. "And *C. G.?* That's new, isn't it?"

"That started last year," Francis Guzman said. "Francisco decided that he'd call his brother 'C. G.,' and Carlos was supposed to call him 'Frank.' "

"Very executive," I said.

With a grunt I sat forward and wrestled off my boots. Freed from a couple of pounds of leather and neoprene, I swung my feet up on the corner of the coffee table and sighed, eyes closed.

"What can I get you, Dad?" Buddy asked.

"No phone calls," I whispered. "What's that stuff you're drinking?"

"A little brandy."

I opened one eye and looked his way. He held up the glass, tantalizing. I rocked my head from side to side. "If I start on that, it'll put me right to sleep."

"That's the object." Francis laughed. "You've had quite a day."

"Days," I said. "Days and days. But we're making progress." I sat up a little straighter and opened my eyes. "Actually, we're not, but it sounds better, especially during an election."

"Alan Perrone was telling me that he wasn't a hundred percent sure about Sosimo Baca, either," Francis said, and I looked at him sharply.

"When did you talk with him?"

"He called here a while ago. He just wanted to chat. During the course of things, we got to talking a little bit about the case."

"He told us earlier that he thought Sosimo got punched in the gut. Or hit, somehow. He doesn't think that anymore?" I felt a rise of irritation. If the coroner had new information, I would have liked to have heard it myself.

"No, he still thinks that. But we were talking about aneurysms in general. You just can't predict." He made a small explosive gesture with the hand that wasn't holding the brandy glass. "Some just pop, no warning."

"But he thinks Sosimo was struck, somehow."

"Yes." He sipped the brandy. "I thought I might swing by the hospital tomorrow and have a chat with Alan. See how things are going with him."

"Things are going fine, as far as I know," I said. "He'd like to see you, especially if there was a little business mixed in with the visit."

Francis flashed a broad smile just as the blocks in the bedroom crashed to the floor again. The tower must have been spectacular, with enough force to send one of the key components skittering out into the hall. Francisco emerged on his hands and knees, grabbed the block, and disappeared.

"Maybe I will," I said to my son, pointing at his brandy glass. "With my house falling down around my ears, maybe I'll need something to help me sleep."

"They wind down eventually," Estelle said.

In a moment, Buddy handed me a large snifter with a dark, fragrant puddle in the bottom. "Thank you," I said. "I keep rediscovering things I'd forgotten I had." I admired the glass. "These haven't been out of the cabinet in God knows how long." I took a sip and remembered why I didn't bother to buy much brandy.

I swirled it a little, and decided to just plunge in.

"Are you toying with the idea of going back into partnership with Perrone?"

Caught by surprise, Francis Guzman paused with his glass halfway to his mouth. *To hell with it*, I thought. I'd been about to add something to soften the question, to ameliorate it, to give him an easy out with a quip. But I didn't. I let it hang there, unadorned and blunt.

Francis Guzman took a sip and set his glass down. "He made an offer in early August that I turned down," he said. He folded his hands in his lap. "They finally got the bond issue straightened out, so the day after tomorrow they'll know if there's going to be the local share of four million bucks for the hospital renovation."

"A good chance," I said. "A bond issue hasn't gone down in flames in quite a while. The schools got two million last year."

"Well, there's always the risk that the voters will say enough is enough." He shrugged. "Anyway, when it looked like that would go through and make it to the ballot, Alan started bugging me a little bit."

"Good for him."

"Well, it was bad timing," Francis said. "And then I had my little accident…"

"Not so little," Estelle said.

He flexed his hand, regarding the scar with detachment. "It's kind of like, one thing happens and that snowballs. Sophia paid us a visit toward the end of summer. You remember my aunt?"

"Indeed I do," I said. Sophia Tournal, the semiretired attorney from Veracruz, was hard to forget.

"She thinks we ought to relocate down there."

"Jesus," I said. "Talk about extremes. From Rochester, Minnesota, to Veracruz, Mexico."

"Lots of advantages," Francis said. "The ocean, the culture." He leaned forward with his elbows on his knees. Estelle had nestled beside him, and looped her arm through his. "We talk about this all the time, Bill. And the one thing that we keep circling back to is the language. Just in the six months we've been up north, I see both Francisco and Carlos using Spanish less and less."

"I don't think they'd ever actually forget," I said.

"Oh, yes. They forget. We can see it. First, they lose the edge, you know what I mean? They lose the depth, the fluency. Next thing you know, all they can say in Spanish is the daily around-the-house stuff." He leaned forward some more and drilled his right index finger into his temple for emphasis. "Or worse yet, the street slang, the Spanglish. They lose the capacity to be truly bilingual. To be able to *think* in either language, at any level."

"So you got an offer from Sophia, too."

He nodded. "Basically a blank check. She plays hardball."

"I bet she does. I can understand how she'd be delighted to have you guys in the neighborhood. I'm a little surprised that you'd consider going from big to bigger, though. If you think Rochester is a busy place, imagine Veracruz. What is it, about five times bigger?"

"About four times," Estelle said, and I felt a little pang of comfort that she'd taken time to check.

"Not to mention about fifty times bigger than Posadas on a busy day," I added. "What did Sophia offer?"

"Like I said, basically a blank check," Francis said. "She owns a building that would make a nice clinic. One block from the beach." He flashed a smile full of perfectly regular white teeth, and I had no trouble imagining the young doctor on a surfboard, beard dripping salt water, arms spread for balance. "More important, there's a real need there."

"I'm sure there is. There's a need anywhere that there are human beings. It just depends what you want."

The smile spread wider. "Counteroffer?"

That took me so by surprise that for a moment the words didn't register. To stall for time, I took a second sip of the powerful brandy. No sounds issued from the bedroom. Either the combatants had all fallen asleep, or the game was getting to the deadly stage where a single hand tremor could send the tower crashing to the floor amid high-pitched cries of *"Idiota! Idiota!"* I set the brandy glass down with care.

"I didn't realize that you would seriously consider coming back to Posadas," I said.

"We haven't ruled out anything yet," Francis said.

"What would be the attraction?" I asked, and even as I spoke the words, I wondered if there was anyone who had lived for any length of time in any of the thousands of tiny communities around the country, or for that matter the millions around the world, who hadn't been asked that question at one time or another.

"It's small," Estelle said quickly, and I sympathized. I couldn't imagine her finely tuned senses bombarded by city life. The edge would dull quickly just to protect itself from sensory overload.

"And quiet," I said.

"There's a need, with more to come," Francis said. "But most important, it's close to home for Mama, and for Estelle. Even for me. And *los niños* like it here." He relaxed back. "And we've got a lot of friends here, you know."

"A few," I said. "One or two."

"Now would be the time to establish something," Francis said. "There's going to be more and more interaction at the border. You're going to get a twenty-four-hour crossing at Regal sooner than later…"

"That's coming in January," I said.

Francis held up his hands. "See? That opens up the culture crossover even more. The medical services in those border towns are pathetic. A good, comprehensive clinic here would be only thirty miles away from Mexico."

"That would please your mother," I said to Estelle.

"But not so much Sophia," she said. "But she understands."

"The new track would help you some, I guess," Buddy commented.

"Sure," Francis agreed, and I looked at my son, puzzled. "What new track?"

"You need to read your own paper." My son laughed. He stretched backward and hefted the bulk of the Sunday El Paso daily from where it had been resting behind the lamp. He shuffled sections until he found the one that passed for regional news, folded it to manageable size, and handed it to me. "Lower left."

I took the paper and shifted my glasses. The article was nothing more than a small squib, boxed in the corner and buried by a feature story about a threatened minnow in the Rio Grande. I would have skipped it even if I'd been reading the paper carefully. As it was, I'd forgotten that the damn thing had even landed on my front doorstep.

Study Given Nod

(Posadas, NM) New Mexico State Gaming officials have approved preliminary study plans for a proposed facility in southern Posadas County that would include horse racing with para-mutuel betting, offtrack linkups, and limited casino-style gambling.

When completed, the facility would join El Paso and Ruidoso as a premier recreation area for enthusiasts from Mexico and the Southwest, promoters say.

"Competition for recreational dollars helps everyone," developer R. Robert Waddell of Newton said.

"I'll be damned," I said, and read the article again.

"You hadn't heard about that?" my son asked.

"No. Then again, I've been living under a rock lately." I read the article a third time. "Well, that slimy son of a bitch," I said.

Buddy pointed at my glass. "You want that stuff?"

"No. Help yourself." I handed him the glass.

"Hate to see it go to waste," he said. "That track thing might explain a little bit why Cliff Larson thinks it's a good time to retire, Dad. It's going to be a busy place if that racetrack starts up."

"It doesn't look like an 'if,'" Estelle said. She handed the paper to her husband, who tossed it back on the table beside Buddy.

"Buddy showed me that article earlier," Francis said. "Who knows? You might be able to lease out some of your back acreage for horse barns. I remember you were thinking about that once upon a time."

"That's just what I need," I scoffed. "And I said I'd give Cliff Larson a couple of weeks to help him out. This thing won't open a gate for two years, even without any snafus. It won't be my problem." I put my feet back up on the table. "Anyway, a few minutes ago, you asked me what my counteroffer was. Leave me half an acre around this house, without touching any of the cottonwoods out back of the kitchen. You can have the rest."

Francis didn't say anything. It wasn't the first time in the ten years I'd known the Guzmans that I'd offered them my property. But circumstances had been different. "You've got room for any sized building you want, a new water line and sewer hookups on Escondido, space for parking, easy access to the interstate frontage road—and you're less than two miles from the hospital."

"Don't forget the helipad," my son added with a laugh. "That's right…and room for a helipad." Another crash came from the bedroom, followed by a screech.

"It's time the kids settled down some," Estelle said, and untangled herself from her husband. "Otherwise we'll never get them to bed. They'll be going all night."

"You think on it," I said to Francis, trying to sound more reasonable and calm than I felt. The suggestion was as much for my benefit as the Guzmans'. I didn't have the expertise of a good car salesman, and had no idea what I could say that would be just the right words to close the deal. I swung my feet down off the low table. "Anyone want some coffee besides me?"

Chapter Forty-two

That night, even the coffee couldn't keep me awake. I closed my bedroom door, content to have a dark corner for retreat. My mind was a jumble of possibilities and anticipations. But instead of lying there in the dark staring at the ceiling, I fell into an exhausting series of cinematic dreams, each more ridiculous and disjointed than the first.

I awoke at one point—at least I assume I awoke...the three-inch-tall red numerals of the clock made sense and told me it was 3:47—after arguing with Francis Guzman about where he should park his Porsche. He had reserved a spot in the new clinic's freshly paved parking lot, but it was hidden from my kitchen window view by one of the large cottonwoods. I tried to explain to him that if he wanted me to keep an eye on his exotic machine while he was busy inside, then he needed to park it where I could see it. He didn't appear to understand.

The next time I awoke, the clock announced 5:12. I stared at it for some time, trying to will my eyes into focus to make sure that either the numbers weren't lying or my tired brain wasn't scrambling the signals. For a die-hard insomniac, a full night's sleep can be a rare thing.

The house was dark, and if the children were up to mischief, there was no way to hear them through the thick adobe walls and the massive wooden doors. I turned my back to the clock, enjoying the silence. I tried to imagine what early morning was like in a busy city like Veracruz. The place probably never went to bed at all. Traffic up and down the coast, or inland to Cordova, would be as constant as the flow on any inner loop in any large city. The Guzmans couldn't sit out on a patio in the evening and expect to be wrapped in such companionable silence.

I knew I was kidding myself, of course. My bedroom was surrounded by two feet of dense adobe. If I got out of bed and went outside to my own patio, what I'd hear would be the traffic going by on the interstate a quarter of a mile away.

I grumped in disgust and rolled back over, swinging my feet to the cool tile floor. I slipped into a robe that Maria always folded over the back of the chair at the foot of the bed. She had high hopes of civilizing me. Normally I wouldn't have bothered, but the house was full of people.

The single light over the kitchen range didn't broadcast light down the hall, so I snapped it on and went about the routine of preparing the coffeemaker. When I was sure it was working hard enough to push water past its calcium-plated innards, I returned to my end of the house, showered, and got dressed. I hadn't worn a uniform since I'd accepted the appointment to the sheriff's post the previous spring, and the green and brown flannel shirt with heavy brown corduroy trousers looked like a good choice for the fitful autumn weather.

By 5:40 that Monday morning, I was standing in the kitchen again, fully dressed, a cup of steaming coffee in hand. The pull of my normal routine was powerful—to slip out the front door and spend the early morning hours cruising the highways watching the county wake up. This time of year, the sun would sneak around the northeast end of Cat Mesa, striking diagonally through the tawny prairie grasses, hunting shadows. Dawn was a few brief moments when everything in the county stood out in sharp relief.

I sighed. I cherished every soul in the house at that moment, and didn't begrudge their visit one iota. But I liked my own company and I liked my own schedule. With six o'clock coming up, I was already several hours behind. Hell, half the county would be up and at 'em before I was even out of the house.

After refilling my cup, I stepped out the back door, closing it gently behind me. The air was crisp and still, the thermometer by the kitchen window touching thirty-eight degrees. I stepped away from the house, away from the light in the kitchen, and looked up through the cottonwood limbs. A billion or so stars looked back, just beginning to fade as dawn worked at the horizon.

I heard the doorknob rustle and turned to see my grandson.

"Hey, there," I said. Tadd was wearing blue jeans, a T-shirt, and no shoes. "There are goat-heads out here, by the way." He stopped short, aware of the awful pain that those little, triangular seed spikes could inflict. I ambled back to the patio and gestured with the cup. "There's coffee."

"Smells good," he said, and stretched. "And five minutes, by the way."

"Until what?"

He grinned. "The boys are awake. I could hear them talking and plotting."

"Ah. Thanks for the warning. Is your dad up?"

"Yeah. He's in the shower."

"How about breakfast out," I said. "The Don Juan opens at six. My treat."

Tadd frowned. "Well, I was gonna do pancakes, if you didn't mind."

I laughed. "Why would I mind, Tadd? I was just trying to save you a little work. You're supposed to be on vacation."

Tadd shoved his hands in his pockets and hunched his shoulders against the bite in the air "Francisco said he didn't think I knew how to make 'em. In his mind, only his mother knows how to do 'em right."

"That's how it goes," I said. "Is there anything you need from the store? They're open by now."

He shook his head. "You didn't have any syrup, but we got some yesterday."

I regarded my grandson with affection. "You're good at this planning business, you know that? I don't know what I'm doing from one minute to the next. Come on inside, before you freeze."

Opening the outside door to the kitchen was the signal. *"Padrino!"* Francisco shouted at the top of his lungs. He rounded the corner of the kitchen island and collided with my legs. I had enough warning that I was able to hold the cup well away, only a minimal amount of coffee hitting the tiles.

"Easy, you little brute," I said. "Where's your brother?"

"C. G. went to wake up Mama and Papa."

"I bet they appreciate that."

"He always does," the little boy said, as if that's just the way the world turned.

"As soon as everyone's up, we're going to make some breakfast. What do you think of that?"

"That will be okay," he said, and transferred his attention to Tadd, who was rummaging in one of my cabinets. "My mama will show you how to make pancakes," he announced. He crouched and peered into the lower cupboard, one hand resting on Tadd's shoulder.

"I know how to make pancakes, Frankie," Tadd said.

"No you don't. And my name's not Frankie. Use that bowl there." The two of them emerged with a large mixing bowl in hand.

"This ought to be something," I muttered. "In case of emergency, the number of my insurance agent is right there, above the phone."

Tadd grinned. "Under control, sir." And I guess it was, since the seven of us sat down promptly at seven around the large kitchen table. Francisco and Carlos looked on wide-eyed as Tadd showed them the proper way to construct a pancake sandwich, a mammoth thing that combined eggs, pancakes, bacon, butter, and syrup in meticulous order. All that was missing was green chile, but I didn't mention that.

I had cut a forkful of pancakes that reduced my stack to exactly half, following Francisco's instructions on how to preserve the symmetry and integrity of the stack, when the telephone rang.

Tadd was up at the moment, returning to the table with the coffeepot.

"Shall I get that?"

"Please," I said, and sighed. I had enjoyed a pretty good run—a decent night's sleep and half a breakfast without interruption. "After Tuesday night, I'm just going to pull the damn phone jack out of the wall," I muttered.

Tadd answered the phone in his usual efficient style, listened for a couple of seconds, and nodded. "Just a moment, sir," he said, and turned to extend the phone toward me. "It's Deputy Wheeler at the Sheriff's Office, Grandpa."

With one hand on the table and the other lightly on top of Francisco Guzman's little head, I rose to my feet and maneuvered my way around to the phone.

"Gastner."

"Sir, we've got a bad situation down south involving some hunters. Undersheriff Torrez has responded, but he asked that you come into the office ASAP."

"I'm on my way. Give me about four minutes."

I hung up and turned to look at the six faces. "Sorry about that," I said.

"Anything we can do?" Buddy asked.

"Nope. Well"—and I stopped in my tracks—"there is. Show Dr. Francis the back acres. I'll be back as soon as I can."

"Regal?" Estelle asked when our eyes met.

"I don't know, sweetheart."

For a heartbeat or two, she looked as if she might want to ride along, but I shook my head. As I left the kitchen, I pointed at Tadd. "Lunch today is my treat," I said, and left before he had time to answer.

Chapter Forty-three

Ernie Wheeler was standing by the dispatcher's console, a cup of coffee in one hand and a pencil in the other. He was in the process of saying something to Deputy Jackie Taber as I walked in—and both of them laughed. Ernie saw me walk through the door and his face immediately went serious.

"Sir," he said, and set the coffee down on a small table behind him, well away from the console and all of its sensitive electronics equipment. "There's a hunting accident of some kind down at the head of Borracho Springs."

"Who's on the way?"

"The undersheriff, Deputies Pasquale and Bishop, an EMT crew, and we just heard that Doug Posey is on his way with another Game and Fish officer. They were running a roadblock over near Animas. Oh, and Linda Real just headed out."

I turned and looked at Taber. "Stick around for a bit, all right?" She nodded.

"Do you know what happened?" I asked.

"All we have is the original call-in, sir. It's a cellular phone call from a Jerry Walsh. Here, I can play it for you."

I waited while he manipulated the autotape. It was a slick gadget, allowing us to record all telephone or radio communications, and play back at any time, with the record feature still engaged. If someone called while we were listening to a previous recording, even that call was locked in and recorded.

"What time did this come in?"

"I logged it at seven-oh-two, sir."

The first thing I heard was Deputy Wheeler announcing himself, followed by a bunch of static and unintelligible voices. Wheeler's voice was loud in comparison.

"Sir, I can't understand you. Please try to speak slowly and distinctly."

"God, I need help," a man's voice then said, and we could hear loud breathing, as if he were running and trying to talk at the same time. "He's pushed her off, and now he's taken a shot at me."

"Where are you, sir?"

"I'm...just a second...I don't think he can see...oh, shit." Sounds of scuffing and scraping followed, with more unintelligible background. "Hello?" the voice said finally.

"Sir, where are you?"

"Listen," the man said, sounding more in control. "This is Jerry Walsh. I need help, before my stepson goes crazy and starts up again. There's no time..."

"Where are you, sir?"

"I...I'm not sure. I think we're in a ways from Borracho Springs. That's just past the camp. About three miles off...no, five or six miles in from Fifty-six, then on Forest Road 122, I think it was."

"Has someone been hurt, sir?"

"My stepdaughter," Walsh said. "She fell. He pushed her right off those rocks...no, wait a minute." More loud breathing and scuffling followed. "That son of a bitch is trying to work his way around so he can get another shot at me." A loud noise in the background could have been a muffled gunshot or a car door slamming. "Son of a bitch."

"Sir..."

"You gotta send help. Oh...Christ...what's this?" For the count of five, the phone was silent. Then the voice whimpered, "Not now. Come on..."

The recording went dead.

"We weren't able to raise anything else, sir," Ernie said. "The caller identification says it's a cellular number issued to Jerry Walsh of Del Rio, Texas." He paused to see if the name registered. It didn't for a moment, and without waiting for me to plod through all my memory files, Wheeler added, "Scott Gutierrez's stepfather."

"There's nothing else on the tape?"

"Nothing, sir. That's all we know."

"Hunting accident, hell," I said. "They're down there shooting at each other, for Christ's sake."

"Yes, sir."

"Jackie, let me have the keys to the Bronco."

She handed them to me, and Wheeler was in the process of saying, "Sir, do you want..." but he was talking to my back.

"Jackie," I said over my shoulder, "the unmarked unit is right here by the door. Make sure it's got a full tank. Then stay put. I don't know if someone's going to be heading back up this way or not, but I sure as hell don't want any door out of the county left open."

The Bronco smelled a little of perfume when I slid in, and I had to kick the seat back so the steering wheel didn't hit me under the chin. It was one of our newest units, and I headed south on Grande with the engine screaming.

"Three oh eight, this is three ten." I rounded the curve onto State 56 just as Torrez came on the air.

"Three ten, three oh eight. Go ahead."

"Three ten is just leaving the village. Ten-twenty."

"About..." Torrez said and hesitated, judicious as ever. "About a mile on Forest One Twenty-two off Fifty-six. Coming up on Borracho Springs. Three oh six is right behind me."

"Did you copy that shots were fired?"

"Ten-four."

"Then be careful."

"Ten-four."

"Three oh six, did you copy?"

Pasquale's voice didn't carry the same note of glacial calm, but he managed to make his cryptic, "Ten-four, three ten," sound as if he were responding to a minor fender bender in a parking lot.

Three miles east of the Broken Spur Saloon, a dirt road intersected State 56 and angled off to the south. The county didn't bother to blade it, since school buses didn't make pickups anywhere along its length. After less than a mile, the road cut into Forest Service property and became Forest Road 122. Once a year in late summer, the U.S. Forest Service drove the grader along it to knock the rocks off and fill the ruts as far as Borracho Springs, one of the premier camping spots for hunters.

The spring hadn't dripped out of the rocks in years, but it was obvious by the litter and trash that water wasn't the drink of choice anyway when a day of hunting was over.

The terrain rose swiftly after the campsite, blending into the rump of the eastern slope of the San Cristóbals—rugged canyons with jagged and crumbling granite that had killed its share of careless hikers and hunters.

Fourteen minutes later, I braked hard for the turnoff onto the dirt road, damn near sliding past it. The Bronco jounced across the cattle guard and fishtailed on the loose gravel.

For the first mile, I didn't need to lift my foot. The road was the width of the Bronco and fairly smooth. I rounded a sweeping corner where the road avoided a deep arroyo and came upon a Posadas County Emergency Services ambulance parked by the fence in front of the Forest Service cattle guard.

An EMT stepped out of the unit and across the road. I opened my window and slid the Bronco to a stop.

"Sir, the undersheriff told us to wait here until he was sure of the situation," she said. I didn't bother to take time trying to remember who she was.

"Outstanding," I said. "Stay put." She nodded and stepped back. "Were you behind Linda Real?"

"Yes, sir. She went on ahead."

"Wonderful," I said. In another mile, the Forest Service road cut its way up out of the bunchgrass and creosote bush into the few scattered live oaks, juniper, and cholla. Why the deer liked the area, only they knew.

Gigantic boulders dotted the rising slope. Many of them were large enough to hide a house—much less an unbalanced young man with a high-powered, scoped rifle. The route wound this way and that and finally, just after the road reared damn near vertically to climb over a massive granite dike, it cut hard to the right, around the flank of mountain that hid Pierce Canyon and Borracho Springs. A bullet-riddled sign announced BORRACHO SPRINGS, 1/2 MILE, with an arrow pointing off to the right.

There was no way to guess where the path went just by guesswork. To the uninitiated, the road would have to levitate straight up, but the original bulldozer driver had been adept at finding the various slices and dices that wound the road up the hill.

"Three ten, three oh eight. You're coming up on us in about a quarter mile."

I had just enough time to consider the brake pedal before I went around a final rock outcropping and saw a collection of county vehicles. As I slid to a stop, I quickly counted heads. Linda Real was sitting in her own Jeep, and the other four marked units were all nosed into the same collection of trash cans that the Forest Service provided, and that no one apparently used.

Off to the side was the white Durango with Texas plates that Scott Gutierrez had been driving when my son and I had crossed his tracks in Regal during the early morning hours on Sunday. To the left of it was one of those small pop-up campers. If it had been used the night before, it wasn't obvious. All the gear was still neatly stowed.

What must have been one giant, spectacular crash eons before, had left a series of boulders that provided a barricade for the springs. At one time, water had even pooled beneath the boulders' knees, but that had dried up sometime in the 1880s. The rocks afforded adequate cover for us, protection from someone who might be up the hill and trigger-happy.

I saw Torrez and Pasquale standing together with New Mexico Department of Game and Fish officer Doug Posey and another young man in civilian clothes. Sergeant Howard Bishop was in the process of plodding toward them from his unit, a rolled-up map in hand. Torrez was talking on the phone.

Jackie Taber's binoculars were on the passenger seat, and I scooped them up as I slid out of the vehicle. The mountainside loomed above us, massive and silent.

"Sir," Torrez said as I approached, "I got Walsh's mobile number, but it's busy. I'm seeing if the cellular operator can patch me through as a third party."

"Any sign of anybody up there?" I scanned the rocks with the binoculars.

"No, sir."

I continued my sweep across the mountainside with the binoculars. "Do we know anything about this situation other than what we heard on the initial phone contact?"

"No, sir." Torrez dropped the phone from his ear and regarded it with impatience. "Nothing."

"And nobody's come out since that call?"

"Not as far as we know."

"We came in from the west," Posey said. His was the slow, measured cadence of West Texas. "By the way, sir, this is Officer Wade Kearns."

I shook hands with the young critter cop, then stood with my hands on my hips, gazing up at the mountainslope. "Well, this is a hell of a deal," I said.

Torrez nodded. "If he was calling from a spot just beyond the springs, then he should be just above these rocks. He should have heard us approach."

"Give him a holler," I said.

Torrez nodded and slipped into his unit. The public address system was spectacularly loud, and all of us stared uphill as if we could see the undersheriff's words bouncing off the rocks.

"Mr. Walsh? James Walsh? This is the Posadas County Sheriff's Department. Can you hear us?"

We waited, straining. There was no breeze to tickle the vegetation, just the sound of our own pulses in our ears.

Torrez repeated the message, waited a minute, then said, "Scott Gutierrez, can you hear me? This is Undersheriff Robert Torrez. Can you hear me?"

The hills remained silent.

Torrez tossed the mike onto the seat of his unit. "We need to go on up," he said.

Chapter Forty-four

I knew that the undersheriff was right…we couldn't sit around
the campfire drinking coffee until someone decided to roll down
off the mountain. Still, we held none of the advantages. The 911
call had involved three people, and every one of them had reason
to be armed with a high-powered rifle that could fire a round
farther than any of us could see on the best of days.

There was every possibility that our movements were being
watched at that moment through a nice, clear telescopic sight.

Sergeant Howard Bishop, who normally spent his days
managing the department's civil caseload, looked up the steep,
rugged canyon and shook his head. "You're shitting me, right?"
he mumbled.

"Channel three," Torrez said. He checked his handheld radio
and slipped it back on his belt. "Tom and Wade, go right. I'll go
left with Doug. Howard, why don't you follow the water course
right up the middle."

Bishop nodded without enthusiasm. If we had to climb all
the way to the summit, where the view of northern Mexico was
terrific on a clear day, that would mean nearly three miles—all
of it steep, all of it treacherous. Not all of it would be uphill.
Like an old blanket dumped on the floor, the terrain was a series
of folded saddlebacks, each one progressively higher and steeper
until it reached the final ridge. It was a matter of hiking up, then
down, then up still higher, then down, then up again.

He patted his ample belly as he regarded the task. No one had thought to bring a cooler of beer, either.

I lagged even farther behind, in no hurry to have my heart explode trying to solve a family dispute that—considering the silence of the mountain—had already been resolved one way or another.

Ten minutes later, I had ambled my way far enough up the hill, a hundred yards or so, that I could look back and see the road that snaked into Borracho Springs from the state highway. It tracked about as straight as a snarled ball of grocer's string.

I found a comfortable boulder and leaned my back against it. By supporting my shoulders, I could hold the binoculars still. I swept the hillside, finding each officer in turn. Tom Pasquale and Wade Kearns were already approaching the crest of the first saddleback.

Off to the left, I saw Robert Torrez striding around a jumble of boulders about the size of a Motel 6. Ahead of him was a promontory of bare granite that would afford a commanding view. Doug Posey had split off, circling the rock motel in the opposite direction.

Howard Bishop plodded a hundred yards ahead of me. He stopped, hands on both hips, considering a route.

"Sergeant Bishop." It was Tom Pasquale's voice on the radio. I took mine off my belt and turned the volume up.

"Go ahead," Howard said. He was breathing hard.

I swung the binoculars to the right and picked up Pasquale. He was standing under a gnarled juniper, his own glasses glued to his eyes. He was looking downhill toward Bishop.

"About fifty yards in front of you at eleven o'clock," Pasquale said. "There's a man sitting under a grove of scrub oak."

I swung to my left, but the terrain blocked my view from below. Bishop hadn't moved.

"How clearly can you see him?" he asked.

"Full view," Pasquale said. I turned to watch him again, and saw that the young deputy had dropped to one knee to steady his hands. In a moment, Wade Kearns appeared beside him.

"So what's he doing?" Bishop said. He hadn't moved and I'm sure didn't relish being a big, slow-moving target.

"Nothing. I can't see his face, though. He's wearing a red vest over blue. Blue jeans. There's a rifle on the ground beside him."

"He doesn't have it in his hands?"

"Negative. His arms are folded."

"Howard, we're headed that way," Torrez said. "Tom, you stay right where you are and keep us posted, all right? If he makes any move at all, you let us know."

"Yes, sir. He's covered." Pasquale was being literal. He had replaced his binoculars with the scoped rifle that had been slung over his shoulder. Kearns had left the position and was working his way east toward Bishop.

"Okay, I see him," Torrez said after a couple of minutes. "Has he changed position? Any movement at all?"

"Negative, sir."

We converged on the man, but as we approached from three directions, he never made a sound.

"Bob," Pasquale said at one point, "he just moved his right hand to his right knee."

The radio clicked twice in response. I stopped, breathing hard, and said, "If he makes a move toward that rifle, you let us know, Thomas."

"Yes, sir. He's not doin' anything at the moment."

"So don't blink," I said.

If he'd been in the mood or condition to enjoy it, James Walsh had a marvelous view to the north, looking out over Posadas County on a crystal-clear November day. But the view just then was the last thing on his mind. I was the last to reach his position. By the time I pulled myself around the last interruption of rocks, Torrez was on the radio to Linda Real. In that rugged country, the little handheld radios were only slightly more efficient than pitching rocks with messages rubber-banded to them.

"Linda, have the EMTs bring their unit forward," he said. "Tell 'em we'll have at least one to transport, but they're not to start up the mountain until we give the all-clear."

I didn't hear her response because I was too busy wheezing air into my own lungs. I reached out a hand to the nearest rough granite face and steadied myself, looking James Walsh in the face. He opened one eye and saw me, and we both knew exactly what was wrong with him.

His arms had been crossed over his chest in an effort to control the crushing pain that must have felt as if his Dodge Durango were parked on his ribs. His bluish lips were frosted with a pink froth. Sweat beaded his ashen forehead. First on his knee, his right hand now dropped down to the ground for support.

"Glad you could make it," he murmured and tried a wan smile. Torrez knelt by his side and checked his pulse at the wrist while he scrutinized the man's face. Walsh kept his eyes closed. "He's up there," he whispered.

"Mr. Walsh, the ambulance is on the way," Torrez said. "Before I let 'em risk coming up the hill, though, I have to know what happened. Where are the others?"

Walsh slowly opened his eyes, having a hard time focusing. Torrez moved slightly so that Walsh could see him without turning his head. "Off to the east," he said, and gagged. Wade Kearns handed Torrez a small water bottle, the kind cyclists carry clipped to the bike's frame. Walsh took a sip and pushed it away.

"How far?" Torrez said.

"About half a mile. Maybe less." I looked to my left, squinting against the sun. The terrain to the east was, if possible, worse than where we stood, the San Cristóbals jumbled into vertical chimneys of granite extrusions that resembled a giant's attempt at building a massive pipe organ.

Down below, the ambulance picked its way up to the springs and stopped.

"The ambulance is here, sir," Linda's voice said.

"Tell 'em to wait," Torrez replied. "Mr. Walsh, what happened? Where's Scott Gutierrez?"

"I...I think that I hit him," Walsh managed. His eyes opened wide with urgency. "I saw him and Connie together. They were across a canyon. At first...it was their voices. They were arguing."

"How far away were you?"

"Across the canyon. Maybe fifty yards. Maybe more. I don't know." He closed his eyes and turned his head away. "They were standing out on a...kind of a spurlike thing." He raised his right hand weakly. "It dropped off. I could hear them talking." He shifted position, opened his mouth, and stuck out his tongue, as if something really foul-tasting was glued to the back of his palette.

"And then they were shouting at each other. And then... he pushed her. Really hard. She fell backward." He closed his eyes again and his face scrinched up, either with the pain of the memory or the pain of what his innards were up to.

"You saw her fall?"

Walsh nodded. "I saw her...fall. She didn't even have time to cry out."

"And it was Scott Gutierrez who pushed her? You're sure?" I asked.

Walsh opened his eyes and looked at me. "Oh, I'm sure."

"I'm on my way up there," Tom Pasquale said.

"Wait a minute," Torrez snapped, and it looked as if he'd jerked an invisible line. Pasquale stopped in his tracks. "What did Gutierrez do after that?"

"I shouted at them." He grimaced. "I mean, what could I do? I shouted and he turned around, raised his rifle, and fired at me. Just like that. He fired at me." Walsh's gaze fastened on the horizon, his breath coming in short, quick little gasps.

"You need to get the EMTs up here," Posey said.

"Not if somebody's out there with a rifle."

"We've got cover here," the officer said. "If they don't get some oxygen up here, he's not going to make it."

Torrez frowned and then nodded. "Route 'em right up the middle so we can keep an eye on 'em," he said. "But hold on a minute." He rested a hand on Walsh's shoulder. "Did you see where Gutierrez went after he shot at you? What direction?" Torrez turned and looked at me. "He's got to be circling around to the vehicles, sir. That's what worries me."

"No," Walsh said. "He shot at me twice. I didn't even imagine that he'd do that. I had nowhere to go. I tried to dig in behind a rock, but he shot at me again. That's when I shot back. Three times, I think." Walsh sagged backward, exhausted from the effort.

"Did you hit him?"

Walsh nodded. "I think so. I'm not sure. But I think...that I did. He fell backward. Maybe he just tripped. But I think that I hit him."

"Jesus," Pasquale muttered.

"Okay," Torrez said, stretching out an arm and pointing east. "I see a sort of jagged pinnacle over there maybe a thousand yards. Is that where they were, Mr. Walsh?"

Walsh nodded faintly without turning his head to look. "I... think so."

"Tom, you and Wade circle around, come in from above," Torrez said. "And be goddamn careful. Me and Doug will go straight across." He stood up and peered down the hill. "Linda," he said into the radio, "who's got the gurney?"

"Judy Parnell and Al Langham, sir."

"Okay. Radio dispatch and tell them that we're going to need another unit out here with four people. Tell 'em it's a real bad climb in rough country. They may want to pick up some folks from Search and Rescue. When they arrive, keep them at the bottom until I give the all-clear. Understood?"

"Yes, sir."

"Go ahead and tell Judy and Al to come up. Al, are you listening?"

"I'm here." Langham's voice was tense.

"You two be careful. I think it'll be all right, but don't be standing around out in the open. Keep in the cover of those rocks there in the old streambed as much as you can."

"We'll do it."

"You've got a coronary to transport." Torrez surveyed James Walsh. "We need you up here ASAP. Make sure you bring some air with you."

"Ten-four."

"Howard and I can give them a hand," I said.

Torrez nodded. "You hang in there," he said to Walsh, and he glanced at the others. "Let's boogie."

In a matter of minutes, the only sign of the four officers was the occasional clatter of their boots on loose rocks. Below us, the two EMTs, casting nervous glances up the side of the mountain, wound their way up toward us. They were within a hundred yards when James Walsh said, "Oh, my gosh."

Chapter Forty-five

Sergeant Howard Bishop moved with surprising speed for such a big man. Even as James Walsh's eyes rolled back in his head and his hands spasmed up against his chest, Bishop leaped forward, grabbed Walsh by the coat at the shoulders, and swung him away from the small tree against which he'd been leaning.

Striking out with his boots, he cleared the largest rocks while I scrabbled an almost clear patch of ground. Of average build weighted down by an expanding beer belly, Walsh was no child. Bishop handled him as if he were, and stretched him out on his back.

With practiced motions, the deputy lifted Walsh's chin, cleared the airway, and took a deep breath. I dropped down on the strickened man's right side. His carotid artery was easy to find, but instead of a nice, steady pulse, the artery jiggled under my touch as the man's heart spasmed into a string of fibrillations.

It'd been a long time since I'd done chest compressions on a human being. The mannequins that the EMTs entrusted to us during the CPR refresher courses didn't complain about mangled technique, and they didn't die. I felt for the xiphoid process at the end of Walsh's sternum, moved up a bit, took a deep breath, and used my considerable weight behind straight arms to do the work.

For what seemed like the rest of the day, I pumped while Bishop breathed, the two of us working in sync while I prayed that the two EMTs would just levitate up the hill. In reality, we worked for no more than three minutes before Al Langham dropped down beside me, puffing like a steam engine.

"Jesus, what a place," he said.

"You ready for me to get out of your way?" I gasped. He listened with the stethoscope and even as he did so, his eyes were as much on me as on Walsh.

"You all right?" he snapped.

I nodded, continuing the compressions. The sun was almost hot, bouncing off the rocks.

"Then just keep doin' what you're doin' for a couple of seconds." Even as he said that, the radios barked.

"Sheriff?" Torrez said. "Call me when you can." He was either a mind reader or was watching us through binoculars.

"He's going to have to wait," I panted.

Langham turned to the large aluminum case that he'd lugged up the hill, and then he and Judy went to work. But James Walsh had chosen a bad spot to have a coronary. In another minute, his heart gave up on the wild, run-a-way rhythm and flat-lined. The EMTs went the whole gamut for the next ten minutes, but eventually we sat back, exhausted. I touched Walsh on the neck, feeling skin that was already going cool to the touch.

"Shit," I said.

"That just about covers it," Al Langham said. "Where's the rest of the hunting party?"

"I wish we knew," I said. I pulled the radio from my belt. "Linda, call dispatch and tell Gayle she'll have to reach us by phone. Then come on up."

"I'm on my way," she said. She was more eager to climb a rugged mountain than I was just to shift position to rest an aching knee.

"And there's no point in you two heading back down yet, Al," I said. "Not until we know what they find up above."

"That's good news," Al said, and lit a cigarette. He'd unpacked a black plastic body bag, and he and Judy stretched it out.

Bishop nodded at Walsh's rifle, still lying where he'd dropped it under the oak scrub. "I want pictures of that before it's touched," I said. "Of this whole area where he was sitting." I straightened up with radio in hand, taking time to suck some air into my lungs.

"We've got some O^2 with us, Sheriff," Langham said, my actions not lost on him.

"No, I don't need oxygen. I'll be fine. Mountain climbing is not my thing." I raised the radio. "Robert, what did you find?"

"Sheriff," he began, but his radio barked a long complaint of static. "Sheriff," he said again, "we've located Connie French."

"Is she alive?"

"Alive but unconscious. My first guess would be multiple fractures and internal injuries. A helicopter would sure make things easier."

"All right. Any sign of her brother?"

"Negative, sir. Tom and Wade are working the area, but nothing yet."

"All right. Linda, did you copy that?"

She didn't respond immediately, but I'd probably caught her between boulders. "Yes, sir," she panted after a minute.

"Let me see if I can reach dispatch by phone. If not, we're going to have to keep you down at the radio."

"Yes, sir."

A dinosaur when it came to most new gadgets, I still viewed the little cellular telephones as nuisances that distracted motorists. This time, the gadget served its purpose. Gayle Torrez's voice came through perfectly.

"Gayle, I've got a list for you," I said. "First of all, we're going to need a helicopter. It's rugged, high country, so you better see if the State Police Jet Ranger is somewhere in this part of the state. While you're at it, find where the Med-Evac plane is. And then see what personnel you can rustle up. We may need to cover a lot of ground before this is over."

"Yes, sir," she said. "Do you want me to put in a call to state police for ground support as well?"

"Hell, yes. Whoever you can find. Jerk the Forest Service out of bed, too."

"Yes, sir."

"I'll get back to you in a little bit." I shifted to the handheld radio. "Robert, is Connie stable?"

"That's negative, sir. She's got an open compound of her right arm, what looks like a broken hip, and a really nasty injury to the back of her head. I would guess a fracture."

I looked at Al Langford. "We'll get some help up there, Robert. Al and Judy are on their way. You think it's going to be all right?"

"Probably," Torrez said. "There's no sign of Gutierrez in the immediate area."

"What the hell is going on here?" Langford said.

"I wish we knew," I said, and lifted the radio again. "Robert, are you and Doug going to need more help with Connie in addition to the EMTs?"

"That's negative, sir. But they need to hustle. She's in deep shock, and her position is head down and really awkward. I don't want to move her until we can stabilize her neck, but we don't have any way to do that."

"Ten-four. They're on their way. And Gayle's looking for the chopper."

James Walsh was bagged and ticketed for his trip down the hill, but he was going to have to wait. The backboard went up the hill with Al and Judy.

"I'll go on over with them and see what Bobby wants to do next," Bishop said.

"Well, wait a minute. I'm going to go back down to the vehicles and sit the radio," I said. "Linda needs to be up here where she can do some good, but somebody needs to be able to communicate." I slipped the phone back in my pocket. "All I need is to have us all up here, and the battery in this thing goes dead. I'll send her up. Show her what we need."

"All right." Bishop didn't sound overly eager, but that was understandable considering his choices. He could either scramble over rocks until he was purple in the face with bruised hands and barked knees, or sit in the sun with a bagged corpse.

"Sir, this is Linda," my radio crackled.

"Go ahead."

"Gayle said that John Rivera was en route from the Forest Service office, and that the chopper is in Las Cruces, sir. Their best ETA is less than an hour."

"Copy that," Torrez's voice interrupted. "Tell 'em to firewall it. Make it a short hour."

"Yes, sir and sir? The Med-Evac plane is in Deming. They'll meet the chopper at Posadas."

"Outstanding," I said, "I'm coming down. We're going to need you up here."

"Affirmative."

I craned my neck and looked uphill, spotting a patch of brown. "Thomas, do you copy?"

"Yes, sir."

"Were you able to find the location where Connie was standing before she fell?"

"That's affirmative, sir."

"How far did she fall?"

"It looks to be about thirty feet, sir. And that's with a strike about halfway down. There's a ledge that she would have hit. We found her rifle and a little day pack partway down."

"Any sign of Scott?"

"That's negative. A little patch of blood, though."

"Is there any way to tell what direction he might have gone?"

"Negative, sir. And the way this terrain is, he could be anywhere."

"Make sure nothing is disturbed. Linda's on her way up. One of you guys needs to be with her."

"Yes, sir."

I holstered the radio. Down below, I could see Linda Real standing beside one of the county units, waiting for me. I glanced at my watch. I had twelve minutes before Judge Lester Hobart would expect me in his chambers. If I hurried, I could be halfway back to the trucks by that time.

"Linda?"

"Yes, sir."

"Have Gayle give Judge Hobart a call. Advise him of the situation, and tell him that Cliff Larson will be attending the hearing this morning instead of me. If that's not going to work, he'll just have to reschedule."

"It's a hell of a good time for somebody to rob a bank," I said to Bishop as I turned to start down the mountain.

Chapter Forty-six

"Use lots of film," I said to Linda as she drew near. I was sitting on a rock a third of the way down—and her rapid progress up the canyon was an acute reminder that this was a young person's game. She paused, cheeks flushed and eyes bright, the massive camera bag slung over her shoulder.

"I want details of the spot where Connie was standing when she fell, and anything else in the area. They say they've found her stuff, so that will be important. And"—I nodded back up the hill where Howard Bishop was waiting patiently—"that spot there, where we found Mr. Walsh."

"Okay," she said. "I'm on my way."

"Take your time," I said. I was talking more to myself than to her, since there was no reason for a healthy, hearty twenty-six-year-old to take her time with something as insignificant as a little mountain and a few boulders. I stood up and started downhill again, rediscovering for the umpteenth time that if I held my head just right, the lower portion of my bifocals blurred the rocks so that I couldn't see a damn thing.

"Sir, we found his rifle," Tom Pasquale's voice was sharp and excited. I had just broken out onto the stretch of relative level ground by the vehicles, and I turned to look back uphill. It wasn't clear who Pasquale was talking to, but that didn't matter.

"Don't touch it," I said.

"No, sir."

"Anything else?"

"No, sir. It looks like the rifle was dropped, sir. He didn't just lean it against a tree. It's jammed down between an old tree stump and some rocks."

"Let Linda get pictures before you touch it or move it," I said. "Are there any scuff marks that might show which direction he went?"

"It's solid rock here, sir. Wait a sec." I did, and then Pasquale added, "It looks like a blood smear, maybe. I don't know for sure."

"Robert, do you copy?"

"Sure do. And, sir, we've done all we can for the girl. Doug is going to stay with her and assist the EMTs when they get here. If you could get someone to light a fire under that helicopter, it'd be appreciated."

We both knew that magic couldn't be counted on, but it never hurt to hope just a little. It was more than eighty miles to Las Cruces as the Jet Ranger flew. If the state police pilot had been strapped in with fingers poised to throw switches when he got the call, that still meant that Connie French had an hour of agony to wait. It would be just as well that she was unconscious.

A steady stream of law enforcement personnel continued to arrive until the campground looked like a goddamned discount store parking lot. We had a string of Search and Rescue civilians, state police, Forest Service, Game and Fish, and Posadas County sheriff's deputies daisy-chained across the lap of the San Cristóbal Mountains, scouring the rocks for some trace of Scott Gutierrez.

The list also included three grim-faced members of the United States Border Patrol. One of them was Taylor Bergmann, and I beckoned him off to one side.

"So, tell me," I said, "do you know anything about this?"

Bergmann's icy blue eyes surveyed the mountainside, and the various specks of color that inched across its face.

"Clueless," he said and shrugged. "We'd only met a few days ago. In fact, the night of the accident when the kid got killed? That was the third time I'd met him."

"You had no knowledge that his sister might be involved in something? Or that he might be?"

"No, sir, I did not."

I turned to see a Suburu station wagon wending its way into the symposium. Frank Dayan leaned forward against the steering wheel, eyes big. I waved him to a spot where he wouldn't block the ambulance.

"What we need to do, Agent Bergmann, is find Scott Gutierrez. He's up there somewhere, he's hurt, and he's the one with all the answers just now. Undersheriff Torrez is right about there," and I pointed past Bergmann's shoulder. "They're right at the base of that thing that looks like a petrified ballistic missile. Check in with him, and he'll tell you what he wants you to do."

Bergmann responded with a curt military nod and set off up the hill at a fast jog trot.

"What the hell's going on?" Dayan asked. He had a camera with a large lens hanging from his neck. The light cotton jacket, polo shirt, and chinos would work just fine, but his penny loafers would serve him for about thirty seconds up on the rocks.

"Frank, we've got a mess. One man is dead from a heart attack." The newspaper publisher pulled a small notebook from his back pocket. "Where's Pam?" I asked, referring to the stout girl who served as his editor.

Dayan looked pained. "Who's the victim?"

"His name is Jerry Walsh. We haven't even had time to check his license for the correct spelling of his name. He suffered a coronary, and died while we were talking to him. The second victim apparently fell a distance of about thirty feet. She's in bad shape, and we've ordered a helicopter from Las Cruces."

"Med-Evac?"

"No. State police. Right now, the problem is getting her down off the mountain. Then we'll transfer to Med-Evac at Posadas."

"How did she fall?"

"I'm not sure yet," I said. Dayan looked up quickly, his pencil poised. "I'm not sure yet," I repeated.

"And that's it?" He scanned the mountainside as if counting all the people.

"Evidently not," I said. "Ah, thank God." The heavy *whup-whup-whup* of the Jet Ranger's blades carried for miles.

"Where is she?" He squinted and leaned forward. "Over by that group of people up there?"

I nodded. "It's going to be a trick."

"I need a picture of that," Dayan said. "Can I go up there?"

I looked down at his shoes. "I've got some gear in the car," he said quickly.

"Have at it, then."

As the helicopter approached, I realized I was hearing two aircraft. Coming in from the west, a Cessna Sky-Master, that strange hybrid beast with one engine pushing and the second pulling, moaned over the top of the mountains and settled into a wide orbit over the area. It was a state police unit as well, and his cautious approach told me that he was already talking to the helicopter pilot.

I turned up the state police radio in the Bronco just loud enough that I could hear the conversation, and then settled against the fender of the unit to watch the show. There wasn't much I could do *except* watch—and wonder where the hell Scott Gutierrez was hiding.

Jerry Walsh had called 911 just about the time I took my first bite of pancakes. Dispatch had logged the call at 7:02. It was hard to choreograph the skirmish, however it had happened, with the little information we had, but while domestic disputes may brew for days, weeks, even years, the actual violence that culminates is initiated and concluded in a matter of seconds.

Why they were hunting in such rugged country in the first place was something any eager hunter could explain...that's where the deer went when hunting pressure increased. James Walsh hadn't had time to fill us in on all the details, but their morning hadn't been one of pursuing the wily eight-point buck. The image that had stuck in his mind was that of his two step-children up above him, their voices raised in argument. And then he'd witnessed Scott Gutierrez push his sister off the rocks.

Part of that story made sense. The two younger hunters would be farther uphill, eager to hunt—maybe eager to argue. Walsh himself might have been feeling the first uneasy symptoms of the cardiac attack that was going to kill him in a few minutes.

Shortly before seven, then, he had witnessed the episode. Perhaps it was 6:55, with the sun just peeking over the eastern horizon. When Connie had pitched over backward to slam into the rocks below, Jerry Walsh had shouted—screamed something—to attract Scott Gutierrez's attention. Realizing that his stepfather had witnessed the deed, Gutierrez without hesitation had thrown his rifle to his shoulder and let fly.

The roar of the heavy hunting rifle must have reverberated across the slope of the mountain like a howitzer, and as the jacketed slug crashed into a rock near Walsh's head, his pulse rate would have leaped exponentially.

I tried to imagine him diving for cover, wild-eyed and gasping for breath. The little grove of stunted oak was all he had. He said he'd pumped a few rounds back up the hill, and through the brown leaves had seen his assailant take a tumble.

That was how I imagined it. And by the time the last rolling echo died away, Walsh was left lying there, wondering what the hell to do as his pulse hammered and skipped. And then he'd remembered his cellular phone, and fumbled it out, punching in 9-1-1. At 7:02 a.m., Ernie Wheeler had picked up the call.

And where was Scott Gutierrez now? Bob Torrez had been first on the scene, sometime around 7:30. That would have given Gutierrez almost half an hour…and with the terrain, it was conceivable that he'd continued to move, unseen, even as the troops gathered down below.

I scanned the side of the San Cristóbals. The ground lay in a series of wrinkles and folds. A strong back-country hiker could cover a lot of country in a half hour, could easily travel far enough to be out of sight. Off to the west, a large ridge folded down toward the state highway, four miles away, hiding where the pavement curved up through the mountain to Regal Pass. To the east, the terrain sloped gradually toward the flat country just north of the little village of Maria right on the border.

My watch said that it was twelve minutes after nine. The young man could have been hiking for more than two hours. He could be damn near to the border if he had headed south—straight up to the peak and over the other side.

There was no reason for Scott Gutierrez to go in any of those directions. What made sense was that he'd come back down the mountain the same way he'd gone up—making sure that James Walsh was no longer a threat. He'd come down to find that he hadn't hit Walsh with a stray shot—the man was stricken with a coronary. Gutierrez would return to the camp and make his decision there. His sister had fallen, his stepfather had had a heart attack. Nicely done.

But that hadn't happened. For one thing, that scenario didn't account for James Walsh still being alive to tell his version of the story. Second, the Durango was still parked down below. Scott hadn't taken it.

Instead, one of those high-powered bullets that had been singing across the canyons had clipped Gutierrez solidly enough that he'd dropped his rifle, left a patch of blood on the rocks—and then staggered off, disoriented and out of control.

I took a deep breath. That's what made sense to me. There would be no way to predict in what direction Scott Gutierrez was moving, if in fact he was still moving at all. He had the answers that I wanted. Now it was a question of whether he bled to death before he was found.

Chapter Forty-seven

The sky was clear and calm, sunshine streaming in at angles that carved dramatic shadows on the rocks. The helicopter extraction of Connie French went like clockwork, once she'd been gently neck-braced and IV'd and splinted and then strapped securely into the lightweight aluminum gurney. Nevertheless, it must have been a hell of a ride, dangling far below the chopper as it swung away from the mountain.

The state police chopper pilot made it look easy, the brightly colored helicopter appearing as if it had been painted in place against a canvas backdrop. Less than two minutes later, the ground team caught the gurney as it hung suspended near the ambulance. The transfer to the ambulance went just as quickly. An occasional dust devil was kicked up by the blades' downwash and spun off to dissipate among the rocks.

In minutes, the chopper angled away, and the ambulance was easing out the dirt road for its rendezvous with the Med-Evac plane waiting at the Posadas Airport with Deputy Taber.

Odds were slim that Connie French would regain consciousness, but if she did, her version of the story would be interesting to hear.

James Walsh's body came down the mountain less dramatically.

All the possibilities and images kept parading through my mind in an endless cycle. "Goddamn useless," I muttered. I hauled out the heavy binoculars again and rested my elbows on the hood of the Bronco with my belly braced against the fender.

With my glasses off, I scrutinized the mountainside, scanning ahead of each member of the search party.

My cell phone chirped to interrupt my concentration. It was the undersheriff.

"Sir," he said, "this doesn't add up."

"No shit," I said. I couldn't have told him *why* it didn't, but I was glad someone else shared my apprehensions. "Where are you?"

"I'm still at the original site. Up on top." I swung the binoculars and saw him standing on the promontory from which Connie French had launched—or been launched. Torrez's use of the phone, rather than the very public radio, wasn't lost on me.

"What have you found?"

"Not much," he said. "But Scott's rifle is a hundred and sixty feet from where Connie fell." He paused, and I could see him moving off in that direction. "That's where the blood is, too."

"Right."

"It would take a few minutes to get over there from here, sir. That's one thing. If it happened the way Walsh says it did, that doesn't add up. Scott pushes Connie, she falls, Walsh yells, Scott fires. Walsh ducks for cover, and returns fire. All in a matter of seconds. These aren't two guys who are hunting each other, jockeying for position. You know what I mean?"

"Yes. More of a reflex thing."

"Exactly. But somehow, Scott gets hit. At least, that's what Walsh says. He manages to travel a hundred and sixty feet before dropping his rifle."

"Or his blood."

"Yes, sir."

"A hundred and sixty feet isn't much, Robert."

"Up here, it is. And it's on an angle, uphill." I saw him stretch out his arm. If he had taken a step or two away from the edge of the rock, I'd have been happier.

"All right. I'll buy that. What makes sense to you?"

"I think that *if* Scott was hit, he was struck near the place where he dropped his rifle, and where there's the trace of blood. Not way over here. But..." He stopped.

"But what?"

"His rifle fell eight or nine feet, down in a jumble of smaller rocks. It wedged up against an old stump."

"That's what Pasquale said."

"And it hadn't been fired, sir."

"What do you mean, it hadn't been fired?" I asked, too frustrated to keep the really stupid questions from slipping out.

"Just that, sir. This rifle hasn't been fired since the last time it was cleaned. There was even a trace of lint just ahead of the front sight, near the crown of the barrel. Probably from the rifle case."

I didn't say anything.

"Sir?"

"I'm here. I'm listening."

"The rifle wasn't fired."

"Was there a round in the chamber?"

"No, sir. Five in the magazine."

"Hold on a minute." I pulled my radio off my belt. "Howard, do you copy?"

"Yes, sir." Bishop sounded bored.

"Did Linda take all the photos of Walsh's rifle that she needed?"

"I believe so."

Linda Real's voice broke in. "Sir, I think I covered it from every angle."

"Good. Howard, have you bagged it up yet?"

I heard him chuckling as he pressed the transmit button. "That's negative, sir. I didn't bring any evidence bags up here with me."

"I need to know if it's been fired."

"Walsh said that he did, sir."

"I know he *said* that he did. Check for me."

"Just a minute."

I could picture the slow, methodical Bishop trying to figure out how to handle the rifle without ruining whatever prints might be on it. In a moment, the radio crackled to life. "Sir, that's affirmative."

"Round in the chamber?"

"Affirmative. One in the chamber, one in the magazine. Safety is off."

"Linda, did you take photos that would show the position of that safety?"

"Yes, sir."

"Good. Howard, put the safety on. Otherwise, leave it alone. I'll get someone to run up a large evidence bag. Don't let anyone else near the thing."

"Yes, sir."

"So," I said into the phone.

"I heard," Torrez replied. "Walsh fired, Gutierrez didn't."

"Unless he had another weapon with him. He'd have a handgun, I'm sure."

"Not a weapon of choice for up here, sir," Torrez said.

"So why would Walsh lie?"

Torres hesitated. "I don't know. Maybe he saw Scott push Connie, and took a shot at him right then, without giving Scott time to react. That's possible. And then he got to thinking… his actions would seem more justified if Scott had fired first."

"Think on it," I said. "I told Howard I'm sending up some evidence bags. Be really careful how you treat that rifle."

"Oh, yeah," Torrez replied. "I'll be careful."

A kid barely old enough to vote and wearing a Forest Service uniform shirt had picked his way down the hill and was headed toward his pickup, whether to find a smoke, or toilet paper, or just water, I didn't know or care. I sent him back up the mountain with a supply of large black plastic evidence bags and tags, and then called Gayle Torrez.

"Gayle, call the medical center in Las Cruces for me. Tell Jackie Taber that I need to know the extent and nature of Connie French's injuries the instant that information is available."

"Yes, sir. I just got off the phone with them, and the Med-Evac's ETA is about ten minutes."

"All right. Make sure Jackie understands the urgency of this."

"Yes, sir. You want extent and nature of injuries."

"That's it."

"Any word on Scott Gutierrez yet?"

"Nothing. He's evaporated. We've got fifty people on this mountainside, in broad daylight, and an aircraft circling overhead. We can't find him. Not a damn trace."

"Estelle stopped by for a few minutes a little bit ago. She asked if there was anything that she could do."

"I wish," I said. "There are certainly other places I'd rather be, I can tell you that. Have Jackie get right back to me the second she knows something."

I tossed the phone on the hood of the Bronco and was reaching for the binoculars when I heard the shout, far over to the west. It was too far to recognize the voice or the words, but in an instant my radio brought confirmation.

"Sheriff, we've got him."

Chapter Forty-eight

What kept Scott Gutierrez staggering west might have been as simple as the warmth of the sun on his back and the gentle downslope of the terrain as one fold blended into another. He might even have imagined that he was making his way downhill toward Borracho Springs.

More likely, he'd just *moved*. His instincts drove him to put distance between himself and the man with the rifle down below, and that's what he had done—for 890 yards.

Deputy Thomas Pasquale found Gutierrez curled up in a tight ball, deep in a thicket of mountain mahogany. Each stem was about the diameter of a finger, tough and resilient. The young man had wedged his way into the thicket by feel, laid his head on his arm, and passed out. The brush provided a canopy, shielding him from view from the air.

I watched the rescue effort through binoculars, and quickly picked up Undersheriff Robert Torrez. He stood perfectly still just west of where the rifle had been found, and examined the route across to where Pasquale waved his arms. The EMTs had already started clambering their way toward the victim, moving as quickly as the rugged terrain would allow.

Torrez picked his way across, stopping frequently to readjust his route and peer at the ground. After a minute, I realized what he was doing. Ever the hunter, he was following what little sign Gutierrez had left behind—telltale spatters of blood that to a less trained eye simply blended with the earth or the lichen on the rock faces. Now that Gutierrez had been found, and emergency help was on the way, Torrez took his time, reconstructing the route.

The seventeen minutes that it took Al Langford and Judy Parnell to reach Scott Gutierrez after Tom Pasquale's first triumphant shout seemed hours.

People converged on the spot from the east and from below, including another backboard raced up the mountain from the waiting ambulance. I waited patiently, watching. Eventually, my telephone chirped and I snatched it up eagerly.

"Yes?"

"Sir," Robert Torrez said, "we're bringing him down now. Al says he's stable. He's sedated pretty good."

"He'll have to be, for that trip," I said. "Whoever is carrying that gurney better be surefooted."

"They're doin' all right," Torrez said.

"How is he?"

"I can't tell, sir. It looks to me like the bullet came at him from the left, but it's hard to tell. Took a chunk out of the bridge of his nose, and then did a tap dance over his right eye. Kind of a grazing shot. A quarter inch more and it would have blown his face off."

I winced. "Just the one injury?"

"As near as I can tell, sir. That one's sure enough, though. He wouldn't have had a clue about where he was going."

"He wasn't conscious at all when Pasquale found him?"

"No, sir."

"Well, be careful. Bring him down easy, Roberto."

"You betcha."

◇◇◇

The last vehicle drove out of Borracho Springs at 11:05 that morning. Shortly before that, two of Scott Gutierrez's supervising officers from the U.S. Border Patrol had arrived. They didn't stay long.

They would have left a lot happier if I could have told them exactly what had happened, and been able to explain Gutierrez's role in the whole affair. As it was, they lingered just long enough to satisfy themselves that it had been a family quarrel of some kind, and to receive a guarantee from me that as soon as we had details, they'd be among the first to know. Driving into Posadas and waiting at the hospital didn't appear to be on their agenda, but that was their business.

Of more interest to me were events in Las Cruces. I had heard no word from Deputy Taber, and the deafening silence made me nervous.

Shortly after eleven-forty, I closed the door of my office for a few moments of peace and quiet, ignoring the lengthy list of return calls that Gayle Torrez had kindly organized for me. I had looked at all the notes, and then at her. "But Taber hasn't checked in yet?"

"No word," Gayle said. "I talked to her a few minutes ago, and Connie was still in surgery."

"You have the number handy?"

"Sure."

With that in hand, I retreated to my office. The young man who answered the phone in Las Cruces sounded polite and efficient, and it took him less than a minute to find Jackie Taber.

"Sir, Connie is still in surgery," the deputy said. "The head injury is not real good news, I guess."

"Nothing else so far?"

"No, sir. She's been in surgery for almost three hours, and they haven't looked up once."

"If you get a chance, try to pry one of 'em loose long enough for a progress report. They found Scott, by the way. He'll probably be okay. One bullet hit him a grazing shot across the face. He'd wandered about a half mile west of where we found Connie."

"Was he able to tell you anything?"

"Not yet. So you stick close at that end, and we'll see what we can find out up here."

"Yes, sir."

I hung up and leaned back in the chair, letting the old, soft leather upholstery cushion my sore joints. I was allowed no more than five seconds before the phone buzzed. I groped for it without opening my eyes. "Yes?"

"Sir," Gayle said, "your grandson is on the phone. He wanted me to make sure I wasn't interrupting anything before I put him through."

I looked at my watch. I'd made some vague promise about lunch, but I couldn't remember what it was. In any case, I had eight minutes to make up my mind.

"Put him on," I said.

The phone clicked. "This is Tadd, Grandpa."

"How was your morning?" I asked.

"Neato," the kid said. "We messed around all morning, and I kinda lost track of time. I wanted to check with you about lunch, but I asked Mrs. Torrez not to bother you if you were awful busy."

"I'm not." I spread out the callback notes, scanning the names. They could all wait. "Are you guys ready to eat, then? Are the Guzmans there?"

"Sure thing. Well, Dr. Guzman isn't. He's over at the hospital, I think. I called to ask you if you wanted me to put something on the grill?"

I gathered the notes and tossed them to one side. "Save it for supper, Tadd. I'd hate to see you rush a masterpiece. Let's grab a burrito at the Don Juan."

Tadd laughed. He muffled the phone, but I heard his bellow anyway. "You owe me five bucks!" A voice in the background mumbled something that I couldn't hear.

"Who was that?"

"My dad," Tadd said. "I made a bet with him that you'd suggest that."

"It's terrible to be so predictable," I said. "I tell you what. There are a number of odds and ends hanging right now. How about if you guys just meet me there rather than me driving over to the house? I'm heading out the door right now."

"You got it, Grandpa."

As I left the office, Gayle's phone was ringing, and I paused as she answered it. "If it's Jackie Taber, I'll take it," I said.

She nodded, listened for a few seconds, and shook her head, then she put her hand over the receiver. "It's Leona Spears," she mouthed, and her eyes twinkled as I raised the corner of my lip.

"Tell her highness that it's all a right-wing conspiracy, and the election has been called off," I said over my shoulder.

Chapter Forty-nine

I hadn't been completely accurate, of course, when I told my grandson that there were just some "odds and ends" to wrap up. What we had was one man dead of a coronary, a young girl still under the surgeon's knife after being pushed from a cliff, and her brother with his head nearly split open by a high-caliber rifle bullet. That was an impressive list, but one crucial element was missing: the why.

Until either Connie French or Scott Gutierrez could put together a coherent sentence, we were stymied. I had discarded James Walsh's version. The ballistic evidence said that he was a liar, dying words or no.

As a first step, Robert Torrez was concentrating on Walsh's background. The man had lied—even when he knew that he was having a heart attack. Of course, he didn't know just that moment that he was about to die, but it takes some cold calculation to bring off tall tales when the old ticker is bouncing in your chest.

Walsh had said that Scott Gutierrez fired first, after pushing Connie off the rocks. The young man hadn't fired first. In fact, he hadn't fired a shot all morning.

The hunting rifles didn't lie: Walsh's .270 Winchester had been fired at least three times: Sergeant Bishop had found two empty casings on the ground about twenty feet east of where we'd found Walsh, along with the casing still in the chamber. Connie French's little .243 had gone airborne over the rocks with her. The cheap scope was smashed to a million pieces, the stock was busted, and the chamber was empty.

That left Scott's Remington .308—clean as a whistle, with a full magazine.

Torrez turned his attention to Del Rio, Texas—an interesting little resort city of thirty thousand people at the south end of Amistad National Recreation Area. Across the International Amistad Reservoir lay the Mexican town of Ciudad Acuña—and another thirty-eight thousand people. An interesting place, with lots of opportunity.

By the time I had walked out of the Public Safety Building heading for lunch, the undersheriff had already been on the phone with Lieutenant Leo Nuñez of the Del Rio P.D.

I pulled to a stop for the red light at Grande and Bustos just in time to see the Guzmans' rental van gliding northbound on Bustos. They caught the light, and I tailed them west on Bustos to the Don Juan.

Francisco and Carlos were wound up like two little springs. "They should have been running up and down the mountain this morning," I said to Estelle. As I opened the restaurant door for them, I tapped the sign taped to the glass.

"They're closed tomorrow?" Estelle asked. "How's that possible?"

"I don't know," I replied. "The one day that we need a place to celebrate, they close. Tadd's going to have to dream up something."

"No problem, Grandpa," Tadd said. He had a firm grip on two little hands as he herded the kids inside.

We'd hit the place at high noon, a busy time for the Don Juan on any day, but especially on a Monday with the Lions Club meeting in the Conquistador Room. We found a quiet spot on the other side of the restaurant where we could pull two tables together.

"Is Francis going to make it?" I asked.

Estelle shook her head. "He's playing golf with Alan Perrone...at least he was supposed to."

"Then he's going to be a while. I imagine Perrone's got his hands full." In between mock skirmishes with Francisco to keep him out of my chips, I recapped the morning for Estelle. "And I didn't know that your husband played golf," I added.

"All doctors play golf," Buddy said. "It's a rule. If you look at their license to practice, it's got a little space down at the bottom to record their current handicap."

"The Posadas Country Club might change all that. And if Francis eats out there, you may never see him again."

"They actually built that course? The one over by the high school?"

"They actually built it, rattlesnakes, antelope, wind and all. Nine holes. The only real difficulty has been training the prairie dogs to dig the pin holes straight down. They're a little sloppy."

I looked across at Estelle. "Did you guys get a chance to look at the back property this morning?"

"We built a fort in the leaves," Francisco announced around taco chip crumbs before his mother had a chance to answer.

"A leaf fort? How does that work?" I asked.

"It's a long story, Grandpa," Tadd said with a sad shake of his head.

"Well, you cheated," Francisco said, and butted my grandson's arm with his head. His younger brother nodded in sober agreement.

"Francis, Bill, and I walked the whole thing," Estelle said. "It looks like they're planning to build something down on Escondido a ways where they extended the water line."

I nodded. "I've heard fifteen different stories about that, everything from another trailer court to a new truck stop. Whatever it is, I don't think it would affect my property much, except by increasing the traffic around the back side. So what did you guys think?"

I reached out with a chip, loaded it with salsa, and was navigating it to my mouth when I saw one of the county cars pull into the parking lot. Deputy Tom Pasquale got out and strode purposefully toward the Don Juan's front door.

"They found me," I said. "Pasquale isn't coming here for lunch." I poked Francisco in the ribs. "Excuse me, *niño*. I need to slide past you." I managed to navigate myself away from the crowded tables without disaster, and met the deputy out in the foyer.

"Sir, Jackie Taber just called from Cruces. They think that Connie French is going to make it."

"That's good news." I looked at him expectantly, since the eager expression on his face told me that he hadn't driven to the restaurant just to tell me that.

"And there was something else, too," he said. "She's got a bad skull fracture, a smashed lower right arm, a broken left shoulder, a fractured pelvis, and a broken knee. The left knee." He ticked the list off on his fingers as he made his way down the injured girl's anatomy.

I grimaced. "That's quite a 'something else,' Thomas. There must be a bone or two that she didn't break. No spinal damage?"

"They think not. But she had a bullet wound in her right calf."

"A bullet wound?"

"That's what they said. Not too serious, like maybe from a ricochet. They removed a pretty good chunk of brass jacket that was wedged up against the bone."

"Enough there for a rifling match?"

"Bob says that it's worth a try. In the meantime, me and Linda and a couple of the others are going back down to look for the bullet strike."

"Walsh is the only one who fired," I said. "So who was he shooting at? You can't intentionally hit someone with a ricochet. He was either aiming at Connie and missed, or he was aiming at Scott—and missed." I shook my head, perplexed. "Keep me posted, all right?"

He nodded and turned toward the door, eager to be on the road. I turned to go back inside. I'd asked Estelle a question. I was eager to hear an answer.

Chapter Fifty

Hell, I knew that Posadas was a meager, dusty little place, a dinky watering hole in perhaps the most bleak part of New Mexico. I knew that where Dr. Francis Guzman and his family ultimately decided to settle was none of my affair. And depending on the current definition of "opportunities," there were probably more of them in a myriad of other places.

In all fairness, Estelle Guzman's answer was the best that I could hope for. "We've got so much to think about," she said.

"Yes, you do," I said, and let the conversation drift to other topics. The six of us ate enough for twelve, a leisurely, sloppy grub fest that ended with sopaipillas squirting honey in all the wrong places.

As I was starting my third cup of coffee, Fernando Aragon sauntered around the small island where the coffee machines lurked. He picked up one of the decanters and brought it to our table. I covered my cup with my hand but quickly moved it when he showed every intention of pouring anyway.

"How was everything?" he said.

"Awful, as usual," I replied. "The chile was green, the sopaipillas were full of hot air...all that sort of thing."

"Good, good," he said, and favored the two wide-eyed children with a vast, perfectly capped grin. "Those kids are sure growing up, eh?"

"Kids do that," I said. "And by the way, what's with the sign on the door? How can you do that to me?" I nudged my empty plate.

"What's life without a green chile burrito, especially tomorrow?"

"How's it feel, eh?" Fernando said. "You finally going to do it?"

"I have no choice." I grinned. "And it's a good time, Fernando. Robert will do a fine job."

"I'm sure he will. So what are you going to do with yourself? All this time on your hands."

"I don't need to worry about that until tomorrow," I said.

Fernando grinned. "I hear that you're going to take over Cliff Larson's job."

"This is indeed a small town," I said. "I'm going to help Cliff out for a few weeks. That's all. It's a favor."

He regarded me through narrowed eyes, and then swung his gaze to Estelle. "What do you think about this guy?"

"*El resolvera su problema aunque le lleve toda la noche,*" she said.

Fernando Aragon laughed and clapped me on the shoulder. "This guy," he said, and if possible his accent thickened for the occasion. "At six o'clock in the morning, he's at the door, wanting dinner."

"That's because you don't open at five," I said. "When ordinary people eat."

"That's okay," Fernando said. "When you stop coming in, that's when we sell the place. To hell with it." He smiled widely again. "People today don't appreciate what it takes." To Estelle he said, "*El esta en ayunas de mañana?*"

She shrugged and said in English, "I think so."

"You think so what?" I asked.

"We're painting the kitchen ceiling tomorrow," Fernando said. "That's our excuse for closing. I told her that if you're starving to death, drop by and knock on the back door. I'll fix you something."

"Paint chips and all," I said. "Thanks, anyway. I can survive a day."

He patted me on the shoulder again, and nodded around the table at each one of us in turn. "Take your time. I have to go back in the kitchen and mix paint, but if there's anything else you want, just ask Janalynn." He held up a hand in salute. "*Hasta…hasta cuando.*"

"Thanks, Fernando. Give my regards to your lovely wife." I watched him saunter back to the kitchen, sliding the coffee decanter back in place with one smooth, practiced motion without breaking stride.

I turned to Tadd. "So tell me what they *actually* said, Tadd."

He grinned at Estelle, who raised one eyebrow in that characteristic expression that said she was waiting for someone to dig a deep enough hole.

"She said that you'd figure out what you wanted to do if it took you all night."

"Uh-huh. And he said?"

"Uh…that he'd see us whenever." He shrugged. "*Hasta cuando* means sort of like that. See you whenever."

"I see." I studied him through my bifocals for a minute. "You're pretty good in that language, son."

"Yes, he is," Estelle said, and took a deep breath. "Well… they probably want some peace and quiet around here. What's on your docket for the rest of the afternoon?"

"I need to run by the hospital for a few minutes," I said. "When Scott Gutierrez comes out of it, I want to make sure he knows that he's not going to have to wade through this mess all by himself."

"If you see Francis, would you tell him that we were going to go over to the Twelfth Street house for a bit?" She looked at Buddy. "Do you want to come with us?"

"Tadd might," my son said. "I've got a few things I need to do. If you'd drop me at the house, that would be fine."

"Let's play it by ear for dinner, then," I said.

"I was thinking of green-chile cheeseburgers on the grill," Tadd said instantly, and Francisco's eyes bugged with delight.

"Arg," I said. "More food."

Janalynn Torrez waited by the front register, and I expected to see her start digging for the ticket. "It's on the house today," she said with a smile.

"You're kidding," I said.

"We hope you enjoyed it."

"Well, of course we enjoyed it," I said, flustered. "Thank you very much." I slipped a twenty out of my wallet and put it in her hand. "That's for putting up with all the mess, Jana."

She blushed. "Thank you, sir."

"Hasta cuando," I said.

Tadd was holding the door for me. "That's pretty good, Grandpa."

"It's just that natural Gastner ear for language," I said. Estelle heard me, but made no comment.

⟨⟩⟨⟩⟨⟩

I exchanged the aromas of the Don Juan for the sterile bouquet of disinfectant at Posadas General Hospital, where instead of black velvet renditions of the conquistadors, the artwork consisted of light green walls and the reflections in the polished floor tile of the Danish-style furniture.

Anne Murchison Shalley looked up from the nurse's station, saw me, and beckoned. I'd known Anne since she was in grade school. Her mother, Helen Murchison, had been head nurse for years at Posadas General, and knew my insides better than I did. While I had often described Helen as an old battle-ax, Anne was a delight for the eye.

"Sir, Dr. Perrone said that if you came in, I should tell you that Scott Gutierrez would be able to speak with you for just a few minutes."

"Just a few is all it will take," I said.

"He's going to be in a lot of pain," she added, and her sympathy was genuine.

"Where's he at?"

"Intensive care recovery," she said. "You can't miss it."

She knew how often I'd been there myself. I turned the corner at Radiology and saw Sergeant Howard Bishop down the hall, leaning against the wall with one hand, deep in concentration. He looked up as I approached.

"All the docs just left a few minutes ago," he said. "Is Francis Guzman working back here again? I saw him with Perrone."

I shook my head. "No. Golfing buddies. They're just visiting. They're staying over at the house."

"Estelle, too?"

"Yep. Her too." I thought Bishop's expression was a touch wistful. "Is he conscious yet?" The facility had glass partitions, but the sliding curtain had been drawn around Gutierrez's bed.

"I heard one of the nurses talking to him a bit ago, so I guess he is. I haven't been in. Bobby said to post a watch in the hall, so here I am."

"Long day, huh." I didn't wait for his reply, but stepped past and pushed the door open. I didn't recognize the nurse at the ICU desk, but she apparently knew who I was. She nodded and remained seated, caught up in paperwork.

I stepped around the curtain and looked at Scott Gutierrez. His head was bandaged down to the tip of his nose, and he had enough lines and hoses plugged into his system to support a fair-sized village.

He raised his right hand a few inches off the sheet, as if he could sense who had invaded his domain by the change in air pressure.

"Scott, it's Bill Gastner," I said.

"Hi," he replied.

"Can you talk with me for a few minutes?"

After shifting a tiny bit on the bed as if winding up for the effort to speak, he said, "Yes." He sounded almost normal, like a person with plugged sinuses. He was lucky he still had sinuses. He reached up and touched the bandages lightly. "This is not going to be good, is it?" He spoke slowly, trying his best to make each word come out right with a minimum of movement.

"You're going to be fine," I said, unable to think of anything more creative than the standard line. I didn't know—and Scott probably didn't, either—if his vision had been saved or not. "Connie is doing all right, too, Scott. She was banged up pretty badly, but she's going to be all right."

"I couldn't catch her," Gutierrez said. "I remember that. I couldn't catch her." He took a deep breath, very slowly. "I remember the look on her face."

"She's going to be fine."

"Walsh?" It wasn't "Dad," or "my stepfather," or anything else that might be tinged with affection.

"He's dead, Scott."

He lifted his hand again, then let it drop on his stomach. "How?"

"Heart attack. We found him just a few feet from where the shots were fired."

"He shot twice," Gutierrez said. "Really fast. I heard the snap of the first one. Right over my head."

"Then what happened?"

"Before we could move, he shot a second time. The bullet hit the rock." He stopped and seemed to be marking time, his index finger tapping the sheets. "I thought that it hit Connie. She kinda jumped. She lost her balance. I couldn't grab her."

"She's going to be all right, Scott."

"She went right over backward."

"He shot again, though. Do you remember that?"

"Oh, yeah. I remember that." He fell silent again and I watched as he lifted his right hand as if in slow-motion. He carefully ran his finger under the edge of the bandage on his right cheekbone. "Uh," he said and took another deep breath.

"Do you want me to ask the nurse to get you something?"

"No." He lowered his hand to the automatic morphine dispenser's plunger that was clipped to the bed rail. He didn't press the button. "I could see…see that he was trying to line up again, and I dove off to one side."

"Did you try to shoot back?"

"No." His left hand lifted an inch off the sheets. "I didn't even think about that. Can you believe it? I didn't even remember I had a damn rifle in my hands. And then it felt like somebody hit me in the nose with a baseball bat. I couldn't see, I didn't know what the hell..." He pulled his right hand away from the morphine dispenser.

"Do you remember dropping your rifle?"

"No. I don't remember that. I don't remember much else, except I couldn't see where to go."

I reached out and touched the back of his hand, just a couple of fingers, just enough to make contact. "Why did he do it, Scott?"

"Because Connie was going to quit."

"Quit what?"

"She was making fake licenses for him."

"Driver's licenses, you mean?"

"Yes. Like the one Matt Baca had."

"He told you this?"

"No. Connie did. She told me last week what she'd done. That she'd run one once in a while for Walsh. He paid her eight hundred bucks. He lines 'em up down south, in Acuña. They come up here when she's working by herself. She'd help 'em with the test, whatever they needed."

"Fake addresses?"

"Yes. And especially commercial tickets. You'd be surprised..." He stopped suddenly. His right hand moved halfway to his face and stopped. "Jesus," he breathed. "You'd be surprised how many truckers down in South Texas live in Posadas, New Mexico." He made a little snuffling sound as if the laugh had been stopped short, followed by a groan of pain.

"I don't understand about Matt."

"She made him a fake license."

"For eight hundred bucks? You're kidding."

"No. No money. She was hot to trot as far as he was concerned. For a little while, anyway. Then she got nervous, and realized that Matt was going to really screw things up if he wasn't careful."

"And she told you this when?"

"Last week. She was scared, sir. Walsh had a good thing going. An easy place to get the right paperwork."

"Why did he do it?"

"Money for one thing. For another, it was easier to sell 'em a car if they're citizens. A lot of 'em wanted it registered in this country."

"Banks fall for that?"

"No. It was used cars and trucks. He carried the papers. Right at the dealership."

"So Connie panicked and told you about all of this?"

"Right. I thought maybe I could just nose around, you know, and straighten things out. I guess I thought wrong."

I felt a presence behind me and heard the curtain. I turned to see the nurse hovering. "Give us just a few more minutes, all right?" She retreated after closing the curtain. Scott took another deep, careful breath. "Walsh was coming up here to go hunting. He's done that for a long time. This time, though, he probably figured to calm Connie down. Tell her she had nothing to worry about. And then the thing with Matt happened. She flipped out when she heard about it. And then Matt's father on top of it."

"Were you involved in that?"

"Yes. I saw Sosimo walkin' on the road. I thought maybe I could go in and get the license back. I didn't count on old...old Sosimo having a thing about the U.S. Border Patrol."

"You mean he didn't let you in?"

"Oh, he accepted the ride, and he let me in the house. I had to promise to drive him into Posadas so he could get his old truck. But when I asked him if I could look for Matt's license, he went ballistic. We struggled a little, but it was mostly me just trying to calm him down. He lost his balance and broke the window in the back door, and then he popped. That was it."

"Why didn't you tell us this?"

"I thought there might still be a chance to find that license. If I had that, then there was no evidence for you guys against Connie. But you told me you'd found it, so..." His right hand moved slightly in lieu of a shrug. "But she heard what had happened down in Regal, and went off the deep end."

"With all that, you decided to go hunting anyway."

"Sir, it's the truth. We figured that we'd get out of town, just the three of us, and work it out. We'd just explain to Walsh. We didn't have to involve any of the authorities. I told Connie…" He stopped and raised his hand to his head. "Jesus, this hurts," he whispered. "I told Connie that I'd just lay the cards out on the table. The license deal was over. He'd stop pushing Connie about it, and I wouldn't go to the authorities."

"He didn't go for that?"

"He would have. It was Connie who couldn't handle Matt's death, and then the old man's dying on top of that. It's just something that she couldn't handle. It was obvious to me. It would have been obvious to Walsh."

"So he thought a hunting accident was going to work?"

"Stupider things have been done, sir. He must have seen the two of us arguing, and took a chance. I think he wanted to hit her, but it worked out even better than he planned. He knew he didn't hit Connie, so now he could say that she fell. He'd nail me, and that's it. Self-defense."

"But you never fired."

"No. He could have climbed up to where we were, and fired my rifle a couple of times. He could have done that."

"Had his heart been in it," I said. I stood silently for a while, looking down at the young man. "Scott," I said finally, "somebody's going to ask this. It might as well be me." The silence lingered for another few seconds.

"Walsh said that he saw you push Connie off the rocks. That he heard you two arguing. He saw you push her, and he then yelled at you. We know you didn't fire your rifle. But what about Walsh's claim that you pushed your sister?"

Scott Gutierrez remained silent.

"How would you answer that, Scott? If Dan Schroeder puts those questions to you?"

He lifted his right hand, making a pistol out of his thumb and index finger. "I didn't push my sister off that rock, sir. If everyone thinks I did, then I wish this had been a couple of inches farther back." He put his index finger to his skull just above the ear and dropped his thumb. When I didn't respond immediately, Gutierrez stretched out his right hand toward me. I took it, and his grip was surprisingly strong.

"You haven't talked to Connie yet, have you?"

"No. I haven't. She's in Las Cruces. It's going to be a while."

"Oh, Christ," he murmured.

I gave his hand another squeeze. "You hang in there, Scott. Give us a chance to work this thing through."

"I guess I don't have much choice, do I?"

Chapter Fifty-one

"Do you believe him?" Undersheriff Robert Torrez waited by my front doorstep while I thought through my answer. There were too many angles still to be explored, but my intuition had made up its mind.

I'd had all afternoon and evening to think about Scott Gutierrez, his sister Connie French, and their stepfather, James Walsh. I knew what my gut feelings were, but I didn't want to bulldoze over the soon-to-be-sheriff's investigation. He had his men placed where he wanted them, and he'd proceed with his investigation at his own speed.

He didn't need me barking at his heels for the next few hours. If he was good enough to lead the charge up through the rocks without knowing if a high-powered rifle was trained his way, then he could manage the wrap-up, too.

In fact, all Robert Torrez really needed from me was to make sure that I voted the next day.

The undersheriff had driven to my home on Guadalupe late that evening. I hadn't crossed paths with him all Monday afternoon. I didn't want to leave messages for him at dispatch, interrupting his day just so that I could tell him, "Hey, I think this," or "Listen, I think that."

Even if I were completely wrong, even if I were hoodwinked by sincere-sounding answers from behind the convenient mask of Scott Gutierrez's bandages, neither he nor his sister were going anywhere. Deputy Jackie Taber was keeping Connie French company in Las Cruces, along with assistance from the Las Cruces Police Department. At four that afternoon, Deputy Tony Abeyta had relieved Howard Bishop outside the Posadas ICU. It had been at that point that I stopped hovering and went home.

I held the door open and gestured for the undersheriff to step inside. "Come on in, Roberto." He did so, and as he stepped past me, I said, "And for the record, yes, I do. I believe him. I think he was genuinely concerned for her welfare." I closed the door. "The last thing he'd do is push her backward off some rocks. It would serve no purpose."

Torrez took off his Stetson and rolled the brim in his hands, frowning at it. "Unless she was threatening to blow the whistle on him. If the license thing was his scam all along, then we've got a problem. That's our sticking point."

I shrugged and held up my hands. "Did you make any progress with the Del Rio authorities?"

"Nothing yet, but they arranged a court order putting a lock on all of Walsh's papers—everything at his home or at his dealership. We're going to do some sifting and see what we can come up with."

"I think Scott was just in a bind, Robert. He couldn't just arrest Walsh, because he'd have automatically implicated his sister. And he may have had no proof against the man. He didn't want to do that, if he could get away with it. I didn't ask him flat-out, but my guess is that Scott was looking for some way to put Walsh out of business, at least as far as Connie was concerned, without going to the law."

Estelle and Francisco appeared in the hallway, and the little kid craned his neck to look up at the six-foot-four Torrez. "We had hamburgers for dinner. You shoulda been here," he said without preamble.

"It would have been better than what I had, that's for sure," Torrez replied, and then he turned back to me. "Some interesting tidbits from Neil Sommers."

"That's Connie's current boyfriend," I said for Estelle's benefit. Francisco, seeing that the conversation wasn't going to linger on hamburgers and such, darted back toward the living room.

"Sommers wasn't invited on the trip," Torrez said. "He agreed to go along, but Connie refused, saying that it wasn't so much a hunting trip as a chance for her and her brother and Walsh to sit down and talk over some important family business."

"So he stayed home," I said.

"That's right. He asked if he could join up with them today sometime, and Connie said no to that, too. He said that he got the impression that she was in some kind of trouble with her stepfather."

"You got a signed deposition to that effect?"

"Yes, sir."

"Did he go down to Cruces after that?"

"He said he was going to drive down this afternoon. I don't know if he went or not, but the officers down there have orders that there are to be no visitors, period. Not until she's conscious and has had a chance a talk to one of us."

"I assume that you stopped by and talked with Scott?" I asked.

"Yes. I just came from the hospital."

"Do *you* believe him?"

A trace of a smile ghosted Torrez's face. "Let me put it this way, sir. I'd like to. First, let's see what we find out down in Del Rio. That may take a day or three. By then, maybe Connie will come around. We'll see what she says."

"Fair enough."

"By the way, Judge Hobart turned Dale Torrance loose on five thousand dollars' bond. Herb and the kid went over to Lawton to pick up the livestock. Miles Waddell is royally pissed."

"At what?"

"He thinks that Dale should be in jail."

"Maybe he's right. But I've given up trying to second-guess the judge."

"Gayle said Waddell called the Sheriff's Office and chewed on her ear for ten minutes. He wanted to know what kind of game of favorites we were playing."

I laughed. "Get used to that, Roberto. After tomorrow, that becomes a way of life for you. You'll spend about a third of each day handling crank calls from idiots."

"And relatives," he said. "Same thing. You should have gone to the Baca funeral. That was quite something."

"I bet. And no thank you."

He regarded his hat some more. "I may send one of the deputies down to Del Rio tomorrow, if the lieutenant thinks it's worthwhile."

"Good idea. Make sure he votes first."

Torrez laughed. "Two or three times, sir."

"We don't have to stand here in the foyer, by the way," I said. "You could come in and relax for a while."

"I can't," Torrez said. "I've got a stack of things that need doing."

"There's always tomorrow," I said.

"Well, no there's not, sir. Tomorrow's already booked."

"Is there anything in particular that I can do for you?" I tried to sound sincere, I really did.

He reached for the door. I didn't like the way his forehead was wrinkling. That meant he was thinking, and might actually come up with something. He opened the door and paused. "Don't forget to vote."

"Two or three times," I said, and clapped him on the back. "But for who?"

"I'll let you know first thing in the morning," he said.

Chapter Fifty-two

At 7:04 a.m. the next day I pushed the big red button at the bottom of the voting machine's display. The machine chimed to let me know that I'd made the right choices. I pushed back the curtain, turned, and caught a blast of white light square in the face.

Frank Dayan grinned sheepishly and wound his camera for another take.

"Jesus, Frank," I said, and rubbed my eyes. "There has to be a better way to waste film."

"Posterity," he said. "This is a big moment."

"Just enormous," I grumbled, and stepped to one side so that I wouldn't block traffic. In this case, "traffic" was a tiny, white-haired woman who smiled brightly at me. I tipped my hat and moved Frank out of her way. She'd arrived at the fire station on Bustos just as the election clerk had handed me the little admission stub with the number *6* written on it.

Dayan followed me outside.

"Have you established the connection between James Walsh and Scott Gutierrez yet?"

"No, Frank, we haven't." I breathed in the wonderful air. And then, as an afterthought, I said, "At least Sheriff Torrez hasn't. Investigation is continuing, as we're fond of saying."

"Is Connie French still in a coma?"

"As far as I know."

"I'm guessing that some of the answers lie with her, is that right?"

"That would be right."

"So if she never comes out of it, what happens?"

"The department pursues other avenues of investigation that remain open."

"I understand that Estelle Guzman is visiting."

"That's also correct."

"Do she and her husband have any plans to return to Posadas?"

I laughed. "You'd have to ask them, Frank."

"Fair enough. I had a feeling you were going to say that, but it was worth a try. One last thing. Can I break the news that you've agreed to work with the New Mexico Livestock Board as an interim inspector? Is that official yet?"

"I've been asked, and I haven't given my answer." Another vehicle pulled in and deposited two more voters. I nodded a greeting. "But yes, you can say that I've agreed to help out on a temporary basis."

Frank Dayan looked pleased. Apparently his news scoops came in all sizes and shades of importance.

"I heard—maybe it was you that told me, I've forgotten—I heard that you promised today would be your last day as sheriff. That you weren't going to wait until January. Is that true?"

"That's true. I told the County Commission last spring that was the deal, when I took the job. Assuming both of those voters who just walked into the building push the right buttons, Robert Torrez will be serving as sheriff-elect beginning at midnight."

Dayan cocked his head and studied me. "And so now what? How are you going to spend your day?"

"I can't imagine that the average reader would care." I chuckled. "It would make sense to spend the next seventeen hours being useful. Other than that, I have no plans."

"Will you do me a favor?" Dayan asked.

"If I can, sure."

"As soon as you find out something definite about this mess with Connie French, will you let me know?"

"If something crops up in the next seventeen hours, I certainly will. Otherwise, you'll be talking to Sheriff Torrez." I found myself grinning like a teenager. "I like the sound of that." I turned to go, then remembered the newspaper publisher's trek up the mountainside. "How did your photo of the air rescue come out?"

"Awesome," he beamed. "It's going to be a hell of a front page this week. Full color."

"Outstanding. I look forward to seeing it. Don't forget to vote, Frank."

I was three minutes from home, and didn't waste any time. The Don Juan was closed, but my grandson wasn't one to shirk his duties. He and Estelle had conjured up their own version of breakfast burritos, and when I walked through the front door I was greeted by the wonderful aroma. Eating wasn't the first thing on my mind, though.

Earlier, the telephone had rung just as I was getting ready to walk out the front door on my way to vote. My grandson the answering machine had gotten there first, and surprised me when he announced that the call was for Dr. Francis Guzman. "Your aunt in Veracruz, Doctor G," he said as he handed the physician the receiver.

When I returned home from my electoral duties, "Doctor G" was still on the phone. He'd moved from the busy kitchen to the back patio, where he stood in his shirtsleeves, shuffling the cottonwood leaves with his sandals while he talked.

Estelle reached across the counter and handed me a mug of coffee. "We can eat breakfast in about five minutes," she said.

"Great. Have you had a chance to talk to Sophia?"

Estelle shook her head. "She was hoping that she would be able to break away and come up for a couple of days, but it doesn't sound like it." She glanced out the window. "Very serious negotiations." She caught her husband's eye and beckoned, but he grinned and held up a hand. After another minute or two of animated conversation, he opened the back door and peered inside.

"Ah, you're back," he said to me. "Sophia would like to speak with you."

I joined him outside and he handed the phone to me.

"Sophia," I said. "Nice to hear from you."

"And how is the *padrino?*" Her quiet voice was silky, alto, and strongly accented.

"Better and better," I replied, remembering that the last time I'd seen Sophia Tournal, she'd been lingering over a cup of coffee in my kitchen, deep in conspiracy with Estelle. "Are you able to pay us a visit sometime soon?"

"Sometime soon, yes. I regret not this week."

"That's a shame. We've got quite a reunion going here at the moment."

"Francis told me. You are pleased to see your son after so long, no?"

"Most pleased. And my grandson, as well. He's been keeping the two boys busy."

"Hmm," she said. I wasn't sure if the little sound was a suppressed laugh, a sigh of nostalgia, or a groan of relief that the two Guzman kids weren't tearing *her* house apart. "Your little town," she said, "it holds the attraction for Francis and Estelle, no?"

"So it would appear," I replied, trying to sound as neutral as possible.

"I've mentioned the opportunities to be found in a large city, and of course, they are aware of those."

"I'm sure they are," I said. "After all, Francis did his residency in Houston. And now they've had a taste of the north country and city life up there in Minnesota."

"Yes." The single word came without inflection. "You know, I don't recall the land behind your home, William. When I was there four years ago, I don't believe I ever had occasion to…to explore."

"It's just five acres of trees and brush right now, Sophia. Nothing spectacular."

"One must look far ahead for these things," Sophia Tournal said. "Francis assures me that there is opportunity there."

"I suppose there is."

She laughed at that, a gentle little chuckle that once again was impossible for me to translate. "You don't sound overly… what's the word…enthusiastic."

"Sophia, just the opposite. I'd do anything I could to help them make the right decision. Of course I'd be delighted if they would settle in Posadas again. I happen to think that there's opportunity here, but it depends what a man wants. The area is growing, like all of the southwestern United States. Like many little communities, Posadas is desperate for quality medical care. Francis can write his own ticket."

"Anywhere in the world," Sophia said.

"Anywhere. I'm sure there's some pull here because of Estelle's mother. She's been a good sport about Minnesota, but she'd like to return to New Mexico—or at least close by."

"A remarkable woman."

"Yes, she is. But Estelle tells me that her mother hasn't tried to influence them one way or another. And that's exactly the way I feel. It's none of my business, when you get right down to it."

"You're the *padrino* for the children. It is your business. Just as it is my business."

"I can be their godfather from a distance, if it comes to that." I laughed. "I'd rather not be, of course."

"Well," Sophia Tournal sighed. "I can be an aunt from a distance, too. I have told Francis that I would invest in a new clinic."

"That's most generous of you."

"No, it's not. I'm sixty-seven years old. I have more money than I could spend in three lifetimes. I would prefer that the clinic be located in Veracruz, of course. But if Posadas is what Francis wants, then so be it. You are close to the border. The clinic will benefit a large area of northern Mexico as well. I have told Francis that he must see to that."

"I'm sure he will." I switched the phone to my other ear and realized that my hands were shaking.

"My nephew said that he would call back this evening to tell me what he has decided."

"That's fine. And if it turns out that you can break away, we'd love to have you visit."

"We'll see what will be," Sophia Tournal said. "Take care of yourself, *Padrino*."

I switched off the phone and just stood there for a long minute, looking at the little gadget.

"Breakfast," Estelle said. She held the door for me as I stepped into the kitchen, and then gave me a fierce hug.

"What's that for?" I smiled as she stepped away.

"General principles, sir."

Chapter Fifty-three

Everyone seemed to have something to do, and we agreed to meet for lunch at 2:00 p.m.—that would give the mammoth breakfast time to settle, and Tadd enough time to decide what creation he wanted to try next.

I walked into my office shortly after eleven, with every intention of cleaning the place out. My office was spartan and neat. I was not one to cover every available flat surface under a landslide of paperwork. Besides, I had started the transition process more than a month before, first by taking active files and farming them out to Torrez and the other deputies.

Since there was nothing personal to William C. Gastner in the files, I could have just slammed the file cabinet drawers shut and tossed the keys on Bob Torrez's desk. Instead, I found myself kicked back in my old chair, feet up on the desk, reading each file methodically, as if all the memories needed prodding one last time.

"Sir?"

I looked up with a start. Gayle Torrez stood in the door. "Hi there."

"Excuse me, sir, but can you take a call from a Lieutenant Nunez from Del Rio? He's the officer that Bobby talked to earlier."

"Did I hear your husband say earlier that he was going back down on the mountain?"

Gayle nodded and glanced up at the clock. It was twenty minutes before two. "Yes, sir. They found the bullet mark on the rocks. He went down to help them measure the angles."

"Good deal. Sure, I'll take the call."

I reached out and picked up the phone. "This is Sheriff Gastner."

"Hello, Sheriff! Leo Nuñez in Del Rio, Texas. How's your life way up there in God's country?"

"Things are going well, Lieutenant."

"The undersheriff tells me that you're stepping down today. After how many years?"

"Something like thirty-one, thirty-two. Altogether too long."

"Well, congratulations. Say, we've had a hell of a morning. Boy, what you guys got us into."

"How's that?"

"Well, you know. I have a couple men over at Walsh Motors. The dealership's closed up, and we've got a court order to seize any and all records. Makes for real interesting reading."

"I bet it does."

"Best of all, the floor manager, a fellow by the name of Terry Baggerly, knew pretty much what Walsh was doing. Baggerly would like to stay out of jail, so he's singing a really nice melody for us."

"That helps," I said. "What was Walsh's game, anyway?"

"You know, that's the damned thing about it all. He's makin' just a shitload of money with this dealership through legit sales. For a few thousand, he's willing to risk it all."

"Some people just like to gamble, Leo."

"Well, he kept good records, that's for sure." Nuñez made a sucking sound through his teeth. "I always wondered why crooks went to all the trouble to write stuff down. That's pretty stupid, no? To keep records of just the things that would put you in jail?"

"Even presidents have been that stupid, Leo."

"True, true. You want to send down a deputy? I understand from Undersheriff Torrez that there's a possible tie-in up your way."

"Appears to be. Walsh's stepdaughter worked at the Motor Vehicle Division here. It appears that she was issuing fake licenses for him. That's what we're guessing right now. We don't know the extent of it."

Nuñez laughed, a rich, rolling laugh of delight. "Well, sir, let me tell you the extent. You got a minute?"

"Sure I do." I sat back and swung my feet back up.

"For example, let me tell you about Ejenio Rocha," he said, and for the next ten minutes I listened to the lieutenant's softly accented voice spin the story.

Ejenio Rocha knew that the road to real wealth, the road to the good life, lay across the border in the United States. Ejenio had no family...it wasn't a question of his having to support a wife, five children, and two sets of grandparents. He was twenty-six years old, educated through seventh grade, and ambitious. In addition to that, Ejenio Rocha loved trucks.

On August 8, Ejenio crossed the toll bridge over the Rio Grande at Ciudad Acuña, and then hoofed it the four miles into Del Rio, Texas. At nine that morning, he presented himself to James Walsh at Walsh Chrysler-Plymouth on the outskirts of south Del Rio.

He had visited the dealership several times before. The object of his affections was parked in the back row so that its size didn't overshadow the shiny new vehicles that rolled from the lot with astonishing regularity, making Walsh one of the highest-producing dealerships in its zone.

Ejenio stood in front of the massive, blunt prow of the 1989 Chevrolet C-70 flatbed truck, and imagined the payloads he could haul...watermelons and other fruits, farm machinery, pumpkins, firewood, wrecked vehicles. The list was endless. Tons at a time.

James Walsh knew a hardworking young man when he saw one, and he was immediately impressed with Ejenio Rocha. Rocha was not interested in illegal drugs, or other border contraband. He wanted to drive a *truck*. If he could someday drive a semi and be a member of the union, so much the better. There was a catch. Ejenio was a Mexican citizen, with a Mexican driver's license. He knew that his future wealth lay in the United States. He needed residency, and he needed a U.S.-issue commercial driver's license. The paperwork wall appeared impenetrable. James Walsh agreed to help.

The Chevy, a good-looking machine when detailed, had served a long, hard life with Marathon Building Materials. With more than 140,000 miles on it, it was still a bargain at $9,500. Ejenio knew it was a bargain at $9,500. Ejenio could indeed buy the Chevy in Texas. He could buy it and drive it to Mexico, and license it there. But Mexico was not the place of Ejenio's dreams.

Ejenio could not license the truck in Texas…or anywhere else in the United States, unless he was a resident of the licensing state. Walsh was sympathetic and helpful. Suppose Ejenio had a shiny new commercial driver's license from New Mexico?

Ejenio had never been to New Mexico, and was unsure of why he would want to do that, but Walsh was persuasive. The laws were too complex to explain in just a few minutes, but suffice to say that the Motor Vehicle Division in New Mexico would help the young man through the test, would help him establish residency, would issue him a beautiful New Mexico CDL with his picture and address on it. For all intents and purposes, he would be a U.S. citizen.

The new license was $1,000, cash American. Ejenio hadn't realized that the American government also operated on the theory of greased palms, but it seemed worth it. The thousand dollars was a lot of money, as much as the down payment that Ejenio had scraped together for the truck. But Walsh was quick to point out what Ejenio stood to gain.

If Ejenio licensed the truck in Texas, the license tax was seven and a half percent—$712.50—just in taxes. In New Mexico, the tax was three percent. The $427.50 that Ejenio saved would almost pay for half of his new driver's license—his ticket to all things bountiful in the United States.

Ejenio drove a nifty Mercury Cougar with Texas dealer tags to Posadas, New Mexico, where, on August 9, Connie French issued him a New Mexico commercial driver's license. His address on the license was 110 Country Club Lane, 22, Posadas, New Mexico.

With license in hand, Ejenio received a freshly minted registration for the Chevy of his dreams, along with the license plate and a new sticker. He headed back to Del Rio a happy man.

"And he's made four payments on the truck," Nuñez said. "Regular as clockwork. I've got the payment record right here in front of me. There's also a photocopy of Rocha's license and registration. Talk about a paper trail."

"It never ceases to amaze me what people will do for a few bucks, Lieutenant."

"More than just a few. Walsh is charging eighteen percent interest on the deal. A four-year note at eighteen percent. That's two hundred and fifteen dollars every month."

"It'll pay the light bill."

"For sure. So can you break a deputy loose?"

"Sure can. I'll have him there tomorrow."

"You have the girl—what's-her-name," and I heard papers shuffle. "Connie French? You have her in custody?"

"She's still in a coma. So yes, I guess you'd say she's in custody."

"Too bad. This is going to put a dent in her life by the time it's over."

"She didn't have to do it, Leo. That's the other puzzler. Folks have a hard time saying no."

My earlobe was practically numb by the time I hung up. Ejenio Rocha had another day or two at most to enjoy his apartment in Las Cruces, New Mexico, his amazing Chevy C-70 flat-bed, and the highways of the United States.

I stretched and walked out to dispatch. Brent Sutherland was settled in, and I frowned.

"Aren't you about ten hours early?" I said.

"Gayle had to cut out, sir," he said. "I offered to come in and cover for her."

I frowned. Gayle Torrez didn't "cut out" without damn good reason. "I'm glad you came in," I said. "I've got a question for you."

"What's that, sir?"

"The apartments behind the school? The Vista Del Montaño complex at One Ten Country Club? How many units are there?"

Sutherland grinned. "I happen to know that, sir. A friend of mine lives in the last one. Number twelve."

"Twelve? That sounds about right. I was just curious."

I heard the outer door open, and turned to see Estelle Guzman. Dressed in an outfit reminiscent of the trim, khaki pants suits that she'd favored when she worked for the Sheriff's Department, she looked right at home.

"Hey," I said. "I was just finishing up. They're making real headway down in Del Rio. Walsh had himself quite a scam going."

She hooked an arm through mine. "Tell me about it on the way," she said.

I looked back at Sutherland, who was grinning. "If Bob Torrez comes in, have him stop by the house. I need to fill him in," I said.

"Yes, sir," Sutherland replied.

On the way outside, I recounted a shortened version of what Nuñez had told me, and Estelle listened with her usual frown of concentration until I started to walk toward the unmarked car I'd been using.

"Let's use the van," she said. "I'll drive."

"That's going to be a nuisance later," I said, then stopped abruptly. "To hell with it. I don't need the county car later, either, do I?"

"No, you don't."

We pulled out from the Sheriff's Department parking lot, and instead of turning southbound on Grande, Estelle headed west-bound on Bustos. That reminded me, and I said, "I assume you guys have checked on your place on Twelfth Street?"

"It's fine." A wide smile spread across her dark face. "Until we turn on the water. Then everything will probably come apart."

"Ah, well," I said, and then leaned forward. "What the hell is going on here?" We approached the intersection of Bustos and Twelfth Street. Every available inch of parking space along the curbs and in the parking lot of the Don Juan de Oñate Restaurant had been taken, a vast sea of vehicles that threatened to clog both Bustos and north Twelfth.

"Can you believe that? Somebody's got a goddamn wedding reception on Election Day," I said, and then braced myself as Estelle reached the intersection. Her house was four blocks south.

We turned north instead, hooked in behind the restaurant, and rolled to a stop directly in front of the restaurant entrance, parking beside an immaculate older model Corvette with Texas plates.

Deputy Thomas Pasquale and Linda Real stood by the door. Pasquale stepped forward in a fair imitation of military manners and wrenched open the door of the van.

"Good afternoon, sir," he said.

I sat perfectly still, looking at him. Then I turned slowly and looked at Estelle Guzman. "Is this your doing?"

She reached over and patted my arm. "The doing of a lot of people, Padrino," she said.

I got out of the van and Pasquale slammed the door hard enough to rock the vehicle. "You got pictures of the bullet strike?" I asked Linda, who couldn't wipe the enormous, lopsided grin off her face.

"Yes, sir. We did."

I found myself wanting to continue the conversation so that I didn't have to go inside, but Estelle Guzman's hand on my elbow was insistent.

I took a deep breath as she opened the door. "Torrez sure as hell better win the election after all this," I said. "Otherwise he's going to look damn foolish."

Estelle leaned close so that she didn't have to shout. "This isn't for him," she said. "And besides, Deputy Pasquale is checking for 'I Voted' stickers at the door."

"Why does that not surprise me," I muttered.

To receive a free catalog of Poisoned Pen Press titles, please contact us in one of the following ways:

Phone: 1-800-421-3976
Facsimile: 1-480-949-1707
Email: info@poisonedpenpress.com
Website: www.poisonedpenpress.com

Poisoned Pen Press
6962 E. First Ave. Ste. 103
Scottsdale, AZ 85251

CPSIA information can be obtained
at www.ICGtesting.com
Printed in the USA
LVOW12s1417011116
511179LV00001B/70/P